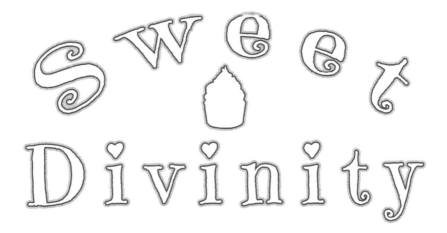

Sweet Divinity

DISCARD

Sweet Divinity

by

Megan Prewitt Koon

Shine

an imprint of

PROSPECTIVE PRESS LLC

1959 Peace Haven Rd, #246, Winston-Salem, NC 27106 U.S.A.
www.prospectivepress.com

Published in the United States of America by PROSPECTIVE PRESS LLC

SWEET DIVINITY

Cover and interior design by ARTE RAVE

ISBN 978-1-943419-97-5

E008

First PROSPECTIVE PRESS trade paperback edition

Printed in the United States of America
First printing December 2019

The text of this book is typeset in Amiri
Accent text is typeset in Emily's Candy

PUBLISHER'S NOTE

Acknowledgments

There are too many people to thank by name, but I can't miss the opportunity to thank a few people on my first ever "Acknowledgments" page!

Thank you to Ryan for choosing to marry a writer (though I'm not sure you knew what you were getting into). Thanks to Marie and Jack for making me smile every day. Thanks, Mom and Lisa, for driving me to theatre rehearsals so I could find my voice. To Nana, thank you for always believing with absolute certainty that I am a writer.

Thank you to all of my teachers, especially Mr. Brian Suits. You once said to sixteen-year old Megan, "Well, Miss Prewitt, I look forward to seeing your name in print." You don't know how many times I heard your words over these years. They kept my words alive.

Thank you to my writing colleagues, especially my writing partner, Imani-Grace King—make note of her name. Her gift is natural, authentic, and beautiful. Also, thank you to my research road trip partner, Jennie. I love wandering with you.

Thank you to all of my early readers: Sara, Jessica, Matt, Emily, Maddie, Sydney, Brian, and Kaitlyn, all gifted, powerful writers. Your encouragement is priceless.

And, of course, thanks to everyone who let me steal bits of their stories to craft this one, particularly Eric, Sebastian, Meby, Louisa, and Julie.

Thank you to Jason Graves and everyone at Prospective Press for taking a chance on a new writer who has tried to be low maintenance and who probably failed. I'm so grateful for you!

And to you, my dear reader. You are part of this story now. Thank you for choosing to dwell in these pages. I hope to see you again soon.

For Nana, who never doubted and always loved

Chapter One

One of my earliest memories of my mother involves pot leaves and sprinkles of dirt raining from the heavens.

The morning began as usual. My mother wasn't in the kitchen when my older brother Michael and I sat down at the table and poured our bowls of cornflakes, which was normal for farm life. I assumed that, as usual, my mother was out surveying the day's work.

But I saw something move out of the corner of my eye, and the next thing I knew, Michael had shoved his chair away from the table and was running toward the back door.

I followed, of course, and when I arrived in the yard, it appeared that the sky was raining dirt. I put out my hand to catch the brown rain and a small, green leaf floated elegantly into my hand. I had never seen a leaf like that before, and I decided I would press it and add it to my collection of leaves and flowers.

"MOM!" Michael started screaming, his hands reaching toward the sky. It appeared he was as fascinated as I was by these little specks of green falling from above. "MOM! STOP! STOP!"

I looked up to find that the leaves were not, in fact, falling from the sky, but from the window of my brother's room. Handfuls of dirt, roots, and pieces of little plants with what looked to me like star-shaped green leaves, were being heaved out of the window by hands unseen, but a glimpse of pink gardening gloves let me know that they belonged to my mother.

After a few minutes of dirty rain, the early fall came to a sudden halt and all was quiet until my mother's voice pierced the early morning calm.

"Michael Roberts, I will not have you growing marijuana in my home! I will NOT allow a drug dealer to live under my roof!"

Michael had blanched and looked to me, as if my six-year old self had any idea as to what was happening.

"Mom, I swear, I was just keeping them for a friend. I swear!"

Silence answered him. He stood in the yard, using his hand to block the light so he could see his window more clearly. Then he bolted inside.

Immediately, the rains began again, and I leapt and danced in the dirt sprinkling from the sky as if it were the water hose and I were in my pink, polka-dotted swimsuit. I could hear Michael beating on his bedroom door, and that was when the pots began to fly out of the window, shattering against the trees that bordered the yard. I stopped my dance and ran for the front porch, taking cover from the shards now scattering the grass.

A lamp smashed against a large pine tree, the black bulb shattering into tiny glass pieces. A flag decorated with one of the star-shaped leaves lightly sailed against the wind, finally resting in the branches of a tree, upside-down. I wondered how Michael would get it down.

"You're INSANE!" Michael came storming out of the house and to his car, where he wrenched open the door and threw himself inside. I watched him peel away and fly down the long, gravel driveway.

I sat on the porch in my pink princess nightie, an intact leaf twisted in my fingers.

The screen door creaked open and my mother emerged, a glass of sweet tea in her gloved hands. She wiped the sweat from her forehead and sat in the rocker.

"Mommy, what is this?" I held up the leaf.

She took a long sip of her tea. "A leaf, baby."

I twisted my mouth in curiosity. "What kind?"

"Poison."

I dropped it as if it were a snake. Being a farm girl, I had battled my share of poison ivy.

"Mommy, why did Michael have them in his room?"

"I have no idea."

We sat in silence listening to the birds chirp in the morning quiet. This was always my mother's favorite time of day, when all of creation was waking up.

"Mommy, why did you throw all of those things out of the window?"

She took another long sip and relaxed into the rocking chair. When she spoke, a smile spread across her lips and she closed her eyes.

"Because your brother needed to clean his room."

❤

I've never forgotten that event because it characterizes my mother perfectly. When my brother arrived home that afternoon, bad attitude still storming, he found his room spic and span with a new set of flower pots resting on the window ledge, filled with fennel seedlings and basil leaves.

But if you were to tell me one year ago that I would be packing my car to return to that house, to return to my mother and her rules and ways, I would have told you that you had completely lost your mind.

Yet here I am.

It was a fresh June morning when I loaded my own little princess, Sylvie, into the car amongst our most precious possessions. The moving truck would follow with the belongings that were now in storage once I figured out where in the world we were going to settle ourselves. I knew I wouldn't live in Po-dunkville, Georgia, forever, but at the time, it was the only place we had to go.

Richard, Sylvie's father and my philandering husband, sat on the front steps as I loaded the car, his face in his hands. I don't know if he thought that tears would make me change my mind, or if he simply wanted me to see that he did, in fact, have a heart, but either way, I felt nothing. I just kept walking past him, silently cursing him for playing the victim right in front of our daughter. She was only five; she didn't yet recognize deceit.

And when the car was packed and Sylvie tucked into her booster seat, I stood, arms crossed, looking down at Richard, the embodiment of pathetic.

"So this is it?" He had tears in his eyes. It made me sick.

I nodded. "You know where to find us if you need us."

"I do need—"

"Just stop." I put my hand out, inches in front of his face. "Let's not play games."

"Amanda, I said I was sorry."

"I know you did. And I'm sorry, too. But we have to go away for a while. We'll be at Mom's. If you want to say goodbye to Sylvie, this is the time." I turned on my heel and marched to the car, waiting outside so I didn't have to hear whatever pathetic words he spoke to our child. My heart was beating so loudly, my eyes were blurred with tears I willed to stay dammed up, and I felt my hands shaking. Damn him.

Without a word, I stepped in the car as he shut the back door, slammed my own, and yanked the car into drive, tears stubbornly flowing down my cheeks.

❤

Stop it. You're better off. You can't stay with someone who is unfaithful to you. You deserve better than this.

"Mommy?" I flipped the rearview mirror down at the sound of Sylvie's sweet voice singing from the backseat where she sat with her pink headphones plugged into the DVD player. "How long are we staying at Momo's?"

"I don't know, baby. But are you excited about going?"

"Yes!" She kicked her legs in excitement. "Momo's! Momo's!"

"I'm excited, too, baby."

"I love you, Mama."

"I love you." I flipped the rearview mirror back into position and wiped my eyes, thanking God that large sunglasses were currently the style.

"Mama?"

I flipped the mirror back down.

"Are we there yet?"

"No, baby."

She pouted. "What's taking so long?"

"Honey, we just left home. It's going to take five hours to get to Momo's house."

"How long is five hours?"

I felt my shoulders tense and took a deep breath, determined to explain *time* in a way she could understand. "Three movies."

"Three movies!" She kicked her legs again. "Three movies! Three movies!" She sang and did a little dance. I felt my shoulders relax. Her happiness was contagious, and it had saved me over the past few weeks in a number of ways.

When I'd found out that Richard was cheating, I'd felt like the world had fallen in around me. I had skipped work one afternoon with my friend Jeannette to go see the new Bradley Cooper movie, as any woman with a pulse would. We felt like high schoolers skipping out of class as we drove downtown with our dark sunglasses, giggling and on the lookout, as if our boss would magically appear on the corner.

When we bought our tickets, I insisted we also get popcorn, outrageously overpriced soda—the works, and so by the time we entered the theatre, the previews had begun and it was dark.

We slipped into a row toward the back so that we wouldn't miss a minute—I mean, the previews are the best part. Well, about five minutes into the movie, I started hearing a distinct smacking sound behind us. I looked at Jeanette and she rolled her eyes. Teenagers. I never did understand what the allure was of paying so much money for a movie just to miss the whole thing because your eyes were closed. Ridiculous.

So we ignored it for a while as I watched Bradley saunter across the screen, looking sexy as all get-out. But when it came time for the on-screen romance, it was time for the romance behind us to end. By this time the couple had crossed the lines of normal decency and sounded like they were honest-to-God sucking each other's faces off. When the girl started giggling "Stop! Stop it! Heheteehee!" I turned around and in my 'Mother' voice, full-volume, yelled, "Seriously?"

And that was when my heart stopped. Just literally stopped in my chest. These were not truant teenagers. This was my husband and some woman I'd never seen.

"Oh my God." Jeannette was standing up now. "You —!" She threw her popcorn bucket at him, smacking the girl right in the face. I suppose I can only take pleasure in this now, but the sight of her extra butter greasing that girl's hair and the M&Ms Jeannette had poured in that were now stuck to my husband's face makes the scene almost comical.

But in the moment I said nothing, just ran. I ran through the lobby and into the bathroom, locking myself into a tiny, disgusting stall. We can all agree that I must have gone momentarily insane, because I sat on the movie theatre toilet—I know, let's just have a moment for the lasting effects of this decision to sink in—and put my face in my hands.

I didn't hear Jeannette come in, her voice just crept in between my sobs.

"Amanda, please don't make me crawl in there on this floor. I'd do a lot of things for you, but I just ask you to please not make me do that. There isn't enough Clorox in the world to get me clean if I get down on this floor."

I flipped open the lock and she squeezed in with me, shutting the door behind her.

"Oh my God, you're sitting on that toilet."

"I—can't—breathe."

She put her hands on my shoulders and looked into my eyes. "Amanda."

She kept saying the words, and I felt my breathing calm as I breathed along with her. My chest loosened and my head, though throbbing good now, began to clear.

"I can't face him right now."

"I'll handle it." She kissed my cheek and left me in the stall to clean myself up. I wiped my nose with toilet paper that went into soggy pieces in my hands and got stuck on my nose. I mean, just add insult to injury. So I stood, made sure that there was no toilet paper stuck to my shoe, and shuffled, head down, out of the stall.

I looked into the mirror and was infuriated with what I saw. I saw a happy, confident woman reduced to a drowning rat. I took a deep breath and stared in silence, willing my red eyes to clear. I felt sad, angry, embarrassed, and sort of homicidal.

And I could hear Jeannette screaming in the lobby. "Get out of here, you cheating bastard! She doesn't want to talk to you right now! Get out of here or I swear to God I'll call the police! GO!"

I couldn't help but smile at myself in the mirror as I listened to Jeannette fight for my honor. I love that woman.

❤

Now here we were, just over a month later, driving into no-man's land. It's not that I don't like visiting my mother, and it isn't that I've become citified and don't like going back to the country, it's that I swore I'd never come back here in a permanent or semi-permanent way. When I graduated high school and moved on to Charlotte, with its museums, and traffic, and buildings, I promised myself that no matter what, I would never go back.

So much for promises, it seems.

I crossed the state line—'We're Glad Georgia's on Your Mind!' Cue Ray Charles—and I swear the landscape automatically changed. You can see it, the minute you've left Carolina. The trees get thicker on the sides of the interstate, the medians grassy and full of wildflowers. It's quieter, and the roads are not nearly as smooth.

I looked in the rearview mirror and saw that Sylvie was sleeping, her head cocked, bottom lip in a pout.

As I drove it became even more apparent that I was closing in on home. With the increasing curves of the mountain roads, the Confederate flag became a common sight, either flying on a pole erected in front of a small mountain home, or through the windows, serving as curtains to block a stranger's view.

But I also saw the flowerbeds—flowerbeds overflowing with yellows and purples. Birdhouses filling the trees. Front porches occupied with men and women waving to passersby as if they were the Georgia welcoming committee.

Eventually, Sylvie woke up, starving of course, so we pulled into a drive-thru, a small cement building on the side of the road fronted with picnic tables filled with workers on lunch break. I turned off the car and rolled down the windows.

"I want to come!"

"I'm just going to walk right up to the window and get lunch, okay, baby?"

"PLEASE!"

"Honey, there's no sense getting out. I'll only be a second."

"PLEASE!" She unbuckled her seatbelt and stood up in the backseat.

"Sylvie, it will be so much easier if Mommy just goes to order the food and you wait right here in your seat."

Cue the tears. Cue the wailing. My daughter was God's own angel, but sometimes I forgot that she was also five years old.

"Okay, okay, please stop crying."

"I'm HUNGRY!"

I sighed. We still had a couple of hours to go, but let's face it. When cabin fever sets in, one must choose her battles wisely.

"Okay, fine." I unloaded my now cheering daughter from the car and she skipped to the building, proceeding to read every item on the menu, a shiny piece of painted metal attached to the cement blocks next to the window.

"Hot dog. Corn dog. Hamburger. Cheeseburger. French fries. Pork rinds. Mama, what are Pork rinds?" Please be advised that she pronounced them, "Pok Winds."

An old man at a nearby table laughed quietly.

Sylvie looked at him, her head tilted in question.

"Young lady, those are the tastiest concoction the good lord ever created!"

Sylvie's eyes grew large. She looked suddenly shy and reached her arms for me to pick her up. She whispered in that not-really-whispering way children have, "Mommy, why doesn't that man have all of his teeth?"

The old man laughed louder.

Embarrassed, I turned toward the screened order window and blurted, "Honey, would you like a hot dog?"

"Corn dog."

"Corn dog, *please.*"

"Corn dog, please!"

I ordered and the kind woman inside handed Sylvie a lollipop. Before lunch, of course. Perhaps this custom explained the old man's lack of chompers.

"Yes, ma'am," the old man had turned toward us and sat back, drinking his Coke out of a bottle. "You're doin' a good job with that there little lady. Real polite, she is. And curious, too."

I flushed. "Thank you."

"You folks from around here?" He raised his eyebrows. I supposed the Ralph Lauren attire gave it away.

"No. From North Carolina."

"But we're going to visit my Momo!" Sylvie stuck the candy into her mouth and popped it back out.

"Your Momo, eh?"

"Yes, she lives on a farm! And we've packed all of our stuff into the car, and we're going to stay for a long time!"

"That's enough, Sylvie." Our order was ready so I claimed it, balancing ketchup and salt packets in my arms.

"Let me help you, ma'am." The man had tossed his Coke bottle and took the drinks from my hands.

"Thank you."

Sylvie skipped to the car and pressed the buttons to unlock it. I felt immediately foolish for locking it in the first place. I guess it was habit.

The old man opened the car door for me so I could set down the bags and then handed me the drinks.

"Well, I certainly hope you ladies have a safe trip to Momo's house."

"Thank you!" Sylvie pulled herself into her booster seat and buckled up.

"And, ma'am, I hope you find the peace you're lookin' fer." He winked at me and shut me in my car, tipping his baseball cap, his toothless smile the most genuine I had seen in a while.

The gratitude I felt at his simple act of kindness I can't really express, but I nodded to him as we pulled away. And despite myself, I couldn't help but think that maybe I was doing the right thing after all.

❤

But if that were so, then why did I pull over on the side of the road next to the county welcome sign and sit silently for fifteen minutes, staring senselessly ahead?

Sylvie was happily singing along to "When You Wish Upon a Star" in the backseat while my gaze was locked on the "Welcome to Carroll" sign, not so much making a wish as having a silent mental breakdown.

And just to make things the very best they could be, flashing blue lights appeared in my rearview mirror. She did nothing to contain the absolute glee in her voice. "The police are coming! The police are coming! Are they going to arrest you?" Somehow it sounded enticing coming from the sweet little voice in the backseat.

"I don't think so, honey. I'm sure it's just a misunderstanding."

"Are you going to JAIL!?"

Seriously, why was she so excited about this concept?

I rolled down the window as sunglasses gazed into my car.

"Everything all right, ma'am?"

"Yes. Yes, sir. I was just on my way home and I pulled over because my daughter was being pretty loud back there."

"No I wasn't, Mommy."

Awesome.

"You ain't from around here, are you ma'am? I seen your license plate."

I leaned my head back on the seat. Was it really that obvious within seconds of meeting us?

"No, we're from North Carolina!" Sylvie has unbuckled and was perched on the center console, bouncing on her knees, her little head rhythmically bumping the ceiling of the car.

"I'm from here originally. Grew up here."

"And we're going to my Momo's house!"

God bless that child. At least I knew that in the future, when Sylvie got pulled over, she'd know how to charm the officer.

The officer in front of us now smiled and sort of chuckled to himself. "Been away from home long?"

"Yes, sir."

"Well, I hope you find a warm welcome."

"I'm sure I will. Thank you, sir."

"Ma'am." He tilted his hat—honestly, he did—and walked back to his car.

Of course he followed me for the next four miles in a twenty-five mile per hour zone with cars speeding past us left and right. Finally, as I entered Carroll proper, he turned off and I was faced with my hometown.

It takes approximately thirty seconds to drive through the city of Carroll, Georgia. Fortunately for Sylvie, we caught both traffic lights and so I was forced to comment on every building we saw.

"Yes, darling. That's the courthouse. The Olympic torch passed through here back in the nineties when the Olympics were in Atlanta." I had a commemorative Barbie from the occasion. I wondered if my mother still had it tucked away somewhere.

"Wow...did it set the building on fire?" Sylvie had a gleam in her eyes that I momentarily considered should have disturbed me. Just what I needed, a pyromaniac daughter.

"No, dear."

"And what's that?"

"That is the jail."

"It's really small."

"There aren't many criminals here in Carroll, Sweetie."

"Good. And what's that?"

"That's where Mommy went to high school."

"I want to go to school there! I want to go to your school, Mama!"

I spoke the words under my breath, "Not over my dead body." My high school had been fine at the time, but in retrospect, the senior prank where everyone drove his tractor or horse to school should have indicated the redneck level a little more clearly to me.

And then we were through town and entering the countryside.

"Are we there yet?"

"Almost."

"How many turns?" It was hard to be annoyed with her, she was so sincere in her excitement and eagerness to get to Momo's house.

"Three."

Of course, the first turn didn't come for five more miles, and Sylvie was getting restless. I looked around, trying desperately to find something that would intrigue her. I realized that what was commonplace to me was something she had never seen except for in books.

"Sylvie, look at the cows...look at all the cows!"

"Wow...aw—w—wesome." Her tone was one of complete and utter awe as she stared at the classic black and white animals, chewing their cud. It looked to me like they were staring at us with an eyebrow cocked, sort of a "Who the hell are you people?" but then again, I had been in the car for quite some time.

The last turn took us onto an unpaved road and we bounced along, Sylvie calling, "Whoa! Whoa! Whoa!" with every bump and jolt. It was a relief to turn into the driveway, still gravel, but recently smoothed over by the tractor.

"Momo's house! YAY!"

We drove past the greenhouse, the bee hives, and the rows upon rows of berry bushes. In the distance, I saw the lake I had fished in as a child, the small garden I helped tend, and the woods where I would disappear for hours, playing Swiss Family Robinson and Boxcar Children.

And then the house came into view, and my childish heart overflowed with all of the emotion I'd been keeping tucked away.

"Momo! Momo!" Sylvie was practically kicking through the seat as I parked the car and unlocked the doors. She ran to the back porch where my mother was waiting, arms outstretched.

My mother looked exactly like herself, which I suppose isn't the most apt description, but it was the thing that struck me first when I saw her. Long gray hair pulled back in a ponytail, tanned skin tight on her face, skirt dusting the ground around her sandaled feet.

"Mom." I smiled through the tears and went to her, threw my arms around her and my daughter, who had already leapt into her grandmother's arms.

"Mommy! You're squishing me!" Sylvie giggled and squirmed to the ground. "Momo, we brought so much stuff! We're going to stay with you for a LONG time!" She ran to the car to get her Hello Kitty suitcase.

"Mom, thank you. I—I can't tell you how..."

"Don't mention it, darling. This is your home." She put her hand on my cheek and smiled in that understanding way she had.

I nodded, the tears burning my eyes.

"Why don't you go up to your room. I'll get Sylvie settled." She wiped my cheek and walked past me to help with our suitcases.

The smell of the house, the smell of cinnamon sticks and sweet, sweet honey filled my lungs and brought a smile to my face as I walked through the door. My mother was not one for change, and so the house looked as it had when I was growing up. My room had changed, of course. No longer did the faces of my teenage crushes paper the walls, my desk was gone and replaced by a new bureau, and the bed was covered in a homemade quilt. But nestled on the pillow was Ramkie, my childhood teddy bear. When I'd left for college, I'd left Ramkie behind, as he was falling to pieces and already missing an eye, and yet here he lay, waiting for me.

In the moment that I saw him, I lost the ability to hold it all together. A sob burst from my lips, and I threw myself on the bed, held Ramkie tight, and wept. Wept for myself, wept for Sylvie, and wept for the teenage girl who had once been so hopeful about love.

❤

When I awoke, I could smell something frying, that sweet, crisp smell of canola oil heated on the stove. I opened my eyes to find that the sun was beginning to set. Good Lord, I had been asleep for four hours.

Sylvie was standing on a chair at the kitchen sink, scrubbing potatoes with a little brush shaped like a potato and clearly sent through the food disposal a couple of times. She wore a tiny apron that I recognized as my own, the one I would wear whenever Mom and I made chocolate chip cookies for Daddy to take on one of his trips to the agricultural conventions.

"Mommy! Look, I'm helping!" Her blonde curls bounced around her face as she scrubbed deliberately, nearly taking the skin off of the potatoes with the brush alone.

"Nice rest, dear?" My mother's hands were covered in flour as she patted biscuits into shape and set them on the buttered baking pan. "You must have been beat."

"I guess I was." I poured a cup of cold coffee and popped it into the microwave. "Sylvie, did Momo show you around?"

"Yes...I saw my room and I saw the basement." She lowered her voice to a whisper. "There were heads down there!" She giggled, dropping a potato with a loud thunk into the sink.

"Mom?"

"You know the boar's head is down there...the ram, the deer. I didn't think about it, but it didn't scare her. Actually, she was really intrigued."

"Did you know, Mommy, that a boar is a wild pig with tusks like an elephant?" Her eyes were wide as if this were the greatest revelation of her short life.

"Really?"

"Yes, and a ram is like a goat, but with HUUUUUGE horns, and they're curvy. Isn't that AWESOME!"

"Indeed." I gave my mother a look but she just shrugged and put the biscuits into the oven.

"Sylvie, could you set the table for us?"

"Yes, ma'am!" She hopped down and began opening drawers, looking for utensils.

I lifted myself so that I was sitting on the counter. It was a teenage maneuver that was surprisingly more difficult to do these days. "Thanks, Mom, for watching her. I didn't mean to sleep that long. I guess I just haven't slept in a while."

She brought the warm mug of coffee to me. "Well, there's no place like home for a good rest. And there's no place like the country for peace and quiet." She winked.

I nodded and took a sip, letting the bitter heat burn my throat.

Sylvie hummed as she set the table, careful to place the knives just so.

Mom motioned for me to join her at the sink. I scooted along the counter. She used to hate when I did that, and she was giving me the same disapproving look now.

"Really, Amanda Jane?" She smiled, and then went back to her work, lowering her voice to a whisper so the young, acute ears wouldn't hear her. "You know, she's doing awfully well. She told me that you and her were having some girl time here, that her Daddy had a lot of work to do, so he was staying home while you spent the summer here."

"It was the best I could do, Mom."

She put her arm around me and I felt her approval. "You're doin' good."

"I don't know how to tell her..."

"You don't need to yet. Just let her be happy right now. She'll ask when she's good and ready."

I pulled away and looked her in the eyes. "Don't you think you're giving her an awful lot of credit for perception? She's only five."

Her eyes smiled. "It's been my experience, dear, that children are the most perceptive of all of us. They have no bias, no history, nothing to distract them from the truth. Believe me, she knows more than she lets on."

"That isn't comforting."

"But it should be!" She took my hands. Hers were so soft, as they always were. "You're doing a great job with her."

"Thanks."

"Momo! Can I have tea with supper?"

I sighed. The usual argument. "Sylvia, you know that you get milk or wa—"

"Of course!" My mother threw her hands up and rushed to the table. "Sweet tea is what runs in the veins around here!"

"Hurrah!"

Mom: One. Me: Zero. Thus it begins.

"Mom, we have a rule in our house…"

She stood erect and gave me her don't-you-speak-like-that-to-me-young-lady look.

"Well, fortunately for us all, we're in MY house now. And so we go by my rules. And my rules state sweet tea at dinnertime."

Sylvie cheered and danced around the table, her apron swinging loose like a dress.

I sighed and gave my mother a sassy look. "Okay, Mom. But when she's up half the night, don't say I didn't warn you."

She blocked her mouth with her hand and whispered. "It's decaf, hon."

Well that stopped me in my tracks. Decaf? My face must have looked completely befuddled, because she immediately explained.

"I'm not sleeping as well as I used to, honey. So I'm cuttin' back on the caffeine. "

I looked down at my mug curiously.

"Oh no!" she laughed. "Good Lord, I could never give up my real coffee! No, no. No fake coffee around here! Do you think I've completely lost my mind?" She patted me on the back and bustled into the kitchen to take the potatoes out of the microwave.

Of course not. That would make too much sense.

Full-tummied and exhausted, Sylvie fell to sleep before I could finish reading her the Berenstain Bears book she'd chosen from Momo's library. I kissed her forehead and watched as she smiled in her sleep, no doubt perfectly content to be here in the middle of nowhere, with nothing but the exciting unknown surrounding her. In that moment, I envied her.

I found my mother smoking on the back porch, saw her cigarette burning orange in the darkness. Curling into one of the unfinished Adirondack chairs worn by years of weather, I sat in silence, listening to the crickets and frogs, the trucks gunning their engines way off on the road, and the critters rustling in the woods around us. It was a clear night, and the stars were easily discernible in the sky.

My mother exhaled slowly. When she spoke, it was very quietly, "How're you doing', baby?"

I heard my voice quiver as I answered. "Not well, Mom."

We sat in silence for a few minutes. I could hear her inhaling and watched the orange glow.

"I saw Donna Reynolds at the Kroger last week. She says Dana would be real happy to see you now that you're back in town.

"I'd like that."

"I got her number for you."

"Thanks."

I closed my eyes and rested my head back on the chair. "I want to be happy again, Mama."

She exhaled slowly. "You will be."

"I hope so."

"I know so. God takes care of us. He always has, always will."

I could never tell my mother that I had given up on God long ago. Of course, she knew we didn't go to church; then again, neither did she. She said that she saw God best when she was working in her fields amongst his creation. She watched a televised service every Saturday night or Sunday morning, depending on who was preaching on each channel. Her latest had been an AME church out of Tennessee. She loved the charisma.

"Mom, how did you know that leaving Daddy was the right thing?"

She stubbed out the cigarette and we were in complete darkness, the moon covered by cloud.

"I didn't. Just had to believe that God wants us all to be happy, that we are allowed to be happy. No one has to live her life in misery. We can all make choices."

"Do you ever regret asking him to leave?"

She waited a few seconds before answering. "I regret not asking him to leave sooner!" She coughed a laugh.

I couldn't help but smile. I remembered when she'd found out my father was cheating. She'd taken a frying pan to his head and chased him halfway down the driveway on foot, and considering the driveway is over half a mile long, you can imagine she had quite a bit of pent up anger to fuel her that far.

He'd come back that evening, tried to make nice, and she'd let him stay for a couple more weeks. Then when he'd mentioned that she really should think about losing a few pounds, she'd traded the frying pan for a rifle, and this time she let him get in the car so he could go a ways farther.

So Michael and I saw our father every other weekend, and we all got together on holidays and played civil, even when Dad got re-married to Sandra Lexington, the town 'you know what.' I think my mother found it poetic that they ended up together.

And now here we were, a couple of jilted women, back where we'd begun.

We sat in silence for a few minutes, listening, thinking. I heard a turtle slip into the pond, the gentle plonk that echoed through the quietness of the evening.

"What do you have planned for tomorrow?"

I wasn't expecting the question. "I have nothing planned for ever."

"How 'bout callin' Dana. Seein' if she can lead you towards a job."

"I thought I'd take a vacation first."

"So you can sit around feelin' sorry for yourself?"

"Yes. Basically."

Mom chuckled. "Can't allow it, sweetheart."

"Can't I help you here?"

"Of course. You know that. But you need to be around people your own age, too. Young people."

"Ha—young." I rolled my eyes and slunk back in the chair, my chin on my knees. "I think when you have a child and officially separate from your husband, you're stripped of the 'young' label."

"Honey, thirty-two isn't anywhere near dead."

"I know. I just don't know how to live on my own, you know? I really thought I was all set." I felt tears burn my eyes and begged them to stay tight.

"Well, that's life, butterbean. You have to be ready for the unknown."

"I don't like that part."

"You're lookin' at this all wrong." The clouds cleared for a moment and I saw her lean toward me in the darkness, her mouth in a broad smile. "It's the best part."

Chapter Two

I shouldn't have been surprised when I awoke to the sound of gunshots the next morning, but something about living in the suburbs for fourteen years had stripped away my casual acceptance of the sound of imminent demise.

What was more surprising was that Sylvie was sleeping soundly right through it, a tranquil look on her sweet face as she clutched Ruthie the bear.

I knew my mother well enough to know that there was no major cause for alarm, so I padded downstairs and followed the echoing shots to the back porch.

There she stood, cigarette dangling from her lips, bathrobe knotted around her, aiming the shotgun into a tree. She pulled the trigger and I looked up just in time to see two fluff balls shoot straight up out of a nest.

"Gotcha," she whispered.

"Um…Mom? Everything okay out here?" I stayed in the doorway lest she be surprised by my voice and fire on me next.

"Yes, darlin'. Come on out. Just taking care of a little pest problem." She was smiling in a self-satisfied manner as she fell back into a cushioned porch chair. She propped the shotgun on the side table next to her. "You see, those damn squirrels have been gnawing away at the wood on the house. They're living up in that crawl space under the attic, and I've been watchin' them come and go for some time. So today…I was ready."

I looked up at the attic, and then over to the nest, raising my eyebrow.

"I can't have them reproducing. For some reason, the only thing they don't find my attic suitable for is breeding. Took care of that, too."

"Well, Mom, what a productive morning you've had."

She stubbed out the cigarette and took a long sip of coffee. "Indeed. And it's only eight o'clock."

I sat in one of the chairs and pulled my knees to my chest, covering my feet with my nightshirt against the morning coolness. This was my favorite time at the farm. I loved the morning with its stillness gently disturbed by nature as it began its business. It was fresh feeling, completely new. I closed my eyes and rested my head against the pillow.

"Son of a—!" Another shot cut through the morning and I sprang to my feet.

"That should do it." Mom put the gun down and rested back in the chair.

"Well, Mom, I guess I won't be worrying about you living out here all by yourself anymore."

"Oh please, you should never worry about me. I can take care of myself."

"Yes, I know, I guess I just thought it was my daughterly duty or something."

"You should hear your brother," she said and snorted, sitting upright and taking another long sip from her steaming mug. "He manages to fret and worry all the way from Colorado. Not much he could do from there, but that doesn't stop him from worrying about it."

"How is Michael?"

"Doin' well. Kids are in middle school now, couple of brats if you ask me, but he'll learn soon enough you can't give them complete freedom. He's designin' a museum for kids out there. Funny, I think. Still so much like a kid himself."

"I remember the day you threw his plants out of the window."

She chuckled, her eyes crinkling with joy. "After I'd been waterin' those damn plants for three months. Do you know—" she sat and stared at me "—that I only found out about those damn plants because of Oprah Winfrey?" She gave me a look of disbelief. "If she hadn't shown those plants on the TV, I would have gone on watering them. Even added fertilizer." She clucked her tongue in disgust.

"That's one of my favorite memories of you, Mom."

"Well, it was one of my better moments, I think. You might fool me 'cause I don't know about illegal substances, but you can't fool Oprah." She smiled. "No ma'am."

MEGAN PREWITT KOON

In this moment, I loved my mother beyond measure.

"Mommy?" The little voice called through the glass doors that led from the porch to the living room. Her tiny face was pressed against the glass, nose smashed like a pig, mouth grinning like a fool.

"Come on out, baby."

She pushed open the doors and scurried across the porch in her bunny slippers, climbing lithely into my lap.

"Did you sleep well?"

She nodded, snuggling her face into my chest.

"Did you have sweet dreams?"

Another nod.

Mom walked over and scratched Sylvie's back. "Sweet girl, do you like being at Momo's house?"

A nod.

"Want to help me make breakfast?"

The curly head snapped up and Sylvie squealed as she leapt off of my lap and took her grandmother's hand.

"I'm going to get a shower, Mom."

"Why don't you call Dana while you're at it."

"Mom," I gave her a knowing look. "Most of the world isn't up at eight in the morning."

"Honey, most of the world works on a Tuesday morning." She kissed my forehead. "Welcome to the world, baby."

I sat on the porch, watching two of my most favorite people practically skip into the house, my mother's words echoing in my mind. What had I been doing for the past five years? Raising my daughter, of course, which is a full-time job. Any stay-at-home mother would tell you that. And yet, she was right in a way. I hadn't really been in the world, and it stung. Sure, I'd gone back to work when Sylvie went to preschool this year, but it was a cushy job Richard had gotten me as an assistant for a lawyer downtown. I went to work at ten, picked Sylvie up at three, never worked a weekend.

And I had Jeannette, who was a wonderful friend. And my husband, and my daughter. So why did I feel like I hadn't been living?

I looked around at the farm, the quiet whisper of morning, the birds singing as they went about their day, the occasional sounds of a fish or turtle splashing in the lakes right below the house's hilltop perch. All of this had been happening while I had been rushing through my days, carting Sylvie here and there, making sure I was on time for my appointments, playing career woman for five hours a day.

I shook my head and decided a good cup of coffee would cure this and all evils, and when I entered the house, the smell of warm dough and cinnamon brought me back to the world of denial I loved so well.

"Mommy! We're making cinnamon rolls!" Sylvie was standing on a chair, rolling dough into a log.

I peered into the oven where the first batch was beginning to brown. "Smells delicious!"

My mother shoved a coffee mug into my hand. "Take it black, darlin'. You're looking a little dark yourself."

"Gee, thanks, Mom."

"It's what I'm here for, dear." She winked at me and moved to cut Sylvie's cinnamon log into smaller buns.

"Look, Mommy, my hands are sticky!" She licked her palms.

"Ew! Sylvie, that's yucky."

"It's yummy!" She hopped off of the chair and started skating around the hardwood floor in her socks, licking her palms like they were lollipops.

Mom laughed. "Adorable. You used to skate around like that."

"Yeah, not licking bacteria off my hands."

She chuckled at my expense. "You've got to take it easy, Amanda Jane. Relax. She's a kid."

I cocked my eyebrow at her. "And I'm her mother."

She put her hands up in surrender. "Mother knows best."

I sighed and picked Sylvie up, carrying her to the sink without getting cinnamon goo on my nightshirt. She was licking furiously, trying to get every bit of dough before I washed it off. She was like a sugar addict. I figured at any moment she'd go rabid on me.

But instead, sweet little darling that she is, she obediently stuck out her sticky hands and let me rinse them.

"I'm going to get a shower now. Can you watch over her please, Mom?"

She sighed, rolling her eyes dramatically at my daughter. "I suppose."

Sylvie's giggles filled the room.

❤

It's amazing, the healing properties of the hot shower. Washing away all the bad, starting afresh. I toweled off and slipped into a sundress, wet hair wrapped on top of my head in a messy bun.

When I came downstairs, Sylvie's fingers were sticky again and she was eating a banana at the kitchen table.

"Good balance." I grinned, grabbing a sticky cinnamon roll for myself.

"See, I follow the rules." Mom smiled, licking her fingertips.

"Mommy, can I work outside with Momo today?"

"Um...I'm not sure Momo needs help..."

"I most certainly do. This one can pick up all of the clippings I drop. It really would save my old lady back."

"Please, Mommy?" She gave me that look she knows gets me right in the heart. Big eyes, batting eyelashes, smile filling her cute little face.

"Fine. Go get dressed. I unpacked your clothes into the dresser."

"In the low drawers? You know I can't reach very high, Mommy." She stood on her tiptoes to show me just how high she was capable of reaching.

"Just the bottom three."

"Thanks, Mommy."

"And wash your hands!" I called after her.

I took another bite of cinnamon roll as I listened to Sylvie's little feet stomp up the stairs.

"Dang, Mom. You can bake with the best of them."

She had a conniving look on her face. "So can you."

I held up my hands. "No, no, no...don't start."

"I'm only saying, darlin', that you have the trainin', the skills, and you don't use them. Now there are plenty of stores in town that need an extra hand."

A realization struck me right across the face. My mouth dropped open and I leaned across the kitchen island so I could look her in the eyes. "You want me to work at the Nut House."

"I simply want you to find something to occupy your mind—"

"You asked Dana's mom if I could have a job at the Nut House, didn't you? Mo-o-om!" I was shocked at the adolescence dripping from my voice.

"Good Lord, Amanda Jane, you just did a time warp!" She started laughing and couldn't stop, tears filling her eyes. "Well, I'll be! I think I've got my petulant teenage daughter back!"

"Very funny, Mom."

Now the tears streamed down her face as she laughed. "Oh but, honey, the fodder for jokes would be endless."

"Very mature, Mom."

"I'm too old to be mature."

I sighed. "Laugh all you want. I'm not working at the Nut House."

Dana's mother owned a nut and gift shop on Main Street that was frequented by the who's-who of our town. You could rent a wooden stork to display in front of your home when welcoming a new baby or a set of foam tombstones to decorate for someone's 'over-the-hill' celebration. You could purchase a faux cat that purred softly on the couch next to you or a bunch of balloons shaped like body parts that were kept in the notorious 'back room' from which Dana and I were banished as kids. And then there were the nuts, of course.

There was no way on God's Green Earth I was working at the Nut House.

But I would call Dana.

I went upstairs and locked myself in my room with the telephone still corded to the wall—and the piece of paper with her number written elegantly with a red pen. The notepad had the imprint of a cornucopia on it and read *Roberts Produce* in black print.

I must have sat there for five full minutes, staring at that paper. I had no idea how Dana would respond when I called.

Dana and I had been best friends since third grade. We had a standing engagement every Friday night of junior high when we would spend the night at one or the other's house, watch Beaches, and cry over our potato chips, cheese dip, and diet soda. When we started dating, the engagements became bi-weekly, and when I left for college, they stopped altogether. I saw Dana exactly three times after I left for school and she stayed behind to go to community college and work with her mom.

I saw her the first summer, when I came home for a week before heading off to be a counselor at a camp for girls.

I saw her at her wedding, when we were twenty. I was the maid of honor when she married Rusty Clemens, who had graduated two years ahead of us and served in the Army. At the wedding, Dana's contact lens fell out and, being the quintessential maid of honor, I popped that sucker in my mouth and held it there until she finished her vows and left the chapel. Now that's devotion.

And then I saw her nine months later, when Annie Louise Clemens was born. I held the mini-Dana in my arms and swore I would be Auntie Amanda.

And I hadn't seen either of them since.

So you can imagine my nerves as I sat on the bed, willing myself to dial the number clutched in my sweaty hands.

In fact, I don't even remember doing it, I just heard the ringing.

"Hello?" Dana sounded just like herself, which I guess is a stupid observation, but I assumed time would have changed her somehow.

"Dana? It's Amanda."

"Amanda Jane?" The disbelieving voice turned into a shriek. "Amanda Jane! Hey! Hey, how are you?"

I released my breath as I heard the excitement in her voice.

"I'm okay. How are you?"

And she was off.

"Me? Oh, I'm just fine. Workin' away, you know. Annie's finishin' elementary school, which is insane, and the boys are in second grade, so you know I've been plannin' to chaperone that horrible field trip to the water treatment plant. Remember that one? Gosh, I think they would be able to get somethin' better goin' after this long, don't you think?"

I felt my whole body relax and I settled back into the pillows, wrapping the cord around my fingers. "Well, it's kind of a rite of passage."

"I suppose so. So I just got so excited when my mama told me you were in town! When can I see you?"

The lazy ass procrastinator in me panicked. "Um...well, I don't know."

"Listen, I'm busy this mornin', but how about lunch? Is that too short notice? The kids are with my mother-in-law while I'm workin' this summer, and I know Mama will let me off a little longer to meet you. Want to meet here at the shop at twelve? Will that work?"

"Um—yeah, sure."

"Okay, great! Oh I can't WAIT! Amanda Jane, I am just so happy you're home! I missed you, girl!"

"Me too, Dana."

"Okay, gotta go...see you soon! Real soon!"

So clearly my fears were unfounded. Dana hadn't changed at all. It's always amazed me how you can be apart from someone for so long and then things can go right back to the way they were. I guess there's something about best friends. God, do grown-ups even use that word? Somehow it still seemed to fit.

I wasn't sure how to spend the next couple of hours, what with Sylvie outside with my mother and there not being another living soul anywhere near the house, so I flopped on the couch and flipped on the TV. Five channels. That was all my mother had. Okay, well, first paycheck I made, that would have to change. My cell phone had lost reception as soon as I had turned onto this road, so that was out, and Mom had dial-up on her desktop. I'm not even going there.

I pulled a book off of the shelf and curled up on the couch. I couldn't remember when the last time was that I had read a book. It seemed sort of arcane, yet also like it was part of coming home. In high school, I'd loved reading. In fact, I spent one whole summer reading all of Hemingway. I had no idea what any of it meant, of course, but I felt really smart trying to figure it all out. As for the book currently in my hands, I hadn't heard of the author, and five pages in I knew why, so I pulled one of my old school books off of the shelf and gave it a shot.

Two hours later I was running late. It would take me at least thirty minutes to get from the farm to downtown, and I was rushing around nervously, with no clue as to how I should dress.

Back home I would have pulled on some dark jeans and a trendy top, but here, shorts and a t-shirt were more typical. But if I saw anyone I knew, I certainly wanted them to be impressed with how fashionable and—frankly—hot I looked. Secretly I hoped every boy I had dated would be, for some unknown reason, walking down the sidewalk when I stepped out of my car. They would be amazed with how gorgeous I was, more slender now than I had been in school—I mean, I think the chips and cheese dip were to blame, but I could be wrong. My hair was blonde now, my sense of how clothes worked together actually existed, and I was confident. Okay, well, I could fake that last part anyway.

I finally chose a khaki skirt and cute purple top, and slipped on some sandals. I spent a ridiculous amount of time on my hair and make-up, blowing my hair out and running mousse through it before finishing with spray. I looked at myself in the mirror and was appalled.

What was I doing? Who was I trying to impress? My best friend who had stayed home while I ran off and decided to do something 'bigger and better'? The boys I dated in high school who were probably married with kids by now?

I turned my head over in the sink, rinsed my hair, and pulled it into a messy bun. Scrubbed the paint off my face. But I refused to change clothes. There was no crime in being cute, after all.

Just as I was about to hurry out the door, the phone rang. I don't know why I picked it up as it was so unlikely someone was calling for me.

"Hello?"

"Amanda Jane!" I would recognize that voice anywhere. "It's David Harrison! Oh my God, you're home!"

"David...how are you?"

"Better now, girl."

"Listen, I'm getting ready to head out for lunch with Dana..."

"I know. I'm coming too...I was calling to see if that's okay with you."

My heart swelled. "It's better than okay."

"Girl, I don't know what brings you back in town, but I will have you know that when Dana called me last night to tell me you were having lunch, I knew I had to get my business done in the city early and so I'm driving down right now. I can't miss this opportunity...it hasn't come in a while!"

"I know, I'm sorry, I—"

"Don't apologize! You're allowed to have a life! Okay, I need to get off the phone before these truckers run me off the damn road. But I'll see you at the nuts! Ha!"

David Harrison was the third musketeer. He had joined our two-some freshman year of high school when he was too 'effeminate' to be accepted by the jock boys and too 'smart' for the skaters. Luckily, he found us.

He had walked up to our lunch table where we sat with a few other friends, put his tray down, and asked, "Okay, so can I sit here because it's really lame to sit by yourself and I am anything but lame." The rest is history. He eventually started joining us on Friday nights, but only at my house; Dana's mom wouldn't let boys stay over, no matter how harmless.

David had, remarkably, returned to town after college. He was an accountant with the largest firm in town, which isn't saying much really. But he loved his mother, and when she'd begged him to come home, he had. I always figured he was just waiting for her to die so he could escape, guilt-free.

I stopped by the fields on my way down the driveway and hopped out to see my mother and Sylvie pruning blueberry bushes. Sylvie had on tiny, pink, princess-themed gloves and was gathering the scraps and loading them into a cart. My mother was trimming away. They were singing "Supercalifragiliciousexpealidocious" at full volume. Two peas in a pod.

"Mom? I'm heading out. Are you two going to be okay?"

She looked down at Sylvie who was wiping the sweat from her tiny brow.

"Will we be okay, Sylvia?"

"Absolutely!"

She looked back at me matter-of-factly. "We're fine. We'll go inside in a couple of minutes and make some sandwiches or a hot dog or—"

"Hot dog!" Sylvie started dancing around the bushes, singing the name of this delicacy to the tune of "Supercalifragilisticexpealidocious".

My mother raised an eyebrow at me. Damn that eyebrow.

"The kid is acting as if she never gets hot dogs."

I didn't reply.

"Hmmm…" She was sizing me up. "I think I'll give her some Spam, too, just for good measure."

I sighed. "Better be sure to fry it."

"Oh, I will…and douse it in ketchup."

I kissed her on the cheek. "Don't corrupt her, Mom."

"Who? Me?" She held the clippers against her heart and looked me earnestly in the face. She was never good at the innocent act.

"Yeah, you. I want my child's arteries clear when I return."

"I make no promises."

Sylvie pushed her hat brim up with her wrist. "Mommy, where are you going?"

"To have lunch with some friends."

"Who?"

"Their names are Dana and David."

My mother looked up from her pruning. "David Harrison? Oh, how lovely! Tell him I said hello. It's been too long since I've seen that boy."

"Will do, Mom. Sylvie, you do what Momo asks of you, okay?"

"Okee dokee, hokey pokey!" She bent to pick up more dead trimmings.

"I'm off."

My mom winked. "Don't get lost."

♥

A bell tinkled gaily as I opened the door of the Nut House and poked my head inside. There was no one behind the counter, so I stepped in and looked around. It hadn't changed much. The stork signs were still lined up along the back wall, tiny glass figures were displayed inside the case next to the cash register, mylar balloons floated freely along the ceiling.

I looked intently at a rather ingenious mouse trap that appeared to be carved out of a small log when someone emerged from behind the curtain separating the store from storage and my name was squealed across the room.

"AMANDA JANE ROBERTS!" And before I could turn around, I was nearly knocked over by an embrace so strong it could only be Dana's.

"Oh I have missed you somethin' terrible!" she said into my ear, thankfully no longer screaming.

"Me too, Dane."

She pulled back to look me over at arms' length, and I found myself looking at the Dana I remembered. She hadn't changed a bit. Hardly looked any older. She had the same shoulder-length haircut with blonde highlights, the same blue eyes hidden behind delicate frames, the same build, short and sort of full around the hips. The apron embroidered with "That's Nuts!" hid the curves, but I was certain they were there. I was always so jealous of those curves. Mine had not been so much voluptuous as frumpy.

"Well, Amanda Jane, look at you. All citified!" I could have sworn there were tears in her eyes. That southern accent cut right to the quick.

"No, no. Don't say that. My mother might have a heart attack and she's watching my little one."

"Still beautiful. And I'll bet you still only use soap and water on your face."

I nodded. This had always been a point of contention between us. Dana had frequented the feed store where Louie Fisher had always been selling a new tonic for acne treatment. It worked, but I always found mystery tubes with no ingredient labels sold at the feed store to be a little suspect. Dana was just desperate; I stuck with bar soap.

"I could have sworn you'd have the adult acne. Lucky girl. And look at those cute shoes. Love 'em."

"Thanks, Dane. You look great as well. I don't think you've aged a day."

She rolled her eyes. "Girl, if birthin' twin boys didn't do it, I guess I'm destined for eternal youth. And how old is your little one?"

"Sylvie's five."

"Oh, fun! I loved five with Annie. Enjoy it because I'm telling you, with all the drama we caused our mamas as teenagers, we are in for it!" She laughed and took off the apron, revealing dark jeans and a tight black blouse. Wow. I was instantly humbled once again.

"David's meeting us at the Maple Grove Café. Hope it's okay I invited him. Figured if this was gonna be a reunion, it would need to go all the way."

"Absolutely! Together again. How long's it been?"

She sighed. "Too long. This is ridiculous. We have to vow to not let it go this long again."

I laughed. "I don't think that will be a problem for the foreseeable future."

She cocked her head. "You stickin' around then?"

I answered far too quickly. "For a while."

"Best news I've heard all day." She threw her arms around me again and yelled into my ear. "Mama! I'm leavin' for lunch. Be back in a bit!"

Her mother came barreling out of the back room, hands covered in sugar.

"Amanda Jane!" She acted as if she would hug me, thought better of it, and so awkwardly pressed herself against me. I patted her arms.

"Oh honey, I am so glad to see you. Your momma is just so thrilled to have you home. Although I am so sorry for the circumstances—"

"Mama!"

Mrs. Reynolds was a stout woman with a personality to match. She went to the beauty salon every Monday to get her hair done up, and to catch up on the local gossip. I could be sure that my name had come up yesterday. But she had a good heart...just loose lips.

"That's okay. Thanks, Mrs. Reynolds. It's surely less than ideal, but we just have to deal with what life sends our way."

"You always were such a smart little thing." And with that, she gave me a loving slap on the cheek. I'd forgotten just how much that hurt.

Dana rescued me, pulling my arm as my hand flew automatically to my cheek to wipe the sugar away. "Okay, Mama. We're goin' out. I'll be back later."

"Okay, dears. Have fun! I want to hear all about it!"

We shut the door on her final words and Dana whispered. "You'll hear nothing'," and burst out laughing, taking my arm in hers.

"So, AJ, obviously I want to ask the personal questions, but I should probably wait until we get there because Dave will just ask them all over again, but I do want to ask one thing straight out."

"Okay."

"Do we need to enact Operation 15037?"

Operation 15037 was a vow we had made when we were fourteen. It stated that in the event of a broken heart, one of us could ask the other to kill the rotten boy or else take the fall for our own personal vengeance. The closest we had ever come to enacting Operation 15037 was when Dana had lost her virginity in the back of Billy Whitmire's 1982 Ford and he'd broken up with her two days later. In the end, we decided that a jail sentence wouldn't be the way to spend the rest of our teenage years, and probably our twenties as well, so we opted for ritualistically tearing his picture to shreds, dropping it into the toilet, peeing, and flushing it down. Certainly not lady-like, but less messy than murder.

"The jury's still out on that one, Dane, but I think we won't have to resort to it."

"Okay. Although I won't lie to you, I'm a little disappointed. I always wanted to recite the action sequence."

I couldn't help myself. "Alpha Shakespeare Shakespeare Hidalgo Ophelia..."

She slapped her hand over my mouth, a solemn expression on her face. "Don't say the words, AJ. If you do, I won't be able to stop myself. It is my duty."

"Thank you, Wise One."

"So in other news, have you heard about David? I have to know before we get there."

Of course I had heard nothing. Gossip might be rampant in this little town, but my mother was no hub of information.

"David's got a boyfriend..." she said.

I was shocked. Never, NEVER in the history of this town, had a man—or woman—been out and proud. Never.

"What? Who?"

"Samuel Grant. Some guy from Chattanooga. He won't admit it, for his mother's sake, but my mama heard it at the salon, so it must be true." She winked. "But lips sealed, he hasn't told his mama, and my mama doesn't believe it and refuses to repeat somethin' that might kill his mama which means no one knows."

"Well I'll be...things are progressing around here."

"Yeah, and we're fighting it tooth and nail. We can't have any progression, AJ, it just wouldn't be who we are." Her tone was serious, but her eyes laughed as she spoke. "But seriously, act surprised if he tells us."

"Do I need to act surprised that he's gay?"

"Honey, anyone who acts surprised about that little nugget of knowledge needs to get some schoolin'. Or else be beaten upside the head."

We'd reached the café and I saw David through the window. He leapt up when he saw us and nearly crashed into a waitress on his way to the door. He looked like his teenage self, but much more put together. The sloppy t-shirts and jeans were replaced by a casual suit, the shaggy hair cropped short, the gangly frame filled out.

Frankly, he looked pretty hot, and that's totally weird for me to say for so many reasons.

"Amanda Jane!" His arms enveloped me and I was taken back to the last time I saw him, on my front porch, hugging goodbye before setting off for NYU, far, far from here.

So much time had passed, and yet here we all were, back in town as if nothing had changed, but still knowing that so much had.

"AJ, I'm so sorry to hear about what happened." He put his hand on mine as we sat. "But seriously, what happened?" He smiled, half of his mouth curving up in his signature up-to-no-good smirk, his hand on mine.

I shrugged. "Richard had an affair."

A collective gasp from the two sitting around me at the little café table. A couple at the table next to us looked over curiously.

"AJ, Mama told me that you were leaving Richard, but she didn't know why. That's horrible."

"I'm shocked the news didn't get around."

"Your mom kept tight lips." Richard leaned back in his chair and shook his head. "Do we need to enact Operation 05468?

"Nice try, Davie. But you don't know the girl code." Dana winked as the waitress came and brought sweet teas all around. No need to order them here; it's like water. An assumption.

David took a long swig. "You know, it doesn't get better than that. The tea, I mean. The affair is horrible. How did you find out?"

"I caught them."

In unison, "No!"

"Indeed I did. Gave it a month to see if I could get past it, and I couldn't. Separation papers signed. Packed car. Here I am." I lifted my glass in a toast.

"So, the obvious question is..." Dana ran her fingers along her glass nervously. I knew why. This was the questions no one wants to ask and I don't want to answer.

But David would ask it, of course. He leaned across the table and looked me in the eyes.

"Are you going back to him?"

I shrugged. "Who knows. I can't imagine it. I don't think I can get past it. But I feel sorry for Sylvie. She loves her daddy."

Damn it. My eyes were welling up with tears. I blinked really quickly and started fiddling with the straw wrapper. I felt about twelve years old.

"Picture time!" Dana reached for her purse and pulled out her wallet, flipping through a veritable photo album to a group shot of her kids. There was her daughter, now nearly in middle school, sitting amidst twin boys with matching bowl cuts and overalls. They all had the same eyes, Dana's, perfectly round and blue.

"Adorable. Dana—what a sweet family!"

"I think so, too."

I dug out my phone and pulled up a picture of Sylvie at soccer last fall. Her jersey hung down past her knees but she had one hand on her hip and the other balancing the ball on her palm as if it were nothing. She was grinning with a knowledge that she was, in fact, the greatest soccer player of all time. The Pele of Charlotte, North Carolina.

"Awww...so cute." David stuck out his lower lip. "I want a baby."

"Well, darlin', there are some problems with that..."

At this moment, the waitress came to take our order. I knew I needed to watch myself seeing as my gym membership was three hundred miles away, but I heard myself speak the words "Fried chicken with greens and mashed potatoes drowned in gravy...oh, and cornbread." My arteries were already feeling claustrophobic and I could have sworn I was having a heart attack just from uttering the words.

Dana leaned conspiratorially toward David. "So...I heard something about yo—o—o—u!"

"And what might that be—e—e—e?"

She looked at him as if it were the most obvious thing in the world, like he was acting ridiculous.

"That you have a boyfriend, silly!"

"Shhhhhhh!" He leaned in. "This town can't take it! Don't ruin their lunches."

I laughed. "This town needs an attitude adjustment."

"Now, now, Runaway Sue, easy to say when you're just passing through." Dana was chastising me, but she did have a point. I really didn't have the right to insult the place any more. I'd renounced my citizenship.

"Anyway," David continued. "It may or may not be true that I've met someone wonderful who lives just over the border in Tennessee and is a lawyer and loves theatre, like me, and who thinks I'm kind of amazing. And since I agree, it may or may not be a really fantastic thing."

"I'm confused," I said, furrowing my brows in confusion. "Are you gay?"

We all cracked up with the total abandon you can only truly feel when you're with the people who know you best. Tears streamed from my eyes and Dana had collapsed onto her arms, sprawled across the table. David's face was completely covered by a thin white paper napkin.

"God, I've missed you guys." I wiped my tears and took a deep breath.

"We've missed you." Dana's voice was so sincere. "And we're glad you're home where you belong."

I didn't know about the 'belong' part, but I had to admit that in the moment, it definitely felt good to be there.

Chapter Three

O n the drive home, I couldn't help but notice all of the changes that had come over this part of the world. Where trees had once formed thick woods on the sides of the road, houses now stood, built in the latest fashion with siding and lanais terraced with wisteria vines. Where a pasture had once brought out my childhood cries of "Moo Cow! Moo Cow!" a Florida-style house now stood remarkably out of place. Orange stucco with a sunbathing slab next to a man-made lake and in-ground pool. Nothing says 'country' quite like a palm tree planted by the front door.

And of course the power company had claimed farmlands right and left, where cows and horses grazed among the power poles and generators.

Yet many of the farms remained. Red clapboard buildings weathered and shedding their paint. Grand silos slightly rusted but packed to the brim with grain. Tractors toiling noisily in the soybean fields, fenced off from the road with white wooden planks. Things changed, certainly, and I knew all about that. But things also had a way of stubbornly persevering.

And speaking of perseverance, no one could drive down these roads, see the mountains off in the distance, and not admire their beauty. I loved the bluish color they kept in the shade, the too-bright green exposed by the sun, their sheer size looking over the valleys and farmlands below. When I saw those mountains, my heart felt whole. They brought me hope. Because some things can't be broken.

I stopped by a hamburger stand on the way home to pick up milkshakes. Really, you haven't lived until you've had a chocolate milkshake or a fudge nut sundae from one of the hamburger stands in my home-town. When I pulled into the driveway I saw a flash of pink through the rows of blueberry bushes and pulled over to deliver my surprises.

"Mommy!" The pink flash emerged amongst the green leaves hold-ing a bucket and a pair of shears. "I'm helping Momo!"

"I see that." I took the shears from her hand, silently wondering if my mother had forgotten that she would never even let me hold scissors at this age. I replaced them with the milkshake and watched as Sylvie jumped up and down in delight. I think she'd had a milkshake once, after a dance recital. Richard had converted me into a health nut, so fat in a Styrofoam cup hadn't really been a staple in the house.

My mother peeked through the bushes, straw hat perched directly on top of her head, bandana soaked through around her neck.

"How was lunch?"

I handed her a cup and she took a long draw, closed her eyes, and smacked her lips together. "Damn, now that's good."

A tiny echo: "Damn! Now that's GOOD!"

I shot my mother a look and she quickly righted her wrong. "No, no, sweetie. Momo used a bad, bad word. You can't use that word."

"What word?"

To repeat, or not to repeat. That is the question.

I knelt down. "'Damn.' It isn't a good word."

Her eyes grew large. "Is it a bathroom word?"

"Worse."

If her eyes grew any larger, I think she would have floated away. "Is it like saying—" her voice lowered to a whisper—"stupidhead?"

I nodded.

She slapped her hand over her mouth and looked at her grand-mother. "Ohhhhh, Momoooooo! You said a bad word!"

"I know dear, and I'm very sorry. I'm glad you're here to correct me."

Sylvie stuck the straw in her mouth and took a sip. "Don't say that word again, Momo."

The solemnity with which my mother held up her right hand and swore not to use such words again forced me to look away.

Sylvie nodded and moved off to fill her bucket with berries.

"Sorry about that, baby. Not used to little ones around here."

"Mom, I think if that's the worst she hears around here, she'll be fine."

She smiled and took another swig, wiping the sweat from her brow with her other hand. "So how was lunch?"

"Wonderful. Like time hadn't passed at all. We just sat around laughing and talking like we'd never been apart."

"I'm so glad to hear that. That's how you know true friends; they never really leave you."

I nodded. "I guess I'll take Sylvie up to the house now so you can get some work done. Thanks for watching her."

Her brow furrowed. "Now you can't go takin' away my helper. She's been great out here, pickin' up clippings for me and collectin' berries to taste."

"Seriously?"

"Honey, don't take this the wrong way, but she doesn't have your phobia of the out-of-doors."

"I do not have a phobia of the out-of-doors!"

She put her hands on her hips. "Then why are you rushin' inside?"

I looked around me at the baking land. "Because it's hot."

She smiled. "Okay then, a phobia of the heat."

"I do not have a phobia. Is it a crime that I just like to be comfortable?"

She took a sip and turned to walk back where Sylvie was plopping berries into her bucket, but she called over her shoulder.

"Amanda Jane loved bein' outdoors. Couldn't get her to come inside, even in a thunderstorm."

And she left me standing alone, holding my milkshake and pissed as hell that she was right.

❤

I wish I could tell you that I had an epiphany in that moment. That I changed into my frog suit and galoshes and went tramping outside frog gigging or some such country thing, at least that I grabbed a pair of shears and went to work. But instead I chose another book from my mother's library and curled up on the couch. I rose to set the table and to put Sylvie to bed. But this was the extent of my daily routine.

I called Jeannette on my third night back in Georgia.

"Amanda, I miss you! Please say you're coming back home soon."

"I don't know. I can't imagine coming back there. Too much to deal with."

"I know it. Bastard." She took a deep breath and her voice suddenly sounded quite pleasant. "So how is the old family farm?"

I shrugged as if she could see it. "Fine. Quiet. Peaceful. Kind of dull."

"Any cute farm hands?"

I laughed. "Jeannette, if there were any, I'd give you a call and let you know."

"You know I like the rugged typed. A Marlboro man, you know? A cowboy." I could swear she was licking her lips.

"This isn't Texas."

"Oh, you're no fun. Let a girl dream! Besides, there must be cute men in Georgia. Isn't Julia Roberts from Georgia?"

"What does that have to do with cute men?"

"Well, she must have a brother. Therefore, there is at least one good-looking man in Georgia. And I would bet there's more than one."

"Well, if I see any, I'll let you know."

"Don't let me know, take him for yourself!"

I felt my heart drop. "Jeannie, I'm still married."

"To a son-of-a-bitch."

"Married is married."

Her voice changed, grew calmer. "Are you staying married, Amanda?"

It was the question that I couldn't seem to drive far enough away from. The reason I left home and came back to the farm.

"I don't know."

"Okay."

There was an awkward pause while I roused the courage to ask the question. I squirmed in the bed, put my face in the pillow, and closed my eyes. "Have you seen him?"

"No, I think he's staying away from me since I assaulted him with a popcorn tub the last time we crossed paths." She knew how to bring a smile to my face. "Have you talked to him?"

"No, neither has Sylvie. He knows where we are. He can call us if he wants to talk to us."

"Good attitude. In the meantime, do me a favor and remember that you're young, hot, and still breathing. It's not a sin to look."

"Goodnight, Jeannette."

"You're separated, not dead!"

"Goodnight, Jeannette."

"Call me soon."

"I promise."

I hung up the phone and cried myself to sleep.

❤

About a week in, my mother staged an intervention. I was sitting on the back porch one night, snuggled into a deck chair, reading the fifth Agatha Christie book I'd pulled from the shelf, when she marched up to me, snatched the book out of my hand, and threw it over the deck rail into the night.

"What? Mom—what was that?"

She sat next to me and leaned in where I could see her very plainly, her face lit by the porch lights.

"It's time, my love. Time to get your life goin' again."

I sighed and rolled my eyes like a petulant teenager. "Mom, I'm just taking a little break from things. Don't you think I deserve a break?"

"A break ain't the same as a funk. You're in a funk." The southern accent almost made this a humorous statement, but not quite.

"If I'm in a funk, I think I have good reason for it." I crossed my arms and then quickly uncrossed them when I recognized this posture as one of my petulant teenager moves.

"You know you can stay here as long as you like, and you know how I love having my Sylvie Bean here, but you need some purpose."

"I have purpose."

"Oh yeah?" She sat back in her chair. Strangely, when she crossed her own arms she looked intimidating, not at all petulant. Totally unfair.

I took on the lamest look of confidence in the history of womankind. "Sure...I'm a mom, Mom." Lame. "I'm a single parent now. That's a purpose."

"You need a job, butterbean."

Silence fell between us. She was right. She was totally right. But I couldn't surrender this one. I had to at least fight it a little bit.

"I can work here. With you."

"Honey, you and I both know you don't want to do that."

"Part of me does." My voice broke and I didn't even believe myself.

"That's probably true. But, honey, I hate to say this..." She took a deep breath and put her hand on mine. When she spoke the words, they had the gravity usually reserved for the diagnosis of a terminal illness. "Amanda Jane, you've been citified."

This was like a curse. If it had been pronounced at a town meeting, a collective gasp would have escaped the crowd. But she was right, as always.

Funnily enough, the first words that burst from my mouth were not defense, they were defiance.

"I'm not working at the Nut House."

"God, no!"

I relaxed. Nothing could be as bad as that.

"What should I do?" I felt tears come to my eyes. "I don't know what to do, Mom. I don't know what to do on my own. I—I haven't had to do this in a while. And I don't even know where to start..."

She smoothed my hair. "Let's make some calls tomorrow. See what we can do."

I nodded and wiped my nose on the back of my hand. "But what can I do? Really? The job I had back home was just a gift from my boss to my husband. I've no work experience, not really. I mean, I hardly doubt scooping ice cream at the Dari-Dip in high school counts in the business world."

"It counts around here."

I laughed dejectedly. "I have no skills."

She narrowed her eyes at me. "Honey, you can bake with the best of 'em."

I rolled my eyes. "I haven't done that in a while."

"It's like riding a bike, dear."

"With training wheels."

She shrugged. "It still gets you where you need to go."

My mother leaned forward and wiped a tear from my cheek like she used to do when I was a child.

"Mama, there's no way anyone in this town will hire an inexperienced baker, culinary arts degree or not."

She winked at me and sat back in her chair. "I think you might be surprised about that, Amanda Jane."

❤

The bell tinkled lightly as I cautiously opened the door of Beulah's Bake Shop. Beulah May Foxfire had gone to school with my mother and had made the cake for her wedding to my father. In fact, she made every wedding cake needed in town. About ten years ago a woman new in town—obviously, or she would never have made such a ridiculous mistake—opened a rival bakery. She lasted a month. Sure, you could buy a cookie from her, but no one in their right mind would dare buy a cake. Okay, fine, one person, a jilted boyfriend of Beulah's from high school, bought a birthday cake from her, but he was the only one. Now that shop was closed and that man could never buy a baked good in town again. Idiot.

The shop was nothing if not tidy. A display case held cookies and cupcakes decorated with flowers, beach balls and the UGA bulldog, UGA. A cookie emblazoned with the American flag sat slightly below a Confederate cupcake.

The walls were shelved with faux cakes of various levels of decoration. My favorite was a *Gone with the Wind* cake—it is the official movie of Georgia, and let no one tell you otherwise—screenprinted with the movie poster. Wedding cakes cascading with flowers, covered in icy laces, and topped with ornate wedding scenes filled the shelved walls.

But the piece de la resistance was the cake in the center of the room, on a table of its own. It was created in the shape of, and screenprinted with the image of George W. Bush. And in large icing letters underneath, it read, "God Bless the USA."

I heard a gasp and then a southern-aristocrat voice drawled, "Amanda Jane Roberts! Come on over here and give me a hug, darlin'!" And there she was. It amazed me that Beulah had seemed not to age a day. It also amazed me that I seemed to be everyone's "darlin.'" Southern hospitality at its finest.

"Hi, Aunt Beulah." Another Southern pleasantry, calling a woman 'aunt' who bears absolutely no genetic relationship to you.

"Oh, sweet darlin', let me look at you." She held me at arm's length and gave me the ol' up-and-down. I hadn't been looked at this way since my single college days.

She clucked her tongue. "Put on a little around the middle, huh? No matter. Just shows you've born a child and lived to tell the tale!" She waved her arms, sending bracelets jingling about. I reminded myself that I needed to cut down on the fried foods.

"Now let's see, your momma tells me you're looking for a job and you've got the experience."

"Yes, ma'am."

"What's your specialty?"

"My—uh…"

She waved her arms again. "Your specialty. Rum cakes, pralines, macaroons, cupcakes. What are you best at?"

I racked my brain, searching back, back to culinary arts school. What had I loved to make more than anything else? Of course.

"Tiramisu."

Her eyes widened and she clucked her tongue. "Hmmm…high fa-lutin' fancy dessert. We don't make it here. Hmmm…"

I shifted awkwardly, wondering if I would seriously not get this job because I made a kick ass tiramisu.

"Can you un-fancify it?"

"Pardon?"

Again with the hand waving. Now her head was getting into the action, too. It was amazing, really, that her hair was so set that it never even moved as she spun into a frenzy before my eyes.

"Can you un-fancify it…you know, make it so people around here could understand what they're eating."

I shrugged. "So re-name it."

She looked appalled. "Now, now, we ain't cheats. No—change an ingredient, too."

"Okay." Not okay, actually, but I needed the job.

"Can you ice?"

"Yes, ma'am."

"Work with curds?"

"Yes, ma'am."

"Build a multi-layered cake?"

I nodded.

"Make divinity so it don't fall flat."

"Um…well I'm willing to try."

She stared at me.

"You can't make divinity, dear?"

"Well, I haven't actually attempted—"

She held up a jangling hand. "You can learn."

"Yes, ma'am."

"Good…when can you start?"

"Any time. I just need—"

"Great. Come back and sign some paperwork and throw on an apron, honey. I've got more cakes to make than I have hands to make 'em. Let's go."

And with that, I was employed.

I called my mother to let her know I wouldn't be home until dinner, although Beulah promised me that since there were such early hours, I could be done by early afternoon as a general rule. Except when there was a city-wide wedding, as most of them were. And summer was wedding season. So I expected long days.

That afternoon, I decorated a wedding cake for Missy May Spencer. I recognized the name as I'd gone to high school with her sister, Angela. Angela had always been pretty nice to me, and I wanted to impress Beulah, so I flipped back through my internal file on icing and pulled out the card for lace. I draped that cake in such beautiful icing lace, and Beulah gave a little manicured clap when she saw it.

"Beautiful! Oh, Amanda Jane, I feel this is gonna be a great thing! Now, honey, come on over here, I've got some little cookies that need bonnets iced on 'em."

I got home at seven o'clock.

But I was getting paid, I had daily tasks, and I had health insurance for myself now that Sylvie was still on Richard's and it was pretty clear that I wouldn't be for long.

In fact, I had to call and tell him he could go ahead and take me off of his policy. I hadn't spoken to him since we left twelve days ago, and I hadn't planned on doing it this soon. But life has other plans, a lesson I had learned oh-so-well by now.

That night I locked myself in my bedroom and made the call.

Please don't pick up...please don't pick up...please. Damn.

He answered before there was even a ring on my end.

"Hey there, it's me," I squeaked. Keep it cool. Keep it cool.

"Amanda! How are you? How's Sylvie?" Was that relief I detected?

"We're fine...great, actually." I slapped myself in the forehead for sounding so stupid and fake.

"I'm glad to hear that." Then the voice changed. He slipped right into 'poor, poor Richard' mode. God, I hated that. " I'm not so good though. I miss you guys."

"Well, I called for a specific reason. I needed to let you know I have a job, so you can drop me from your insurance. But I'd like for you to keep Sylvie on."

Silence. I guessed he knew what I was really saying. This wasn't about a job. This was about forever.

When he spoke, his voice cracked.

"No, I—I'd like to keep you on. I mean, it'll be a pain and if—when you come home it'll just be a pain again."

"Richard…"

"Don't say it. Please don't say it. Amanda, can I come over there and talk to you? Please?"

"No. No, really, there's nothing left to say." I just wanted to hang up but somehow I didn't have the heart. I mentally slapped my wrist.

"I want to see you. Can I talk to Sylvie?"

"She's asleep. It's ten o'clock."

"I know." He sounded defeated. He was.

"Richard, I can't get past it. I can't. I'm sorry."

"No, I'm sorry. I'm so sorry, Amanda."

I sighed, releasing all the anger in that one note. "It is what it is. There's no going back."

"I'm so sorry."

"Stop saying that."

"I can't. I—"

Wrong. The anger swelled inside of me before I even realized it was there.

"You aren't allowed to be sorry!" I yelled into the phone. "That's not allowed. You are NOT allowed to be the victim!"

"I'm not the victim, Manda, I'm just—"

"No! NO! I'm getting off the phone now."

"Please—"

"You've broken my heart." Damn it, the tears were pouring out now. "You've ruined everything. Just stop now. Stop."

Now it was his turn to sigh, a release of frustration, depression. "I know, Manda."

"Don't call me that."

"Please know that I am sorry. I am. And I'll do whatever you want. You deserve whatever you want."

"Take me off your insurance. That's all I'm asking for right now."

"Okay."

"Thank you."

"Will you tell Sylvie I love her? Can I talk to her some time?"

"Yes and yes. I'm not a monster, Richard. I know she's your daughter."

"I never said you were."

"Goodbye. Call any time she's awake and you can talk to her."

I hung up and buried my face in the pillow. How dare he make me feel like I was to blame somehow? Like he'd done something so innocuous like left his muddy shoes in the middle of the kitchen floor and I'd overreacted about it? I was so angry, frustrated, devastated.

There was nothing to do but cry.

Chapter Four

The bakery was closed on Sundays, of course, along with everything else in town. Dana brought her kids over for Sunday lunch since her husband was at the golf course, also known as 'The Other Church' in our town, and Sylvie was in heaven chasing the boys around the front yard with Annie cheering her on.

Dana and I sat on the porch drinking tea and digesting the honey ham and scalloped potatoes we'd just consumed. Did I mention the carrot soufflé? Best. Vegetable dish. Ever.

"Honey, we need to get you laid."

I spat my tea across the porch rail and into the yard.

"Wow. Just come right out with it, Dane."

She shrugged. "Girl, I can't imagine bein' in your position. I mean, I'm gonna tell it straight. You've got life set up, resigned yourself to the fact that this is the only man you'll ever roll in the hay with ever again in your life, and then upsy-daisy, it all goes to hell in a handbasket and you're left cold and alone in a bed made for two." She lifted her glass in a toast.

"Wow. You make it sound so ideal."

"I'm not kiddin', AJ. You're looking a little worn."

"It's probably because I'm leaving home for the bakery at four-thirty every morning."

She gave me the up-and-down. What was it with this place?

"No. No, you look distinctly undesirable."

"Once again, what a pick-me-up." I ventured another sip.

"Honey, I know you're still married. I get it. I'm not suggesting you violate God's law."

"Then what are you suggesting exactly?"

She looked me in the eyes. "I'm saying you need a man, honey! You need to at least WANT to get laid!"

I shushed her as the kids ran past, not that they would know what we were talking about. Sylvie would simply assume that I was in need of nap time. I imagined her telling me that I really needed to go "get laid" in my bedroom for a few hours. Mercy.

"I'm not even thinking about a man, Dane." I inhaled. "I don't need to depend on a man."

"Bullshit. That's therapist speak. Every woman depends on a man for a few things that she just can't do herself, right?"

By now my face was so red I could actually feel the heat radiating from it.

"Why does everyone want me to find a man? Am I not okay on my own?"

"What other genius have I to thank for planting this idea in your stubborn mind?"

"My friend Jeannette from Charlotte. She's a lot like you, actually, but not nearly as Southern."

"Then she's not nearly as fantastic. That's okay, she can work her way up." She winked at me and took a long swig. My mother, God bless her, chose this moment to join us.

"Oh girls, I can remember when the two of you were just about that age, runnin' around the yard, makin' mud pies and playin' castle."

"Thanks for lunch, Mrs. Roberts."

"You are quite welcome. Thanks for nursin' my girl back to health."

"I'm tryin'." Dana winked at me wickedly.

The bell rang, signaling that someone was approaching the house. The driveway was so long we could hear the bell that signaled at one end of it and suppose who it could be for a solid minute before we ever saw the car.

This time it was a black pickup truck, slightly dusty from the gravel road, but modest, not like those ridiculous, little-man-syndrome, over-compensating tanks you see every way you look these days.

"Oh, Jesse!" My mother leapt to her feet, a broad smile playing at her face.

Dana looked at me in confusion and I shrugged my shoulders.

"Mama, who's Jesse?"

"One of my workers. Maintains the pasture out by the river. Said he'd drop by today and deliver some honey. He has some hives down by the blueberries."

A beekeeper. I envisioned a man emerging from the truck decked head to toe in nets and a hazmat suit. I rolled my eyes at Dana and leaned back to let the heat sun my face. I was about to chastise Dana for her completely inappropriate conversation when I heard her exhale.

"Jiminy Christmas, Amanda Jane, that sure don't look like any beekeeper I've ever seen..."

But by God, she was right. This beekeeper wasn't some old man in white. No, this beekeeper was the Marlboro man. Okay, maybe not *tho* Marlboro man, but a reasonable facsimile. He was around my age, a little taller than me with a broad build, tanned from working outside, and green eyes that smiled and sparkled. One word—beautiful.

Dana's mouth had dropped open. "Now we'll find out if you're alive or dead, AJ. Do you see this man?"

"He's not a man. He's a god." I whispered the words quite subconsciously as he strolled up to us with my mother.

"Ladies." He tipped his hat. HE TIPPED HIS HAT. I think I blacked out for a couple of seconds because I don't remember replying, but surely I did.

"Jesse, this is my daughter, Amanda Jane." He reached out a hand and I shook it. It was calloused from work, which for some reason I can't explain I found extremely sexy.

"Ma'am."

Seriously? *Seriously?*

"And her friend, Dana." Dana nearly leapt from her chair as she offered her hand.

"I'm Jesse Gregory. Work for Mrs. Roberts over in the far pasture."

"Nice to meet you. So nice." Dana was still shaking his hand. I gave her a look and she dropped it like it were a snake. So much for her big talk.

"Mrs. Roberts, ladies, I'm sorry to interrupt you on Sunday, but I brought some honey by, like I promised, and I had a bit of honeycomb as well, so I thought you might could use it."

"Thank you, Jesse. That would be wonderful."

He smiled and went to get the flat of honey out of his truck. He moved easily, with confidence.

Dana was in my ear. "Is your heart still beatin'?"

"No."

He set the honey by the back door and wiped his brow. Is it possible that every single move he made was heat stroke inducing?

Suddenly, I was speaking. I must have been possessed. "Would you like some tea?"

He smiled and looked me right in the eyes. I saw his mouth moving, but I have no idea what he said. I was deaf.

"We'll get it." Dana took me by the arm and pulled me into the house. She lowered her voice. "I am a prophet! Seriously! I should go into fortune-telling!"

"I hardly think we're going to just step around back and have sex."

"Is that all you think about, AJ?"

I rolled my eyes.

"I'm just sayin'. Here's a gorgeous man who spends a lot of time here, and he's right in front of you!"

"Dana, I've been here two weeks and I've never met the man. I hardly think that makes a relationship likely. What am I supposed to do? Casually wander into a pasture one day looking like I'm lost? Offering to bring him tea?"

She looked at me as if I were a complete idiot. "Yes."

I took the tea, gave her the most judgmental look I could muster, and strode back to the porch. Jesse and my mother were laughing at the kids who were now acting out the roles of farm animals with Annie as farmer. Sylvie, the pig, was wallowing in the pine needled dirt.

"Beautiful daughter you have there." And his voice was like velvet. This was ridiculous.

"Thank you."

"How old is she?"

"Five."

He nodded. "I have a niece who's five. Wild little thing. But sweet as can be."

"Sounds like Sylvie."

"The name suits her."

"Thanks."

An awkward pause ensued during which my mother and Dana wore looks that suggested they'd both won the lottery.

"Well," he tipped his hat again. I kind of loved that little maneuver. "I guess I'd better be headin' out. Thank you for the tea. It sure was nice to meet you ladies." He smiled at us, mostly at me, I think. "I'll be here bright and early, Mrs. Roberts."

"Thanks, Jesse. Please send your mother my best."

"Yes, ma'am. Dana. Amanda Jane."

As he drove away we three women stared after him in silence. My mother, being used to seeing this gorgeousness, was the first to speak.

"He's such a nice young man."

Dana and I nodded.

"And just about your age, Amanda Jane."

I put my hands over my eyes.

"You two keep forgetting that I am married—MARRIED," I said. "I can't just run after the first man I see."

My mother shrugged. "But you can look."

"You two are impossible!" I stomped back into the house to cool off, watching the conspirers smile at each other as I left. If you want to know the truth, I ran to the front windows and watched him drive away in a cloud of dust.

❤

Working at the bakery was proving to be more entertaining than I would have imagined. Beulah, truth be told, provided most of the humor when she wasn't intending it, but the customers were more than I bargained for.

One day a woman with bright red lipstick matching her bright red fingernails came bebopping into the store, purse on a golden chain swinging as she moved. She looked into our display case and stood with a shock, her hand on her heart.

"Cream broolee! Oh my Gawd! Beulah, you've got cream broolee in here! Honey, you are moving up in the world!"

Beulah smiled with pride as I rolled my eyes.

"I'll have one of them cream broolees, pour favour!"

Clearly the foreign language department at the local high school was in need of some self-examination.

Another morning a boy came in, probably eighteen years old, buying birthday cupcakes for his girlfriend. The head-to-toe camo should have tipped me off, but I try not to judge a cow by its spots.

"Good mornin', ma'am. I—I need some cupcakes, please."

"Certainly. How many?"

"What? Um..." He shifted, his hands plunged into his pockets.

"They usually come in groups of twelve, but I can do a half dozen if you'd like."

"Yes, ma'am."

"Okay. What flavor?"

"Chocolate!" He smiled. This was an easy one. The next—not so easy.

"And frosting...what flavor and what color?"

"Um...what?"

"What kind of frosting would you like?"

He looked around the shop, completely lost amidst the laces and frills, the little sprinkles and coconut grasses.

He ran a hand through his hair.

"Well, what's her favorite color?" I was trying to help, truly I was.

He looked at me and I swear his eyes filled with tears. He looked so pathetic. Not "geez, that's so pathetic" pathetic, but devastatingly pathetic.

"Okay, well, what do you two like to do together?" I immediately regretted the question and prayed the answer wouldn't be TMI.

His face brightened and the hands came out of the pockets.

"We like to go huntin'."

Unexpected, but much better than the many alternatives dancing through my mind.

"Great...so, perhaps camo colored?"

"You can do that?" Seriously, it was like Christmas morning for this kid. His eyes lit up and he clapped his hands in front of his face.

"Sure."

"Thank you, ma'am. Thank you!"

But my favorite customer to date was Joel Farmer. Mr. Farmer was an institution in Carroll. He must have been one hundred years old. And that's saying something, because when I was seven I also thought he was one hundred years old. So we'll just say he was rather advanced in years, but he always had a slew of women around vying for his money—er, affection. Really, he was a lot like Hugh Hefner—sans the velvet robe.

Beulah nearly tripped over herself running to serve him.

"How are you two lovely ladies this morning?" He winked and I threw up a little in my mouth.

"Oh, lovely, Mr. Farmer, just wonderfully. And how are you?" Really, she was all over him with her puckered red lips and batting eyelashes.

"Just fine, my dear."

"How can we help you?"

He smiled and when he spoke it was a cheerful proclamation. "I've come to order food for my funeral!"

Beulah's eyes turned red and she rushed behind the counter, abandoning me with this ladies' man.

He smiled. "And who do I have the pleasure of meeting this morning, young lady?" He took my hand and kissed it. I almost laughed but I was pretty sure I'd be fired, so I set my jaw and replied.

"Amanda Roberts, sir."

"Hmm...any relation to Marilyn Roberts?"

"She's my mother."

He banged his silver-headed cane onto the ground. "Marilyn Roberts! Haw! I couldn't never get her on my arm. Tell me, is she on the market? There's still time in me yet!"

"Um...sorry, sir. She isn't on the market." I knew she'd thank me for the lie.

"Damn. The one that got away."

I intervened before he had a chance to say that her daughter would do just fine. "Yes, sir. Now, about your order."

"Yes, yes. Write this down." Bang with the cane again.

I hurried to the counter to get an order pad and found Beulah wiping away tears by the fridge. I wanted to tell her to get a grip, but that didn't seem like something you say to your boss. So I simply rolled my eyes and walked away.

"Fire away, sir." Pen poised, ready to go.

"Three dozen coconut macaroons. Three—no four dozen chocolate chip cookies. Not the chunky kind, mind you, the real deal. Chips—not chunks. Four dozen cupcakes. Yellow. Green frosting. No sprinkles or any such nonsense. Three cakes. One, chocolate with chocolate frosting. Two layers. Round. My face emblazoned on top. Two, vanilla, one layer. Rectangular. Buttercream frosting. Flowers and whatever looks nice. No pink. My name across in lovely script. Traditional. Three, the grand finale. A three tiered cake! One carrot, one red velvet, one strawberry something-or-other. Gold everywhere!" He was waving his arms as he spoke and they led him to the display case.

"What's this?" He tapped on the case, pointing to my faux-tiramisu.

"Um...ladyfinger delight, sir."

He looked at me as if I were a bug. A stupid bug.

"Looks like tiramisu."

"Yes, sir. Very similar."

"Can you make tiramisu?"

"Yes, sir. It's my specialty."

"Wonderful!" Bang with the cane. "Four dozen tiramisu, each on an individual plate!"

"Yes, sir. Does that complete your order?"

"It does. Delivery date to be announced. Bill me." And, with a wink, he and his cane banged through the door.

I rushed back to Beulah. "This is going to cost him a fortune! A three tiered caked!"

Her eyes were red and mascara had run in two dark streaks down her face.

All this, and as I write, he's still alive and surrounded by women.

❤

That very afternoon as I was elbow deep in a bowl of dough, kneading the base for an orange-cranberry nut bread that I had assured Beulah would bring in those who needed just a touch of sweetness in their lives, I heard her whistling out front. This was not a good sign. The only reason a true Southern woman whistles is as a warm-up to some kind of nosiness, gossip, or unsolicited advice. Unfortunately for me, I was stuck there with no time to rinse off the dough and lock myself in the refrigerator.

"Amanda Jane?" Her head peeked into the back room followed by her whole self. Today she was wearing a pink dress, a la *I Love Lucy*, and the ruffles were just peeking out underneath.

"Yes, ma'am?"

"You been goin' out much since you arrived back in town?"

I had no idea where this was going, but I was certain it wasn't anywhere good.

"Oh, just a bit with some friends. I've been keeping pretty busy between working and taking care of Sylvie in the evenings."

"Mmm..." Another bad sign. This had her thinking. She seated herself on a pillow-topped stool and idly flipped through a kitchen supply magazine.

I continued my kneading, though I realized I was truly tearing at the dough. At one point I shoved it so hard I knocked a canister of powdered sugar off of the other end of the work table. The air was thick with sugary haze and yet Beulah kept on flipping.

"Hmm...maybe we need some new biscuit cutters in here. We can use those for many-a-thing and I just don't think those ol' plastic ones we have are as efficient as these here metal ones I'm a-spyin'."

"I couldn't agree more." I covered the bowl with plastic wrap and set it in an unlit oven to rise. If I hurried and scrubbed the stubborn dough off of my arms, I might be able to escape before...

"Amanda Jane, do you know my son, Robbie?"

Ah...there it is.

"You know, I don't think I do. Did he go to Northeast High?"

"Yes, yes, but a few years before you I'm sure. He's supervisin' one of the carpet mills out there in the county. Makin' a good livin' and just bought him a big, two-story house out in Magnolia Heights."

I made a face as if I were impressed. In truth, I had no idea where Magnolia Heights was. I assumed it was one of those new subdivisions that had replaced the forest down by the Interstate.

"Well he's been so lonesome, workin' so hard to make a stable life, that he hasn't taken the time to find someone to share it with."

And with that, the nausea struck. Dear God above, why was dough so sticky? I considered the mess it would cause in my car if I suddenly declared the necessity of an emergency run to the bank and fled the store.

"Anyway, I think the two of you would get right along, so I passed along your phone number to him."

I was pretty certain this violated some kind of legal or at least ethic code, handing out an employee's phone number without permission.

"Well, that's mighty thoughtful of you, but I am still married, you see."

Her eyes peered innocently over the top of her magazine. "Not for long, though, right, dear?"

I'm not sure what I was feeling. Was it rage? Hurt? Embarrassment? Incredulousness? All of the above?

"Well, that's really not yet determined, Miss Beulah, so I have to say I—"

"He's a catch, Amanda Jane. And remember honey, happy Beulah means happy days."

I didn't remember learning that one in school.

"Mommy, today Momo took me to the Chickamauga DAM Battlefield!"

My mother turned to me with a guilty smile. "I can explain."

"Please do."

"Mommy! Mommy!" She crinkled up her little nose, the curls bouncing around her face. "Chickamauga DAM Battlefield!" She burst into giggles and started rolling on the floor. "DAM is a funny word!" She put her hands over her mouth to stifle the giggles.

When I spoke, my voice was a couple of octaves too high. "Okay, okay, little girl, run into the living room and clean up the dolls you've got scattered all over the rug."

She reached up and kissed me on the lips, then skipped from the room.

I gave my mother a look which threatened a quick end to her life if I didn't get a quicker explanation.

"Well dear, we decided to go on a picnic today at the Chickamauga Battlefield. You always did love it as a child, you know, with the tower and all the monuments…"

"Yes, yes, get to the dam."

"So we drove under a sign for the Chickamauga Dam. Is it my fault your child can read so well? I tried to stop her from chanting it over and over. Somehow she combined the dam with the battlefield and, well…" She looked helpless. I couldn't help but smile.

"Okay, that's kind of hilarious, Mom."

"I know. I explained that this 'dam' isn't a bad word, but she still found it hilarious." She started chuckling.

"CHICKAMAUGA DAM BATTLEFIELD!" the little voice called from the living room. I looked around the corner and Sylvie was doubled-up, rolling around amongst the dolls. By this time, I was laughing so hard there were tears burning my eyes.

"So how do we stop this?"

"Do we have to?" My mother was wiping her eyes with a paper towel.

"I think we do. Sadly."

"Eh, give it overnight. She'll forget about it tomorrow morning."

"I guess we have to stop laughing about it, too."

"That would probably be wise."

I hugged my mother. "I love you, Mom."

"Thanks, sweetheart. I love you, too."

"Can I help with dinner?"

"Sure." She bustled over to the sink and pulled out a package of ground meat. "Go ahead and knead this in a metal bowl for me."

My tired hands ached in protest, but I willed them to pick up the hunk of ground beef.

"Meatloaf?"

"Your favorite."

"Mom, I think I've gained ten pounds since I've arrived. I'm going to have to go shopping for more clothes soon."

"Good! You were too skinny anyway. I knew Charlotte was a city, but I didn't know it wasn't the South."

"Don't let them hear you say that."

She started chopping potatoes. "Seriously, you're skin and bone. You need some meat on you, girl. You look like a scarecrow."

"Gee, thanks."

She paused and looked endearingly at me. "A beautiful scarecrow."

"Not possible."

"Indeed. Marcelle Lewis up the road had a scarecrow in her garden done up like Dolly Parton. It was lovely. Couldn't stand upright, but it was lovely."

"I wish I'd seen that."

"I think she threw it in the river when she was finished with it. It's probably washed down here by now."

I imagined gazing into the placid depths of the river only to be suddenly faced with a limp scarecrow with ridiculously bloated breasts. Dolly would not be pleased.

"That's really scary."

She shrugged. "If that's the worst she's thrown in that river, we're okay."

"What's that supposed to mean?"

She dumped the potatoes in the water to boil and checked the green beans, now wilted and floating aimlessly with the fatback. Good Lord.

"People have started dumping their trash in the river somewhere upstream. Once in a while I see a tire or some metal come floating down, and the water's becoming murky and kind of discolored."

I started waving my meaty hands in the air, flinging pink chunks around the kitchen. "You have to do something about that, Mom!"

"Like what, honey?"

"I don't know…call somebody!"

MEGAN PREWITT KOON

55

"Who?"

"I don't know...the Farm Bureau!"

She looked at me as a teacher looks at the sweetest kid in the class who is also a complete idiot.

"That's not really the Farm Bureau's problem."

"Well, it's someone's problem! They're polluting the river! Killing the wildlife! And how will you water the fields, Mom?"

"I—I don't know. I've just been doing it anyway."

I washed my hands and stormed from the room, my residual frustration finding its outlet. As I crossed the living room, a little voice called out, "Mommy? What are you doing?" Sylvie followed me like a tiny marching shadow.

"Saving the world."

"Wow...you're a superhero."

"No, honey," my mother's voice called from the kitchen. "Just a woman scorned!"

"Mommy, you're a woman scorned!" She squealed the words as if this were the most wonderful thing I could possibly be called.

I turned around and knelt in front of her. "Honey, what happened on Dora when the ocean was all polluted?"

Her lower lip stuck out as she relived the painful memories. "The mermaids had nowhere to live!"

"Exactly. Go tell your Momo that." I heard her run off calling in that tattle-tale tone of voice that only young children can produce.

I ran to my room and picked up the phone.

"Hey, baby, what's shakin'?"

"David, this is serious. I need legal advice."

His tone went deadpan. I could tell he was 'in character.'

"About the divorce. Well, I looked it up, and according to North Carolina law you have to wait one year from the day you officially moved out. So I'd say you've got about ten and a half months to go."

"No, no, not about that. I know all that."

"Oh. Okay then, what is it?"

"If someone is polluting the river such that my mother cannot use the water in the fields, who do I need to contact about that?"

He laughed. "AJ, I don't do this kind of thing. But let me check and I'll call you back...maybe tomorrow? I know some people who might have the answers."

"Okay. Thanks, Davie."

"Hey, how's it going, other than the fact you've polluted the red states with your tree-hugging agenda?"

"Fine. Work's good. Sylvie's being a great help to Mom, actually. So it's all good."

"Have you spoken to Richard—not to bring up a bastard subject."

"Ha—good one. And yes, briefly. Nothing's changed. In fact, it's becoming clearer that I can't go back."

"I'm sorry, AJ."

I shook my head. "Nope. Don't be sorry. I'm not cutting it all off just yet, but I am seeing that I can be pretty good on my own."

"No doubt."

"Also, my boss tried to shove her son on me today."

David burst out laughing. I heard someone in the background ask what was funny. So there was someone in my sweet friend's life...

"Oh AJ, please say it ain't so! That witch's son is the lowest of all human flesh. Why, he goes to the Tipsy Tulip Tavern on Fridays and... and..." He couldn't bring himself to finish the sentence. In my mind I finished it for him—gambles his money away, leaves with a different girl every week, stiffs the bartender, gets in a fistfight over darts...

"He—he sings 'You Were Always on My Mind' every week, drunk as a skunk and belching the whole way through!"

Well this was unexpected.

"He dares to blaspheme the great Willie Nelson?"

David was pulling himself together. "The very same."

"Well, I was planning on marrying him, but now I guess I need to reconsider."

"You do that, AJ."

"Okay, gotta run get dinner together. Maybe we could hang out one day soon?"

"Sure...I might have someone you should meet." I could hear the smile.

"Ooh...aren't I a lucky girl."

"You have no idea. You're before my mother."

"No surprise there."

"No, not really. But I think to make this real I have to introduce him to my life some way."

"I'm the way?"

"You and Dane."

"I'm so honored. So glad I came home."

I could hear the smile in his voice. "We're all glad, AJ. Have a good night. You'll hear from me tomorrow."

"Thanks. Love you, Davie."

"Love you."

I hung up and proudly sauntered back into the kitchen.

"So…filed a complaint?" Mom was mashing potatoes with an electric mixer and yelling over the noise.

"Not yet. But I'm on my way. What's next?"

"Your daughter set the table."

I looked to find the table set perfectly backwards, silverware switched to opposing sides of the plate. But it was a start.

"You can take the cornbread out."

"Yes, ma'am." I grabbed the homemade oven mitts and went to work.

"So, honey, should I take all this as a sign that you're an environmental hippie and a democrat to boot?"

"Mom, I find it shocking that you aren't more upset by this."

"When it starts hurting my crops, I'll find the fire to do something about it. And believe me, heads will roll."

"Well, I don't intend to let it get that far." I flipped the cornbread upside down out of the pan and onto a towel.

"Well, thank you, dear. Truth is I just can't shift my focus when we open in two days."

"How's everything coming together?"

She spooned the potatoes into a bowl. "Sylvie's washed the buckets, I've numbered the rows and set up the tent. I think we're ready."

"Awesome. Want me to take off from the bakery for opening day?"

"Nah…just hurry home. Takes this old body a few days to adjust to sitting around not messing with the berries."

"You got it. All right, Sylvie, supper's on!"

The patter of her feet announced her arrival before the giggles. She folded her hands in prayer, bowed her head, and giggled. "Chickamauga DAM Battlefield!"

Chapter Five

And so my daily routine became: get up at four and be ready to leave by four-thirty. Bake. Sell. Get home by two-thirty, change clothes, and sit in the field while Momo and Sylvie take a break and get supper ready. Close the gates at five o'clock and eat dinner. Love my daughter. Put her to bed by seven-thirty. Love my mother. In bed by nine to read. Asleep by nine-thirty.

And I loved it.

My favorite moment of the day was walking down to the berry stand and having my sweaty, stinky little berry fairy run into my arms and kiss me all over the face. I usually had a little piece of sweet bread in my pocket that she could snack on, and she reached greedily for it each day, squealing in delight.

And so I sat in the afternoons, reading my book, perched on a picnic table, waiting for customers.

After about five days of this routine, before I realized that I should just go into the house between two-thirty and four because it was too hot for anyone to dare come to the fields, I was reading *Death on the Nile*, not paying any attention to my job, when suddenly I heard a car door slam.

What idiot is out here in the heat of the day to pick blueberries?

I shaded my eyes with my hand and saw him walking toward me from that black pickup truck. My heart leapt into my throat and my head started swimming. Was I twelve years old?

"Afternoon." Geez, he was tipping that hat again. I exhaled far too loudly.

"Sorry, you surprised me. I was totally immersed in this book." Way to play it smooth, Amanda.

"A good one?"

I showed him the cover, thankful that I wasn't reading girl smut.

He nodded. "Oh, I read that a while back. Read all of her books, actually. My mom had the whole set and I was bored one summer in high school. Really good writer, that one."

And he reads! I realized I was looking temptation in the bright green eyes.

I cleared my throat. "Yeah, I like her a lot. I've been reading my mom's books this summer. Didn't think to bring any of my own with me."

He sat on the edge of the picnic table. "So you're just visiting then—Amanda, right?"

"Yes. Well...I'm not really sure. I'm thinking of moving back here."

He grinned. "Funny, lots of people can't wait to get out of this town. You're comin' back. I like that. As for me, I couldn't leave this place. Born and raised here."

"Oh really? What high school did you go to?"

He looked at me suspiciously. "What school did YOU go to?"

"Northeast High."

"County."

"Ooh..." I made a pained face. "I'm sorry to hear that."

"Don't be sorry. We hold more state football titles than you do, so I think we're doin' all right."

"Fair enough."

"So where are you movin' back from? If I'm not bein' too forward."

"No, no that's fine. Charlotte, North Carolina."

"The city."

I rolled my eyes. "As I keep being reminded."

He laughed at me, took off his hat and ran his hand through his hair. I noticed it was thick and dark brown and for a moment, I was jealous of that hand. No. Stop it, Amanda! Get control of yourself. Seriously.

"By who?"

"By everyone. Evidently I've been 'citified.'" I made air quotation marks. Mortifying.

He faked shock. "Oh no...don't say the word!" Man, his eyes were pretty when he laughed. "But really, that's not so bad. Being citified isn't something that can't be undone."

"What? Enough frog gigging and handfishing and I'll be back to normal?"

"No. That's just a stereotype."

I felt my face flush. Great, now I'd insulted him. "Oh, okay then, Dr....um..."

"Jesse."

"Yes, Dr. Jesse. What's the prescription?" I felt myself smiling flirtatiously.

"Fishin', for one."

"Never really cared for it."

He looked genuinely surprised. "Okay. Football."

"Okay. That's fair."

"High school football."

"Ew."

He held up his hands in defense. "Now, now. There's more."

"Okay."

He leaned toward me, his eyes sparkling. I think time froze. When I regained the ability to breathe, he was whispering, "Lots and lots of barbecue."

"Mmm...now that's something I can do."

"There's more to come. But that's what I've got for now."

"It's a start."

"Sure is." Cue awkward pause with me squirming on the picnic table while he fiddled with that hat. Thank God he found some words. "So where are your momma and that sweet little girl?"

"In the house. It's my shift."

"Workin' at home, too?"

"I actually work at Beulah's Bakery in the mornings, then I come here."

"How's workin' with Beulah?" There was something devilish in his eyes.

"Hmm...what's the right word?" I dangled my legs from the table, kicking the bench with my heels. "It's unpredictable."

He nodded, a sideways smile playing on his lips. "Good choice. Very fair."

I was feeling brave now. "So what's your story, Jesse? If you don't mind my asking, of course."

"No, no. Happy to oblige. I work for your momma in the far fields, and I run my own little bee business on the side. She's kind enough to let me use her blueberries for the bees."

"Mutual benefit, I guess."

"Yes. That's true. I give her some honey, she lets me trespass on her property." He winked. Winked. I nearly passed out, which is totally lame. And yet it was in that moment that I lost control of my mouth.

"Married?" Bold, Amanda. Bold.

"No, ma'am." He was blushing. I felt my face turn red and begged it to go back to normal.

"Sorry. That was too personal."

"No, no. It's fine. I'm not gonna tell you much more than that, but it's a fair question. You?"

Now, shouldn't I have known he would ask after I so stupidly blurted out that ridiculously personal question?

"Separated. Divorcing. Kind of messy."

He pulled his hat down over his eyes. "Now I'm sorry I asked."

"Well, between the two of us we're just completely inappropriate, I guess." Wow. Good one, Amanda. Good one. Way to insult him and look like you have no self-confidence. Totally attractive.

"I'm in good company, I think."

"Gee, thanks."

"Okay, I gotta run." He hopped off of the table and dusted off the back of his jeans. I can't even bear to tell you what I was thinking then. I assume you can imagine. "Will you tell your momma that I finished up the soybeans and I'll get started on the cow pasture tomorrow?"

"She'll know what that means?"

"Yes, ma'am."

"Listen, Jesse, the ma'am thing is really sweet, but it makes me feel old."

"It's because you've been 'citified.'" He tipped his hat. "My pleasure, ma'am."

I waved as he lifted himself into the truck and drove slowly away into the dust, and when I could no longer see him, I put my face in my hands.

This is trouble, Amanda. This is trouble.

❤

After that initial awkwardness, the second most exciting moment of my day was Jesse's daily stop by the picnic table to give me a report for my mother. Most days he simply drank a cup of water, passed on a message, and tipped his hat in farewell. Once in a while he'd stay and chat for a few minutes, but as the days wore on, more people started venturing the heat and picking berries, thus cutting away at any time we had for private conversation. Of course I say that as if we would have been having deep, meaningful conversations if only we'd had some privacy. Yeah, and the cows would sprout angels' wings.

In other news, David had called me the day after our initial conversation to let me know what I needed to do about the pollution problem with the river.

"I did some research—"

"Let me stop you right there, Davie. You're using your 'lawyer voice'. How about your 'Davie voice'?"

"Sorry...so anyway, there's a law. OCGA Title Twelve, Article Two, Section A-1 states that no one shall, without a permit, 'Construct, install, or modify any system for disposal of sewage, industrial wastes, or other wastes, or any extension or addition thereto, when the disposal of the sewage, industrial wastes, or other wastes constitutes pollution'; and Section A-2 states further that no one shall 'increase the volume or strength of any sewage, industrial wastes, or other wastes in excess of permissive discharges specified under any existing permit.' "

My poor little brain stopped listening at 'Article Two'. "Yeah, great...so what do we do?"

"You need to contact the Environmental Protection Division of the Georgia Department of Natural Resources. The Regional Branch."

"Okay. And what am I supposed to say? That there's sewage running down the river? I'm sure they get that a lot."

"Yeah. So, this is the part I don't think you'll like."

Classic David line. In high school, he would come charging to the lunch table, book bag slinging about, nearly taking the heads off the Snob Squad as he passed their domain, and he'd be breathless as he threw himself into a chair.

"Oh...my...God!"

Cue friends leaning forward in anticipation.

"I heard...that the principal...is going to install a nap room."

"Awesome!"

"Sweet!"

He held up his hand. "But here's the part I don't think you'll like."

Cue friends leaning forward in anticipation once again.

"It's for the teachers."

Wamp wa-a-a-a-a-ah!

So you can imagine my reaction when this Davidism issued from his lips.

"You're gonna have to track down the source of the pollution first."

"Great. And how do I do that? Traverse the river?"

"Pretty much."

Great. Just what I wanted to do. Climb along the river until I found out who was polluting it. Which meant I'd be waist-deep in pollution by the time I got there, and would probably produce only three-eyed children from now on. Not that I was planning to procreate any time soon. I mean, there was no one to procreate with. Well, there was. But wait. No. Nevermind. Nevermind.

"Okay…so when do you want to come check it out?"

Silence.

"Mandy, I love you. I really do."

Another classic. I expected, 'But you just can't pull off the stirrup pants look' to follow.

"But I'm not getting in that river. I've spent most of my formative years trying to get away from this place, and I cannot immerse myself in a central symbol of this cesspool. It's too figurative. Sorry."

I sighed. "Fine, fine. I'll find someone else."

"And I wouldn't ask Dana. She has a child and I'm not convinced you'll come back from this mission."

"I'm rolling my eyes."

"I know."

"And I also have a child, in case you've forgotten."

"So I've heard. But she's newly exposed so there's still hope for her."

"I registered her for kindergarten yesterday."

"She's doomed."

"David!" I fell back on the pillows and covered my eyes with my arm. "We went through school here and we turned out okay."

"Define 'okay.' "

"Normal."

"Define 'normal.' "

"You're making me feel insane."

"My point exactly."

"Okay, I'm getting off the phone now. I'll report back when I have an address."

"I'll make the call then. You go in the field, I'll be intelligence."

"Debatable."

"Ha, ha, AJ."

"See ya, Dave."

I hung up and covered my eyes with both arms. This wasn't good news. I certainly couldn't go marching down the river myself, and the only two people I really spoke to in this town weren't acceptable companions. My mother was too old for this, and the idea of Beulah dipping a big toe in the river was enough to get me laughing. No, I'd have to think of something else....

❤

The next afternoon I was lounging in the hammock I'd rigged between two trees at the U-Pick headquarters alongside the fields, reading a rather scandalous Hemingway novel I'd found on my mother's shelf, when Jesse arrived. Today he made himself comfortable on the edge of the picnic table and poured a drink of water from the cooler we had set up for customers.

"And how has your day been, Amanda Jane?"

I shaded my eyes with the book. "Nightmarish. This morning I was working on an order of fifty cupcakes for Loretta Miller's Garden Club gala and the oven freaked out. Burned the whole batch. Loretta came in and I hadn't added the candied flowers to the tops. She flipped out. Threatened to sue."

"Threatened to sue over candied flowers?"

I nodded. "*Tardy* candied flowers."

"She needs a hobby."

"She has one. It's flowers."

He started laughing and I couldn't help but join him. He had a deep, joyful laugh, and his eyes got really bright and pleasant. It was totally cute. I silently chastised myself for admiring him.

"Well, I didn't get that much entertainment in the soybean fields."

"Entertainment? I'd take the fields. It's quiet and no one yells at you about cupcakes."

"Yeah, well, it's quite all right. A little lonely, too."

It was in that moment that I realized that the answer to my problem was right in front of me. I popped up in the hammock so quickly I almost overturned. Next thing I knew, this fine specimen of manhood was on the ground below me, arms outstretched for the catch.

"Why, thank you."

He nodded and stepped back.

"Say, Jesse, would you like to do me a favor? I swear you won't be lonely." Oh Lordy, it sounded like I was flirting. In my mind the words replayed in a deep, raspy voice: "I swear you won't be lonely… love-rrrrrrrrrrr."

"Sure thing, Amanda Jane. What can I do for you?"

I gave myself a mental slap and focused on the bigger issue.

"I need someone to come with me down the river to check out where all that trash is coming from."

"I'm in. Been tellin' your momma for months now that she needs to do somethin' about that."

I felt my face turn red.

"Thank you."

"When do we go?"

"Um…how about tomorrow morning? I'm off from Beulah's and Mom and Sylvie will watch the fields."

"I'll be here at seven."

I held up a hand. "Let's not get carried away."

He grinned. "Don't you usually get up earlier than that?"

"Yes, that's why I'm NOT getting up that early on my day off. Eight o'clock."

"Eight it is." He tipped his hat again. Man, that was hot.

Of course, it was the peak of summer.

❤

At eight AM, I was zipping up a camouflage frog suit. Sylvie was beside herself with laughter.

"Mommy, you look like a TREE!" She fell over backwards, clutching her sides.

"It's called 'camo.'" I planted a fist on my hip and struck a pose.

"If you go outside, birds will land on your head! They'll build a nest and have babies in your HAIR!" Tears sprang from her eyes. She got that from me.

"I hope not!"

"And then…then…" She could barely breathe. "Then the squirrels will come up in your hair and Momo will SHOOT them!"

"Okay…not funny anymore." I tickled her feet and she writhed around the bed. "Say the magic words! Say the magic words!"

She giggled something that sounded like, "I love muffmees!"

"I can't hear you!"

"I love muffmees!"

"You love muffmees?"

She was screaming in a frenzy. "I LOVE MOMMY!"

"Whew!" I wiped my forehead and climbed off of the bed. "I was afraid you'd forgotten the magic words."

"No, Mommy Tree. I didn't forget, Mommy Tree." She put her hands over her mouth.

The doorbell rang and I carried her downstairs.

"I'm climbing a tree! I'm climbing a tree!"

Jesse stood at the door in rubber fly fishing pants and a flannel shirt. It wasn't sexy. That was disappointing.

I was more disappointed, though, when he burst out laughing at the sight of me.

"What?"

"You look like a tree."

Sylvie lost control of herself and the two of them were laughing hysterically as I stood there, hands on camouflaged hips. My perfectly punctual mother chose this moment to emerge from the kitchen.

"Why, honey, that frog suit looks great on you. I brought your boots." She looked around. "What's everyone laughin' at?"

"Apparently I look like a tree."

She cocked her head. "I disagree."

"Thanks, Mom."

"You look like a redneck."

"MOM!" I had to force myself not to stomp my foot in a teenage act of petulance.

Sylvie tugged on my leg. "Mommy, what's a redneck?"

I thought that Jesse was going to have to sit down. He leaned against the front porch rail and wiped his eyes.

"I hope you're all happy about this. I'm trying to make a positive change and all you fools can do is make fun of my outfit!"

Mom had her hand over her heart. "Honey, it's just that if you'd told me that I would ever see you lookin' like that, I'd tell you you'd had some bad 'shine."

"Is it so shocking?"

"Yes." She couldn't even get the word out before she broke into laughter again.

"And as for you..." I looked down at Sylvie. "We're gonna get you one of these in your size." I plucked at the camo suit.

She adamantly shook her head, but her mouth was smiling. "No way, Mommy! I don't want birds living in my hair!"

I tousled her curls. "You won't look like a tree. A bush, maybe..."

My mother started pushing me toward the door. Literally, she put her hands on me and shoved. "Okay, you two get goin'. Little peanut and I have to get down to the field and open up."

"Ready, Jessie?"

"Sure am, Maple."

I playfully slapped him on the shoulder and pulled a camo baseball cap onto my head, threading the ponytail through as we walked to the driveway.

I pulled myself into the truck and buckled. Jesse was still grinning. "What now?"

"Buckling up to ride down to the river?"

"You never know."

He nodded. "True. If a mad, rabid deer leaps out of the woods, you'll be safe when I swerve off the road."

"Exactly."

He shook his head and started the engine.

"So what's your plan, Mandy?"

I wasn't sure I liked 'Mandy,' but I figured I'd give it some time before I corrected him.

"Well, I figured we'd put in at the ford and then start walking upstream. I mean, the water level's so low from the drought so I didn't think there was need for a boat."

I swear he looked at me with admiration. "Good plan. We'll just climb along the roots on the sides if it gets too deep."

"Sure. Whatever."

"You never went root climbing as a kid?"

"Do I look like I was the kind of kid that went root climbing?"

He considered me. "Yeah, actually, you do."

"Well, I didn't."

"Handfishing?"

"Absolutely not."

"You never went in the river as a kid? You're kiddin' me right now." He looked genuinely horrified.

I lifted my chin defiantly.

"Of course I went in the river. I walked up and down the river."

"That's reassuring. I thought I was gonna have to turn this truck around."

"It's where I took my boyfriends."

He slammed the brakes and I was thankful for the seat belt.

"You took your boyfriends wadin' in the river?"

I nodded and gave him a mischievous look. When I spoke, I felt the old twang working its way into my voice. "And climbin' trees."

I saw a sparkle in his eyes and it warmed me. He liked what he was hearing.

"Well, Mandy. There's a side to you I haven't considered."

"There's a lot about me you haven't considered, Jesse Gregory."

Seriously, Amanda. Stop flirting! You're not doing yourself any favors here.

He looked like he wanted to say something more but he let out the clutch instead and we bumped along the gravel road.

I leaned my face out of the window and felt the breeze. It was a beautiful morning, cool and fresh, the only sound was the engine as we headed for the river.

"I love it here." The words escaped my lips before I could even consider them.

"What's that?"

"I said I love it here." I realized that it was true. I really did love being home. And I loved being in this pickup truck, even if I did look like a tree.

We reached the edge of the river and parked the truck before picking our way through the wooded trail that led to the ford. The path had been cut wide enough for a tractor to fit through, but the terrain was rough and we could walk faster than carefully bumping along in the truck

The ground was damp from the morning dew and my boots squished into muddy places the sun hadn't dried up from a recent rain. At the ford, we headed down the gravel path and into the river. It was so shallow here as to be only a few inches deep, but it quickly deepened again, the rapids carrying it along.

I squealed as we stepped in and I felt the coolness of the water through the thick boots. It seeped into them, soaking through my suit.

"You needed rubber pants." Jesse looked genuinely concerned.

"I'm going to be mature and not make any jokes about what just came out of your mouth."

That smile was killing me. "You're somethin' else, Amanda Jane."

"Indeed I am." I bravely waded upstream, trying to force a smile even as my teeth chattered.

We walked quietly for some time, the only sound the movement of the water and the chirping of the birds. A mist still hung low over the water and as we got deeper my visibility lowered.

"Too deep, Mandy?"

"Um...yeah, I think so." The water was up to my waist and I was having a difficult time maneuvering in my thick clothes and heavy boots.

I felt his hand take mine and heat shot through my body. I was numb, but it wasn't from the cold.

He guided me to the side of the river and put his hands on my waist to lift me to the underside of the bank where I clung to the large exposed roots.

"You know, Jesse, we could have just walked through the woods at the edge of the river."

"Nah, there's too many fences. Besides, we need to see the moment the water changes, and really, this is so much more fun."

I pulled myself along the edge, fitting my feet into the roots and testing them with my hands before clinging to them.

"Doin' okay, Mandy?"

I grunted as I heaved myself along.

"I'll take that as a 'yes.'"

We climbed along the edge until I could tell that the water had grown a bit shallower. Then he dropped himself in and when I did the same he caught me, his arms around me to hold me steady.

Of course when I hit the water I splashed him in the face. I've always been really smooth like that. I'm surprised I didn't just submerge him.

He wiped the water from his eyes and laughed. "Graceful little thing, ain't ya?"

"I get it from my mother."

That broke him up and we just stood in the water, laughing and trying to wipe the water from our faces with wet hands and sleeves.

It wasn't but about twenty yards farther when I saw the first trash bag. It floated down the river and right past us. Jesse grabbed it and hauled it onto the bank.

The tin cans littering the exposed roots sparkled ironically in the morning sun, and a tire was jammed between two large logs that had washed up against the eroded sides of the river's basin.

A piece of metal that looked like a rusty slide hung over the edge of the bank.

"We're here." And now that we were, I had no idea what we were doing.

He took my hand again. It was warm despite the cool morning.

"This way. Let's climb up and see what we're dealing with."

We climbed the exposed roots and hauled ourselves onto the bank. What I saw as I pulled myself upright truly astonished me.

It was a piece of land cleared of trees and littered with trash. In the center stood a dilapidated shack and a car, tireless, propped on cement blocks. The metal was in fact a trash slide, set up against the side of the shack.

"They seriously just slide their trash into the river?"

"Looks that way."

Jesse started toward the shack and I grabbed his shoulder.

"What are you doing?"

"Going to talk to them."

My heart raced. "Are you insane? You'll get shot!"

His eyes twinkled. "You're really cute, Mandy, do you know that?" And he turned and strode toward the building.

I scurried behind him, more out of the fear of being left alone than anything else.

I was sure that his weight on the porch would be too much for the old wood, but it held him and he knocked and then stood back.

Nothing.

"Anyone home?" He knocked again. "We'd like to talk to you about the trash in the river. We want to help you find a better way of getting rid of it."

Nothing.

Jesse sighed in frustration. He leaned toward the window but it was shrouded with a calico curtain.

He knocked once more and then backed off of the porch.

"No one's home?" I whispered.

"Nobody's answerin' the door."

I nodded. "So no one's home."

He looked at me and for the first time, I saw anger in his eye.

"A coward is home. Just not answerin' the door."

"Oh. Okay." I felt foolish standing there in my soaking suit, limp ponytail, and muddy boots. "So what now?"

"Now we go home. Get the address for this place. Make a report."

"Okay."

"We're fixin' this." There was determination in his voice and his eyes and I saw his jaw clench. "We're fixin' this for your mama."

We went back to the river and looked at the trash slide. It was poorly constructed, and I doubted that using it was any easier than just tossing the junk directly into the water. But what worried me was that the metal was corroded as if something acidic had been poured down it.

We climbed back down to the river and lowered ourselves into the water.

"I can't believe people really live that way." It was a stupid thing to say, but the silence was uncomfortable and Jesse still had that determined look on his face.

"Believe it."

Wow. So that was obviously a great conversation starter. I decided on another tactic.

"Jesse, are there snakes in this water?"

"Sure. Moccasins and the like."

I froze. That was supposed to be a stupid city-girl comment. It was meant to be cute, not true!

"Seriously?"

He turned around and looked at me. I must have looked beyond pathetic because the serious look melted off of his face and it brightened into a smile.

"Mandy, you're in the woods. Of course there are snakes. Did you think this was a lifeless river?"

"I didn't think anything. OH MY GOD!" I swear something wrapped itself around my ankle. I started thrashing and leaping around the water, splashing my hands and shrieking. I thrashed so hard I lost balance and went under. It was really quiet under there. With the snakes.

Jesse pulled me up. "Mandy...have you lost your mind?"

Tears filled my eyes. "I—I swear something wrapped around my legs."

He struggled to keep a straight face. "It probably did. It was probably just a plant of some kind."

"It was a snake."

"Doubtful."

I just stared at him, standing there in the river, completely comfortable. Of course I had been completely comfortable as well until I realized there was wildlife traveling alongside me.

"Can you walk, Mandy?"

"I'm so embarrassed."

"He reached out and hugged me. "I'm sorry. Don't be embarrassed. You're fine."

Tears stung my eyes and when I spoke, my voice was a sob. "It's true. I'm—citified, aren't I?"

He let go of me and stepped back to look me over. "Yeah, a little bit."

I slammed my fists into the water. "I hate this! I hate this! I don't want to be this way!"

"Hey, it's the way you are, and it's fine. Besides, it's awful funny."

I splashed him. "Don't make fun of me."

He held up his hands in self-defense. "Wouldn't dream of it."

"Yeah. Thanks for that. Let's go." I wiped at my eyes and started stomping my way downstream, which turned out to be an easy task after fighting our way up.

When we reached the ford we got out and grabbed towels from the back of the truck.

I took my duffel bag of clothes and went around to the other side. "No peeking."

He turned and walked into the woods. "Holler when you're done. I swear I'm a gentleman."

My suit was soaked through and the dry clothes felt so clean against my skin. I pulled on a pair of gym shorts and a t-shirt. Of course I hadn't packed an extra bra so the water soaked through the shirt and gave me a 'wet t-shirt' look which was just swell. I crossed my arms and called for Jesse.

I swear, that man has a team of experts that hide just out of sight and leap into action whenever he needs to freshen up. He'd changed into jeans and a t-shirt and his hair was perfectly groomed. I felt just lovely with my limp ponytail dripping down my back.

We climbed into the truck and he rolled the windows down for a breeze. It was silent for a while until his voice cut through the hum of the motor.

"You know, we didn't get all the answers, but that was kinda fun."

I looked over at him. He was smiling, driving with one arm resting on the window ledge and the other on the wheel.

"Yeah, I guess it kinda was."

"I especially liked it when you started screaming about the snake that wrapped around your leg." He started giggling like a schoolboy.

"It WAS a snake!"

"Sure it was."

"I swear! It was a snake. I almost died." I couldn't keep a straight face.

"You're crazy, Amanda Jane."

"Yeah, well. I get it honestly."

We drove along in silence for a moment. I looked out the window at the fields as we passed. It was so quiet here, so calming.

"You know, your mama saved my life."

I raised an eyebrow. "Wow. That's dramatic."

"I mean it. I was out of school and didn't have a job. My parents had moved away so I was all on my own. I didn't want to leave here and go with them, wanted to start out on my own, you know? And your mama gave me a job."

"Wow."

"Yeah. I love my parents. Go see them every other Sunday. I couldn't tell them they were about to have to support me again, after they'd sacrificed so much to send me to agriculture school. Your mama saved me. Saved my life. I was at the edge."

He didn't look at me, but I saw that his jaw was clenched. It was really taking a lot for him to say all this to me. "Wow, Jesse. I don't really know what to say to that."

He shrugged. "Just wanted to let you know that we all go through things. You and me—we're just lucky we have your mama to help us through it."

I considered that. What would I have done if my mother hadn't been here to give me a home to come back to? Stayed in Charlotte? Moved to the first random city that came to mind? I shuddered. And yet here I was...

We pulled up to the house and I was still in a daze, imagining Sylvie and me in a one bedroom apartment in Atlanta.

"Amanda?"

My attention shifted and I saw this man sitting next to me. And before I even knew what I was about to do, I'd leaned in and kissed him.

He didn't pull back, but let me kiss him, and then he started kissing me, too.

Oh my God, I realized. I'm kissing a boy in a pickup truck.

And suddenly I didn't feel quite so 'citified' anymore.

Chapter Six

Shame. Shame shame shame. That's what I felt. And complete humiliation. I think to myself, what does a self-respecting young woman
do after kissing a devastatingly gorgeous young man in his pickup truck?
Smile sweetly and bat her eyes? Raise an eyebrow and say something
clever like, "That was delicious"? Look alluring and say a simple, "Wow"?
I don't know, but I can tell you what she doesn't do. Say "Oh my God,"
throw open the truck door, fall out of it onto her rear end, and then crab
walk and scramble back into the house. But naturally, that's what I did.

So it wasn't enough that I was completely ashamed of kissing a
man when I was technically still married. No, I had also behaved like a
complete spaz after I did it.

"Okay, Amanda Jane, I'm sure it wasn't that bad."

Dana, bless her heart, was sitting on the back porch with me while
her kids and Sylvie played. Sylvie told me they were making 'caterpillar houses,' but they looked like glorified piles of dirt. There were also
some mud pies made of rocks and orange mud that were served to us
every few minutes. Thank God Dana had also brought some potato
chips and cheese dip with her. Comfort food. I'd already eaten so many
that the roof of my mouth was raw.

"Believe me, it was that bad." I put my hands over my face for what
seemed like the umpteenth time. "Worse."

"Okay, let's think about this." She took a long sip of her tea and
leaned back in her chair, her legs curled up beneath her. "Did he kiss
you back?"

I couldn't bear to relive the memory. "Um…I think so. I mean, he didn't pull away in disgust if that's what you mean."

"No, I mean did he kiss you back? Did he touch your face or stick his tongue in your mouth or something?"

I crinkled my nose. When you put it that way, kissing sounded like assault.

"I mean, I think he touched my face. Or something. He definitely touched something!" I was on my knees in the chair and I could feel my face brighten as if the fact that he touched me somewhere deleted the crab walk of doom.

Dana tilted her head, her eyes softening. "Aw…you look so happy, AJ."

"I don't know. I feel rotten about it. I'm still married."

"Because of the law."

"Is that why?" I couldn't believe I'd said the words.

Dana suddenly looked intensely concerned. "What does that mean? If you could divorce Richard right now, would you?"

What a horrible question. I looked past the porch and saw Sylvie totally immersed in her caterpillar house.

"I guess so."

"You guess so?"

"Dane, we're talking about divorce. That's kind of a big deal."

"I know that, AJ. But we're also talking about your happiness. Would you be happy going back to Richard?"

I involuntarily shook my head. I could feel my body closing in on itself.

"No. I could never trust him again."

Dana's face mirrored my own and I knew she was imagining how I felt.

"I'm sorry, Amanda Jane. But you can't undo the past. What's done is done, no matter how much you wish it wasn't."

I shrugged.

"Has he called?"

"A couple times. I just let Sylvie answer the phone, and then I leave the room so when she says I'm not there she can tell the truth."

"That's really sad. You're literally running away from this."

"I am." My voice broke and I felt the tears. Damn truth.

"Well, I guess when something like this happens, you just have to make a decision. Do you deserve to be happy or not?" She stood and stretched, glancing at the kids. "And you and Sylvie both deserve to be happy."

"I haven't told her yet."

Dana froze. "What does she think is going on?"

I shrugged again. That seemed to be my gesture of choice today. "She thinks we're on vacation."

"When are you going to tell her?"

"I figured I'd know when. I'd feel it."

"You just don't want to do it, do you?" How could she still know me so well after so many years apart?

"I don't."

She knelt in front of me and took my hands. "Can I give you more some advice? Tell her. Go ahead and tell her. She'll probably take it better than you think she will. She's a very smart little girl. I think she probably already knows more than you think."

I looked over at my child, who was clearly the site manager on the caterpillar houses. She was bossing around Dana's kids, having them collect supplies while she tried various configurations of mud and sticks. I was so proud of her, but the sight of her confidence also broke my heart. I never wanted her to suffer the break in confidence I had.

"Dana, how do you tell a five year old that her family is breaking apart?"

She smiled. "With love."

I leaned forward and wrapped my arms around her. "Thanks, Dane."

She whispered in my ear. "And pull yourself together and talk to Jesse."

"Um...okay."

She pulled away and gave me a knowing look. "You'll totally regret it if you don't."

I nodded. That's when the 'Mom Finger' came out and Dana used her grown-up voice as she wagged it at me. "I mean it! Talk to him. You'd be insane not to."

"Okay, okay. I'll do that. Just one thing at a time, okay?"

"Fair enough. Kids! Clean up now. We gotta get home. Mama's got a casserole to put in the oven!" Cue collective groan.

I took Sylvie inside and straight to the shower where I hosed her down and washed away the caterpillar house that had somehow managed to explode all over her.

"Mommy! This is scary!"

"It's like a waterfall."

Her big eyes grew even larger.

"A waterfall! Like in the books!"

I paused, my soapy hands in her hair.

"Would you like to go and see a waterfall some time?"

She nodded so hard that shampoo hit me in the face.

"Please, Mommy! Please, Mommy! Please, please, please, please!"

"Okay, okay!" I laughed at her joy over such a small thing.

"Are there waterfalls at Momo's house?"

"Well, there are waterfalls in those mountains you see when we drive into town."

Complete awe. "Wo-o-o-ow."

I rinsed the little squirmer and wrestled her into pajamas.

When I had her in bed, I turned down the lights and knelt next to her, taking her tiny hand in mine. Sometimes I just couldn't stop staring at her. How beautiful she was, how sweet and good. I loved the sweetness of her smile, the pure joy in her eyes. It hurt, how much I loved her.

"Mommy," she looked out of the corner of her eye, "Why are you staring at me?"

"Because you're so beautiful."

She reached out and touched my face. "You're beautiful. And you're so soft, Mommy."

"Thanks, baby. But I need to talk to you about something."

I smiled, but in all honesty I was pretty certain I was going to throw up everywhere. I made sure there was a wastebasket nearby. Seriously, I did.

"Okay, Mommy!"

I squeezed her tiny hand.

"Sylvie, Mommy and Daddy have decided not to be married anymore."

It was only in this moment that I realized I probably should have let Richard know I was doing this. I mean, I respected him as Sylvie's father. But I'd already dropped the bomb, so...

"Okay."

That was it. She looked at me expectantly.

"Um...okay, so that means we won't all live together anymore."

"Why?" There was no sadness in the question, just genuine curiosity.

"Well, because when Mommies and Daddies decide not to be married anymore, they also decide to live in different places. But that's

MEGAN PREWITT KOON

kind of neat because you get TWO houses!" Wow. Overcompensating much? "Um...yes, for a little while anyway."

She seemed to think about that for a minute. When she responded, it was with absolute certainty, and it absolutely surprised me. "I want to live here forever, Mommy."

"Oh." I was caught off guard. "Okay, well, I'll think about that." This was confusing...why wasn't she devastated? " So do you have any questions about Mommy and Daddy?"

She looked thoughtful. "Will I ever get to see Daddy again?"

"Absolutely."

"Okay. And are you and Daddy having a fight?"

"Not really. We're just going to live in different places now."

"Okay. Should I be sad, Mommy?"

"I—um...I don't think so."

"Okay. Because you look sad, Mommy." She reached up and touched my face. What a heartbreaker. I knew I had to get out of there pretty quickly, but I didn't want to leave until she was finished talking to me. I fought hard to keep those tears in.

"I'm not, baby. I'm actually really happy to be here with you and Momo."

"Good, Mommy. You're prettier when you're happy."

"Thanks." I kissed her little puckered lips and squeezed her. "I love you, baby."

"I love you, Mommy. Night night!"

She pulled the covers to her chin and settled in with the myriad stuffed animals she had unearthed from Momo's attic.

I closed the door and tiptoed downstairs. My mother was sitting in the living room, knitting and watching her preacher-of-the-week.

"Sit down, honey. This guy is on FIRE! AMEN!" She thrust a needle into the air and it nearly caught me as I scooted past her, wiping my eyes.

I looked at the screen. The preacher was sweating bullets and was definitely being visited by a mighty spirit.

"Mom, why do you watch this? This isn't anything like the church you dragged Mike and me to growing up."

"Exactly. This is the real thing."

"Why? Because he's shouting it a little louder?"

Her eyes shot daggers. You didn't mess with my mother and her religion. "I don't like your tone, Amanda Jane. And as a matter of fact, yes. He means it. That's more than I can say for that so-called godly man I sat and listened to for fifteen years."

"I guess he did run off with the minister of music."

She cut her eyes toward me. "Indeed he did."

The show ended and my mother flipped the channel to *Jeopardy* where she could watch her other spiritual guide, Alex Trebek.

"I'm still mad about the mustache."

"Mom, I need to tell you something."

She turned Trebek down a little and moved toward me.

"I told Sylvie tonight that her father and I were splitting up."

Now she muted Trebek and turned to give her full attention to me. She had that 'proud parent' look on her face, with just a twinge of surprise mixed in.

"You did, did you? And when did you decide on this?"

"Well, I figured I should tell her sooner rather than later."

"I mean that you were splitting up."

"What? I mean, I'm here. Obviously I'm not trying to work it out." She shrugged. "I wasn't sure."

She flipped off Trebek and all I could hear was the clicking of her needles. This was serious.

"What are your plans, then, sweet girl?"

"Plans?"

"Yes. Plans. Are you staying here?"

"Here? The house?" I was shifting awkwardly, like I didn't know what to do with my body. My legs were all twisted and my hands were pulling strings from my shirt. I had expected motherly praise and comfort, not an interrogation regarding my future plans.

"No, honey. Here. In town. Are you staying?"

"For now, yes."

"Okay, that's all I needed to know. You know you can stay here as long as you'd like. I like the company and besides, I'm not as young as I like to think I am." She chuckled to herself. "Of course, I'm not as old as some people think I am, either."

"Thanks, Mom."

"I love you."

"I love you, too." It was such an authentic, sweet moment. I reached out and took my mother's hand. She looked into my eyes. "Now call Jesse."

"Mama!" I dropped her hand. "Why is everyone so obsessed with me and Jesse?"

She shot a look at me. "You and Jesse...that's EXACTLY what I'm talking about!"

"Mom, seriously."

"I am being serious, sweetheart. He's a wonderful young man, and not bad on the eyes, either." Her eyebrows wiggled and I fell back on the couch in defeat.

"I know, I know. But everyone seems to forget that I am still married."

"Well, that's true."

"Thank you."

"But you're separated. You deserve to be happy. I don't think God is going to smite you for kissing a good looking man when your marriage is only still valid because of a man-imposed waiting period."

"Wow, you've really thought this through."

"I have."

"More than I have."

"Probably. I think you'll find that your obsession with your children's happiness never goes away. Every day I pray for your happiness. That's what I want more than anything else I can think of."

"Mom, that's...that's..."

She stopped knitting and looked me deep in the eyes. "Love. And I want love for you. Real love."

"Mom, I'm not in love with Jesse. I barely know him."

"Get to know him. There's no harm in that."

My face started hurting and I realized I'd been smiling the entire time she'd been talking.

"Okay, Mom."

"But no frisky business. I do draw the line there."

"Mom!"

She smiled and brushed my hair out of my eyes like she used to when I was a kid.

"You're so beautiful."

"I take after you."

"Damn right you do. Now get along with you. You might be beautiful, but you need a shower."

Have I mentioned how much I love that woman?

❤

The bell tinkled, announcing the first arrival of the morning. My hands were covered in flour so I dusted them off and went out front only to find myself face to face with Jesse.

And of course I looked just fabulous with a messy ponytail and fly-aways covering my face. I had a flour-handprint right over my breasts as I'd emphatically thrown my hand over my heart when explaining to Beulah the glory of fondant icing this morning. In short, I was a hot mess in front of a hot man. Damnation.

"Mornin'." There he was, titling that hat again. It must work with all the ladies.

"Good morning, Jesse. How may I help you?"

He grinned, his eyes twinkling. "I've always heard about the famous Beulah croissants—" he pronounced it 'cruh-sants' and that's when I knew I was smitten, because I found it cute and not horribly repulsive "—and I thought I'd try one."

"You're in luck!" I was putting on a show and it was beyond lame. "They're hot and fresh! You'll like it hot."

Wow....*wow.*

He didn't say anything, but I could see he was about to laugh.

I reached onto a tray sitting behind me and delicately picked up a croissant.

"Would you like honey with it?"

"What do you recommend?"

"Butter and honey. It makes it really creamy and sweet." I had totally lost control of what I was saying, like some sort of crazy person, but I couldn't stop. That must be why I said, "It gets your lips sticky."

Train wreck.

"Is that so?"

I nodded and enacted a vow of silence as I brought the plate to the one small table we had set up in the shop.

"Could you join me for a minute?" he whispered, presumably so Beulah wouldn't hear him from the back.

"Um, I really can't. I—I have a big order of buns for a church lunch."

He burst out laughing and I couldn't help but join him.

"I'm a mess. Really, Jesse. I'm an awkward mess." I couldn't even look at him.

"Well if it's gonna be this hard on you, I swear I won't let you kiss me again."

I dared a look and saw him smiling at me, eyebrows raised in anticipation. I had to say something smooth now. This was my moment. Maybe, "That's okay, you can kiss me next time" or "Then make it easy on me." As usual, my words made me want to sink into the floor.

"It's not hard on me. It's not hard. Not hard at all."

Death. Slow. Painful. Death. By. Humiliation.

He took a bite of the croissant. "Man, this is really good."

I nodded, not even allowing my lips to part.

"Did you make these?"

I shook my head.

"Beulah?"

Nod.

"Well, then, what's your specialty?"

Dear God, guide my tongue to say the words I mean to say.

"Tiramisu."

He nodded. "I know that stuff. My momma always ordered it at the Olive Garden."

Nod.

"Can I have one of those?"

"At nine in the morning?" Watch it, girl.

"Sure."

I shrugged and went to get him a piece. He took one bite and puckered his lips.

"What is this?"

"Ladyfingers, espresso, cheese..."

"That's disgusting."

"Gee, thanks."

"Sorry. I just—I wasn't expecting that." He wiped his mouth furiously.

"It's okay. I won't charge you. Just don't tell."

"Boy Scouts Honor."

I cleared his plate and watched as he tried to erase the taste with the rest of the croissant. I brought him a glass of water and he washed it all down.

"So, Amanda Jane, I was wondering if I could take you out sometime."

The dreaded moment. It occurred to me that I must be the worst parent in the world if I dreaded telling this near-stranger about my divorce more than I dreaded telling my own child.

"Jesse, I—I don't know if you really want to do that."

"I do."

"Yeah, well, you see, there's a little complication."

"You're married. You told me."

"Um, yes, I am."

"But you're separated?"

"Yes, we're divorcing. There's just—a waiting period."

He nodded and seemed to consider all of this.

"Okay, I'll ask again. Amanda, Jane, may I please take you out on a proper date?"

This was unexpected. I didn't know what to say. I could hear Jeannette's voice in my head: 'Are you *insane*? Go, girl! This boy's a hot one!'

"Okay."

He tossed a few dollars onto the table. "I'll pick you up at seven."

"Tonight?"

"Yes, ma'am. I don't see the point in waitin'. We aren't gettin' any younger." He winked at me, tipped the hat, and with a tinkle of the bell, disappeared out the door.

I was stunned. What had I just done?

I heard a whistle behind me and turned to find Beulah sliding a tray of cupcakes into the display case.

"He's a looker, all right. Not like my Robbie, but nothin' to complain about. Wish I could get my hands on one like that!"

I was the envy of a seventy-year-old widow with the self-image of a twenty year old. Things were looking up.

❤

"Hello, Wendell." I saw him walking up the sidewalk and so steeled myself for the daily rejection.

Wendell Jones owned a body shop near my mother's farm. He was about eighty years old and cute as a button. He was a widower, and I guess he'd taken a fancy to my lawnmower-inspired cupcakes earlier in the summer, for now he poked his head in the door every day and asked me on a date.

"Is today the day, Amanda Jane?" His hair was all a mess and covered with the usual greasy baseball cap.

"Not today, Wendell Jones." I couldn't help but smile at his genuine goodness. He nodded, his eyes still twinkling.

MEGAN PREWITT KOON

85

"I've got another day in me yet!" And the bell tinkled as he strutted from the shop.

Wendell Jones made my day. I never knew exactly what time he would arrive, but he seemed to know when he was needed.

At precisely four o'clock I hung up my apron and tossed a hasty farewell to Beulah who had her hands busy with Annie Parsons, a thirty-something single-mother with too much time on her hands and a husband who thought she could bake like Julia Child. They were cooking up a red velvet cake for Mr. Parsons' birthday.

On my way home I dialed Jeannette.

"Girl! How are you? What's new in the sticks?"

Hearing her voice instantly calmed my nerves.

"I have a date tonight."

I heard tires squeal on the other end of the line.

"WHAT? How could you not tell me before now? Oh my God, what are you going to wear?"

"Jeannette, I just got asked today, and I don't know what to wear, that's why I called my resident fashionista."

"Who is he?"

"His name is Jesse." Pause.

"That's all I get?"

I sighed. "Of course not. His name is Jesse. I think he's about my age, give or take. He works on my mother's farm..."

"Oh. My. God. You've got yourself a cowboy!"

"That's an exaggeration. Cowboys drive cattle. He drives a Ford."

"Besides the point! Okay, girl...more! More, please!"

"I don't know. He's really cute and funny. And he sort of kissed me the other—"

"WHAT!" I was beginning to regret calling her cell; it was clear she was about to drive off of the road.

"Jeannie, maybe you should pull over."

"Honey, I just pulled over at the sketchiest gas station on Planet Earth, but I don't even care. I want details!"

"There aren't many. We were walking down the river looking for the origin of some pollution—"

"What the hell are you talking about?"

In this moment I realized just how far away she was. I suppose this could have been dramatic, shocking, depressing, but I was too distracted by the evening's entertainment to care.

"Long story, but anyway...we were driving home. Well, he was driving me home in his pickup truck and we were parked in front of the house and..." I stopped speaking for fear I'd lean forward to kiss the steering wheel by mistake and drive right off the road.

"And..." I could tell this was making her slightly insane.

"And I kissed him."

"YOU kissed HIM?"

"Yep."

Pause.

"Girl, I am so proud of you."

"Why, thank you."

"And then he asked you out?"

"Basically."

"So you need to wear something incredibly sexy. Like that little black lace thing you wore to—"

"Let me stop you right there, Jeannie. I kissed the boy. That certainly doesn't mean anything else is going to happen. And besides, there is absolutely no place in this town he could possibly take me where that dress would do anything but cause heart attacks and make every woman in town hate my guts."

"What kind of place are you trapped in? Do you need me to come over there and break you out?"

I laughed. "Jeannie, it's a different world. But it's kind of a nice one."

"I'll have to come see some time, I guess."

The image of Jeannette stepping onto a gravel driveway in four inch heels didn't quite materialize in my mind. Okay, it did. She fell right onto her ass. But I wasn't laughing at her of course, just at the situation.

"Any time, Jeannie."

"Okay, back to the outfit. What are you doing on this date?"

I shrugged to no one in particular. "I have no clue. It could be anything."

"Hmmm...Jeans. Jeans are always safe. Sounds to me like you need some cowboy boots."

"Once again...he is NOT a cowboy."

"So? Men love cowboy boots. Why do you think so many men have crushes on female country singers? Do you really think it's because they can sing?"

"No, I think it's the size of their—"

"Cowboy boots. Exactly."

"Well, I don't have any cowboy boots."

"Get some."

"There's not exactly a boot store down the street from the farm, Jeannie."

"Okay, fine. Just promise me you'll tramp it up just a teeny tiny bit?"

"I promise."

"Okay. Listen, I gotta go. I want full details. And if I hear that tone in your voice that tells me you're skipping the good part, I'll never speak to you again."

"You'll hear every horrific detail."

"And seriously, you need to do something about your self-confidence. You'll never get a man that way."

"Who said I wanted a man?"

"You. When you said 'yes' to this date. Now get your butt on home and get ready for this boy. And be NORMAL!"

She clicked off and I tossed the phone onto the passenger seat. I loved Jeannette. She always knew when to make light of something absolutely dreadful...like getting ready for your first 'first date' in years.

I pulled into the driveway and stopped at the picnic table where my mother and Sylvie were parked behind magazines, my mother with *Southern Living* and Sylvie with *Ranger Rick*.

"Good afternoon, ladies." I plopped myself onto a bench.

"Mommy, did you know that baby raccoons spend the first two months of their lives in a hole in a tree?"

"I did not."

"It's true. I think that would be awfully lonely. Do you think they get to take field trips?"

"I'm not sure."

"And shouldn't they be out getting used to the world?"

"Maybe so."

She looked very serious. "When I grow up, I'm going to be an animal doctor. I'm going to take care of the baby raccoons in a hospital just like people. It's just what's right."

"That's a great idea, sweetie."

My mother peered over the top of her magazine.

"I think her reading is more exciting. I'm on an article about basket-weaving using the left-overs of your busted rocking chair."

"Seriously?"

"No. But that sounds like a good idea, huh?"

"Absolutely, Mom."

"So tell me about this outing you're going on." I'd called her at lunch to give her the heads up. Secretly, I was hoping she'd have explained this to Sylvie before I got home. No such luck, of course.

"Mommy, where are you going?" There they were, twin sets of eyes staring over their magazines like two women sitting at the beauty shop drooling over gossip.

"Um...Mommy's going out with a friend."

"Mr. Jesse?"

"Yes."

"Are you going to the river again? To find the bad guys?"

I couldn't help but chuckle at that.

"I don't really know. He didn't tell me."

"A surprise! Oh, Mommy, that's so exciting!"

I nodded. My mother was smiling, one eyebrow raised to ask cheeky questions she couldn't voice in front of the five-year old.

"No, Mom. Don't go getting ideas."

"I said nothing."

"You said everything."

"No, Mommy." Sylvie's brows were furrowed. "She didn't say anything. Are you hearing things, Mommy, cause that's real bad if you are."

"No, sweetie. But enough about me. How was your day?"

"Super fun. The wine maker came out and gave Momo a bottle of wine and he gave me a honey stick."

"Is that so?"

"Yep. And we sold fifty gallons of berries."

"Well done."

She hopped up and threw her arms around me. "I missed you, Mommy."

Oh sheesh. So she picks the one night I'm actually going out to pull the guilt trip. Wait. What if this is some subconscious reaction to the idea of her mother going off with someone she doesn't know? Oh my God, I fretted, am I scarring her?

My mother must have seen the look on my face.

"Mommy's got to go get ready, honey. Why don't you go ahead and wash those dirty buckets for me? It's about time for us to go on up to the house and get dinner ready, once this last family leaves."

"Okee dokee." She plunged her hands into the soapy water bucket and started scrubbing.

I drove up to the house and raced to the shower. It had been months since I'd taken the time to actually make my hair look like I cared and I had no idea if my mother had any tools for that kind of job.

I blew my hair dry and started digging around my mother's bathroom for a heating element of any sort. All I found was a set of hot rollers that looked suspiciously like a fire hazard. So I did what any self-respecting Southern woman would do—I said to heck with it and pulled my hair into a pony tail.

I chose jeans and a white peasant shirt, but that looked a tad too *Little House on the Prairie*, so I tried plaid. That looked like I was trying too hard. Like people who go to a tourist trap and wear a t-shirt proclaiming the destination in big, puffy letters. Finally, I donned a red button-up blouse. I remembered Jeannette's plea and unbuttoned a couple of the top buttons. Just enough to make it interesting.

I looked like a plain Jane. And I felt like one. I looked at myself in the mirror with my limp ponytail and pathetic attempt at make-up and felt the tears burn my eyes.

What are you doing, Amanda? You can't do this. Look at you. Downright frumpy.

"Mommy?" The little voice materialized out of nowhere and I wondered how long she'd been standing there. I wiped my eyes and pretended I had something in one of them.

"Mommy...you look so pretty."

God bless my child. I fell to my knees and wrapped my arms around her. I felt her lips on my cheek.

"I can't ever stop kissing you, Mommy."

"I love you."

"I can't ever stop." True, she was on what must have been her fifteenth kiss.

"Me either!" I dug my face into her neck and kissed her, making monster noises as she squealed and rolled onto her side.

"Dinner!" We pulled apart at my mother's voice and I chased her downstairs where she hid behind her grandmother.

"Goodness! What in the world? Are you just getting her all wound up because you know I'm the one who'll put her to bed?"

"Sorry, Mom." I kissed my mother's cheek.

"Wow, you're awfully chipper."

"Mommy looks so pretty."

I kissed the top of Sylvie's little head.

"She sure does, Pumpkin. Here's your hot dog."

"Hot dogs?" There was a reason they'd been on my 'forbidden foods' list back home. I mean, really? Isn't it like a general rule that you shouldn't eat something when you don't know what it is? And I think we can all agree that a hot dog is an unknown.

My mother rolled her eyes. "Don't worry yourself about what we do here. Just go finish getting ready." She shooed me from the kitchen and I went back to my room to find something faintly resembling cowboy boots.

❤

At six forty-nine the doorbell rang and I blacked out for a split second. I couldn't get up from the kitchen table where Sylvie was putting a puzzle together. I was frozen to the spot.

My mother's sing-songy voice filled the room. "I'll get it!"

I knew the symptoms for a heart attack, and I was so convinced that I was experiencing them that I seriously considered tossing back an aspirin.

I could hear Jesse laughing with my mother. It was like they were on the other side of a cave. Come to think of it, Sylvie was definitely saying something to me but I couldn't hear.

And then there he was. Blue jeans. Red flannel shirt. Cowboy Boots. Hot. Damn.

He smiled at me. "Good evenin', Amanda Jane."

I smiled and nodded.

"Miss Sylvie, how are you?"

"Peachy keen, jellybean!"

"Hey, I like that...I've never heard that one before."

She was smiling up at him with those big eyes and curls bouncing playfully. I know she's mine, but she's seriously the cutest little thing in the world.

"It's a good one." She went back to her puzzle.

"Are you ready, Amanda Jane?"

I nodded again. I considered speaking but quickly decided against it. I didn't want to scare him away with my nervous chatter before I even made it to the truck.

"Have fun you two!" My mother winked at me in an obviously 'hubba hubba' way. So embarrassing.

"Thank you, ma'am." He tipped his hat. Have I mentioned yet that this is extremely attractive?

Jesse opened the truck door and took my hand to help me in. I noticed for the first time how clean the truck was. No cigarette ashes. That was good. Not really my thing. No dip tins. Praise the Lord. No trash at all. So he was a clean guy. Good.

"So I have something kind of special planned. I hope you don't think I'm being too forward."

I shook my head and he put the truck back in neutral.

"Are you okay? I mean, you haven't said a word." His eyes looked concerned. "Is this okay?"

I sounded like a frog. Which is just swell. "Yes!" I cleared my throat. "Sorry—yes. I'm just—it's just—I haven't been on a date in a while is all."

"Well, no pressure. I want you to have fun tonight. You work hard, you deserve to be treated to a nice night."

"Thanks." I was blushing like a teenage girl. The ponytail helped with the transformation.

We bumped along the gravel driveway and out onto the road. It wasn't dark yet, but it was a cloudy evening so the light was dimmer than usual.

"What kind of music do you like?"

Small talk. I could do this.

"All kinds, really. I got really into rock when I lived in Charlotte, but back in high school I was a huge country fan."

"Perfect." He flipped on the radio and I was absolutely shocked to hear a classic rock station. What else had I presumed incorrectly about this man?

I was surprised when we pulled off of my mother's road not three miles from the farm. Jesse hopped out and unlocked a metal gate, drove us through, and then locked it behind us. There was no gravel, but the dirt road was smooth and wound through the thick woods.

We emerged into a large field with a classic red barn and a small cabin stationed near the wood line.

"Is this…?"

He beamed. "Home sweet home."

Wow.

"Don't move." He hopped out of the truck and came around to open the door for me. I couldn't recall the last time that had happened, but it seemed completely right that it was happening now.

"Thank you."

He smiled. "Men don't open doors in North Carolina?"

"Not the men I know."

"You don't know the right kind of men, then." He winked and took my hand. My heart burned and my cheeks flushed. I swung his hand nervously as we walked across the field. I hadn't noticed, but he'd set up a picnic blanket right in the middle of the field. It was red and white checked, just like in the movies, and a cooler held down one corner while stones weighed down the others.

"Nothing fancy." He dropped my hand, took off his hat, and ran his fingers nervously through his hair.

"This is perfect." I sat and he knelt and opened the cooler, bringing out a can and a bottle. His eyes were full of mischief.

"Now, you should know that it all hinges on this one question."

"I'm ready."

He held up the two drinks and looked expectantly.

"Bottle."

"Co-rrect!" He tossed the can behind him. "And thank God, cause I only bought one can."

He opened the bottles and passed one to me. It was cold and frothy and something about the taste of it calmed me.

"So tell me a little more about yourself, Jesse. What about your family?"

"They're amazing. Wonderful. They live in the southern part of the state. Mom's a teacher, Dad's a cattle farmer. Little brother lives in Texas with his wife and five kids. He's an insurance adjustor. Didn't exactly buy the whole 'farmer' thing. But I love him. Love those kids. Speaking of which, yours is beautiful."

"Thank you. She's kind of amazing. She's five going on fifteen. Starting kindergarten in just a couple of weeks. It's crazy."

He nodded. "My brother said the same thing about his kids. Amazing how time flies."

In the quiet I began to hear the sounds of dusk chirping around us.

"Let me light this before you regret coming out here with me." He had a citronella candle and a lantern. He struck the match on the bottom of his shoe which I found to be no less than a magic trick.

"How do you do that?"

"What?"

"Light the match that way? That's awesome."

"You are very easily impressed, Mandy."

I shrugged. "I'm a simple girl."

"Doubtful."

"So tell me more. What do you like to do in your free time? Besides dress up like you're quarantined and play with bees."

"Wow. You're just oozing with respect for my vocation." The playful tone of his voice matched the look in his eyes.

I raised an eyebrow. "I just don't enjoy getting stung."

"Me neither. Say, I should put you in one of those suits one day and let you try it out."

My hands shot up in protest. "Absolutely not. I will try many things. But subjecting myself to a bunch of males all trying to survive the wrath of one woman? No thank you."

"You know a thing or two about it." His eyes were laughing and I wondered what I'd said that was so funny.

"A thing or two—that's all. But seriously, what else is there to you?"

He chuckled and tilted his head, gazing thoughtfully into the darkening sky.

"Church. I go every Sunday. If I skipped, I think my momma would know it, all the way down south. She'd be on her way here before you could shout 'Amen.' And I like fishin', football. Oh, and...well..."

I leaned toward him. "Tell me."

He looked sheepish. "I love to cook."

Perfect man.

"And speaking of which..." He opened an insulated bag and pulled out two containers, popping the lids open and setting them between us. "My momma's recipe for fried chicken. I hope it stayed hot enough. It's probably a little soggy."

"Wait a minute!" I narrowed my eyes. " Jesse Gregory, are you trying to countrify me?"

"Dang. You're on to me." He started to take the container away and I slapped his hand.

"Don't you touch my fried chicken, unless you want to lose a hand!"

"Feisty, girl!"

"No one gets in between me and my food."

"I love a girl who can eat."

I smiled. "Then you chose the right girl."

I swear to you as sure as I'm standin' here. That was the best fried chicken ever created on this planet. Mercy. But don't tell my mother.

He'd brought cole slaw and beans, and some fresh cobbler for dessert. And as I sat there, shoveling food into my mouth as if I hadn't eaten for months, all of my self-consciousness fell away and I was authentically Amanda Jane. I kicked off my shoes and licked my fingers clean without a second's thought. What the heck...he either liked me or he didn't. But something told me that you didn't make a meal like this for someone you didn't care for.

We made small talk. Favorite movies, favorite books, best way to spend a lazy day. It was as if I were sitting there with Dana or David, like we'd known each other forever.

"So what's goin' on with the river pollution?" he asked, spooning one last bite of cobbler into his mouth.

"I passed the information over to my friend David and he's pursuing it. Shouldn't be much of a problem. In fact, we should see clean waters any day now. Thanks for your help."

"Nah...I enjoy stalking evildoers."

"Well, they certainly are. David said when he called to report the address, the woman on the phone sounded so angry about the acid residue we saw that she put him on hold to get someone on the case immediately."

"Wow."

"Yeah. I have to go downtown and file a statement next week, but I don't think they'll need you too. One should do. I'm sure when they go out there they'll find all they need."

"Well, just let me know if those people give you any trouble."

This wasn't something I had considered. "What do you mean?"

He shrugged. "If they go all 'Deliverance' on you or something."

My heart was beating through my chest. Why hadn't I thought of this? I didn't know these people. I may have just ignited someone's thirst for vengeance. Oh God.

Jesse laughed at the look on my face. "Amanda Jane, I'm just kiddin' you. They don't know who reported, and if they did, I guarantee you they wouldn't do anything about it. I mean, they just hid in the house that day."

I relaxed. Then I slapped him on the arm.

"Jesse, you scared the crap out of me!"

He laughed. "That's great. And what a great day that was."

I nodded. Was he referring to the walk up the river? Certainly not my thrashing about, fighting my imaginary snake. Or was he referring to the kiss? No way. I think we would both like to forget my graceful exit.

"You know what I loved most that day?" He lay back on the blanket, arms behind his head.

My heart leapt into my throat. I couldn't speak so I let my eyebrows ask the question.

He stared into the sky. "You looked really hot in that frog suit." He burst into laughter and I started hitting him, punching him in the stomach. He rolled over in defense and I stood up so he'd have to look up to me.

"I will have you know, Jesse Gregory, that you looked absolutely ridiculous in those rubber pants."

He held up his hands in surrender. "I meant it. That frog suit..." He whistled.

I started to march away. Cue music. Cue gorgeous man running after me, lifting me into his arms, kissing me long and longingly.

Nope. Cue torrential downpour.

The next few minutes were pure chaos. I started screaming, because that helps. Jesse leapt up and folded everything except for the lantern into the picnic blanket. He held out the lantern and I took it, shining the light on his work as best I could.

Jesse looked around, took my hand, and started running for the barn. I could feel my shoes plashing through the damp grass as I slipped and skidded across the pasture. It was getting dark, faster now that the sky was filled with clouds, and I was like a blind person depending entirely upon this man.

Once inside the old red building, Jesse pushed the barn doors closed and took the lantern from me. He found a second lantern, lit it, and handed it to me.

The rain was loud on the metal roof, but there was something peaceful about this place. The smell of horses—a raw, sweet smell mixed with that of hay and rain that lent the place warmth and coziness that was welcome to my rain-soaked self.

"Sorry, I guess the whole romantic picnic thing wasn't such a good idea after all," he laughed, opening a weathered trunk and tossing me a thick, blue blanket. "You can use this to dry off."

I wrapped the cloth around me. It was scratchy and rough, but I had a chill and was suddenly longing for that frog suit.

He leaned against the doors, catching his breath.

As I looked around at the horses grunting in the stalls, the various farm tools hung on the walls, I grew curious. "So I have to ask...why did you run to the barn and not the house? Maybe there's something you're hiding from me? A lady, maybe?"

He looked sheepishly down at the ground as he wrapped a matching blanket around his own shoulders.

"No, I—I thought it would be too presumptuous. I was worried it would make you uncomfortable. There's only one room, you see, so..."

"How gentlemanly."

He shrugged.

In the silence I heard the rain pounding on the metal roof. It sounded like hail, tiny pebbles beating down, trying to force their way in. I don't think either of us knew what to say, not like when we'd been in the field and we'd both felt so open. Now trapped in the barn we were closed up as well.

I started stroking the mane of a horse whose nose was stuck out of a stall next to me. It was a beauty, reminded me of Chessa, the pony I'd taken riding lessons with as a child.

I didn't hear Jesse come up behind me and I jumped when he spoke. "That's Rusty. He's about a hundred years old..."

"Sweet boy."

"Yeah." His hand touched mine as he reached through to smooth Rusty's mane. I felt as if I'd been electrified and I'll be dad nabbed if a bolt of lightning didn't strike right at that moment. Thunder shook the barn but the horses stayed calm.

"I think we're gonna be here for a while." Really, I'm smooth like that. The obvious is totally attractive.

"Yes indeed."

I slid down onto the ground, my back against the stalls.

Jesse shone the light into my face. "Are you seriously comfortable there?"

I pushed the lantern away. "Not exactly. The ground is hard as a rock, but it doesn't exactly look like there's gonna be a couch in here somewhere."

"No. No couch. But there's hay at least." I saw his had come into the light and he pulled me to my feet.

"Here, I'll help you up. Hand me the lantern." He was shining light on a ladder that clearly led to the hayloft. I had serious concerns. Dana's cousin Mindy had lost her virginity in Billy Whitmire's hayloft when we were in twelfth grade. Jenny Smithson had been caught in the hayloft with her boyfriend in tenth grade and her daddy had stormed in with a shotgun. She never got asked to Prom. Was climbing into the hayloft with a boy in the country the same as going to a sleazy hotel in the city?

"Um...what's wrong?"

I lifted one of his arms so the lantern lit both of our faces. "If I climb into this hayloft with you, I want you to still believe that I am not the kind of girl that climbs into haylofts with boys."

"Okay. That's confusing."

"I mean that I'm not some easy peasy sleezy. I'm not climbing into this hayloft and suddenly reverting back to a stupid teenage version of myself."

"Okay...if this is going to bring back some traumatizing memory—"

"No! Don't you see? I'm NOT a hayloft kinda girl."

"Okay, well, I can throw some hay down and...'"

"Dammit, Jesse, just help me up." I don't know how I could have been any clearer. Obviously I'd just have to show him what I meant.

I tossed my blanket up before me and hauled myself up the ladder as Jesse lit my way. He handed me the lantern and I crawled to the back wall near a shuttered window and wrapped myself up like a mummy, only my face exposed and my hand sticking out, clutching the lantern.

I saw a light and then his dark form crawling towards me.

He looked at me and laughed.

"Okay, I get it. No access. Geez, what kind of guy do you think I am, Mandy?"

I felt horrible. Here was Jesse, setting up this romantic date only to have it ruined by the rain, rushing us to a barn so as not to make me feel uncomfortable, and now I was insulting him by acting as if he'd planned the whole thing to get me into a vulnerable position in a hayloft. I was dirt.

"I'm sorry." I unwrapped myself awkwardly and draped the blanket simply around my shoulders. "I'm just nervous, that's all. I haven't been on a date in a while." Hadn't I already said that? Geez.

"That's pretty obvious." I couldn't see his face, but I could tell he was smiling.

I scooted sideways until our shoulders were touching. In the dim light I could see him looking down at me. My heart fluttered and I started breathing really heavily. Thank God the rain was loud so he couldn't hear me practically panting next to him.

"Jesse, this has been the best date I've ever been on."

He burst into laughter. "I am SO sorry to hear that."

"What can I say? The last time I had a first date in this town we went to the Chinese buffet and then he took me cow tipping."

"No."

"Yes."

"Okay, that's pretty awful."

"It was. There was no date number two."

"I guess not. Okay then, I'll take it. Best date ever, huh?"

"Yep."

We were quiet and I could tell that the rain was letting up. The patter on the roof had quieted and the horses were getting restless. Then lightning flashed outside, and I was thankful. Because I realized that I had no desire to leave this place, this man. I prayed that time would slow down, that the hail would come back, anything to prolong this night.

I felt Jesse shift next to me and then I heard his voice, low and soft.

"I really like you, Amanda Jane."

I smiled so hard my face began to hurt. I felt his arms slip around me and my chest tightened. I hadn't felt this way in so long...it was magic.

"I really like you too."

And then it happened. I kissed him. I took his face in my hands and I kissed him.

Amanda Jane Roberts was kissing a boy in a hayloft.

Amanda Jane Roberts was lying in the hay, letting a boy kiss her in a hayloft.

Amanda Jane Roberts was making out with a hot guy in a hay loft.

Amanda Jane Roberts was countrified.

❤

I opened the door as quietly as possible, but the catch sounded like a bullhorn announcing my arrival home at two in the morning.

I tiptoed across the living room and had just turned to climb the stairs when the light flipped on and I went blind.

When my sight returned I saw my mother standing in the doorway to her bedroom, arms crossed, hair loose around her shoulders, the hint of a smile on her face.

"Why, you're mighty late, Amanda Jane."

Why did I feel like a sixteen-year old sneaking in after curfew?

"Sorry, Mom."

"No—no apologies. You're a grown woman now. I was just wonderin' if you'd been caught in the storm."

"Yeah, we were actually. Kinda put a damper on the evening."

She nodded.

"Well, goodnight, Mom." I turned for the stairs.

"Um...Amanda Jane?"

Oh Lord, what did she know? What did her maternal instincts tell her? I turned slowly, knowing full well that there was a look of pure shame on my face. And yet I wouldn't take back this night for anything in the world.

"Yes, Mom?"

She was smiling outright now.

"Why is there hay stuck all in your hair?"

My face caught on fire. Really. It was on fire. And then it was as if I were vomiting words.

"Well, when it rained we had to run—and, um—we ran to the barn—and, um—well, we were there for a while so I—"

She held up a hand.

"I don't need to know any more."

"Mom! It's not like we, you know." Oh my God, this was so awkward.

"Well, that's reassuring. I like to think you're still pure, even if there is a sweet little babe upstairs. Now go check on your daughter. I promised her I'd have you come give her a kiss when you got home." She winked at me and turned back to her room. "Goodnight, Amanda Jane. You might want to brush your hair out before you get into bed."

Shame. Shameshameshame. How do parents have the everlasting ability to shame you, no matter how old you get?

I climbed the stairs and peeked into Sylvie's room. She was sprawled across the bed, one leg hanging over the edge, arms flayed out, mouth open. I sneaked into the room and leaned down to give her a kiss. Her cheeks were irresistibly kissable.

What I didn't expect was for her to speak to me.

"Mommy, you smell like poop." Her eyes were still closed but she'd managed to pinch her nose.

"Sorry, baby, go back to sleep."

"Mommy, you need a shower. You really smell like poopie."

"Okay, love you."

"I love you, Mommy. But you smell so bad."

"Okay, okay, go to sleep."

"Night night."

I took her advice and showered before climbing into bed. When I slid under the sheets, the coolness felt so good on my achy body. I hadn't stayed up this late since college. For years it had been Friday nights at home, on the couch, catching up on the shows I'd recorded during the week while Richard sat on the opposite couch, computer on lap, watching everything but me. We'd gone to bed at eleven on a late night, lying still on opposite sides of the bed, coming together only out of a sense of obligation.

And now here I was, alone in my childhood bed, my body feeling anything but obligated.

Chapter Seven

The following Monday I met Dana and David for lunch. David saved me the hassle of being center-stage by bringing along his boyfriend. Which also meant that we didn't dare have lunch in town. No, no, we fled the state, north to Tennessee, to a little artsy coffee shop by the river walk.

Dana and I rode together and I filled her in on the details of my date. I had called Jeannette the night before and she had screamed over every detail. And when I say 'scream,' I mean 'scream'—shrieking, high-pitched, glass breaking screaming. Dana was slightly more reserved.

"Amanda and Jesse sitting in the loft...K-I-S-S-I-N-"

"Enough!"

"Oh, sorry. Amanda and Jesse layin' in the hay..."

"Seriously!" I banged my fist on the steering wheel.

"Whoa there, lady. Touchy, touchy." She leaned back in the seat and gave me one of her "Who's goody-two-shoes now?" looks.

"Nothing happened, Dana."

"What? You're too good for a hayloft?" Her voice belied the fact that she was about to burst into laughter.

"No. No." I had to choose my words carefully here. "I'm just—I don't know. Just nothing."

"Is it lo-o-o-o-ove?"

"I think it's a little early for that."

She shrugged and her eyes sparkled devilishly. "He's a hot one, you know. Don't let him go. Some bedazzled chick'll come along and snatch him up."

"I'll keep that in mind." I turned up the music and rolled down the windows. Dana quickly changed the station to country, of course, but as luck would have it, it was Reba. Who doesn't love Reba?

So there we were, singing 'Fancy' at the top of our lungs, hauling it down the interstate, like two teenagers without a care in the world.

I think my favorite memory with Dana would have to be the time we decided to screw the winter formal and go on our own date. I had been asked by Hawkins Carter, drummer in the marching band—and if you were ever in the marching band, you know what that means. However, a week before the dance I had sort-of, kind-of held hands with Matthew Scott in the backseat of a school van coming back from a quiz bowl tournament, and Hawkins had found out. So I was sud denly dateless. Dana had been asked by poor little Nivens Smith, a sweet but terribly awkward boy who was the sole reason we couldn't wear sweatpants to school on athletic dress days. Sweet boy. No self control. Needless to say, Dana had said she couldn't because she wasn't planning to go to the dance.

There are so many girls in this world who have fallen into the sorry-I-really-wasn't-planning-to-go trap. You're asked. You panic. You say you're not going. Now you can't go.

So here we were, sixteen, sassy, and completely lame-o.

So we did what any two self-respecting single girls would do—we went on a date with ourselves. We dressed up in our formal gowns—purchased weeks in advance, of course—did each other's hair, and drove forty miles to the Red Lobster just over the state line.

On the way, we blasted hip-hop music as loudly as possible and sang even louder. Of course we knew all the words. I mean, I loved rock and Dana was a country girl, but really, there's nothing like some hard-core rap to bring people to the middle.

So there we were, sitting at a red light, blasting some Coolio, rapping in our sparkly frocks, and a guy in a red convertible next to us starts laughing. Never one to be showed up by some jerkfaced condescending nitwit, we rolled down the windows and had ourselves an audience. It was freezing, the wind whipping through our perfectly coiffed up-do's, but the hell with it. This was our show.

The light turned green and no one moved. It wasn't until the cars behind our audience began to honk away that he finally nodded in approval, waved, and tore off into the night.

I rolled up the windows, laughing so hard I was crying, and hit repeat.

It was an awesome night. And those Red Lobster cheesy biscuits. Sweet mother-of-pearl, I've rarely met a bread I loved more.

And now here we were, on the same road, a little older, certainly a tad wiser, but still the exhibitionists we always were.

I parked on the side of the road and we walked through the art district to the coffee shop. As soon as I opened the door, I saw David's face. He was lit up like the middle of the day.

The man standing next to him was tall, good-looking, and joyful. But I soon realized why we hadn't met in town. Not only was he gay, he was black. David had failed to mention the small detail that this man had two strikes against him in a town where the Klan still marched and people still used the word 'fairy'. But I had to hand it to David. This guy was a looker.

"Dana, AJ, this is Lawrence. Lawrence, other than my mother, these are the two most important women in my life."

"Wow. No pressure." He had a firm handshake. Another good sign.

We found a table and ordered sandwiches and drinks, and then I recounted for David and his boyfriend the drama of my date with Jesse. Poor Lawrence, this was trial by fire.

"He took you to the barn?" David glanced knowingly at Dana.

"Yes, he didn't want me to feel uncomfortable."

Lawrence piped in. This was when I knew I like him. "So, I don't know you very well, but you don't look like the kind of girl who would be more comfortable in a barn than in a house."

I sighed. "Do I still look like I just stepped out of the city?"

"No. You look sane."

I smiled and nodded. "You know, you're okay, Lawrence. David, I think you have a keeper here."

Lawrence told us about his parents, who lived in Kentucky, his brother who was serving at Parris Island, and his road to the law. He'd started out to become an architect and then realized he hated math.

"But who knows, maybe I'll have a mid-life career change. I always wanted to be a writer. A journalist."

David leaned away and looked over at him. "A writer?"

"Sure. It's a hobby for now."

"I had no idea."

Watching them interact, it was so obvious that they were crazy about each other. I felt sad for David's family, the ones who were missing out on his happiness.

"So how did you guys meet?" Dana could always be counted upon to go in for the juicy bits.

David blushed and looked at his hands. "This is so cliché."

Lawrence put his hand on David's shoulder and smiled, a twinkle in his eye. "Nothing to be ashamed of, sweetheart. Ladies, we met at the gym."

Dana and I giggled and simultaneously covered our mouths.

"I was on the elliptical. Your boy Dave here was *crawling* along on the treadmill."

"I object! I was not crawling. I was in cool-down mode."

Lawrence held up his hands. "Fine, fine, but as he was 'cooling down' he was also watching reruns of *The Andy Griffith Show.*"

Dana couldn't help herself, "And exactly which part of this was attractive?"

"Thanks, Dane."

"Love you, Davie."

Lawrence laughed. "All of it. He just looked...nice, you know. And nice is hard to find."

"Tell me about it." I really was trying to not be the token 'friend going through the end of a relationship.' That one just slipped out.

"So I walked up to the treadmill, handed him a towel, and asked if he wanted to get a smoothie from the juice bar."

"I'm glad you did."

Dana and I sighed, tilting our heads at this adorable couple.

"So what about your mama? Gonna break the news?" Dana again.

David looked exceedingly uncomfortable. "Well, I'll need to set aside some cash to pay the medical bills she'll accrue as a result of the heart attack or stroke she's sure to suffer."

"You might be surprised, " I said hopefully.

"That's what I told him." Lawrence was holding David's hand on top of the table now and looking emphatically in his eyes. "I thought mine would freak out, but remarkably they weren't that surprised."

We all had a good laugh and David gave Lawrence a quick peck on the cheek before running his fingers nervously through his hair.

"I'm thinking on it. I just have to do it the right way."

Dana reached across the table and took his other hand. "We got you, Dave."

It was a refreshing lunch, and Lawrence passed the test, fitting in as if he'd always been a part of the group. Being with my friends made me feel like Amanda Jane, and it was so refreshing. But as wonderful as it was to spend the afternoon with them, when we were driving home, I suddenly felt the urge to take Sylvie in my arms and squeeze her endlessly.

I walked in the door and found my mother and Sylvie parked on the couch with a plate of watermelon between them. They were rapt by the screen.

I walked in the room and looked to see one of my mother's preachers marching across the stage, hollering about the Lord.

"Hey, guys, what are you doing?"

"Mommy, do you believe in God?"

Okay. Buzz kill.

I sat down next to her and popped a piece of melon into my mouth. She still hadn't looked away from the screen.

"Sure, Sylvie."

"Do you believe that Jesus Christ is your personal Lord and savior?"

I shifted uncomfortably and looked over at my mother who had plastered on her best poker face.

"Do you, Mommy?"

"I don't know."

"I do."

"Why? Because someone on TV told you to?"

She pouted. "No. I can make my own decisions, Mommy. And I feel it in my heart." She defiantly beat her little fist into her chest.

I looked at the TV. To my mother. To my daughter.

"Okay, sweetheart. You can believe what you want."

"Did you know, Mommy, that Jesus loves you? That he loves everyone? Even the bad people?"

"I did."

"Did you know, Mommy, that Jesus brought someone back from the dead? That's AWESOME!"

"I did."

"He's like, a superhero. A superhero in heaven. He's like Superman, Mommy!" Her smile was so bright, it nearly converted me right then.

"He is."

My mother chanced a glance at me and raised her eyebrows to ask if I was about to strangle her right there in front of the preacher.

I shook my head and smiled. It never hurt anyone to believe in something like this. And though I'd lost my faith, I secretly loved that my mother watched these shows, that she believed in something beyond herself.

I wrapped my arms around Sylvie.

"Mommy, I want to go to heaven and live with God."

"Can you wait for a while, sweetie? I'm not quite finished with you yet."

"Okay, Mommy. But you can come, too."

"Thanks."

"How was your lunch with Aunt Dana?"

"Wonderful. How was your day with Momo?"

"Wonderful."

We sat in silence as the preacher called the poor lost souls to the mourner's bench. Sylvie snuggled into me so that I couldn't see her face.

"Mommy, I don't want to go to el—e—o—mentary school."

Well this was just a hum-dinger of an afternoon.

"Why not, baby?"

She shifted and looked up, her eyes so bright and blue and yet a bit sad.

"I'm scared."

"There's no need to be scared. We're going to orientation tomorrow and then we'll go get your backpack and lunch box and all your supplies. That'll be so cool."

"Can I have a Princess lunch box?"

"Of course."

She smiled and closed her eyes, nestling her head against my chest.

"Thanks, Mommy. You're the best mommy in the whole world."

"You're the best daughter in the whole world."

"Mommy, I love you more than you love me."

"Impossible." I tucked a curl behind her ear and she closed her eyes.

"No. It's true. I love you more than the whole world."

"I love you to infinity."

"I love you more than infinity."

"That isn't possible. Infinity is the biggest value."

Her eyes popped open. "Wow. Okay. So I love you like you love me."

"Okay. Close your eyes, baby." She curled up in my lap and in minutes, she'd fallen asleep.

I looked at her, the vision of sweetness. This was a perfect moment.

Then my mother broke the silence. "I see your ability to fall right asleep in church has rubbed off on her."

"Well, what can I say? It's soothing."

She nodded. "How was David's friend?"

"Wonderful."

"I'm so glad. That boy deserves to be happy."

"He does. We all do, Mom."

So since this afternoon was shaping up to be dramatic in so many ways, I figured this was as good a time as any to tell her what I'd been thinking about for a few days now. I lowered my voice so as not to wake the recently converted on my lap.

"So Mom, what do you think about us staying here for a while?"

"I thought you were staying...I mean, Sylvie's starting school next week."

"I mean—at the house. You're not getting any younger—no offense—and Sylvie loves being with you. I love being with you."

She seemed to give it a good deal of thought. She took a deep breath and closed her eyes as she did when she was really considering something.

"I'm trying to decide if it's what's best for you."

"I think it is."

She sat silently, eyes closed, jaw tightened in thought. When she spoke, it was quiet but direct. "I remember when Michael left. He was so excited to move out west, to get away, and yet on the day he left he cried as he hugged me goodbye. But it was still what was best for him."

"Well, Michael's never been one for the best decisions so I'm glad that was the right one."

"He made a good decision marrying Rachel."

"He did. She's a saint...I didn't choose very well, I guess."

She waited a moment before answering. Then her eyes opened and she looked right at me. "You chose right at the time. Honey, people change. He changed, but you changed too. For the better. You're more mature now, more independent. It's wonderful for a mother to see."

We sat there just enjoying the silence for several minutes, and then she spoke the words I'd hoped for.

"You can stay as long as you'd like, darlin'. You can stay forever. I can think of no one I would rather spend my days with."

I reached out a hand and squeezed hers. "Me too. Thank you, Mama."

♥

I'm not sure what the highlight of Sylvie's elementary school orientation was. Perhaps it was the mascots roaming the hallways, mussing the parents' hair and trying to high-five us when clearly they could not see what they were doing. Or perhaps it was in the classroom visit when I saw that the class pet was a hamster named Richard and I spent the boring parts of the presentation making all kinds of rodent-comparison jokes in my mind. But I think that the end of the evening was the true kicker. At the end of the all-parent meeting I found Sylvie on the playground sitting under a tree, crying her poor little eyes out.

"Mommy, I got in trouble."

Now you should know that my daughter is perfect. I realize that all parents believe this of their children, but in my case, it's actually true.

"What happened, baby? Tell me." I crouched down and took her in my arms.

"We were playing tag, and when I wa—was out, the teacher t—told me to go sit on the 'beench'. I didn't know wh—what that was so I asked her what a 'beench' was and she said to stop sassing her and go sit under this tree."

Time stopped. I'm not sure I'd actually ever felt rage, even that day in the movie theater, but in this moment, the feeling was clear as crystal.

"Mommy will handle this. Which teacher was it?"

Sylvie pointed across the playground to a petite blonde with a teacher dress and cheap plastic sunglasses. I know. I try not to judge, but when you've attacked my child, I will judge your clothes.

I took Sylvie's hand and marched up to the teacher.

"Excuse me, I'm Sylvie's mom. Apparently there was a misunderstanding and I just want to get that worked out." I had put on my 'angry mom' voice that was usually reserved for Sylvie alone. But I figured this lady worked with children all day, so she'd know the tone of my words and respond accordingly.

The accent was thick as the make-up on her face. "Yes, Sylvie acted as if she cou'n understand what I was askin' her ta do. I asked her to sit on the beench. She refused."

I was seething. Seriously, the fire department must have been on notice because there was steam shooting from my ears.

"She didn't understand your accent. That's all. Where she's from, people say words differently and so she didn't understand that you meant the 'bench.'" I envisioned myself pinching her little head off. It felt very satisfying.

She lowered her sunglasses and took me in from head to toe.

"Are you—are you Amanda Jane Roberts?"

Suddenly 'angry mom' turned into 'oh, crap mom.' Oh God. Who was this?

"Um—yes."

Sylvie, God bless her, piped right in. "Amanda Jackson. That's my mommy."

"Oh!" the blonde cooed, a note of falsity in her voice. "And I suppose you don't recognize me, Amanda Jane."

Now, I really hate it when people do this. It isn't enough that I obviously do NOT recognize you. No, you have to ask me point blank so that I embarrass myself by admitting out loud in front of your friends that you didn't mean enough to me whenever it was we knew each other to go in the permanent memory file.

"I'm sorry—I don't."

She frowned. "Patsy Cherry. We graduated together from Northeast."

And then it all came rushing back.

Sophomore year. Cheerleading try-outs.

Okay, so it wasn't the best idea. Twirling a flag in the marching band for a year, even with a streamer solo, does not make one nimble and lithe. But in a moment of insanity, I decided to try out for the team.

I had been practicing my kicks and cheers for a week, ever since clinic day when we were taught our try-out routines. And then the day arrived. I took number thirteen—should have been my first clue—and pinned it to the leg of my cute, red gym shorts, knotted my white t-shirt in back so it would be tight—I mean, big boobs is sort of a cheerleader requirement in this town—and pulled my hair into a ponytail so high on my head I looked like a genie.

When I walked into the gym, the current squad was seated at a long table in their warm-up suits, the ones with names embroidered across their large left breasts, their ponytails not only on top of their heads, but glittery.

I walked to the middle of the gym, fists on hips, and smiled.

Patsy Cherry was on the left end of the table. I don't know why I remember that. Yes I do. People often remember pointless details in the wake of true tragedy.

"You may begin, number thirteen." As if they didn't know who I was and this was a totally unbiased audition.

"Ready? Okay!" I clapped, I bopped my head, I smiled so hard my face hurt, I projected.

I was awesome.

"Great. Okay, number thirteen, let's see your jumps."

Okay. Fine. I started the rote series of jumps. Herkey. Pike. Russian.

Patsy Cherry leaned forward. Her voice was dripping with sarcasm. "That was an awesome Spread Eagle. Can we see your Russian, though?"

What. A. Bitch. I should have screamed, "That WAS my Russian, you twit! So I'm not super-flexible! I'm a virgin! Get OVER it!" But instead I did it again. They stared at me. I could feel sweat under my armpits and prayed they wouldn't make me raise my arms again.

They looked at each other and smiled. Then they asked for my tumbling.

I rounded-off and walked out of the gym, dejected and humiliated.

I don't know why I came back thirty minutes later to check the list. My name was not on it.

And now here she was. Miss Cheer Captain. Miss Prom Queen. Miss Heart-breaking Bitch.

I guess I had some pent up frustration.

"Ohhhhhhhh...Patsy! Of course!" I could play the part though, for Sylvie's sake.

She smiled and threw her arms around me, then introduced me to her fellow teachers as 'an old friend from high school.' I disgusted myself with my sweet smile.

"So, Patsy, I came over because there seems to be a misunderstanding with my daughter."

I motioned Sylvie towards us and she shyly walked over and took my hand, studying her shoes.

"Sylvie was punished today because she genuinely misunderstood what you had said."

Patsy cleared her throat. "That was me. And I'm sorry, but she didn't misunderstand. She was being disrespectful and she needs to learn to treat adults differently than she treats her friends." I was on fire. I knew that my face had turned red.

"I'm sorry, Patsy, but you don't know my daughter. And the fact is that she's grown up in a city devoid of a country accent. So when you said 'bench,' she honestly had never heard someone pronounce it that way."

She crossed her arms and in that moment I saw the teenager inside of her.

"Are you suggesting that my accent is so thick people can't understand me?"

"Certainly not. It's just that we're talking about a five-year old girl. She doesn't have much experience with different words. The first week here I had to explain 'y'all' to her."

A collective gasp from the teachers. I had to force my eyes not to roll to the sky.

Patsy plastered a false smile on her face. "I see." She bent down to Sylvie's height. "I'm sorry, Sylvie. I thought you were being unkind. I didn't realize that your verbal skills were just...underdeveloped."

Is it wrong to want to kill someone for insulting your child? I think there must be an asterisk in the Ten Commandments to make an exception for this kind of case.

Sylvie lifted her face. She had a determined look. "Mommy, what does she mean?"

I breathed deeply to calm my frustration.

"She's suggesting that you aren't good with words."

She looked so sweetly at Patsy that I saw a change occur even in that ice queen's face. "I can read already. I can write words. I can say words in Spanish. I'm pretty good with words. Oh, and I can say 'thank you' in French. *Merci.*" She smiled so sincerely.

Patsy looked at me. She looked at the other teachers. She looked at Sylvie.

"Oh, um...okay. I'm sorry, Sylvie. I guess I'm just used to children around here being familiar with...colloquial speech and regional accents."

Now Sylvie looked at her as if this woman were speaking Latin. I had to wonder if Patsy even knew what 'colloquial' meant.

"But I'm very excited for you to tell us all about where you come from."

"Charlotte."

Patsy stood and looked at me quizzically. "North Carolina?"

I nodded. "She was born there. I moved there after college."

"Oh. Are you married then?"

Really. This conversation was not helping me get into heaven. I won't tell you what I thought at that moment. I'm sort of ashamed. Not really.

"My husband and I are divorcing."

Collective *tsk-sigh* from the teachers.

Patsy looked at Sylvie as most people would look at a refugee.

"I'm so sorry to hear that. But I'm so glad you're at our school!"

Sylvie wasn't buying it. An elementary school teacher should realize how perceptive children are.

And then that twit looked me eye for eye. "I'd heard you were back in town, Amanda Jane. And I also heard that you were makin' eyes at Jesse Gregory. Best watch yourself there."

I wasn't sure what to make of that statement, so I took Sylvie's hand and smiled as graciously as I could.

"Okay, well, it's been nice catching up with you, Patsy. I'm sure we'll be seeing a lot of each other now."

"I hope so."

I nodded farewell and took Sylvie by the hand.

When we were far enough away, I whispered to her. "I'm so glad you have Mrs. Wright."

"Me too, Mommy. Those teachers were super scary."

"Now, I don't want you to be scared of them—"

"But Mommy, did you see how much make-up they had on? It was like a scary mask."

I kissed her head and, in that moment, felt that my cheerleading humiliation had been redeemed.

❤

And so began Sylvie's elementary school years. The next day I stood in the cafeteria crying into muffins with the other moms.

"They grow up so fast!"

"Next year she'll be in college!"

"I can't believe this...my baby!"

"Bwahhh-hoo-hoo-hoo!"

Beulah let me work in the back with the ovens since I would randomly burst into tears at any moment. At one point an order of baby bootie petit fours for a shower came across the desk and as I piped icing laces on the teeny pink booties I burst into tears and the laces turned into a swirling bird's nest that took out three of the petit fours. Then I was tortured by having to make three more from scratch.

But I made it through the day and when I picked Sylvie up from school she ran into my arms, pigtails bouncing, arms reaching for me before I even got to the sidewalk.

"Mommy!"

Best moment of the day.

Of course she loved school. Loved the teacher, loved her cubby, loved Richard the Hamster—"His name is the same as Daddy's!"

"Is it now?"

"Yeah—isn't that awesome!"

"Oh, honey, it is beyond 'awesome.'"

She couldn't wait to do her homework—write her name three times and copy her sight words onto elementary lined paper. She sat at the kitchen table working diligently, tongue stuck out in concentration while my mother and I made supper.

Richard called right after dinner and I listened as Sylvie gave him all of the details of her awesome day—including the discovery of Richard the Hamster. She laughed when she told him, and I imagined the slightly offended look on his face. It made me smile.

I left her to her father once she started in on the play-by-play of lunch in a cafeteria. Evidently there was a large traffic signal on the wall. If the light was green, the kids could speak, if it was yellow, they had to whisper, and if it was red—silence. Pretty clever, I thought, until the kids start thinking that would be a fun game to play in the car.

My mother was finishing the dishes so I picked up a towel and started to dry. She had a dishwasher but still preferred to wash by hand. Said she did a better job than the machinery.

"Where's Sylvie?"

"Talking to Richard."

"Good. I'm glad she's excited to tell him about school. She must miss him, you know. Hasn't seen him since the beginning of the summer."

I was somewhat offended at the suggestion that I had kept my child from her father.

"He knows where she is. He could come see her whenever he wanted to."

She nodded in a way that suggested a knowingness that I did not like.

"Have you spoken to him lately?"

"Why would I?"

"I don't know. Maybe he'd like to come see her. Maybe he'd like for you to bring her home to visit him."

"I'm sure he'd tell Sylvie."

"True. So on to a better subject—what's new with Jesse?" Now she was wiggling her eyebrows. Strangely, it seemed to be an automatic gesture whenever she said his name.

"Nothing. I talked to him briefly on Monday night but I haven't seen him since Friday."

We worked in silence. She had the kitchen window cracked and I could hear the crickets chirping outside. It was so peaceful.

"You know, the other night I saw Patsy Cherry at the orientation and she mentioned Jesse."

"Is that so?"

"Yeah. She didn't seem very happy to hear I'd been talking with him"

"Well I'd imagine not. Those two were together for some time. Engaged I think."

My heart stopped beating and hung heavy in my chest.

"Jesse and...and Patsy Cherry?"

"Not one of his brightest moments, I agree."

"Engaged? To Patsy Cherry? To that—"

"Now, butterbean, I'm not sure we should be passing judgement on those with bad taste in relationships."

I nodded. She was right. And yet I couldn't get past the fact that the same man who would ask a harpy like Patsy Cherry to marry him could also be interested in someone like me. She was everything I was not—at least I hoped she was.

"When was this?"

"Oh, I'd say about a year and a half ago."

"And would you say that they were in love or was it just that she cast a spell over him with her dragon-like—"

"Amanda Jane Roberts. That was then. This is now. You aren't the only one with a history. Jesse's allowed to have his as well. If he wanted to be with Patsy Cherry, he would be."

"So he was the one who broke it off."

"Amanda Jane, I am going to whack you upside the head with this wooden spoon!" She took a practice swing.

"Sorry, Mom." We worked in silence, my mind going over and over this new information. And my remarkably unfair feelings about it.

"Mom, do you think I'm making the right decisions?"

She started laughing, not exactly the reaction I expected.

"Oh, honey, how far we've come. Do you know when you were a little girl you would rather die than ask me that?"

"I know. I'm smarter now...I think."

"Wiser anyway...there's a difference. And only you know the answer, sweetheart. This is one question I can't really answer for you."

"I know. But I just need to know that you don't think I'm making some major mistakes here, that I'm thinking this through and I have my priorities straight."

She thought about that. I could tell she was giving it serious consideration because she stopped scrubbing a pan and let her hands soak in the water as she stared out the window.

"Honey, your first priority is your daughter. Second is you. Third is me, of course. So as long as you're putting your family first, I think you're doin' right."

"I think I'm doing what's right for Sylvie, but sometimes I second guess. I think she's happy here, she still has her father...sort of." Oh no, the realization. I hung my head and shook it as the truth came out of my mouth. "I should ask if he wants to come see her, shouldn't I?"

"Perhaps."

But I didn't want him to come and take her away. I didn't want joint custody with divvied up weekends and holidays. The idea of Christmas without Sylvie made tears come to my eyes. Then I realized that maybe Richard felt this way, too. The fact that he loved her never crossed my mind. The fact that he longed for her never entered my thoughts. Oh no! Had I become the selfish one?

"I guess I'll call him tomorrow. But—Mom, do you think I'm doing the wrong thing for Sylvie by going on dates with Jesse?"

She dropped the pan and water splashed onto her shirt.

"Honey, people are meant to live two-by-two. You think of Sylvie first, but you think of yourself, too. And if Sylvie isn't bothered by it, then it's just fine. And believe me, she isn't bothered by it."

"Should I talk to her about it?"

"Hmm...not yet. I'd wait and see if there's something worth talking about first. Of course, you did get up in the hayloft with a boy and around here that's a pretty serious commitment. "

"Mama!"

She raised her soapy hands in surrender.

"Hey, you asked my advice. I always tell it like it is, straight-forward. And I'm telling you that you light up when that boy's around. You were a raincloud when you got here. Now we've got a little bit of sunlight peeking through and, as your mother, I gotta say I really like it."

"Thanks, Mama."

"Of course. Now you'd better be getting' that child to bed. You've both got an early mornin' tomorrow."

I tossed the towel aside and kissed her on the cheek. As I walked away I heard her say, "And I like it that you're callin' me 'mama' again. That whole 'mom' thing sounded so Yankee."

❤

The routine became that I would get up and go to the bakery and my mother would drop Sylvie at school now that the farm was closed for the season. This worked perfectly because leaving her was the hard part, and I got the joy of having her run into my arms every afternoon.

By the end of the week, things had settled into a pretty good rhythm. But like all rhythms, there had to be a full stop.

Let me set the scene for you—It's Friday afternoon, just after lunch. In two hours it will be the weekend for me, and yet I absolutely must finish this ridiculously large order of cupcakes for Penny Sue Darlington's sweet sixteen birthday party that night. Her mama's coming to pick up the cupcakes at four o'clock, so I have to finish them before I leave to pick Sylvie up from school at two-thirty.

I'm just starting to ice the first cupcake when the little bell tinkles and I hear Beulah call me up front. She does it in a cheerful, 'I'm in on a secret' kind of way, so I know it is Jesse and I quickly run my hands through my hair, covering it in flour, of course, but after all, it does make me look more legitimate.

And sure enough, there he is, leaning on the front counter, looking at the delicious crème brûlée I fired up this morning. Patsy who?

"To what do I owe this surprise visit?" I am so smooth with my sweet voice and fluttering eyelashes. And floured hair.

Oh the smile.

"Well, ma'am, I was wonderin' if I might take you out again this weekend. No rain in the forecast."

Well, that made me smile. And then I thought of the hayloft and, God help me, I smiled even bigger.

"Sounds great—tomorrow night?"

"I'll pick you up at seven."

"Make it six?"

Ooh, feisty me!

His eyes twinkled. Really, they did.

"Perfect."

The bell tinkled but I didn't even notice because I was literally staring longingly into his eyes.

Yet the voice that spoke sent a chill up my spine. "Amanda?" I felt every muscle in my face go lax and I slowly shifted my eyes toward the door.

Richard.

Oh God. Richard.

"Um...uh...Ri..."

Jesse turned and I saw them look each other up and down. And then the simultaneous recognition. The situation was very clear to both of them and yet, for me, the world suddenly made very little sense.

"Excuse me," Richard sneered. "Can I please speak with my wife in private? Amanda?"

Jesse stood up straighter. "Certainly. But I wouldn't call her that, friend. As I understand it, the two of you are legally separated." Oh the southern 'friend.' It's like our version of 'asshole,' but more hospitable, as is the southern way.

Richard's face turned red. I had only seen it that red once before, and that was in a dark movie theatre. So you imagine how red that must be.

"I'd like to speak with her in private."

I came around the counter and took my soon-to-be-ex by the arm. "One moment, Jesse." He nodded.

I led Richard to a corner behind a display case of muffins.

"What are you doing here?" I whispered.

"I came to talk to you...to see Sylvie. Amanda, I miss you."

My hands were flapping uncontrollably as I began to freak out. "You're not allowed to miss me! No! You're not allowed." I put up my 'mom finger' and wagged it at him. "You broke the rules! You're not allowed to come groveling back here."

He looked furious. "Is that your boyfriend?"

"What! No, that is not my boyfriend, Richard. Not that it would be any business of yours. I know that you and the blonde are an item."

"How do you know that?" Ha, genuinely surprised!

"I still have friends, Richard. Friends who care about me."

"I care about you."

"Stop it!" I wasn't whispering now. I was shouting. Shouting from behind fifty muffins in a glass case. "Stop! You are NOT allowed to care about me! You can care about Sylvie, and I know you do, but you do NOT and will NOT care about ME!"

I stomped around the case and back to Jesse who looked ready to pounce.

"I'm sorry, Jesse, can we discuss this later?"

"Sure."

"Thanks." And then I pushed the swinging doors to the kitchen open and nearly smacked Beulah in the face. I guess I can't blame her for listening. Usually you had to pay for this kind of entertainment.

Her voice was scandalized. "Oh dear, Amanda Jane...is that you husband?"

"Soon to be ex-husband." I snatched up my icing bag and set back to work on the cupcakes. I was sort of proud of myself. I had handled the situation with calm and reserve. Well done, Aman—

That was when I heard a deep voice yell something profane and then the oh-so clear sound of fist on face.

"Oh Sweet Jesus!" Beulah slapped her cheeks and ran through the doors with me right behind her, clutching my icing bag and thus trailing pink frosting.

Sweet Jesus indeed. At that moment Richard picked up a pink frosted cupcake from a display stand and smashed it hard into Jesse's nose, the palm of his hand working to break it on the way.

Jesse threw a punch which Richard lithely avoided—had he been working out?—but which connected with the display tiers, dumping cupcakes all over the ground in a slippery, sticky mess.

Richard threw another punch but Jesse, who was much bigger—and better-looking, for what it's worth, ducked and upper cut him in the jaw, sending him to the floor where he landed in a pink mess.

The bell tinkled and Wendell Jones stuck his head in.

"Amanda-a-a-oh!" And he disappeared.

"Sweet Jesus!" Beulah declared again, ducking behind the front counter.

Jesse was standing over Richard who was trying to get to his feet but continuously slipping back to the ground. I guess I was just standing there, a bystander to this ridiculous display. There was a stunned silence as we stared at one another.

Beulah was the first to speak, her head peeking up from behind the counter.

"I certainly hope you young men plan on cleaning up this mess."

Silence.

She turned to me. "Amanda Jane, you go on home. I'll finish the cupcakes."

Without a word I walked into the back, took off my apron, washed my hands, and went to my car.

On the way to Sylvie's school I kept replaying the scenario in my mind. What had been said to make Jesse and Richard act like Neandertals? I couldn't imagine. And yet whenever I saw Richard slipping over and over in the pink icing, a smile forced its way onto my lips.

It was still quite a while until pick up, so I called Dana and asked her to meet me at the Cremo Drive-in. It had been there since my mother was a teenager and had the most suspicious hot dogs and the most absolutely delicious chocolate milkshakes on the planet. I was sucking one down, perched on a metal picnic table with peeling white paint when Dana pulled up.

She got herself a shake and then sat down with me. The fact that I had almost finished mine in what must be record time surely indicated that something troubling had happened.

"Okay, AJ, spill it. What's goin' on?"

"Richard's in town."

She coughed up a perfectly good sip of milkshake. "Excuse me?"

I nodded as I sipped.

"What? Why?"

"I don't know. I didn't get much of a conversation in before the next thing I knew Jesse had punched him and he'd smeared a cupcake on Jesse's perfectly handsome face."

Dana was frozen in an expression of confusion.

"Jesse? What on earth? Girl, you'd better start from the beginning."

And so, as Dana sucked up her chocolate perfection, I related the drama, pausing only to slurp out the dredges of my own and to consider ordering a second. Instead, I chose a slaw dog. Might as well eat away my worries.

"This is insane, you know." Dana was always full of helpful advice.

"I do know."

She watched her feet dangling off the edge of the table.

"How did it feel to see Richard?"

"Awful."

"Awful mad or awful sad."

I thought about that. It really got right to the heart of it, huh?

"Awful frustrating."

She nodded. "And with Jesse there, too."

"It's like…" I looked to the sky for answers. "It's like the two paths of my life right there in front of me. The past, the future. And then a big cupcake just crashes in there and causes a big ol' rotten mess."

"I gotcha."

"But one thing's for sure. There's no fixing Richard and me."

"Sure?"

"Absolutely."

"What do you think Sylvie will say?"

"I don't know. I mean, I want her to love her father, but part of me wants her to be mad at him, too, and that's not quite right, you know?"

"I can see why you'd feel that way, though."

I shoved the last bit of hot dog into my mouth to keep from crying.

"Om uhfwayed ee mot tok huh."

Dana put her arm around me. "He won't take her, AJ. He'll just— share her."

"I don't want to share her."

"I know. But he loves her, too."

The tears came. Damn you, emotions!

"I know."

"Sweet AJ, this will all work itself out. Have a little faith."

"Ha—faith in what?"

"Well, in yourself for one. In Sylvie. In God."

"This sucks."

"Yes it does. But you will get through it. I promise you will. With some scars, of course."

"Battle wounds, we used to call them."

She laughed. "Yes, of course that was when we fell out of a tree or tripped on a rock playing Blitz."

"True. And these are real."

"Even more real."

I felt so frustrated. Just when everything seemed to be fitting into place, dumb old Richard had to show his slimy face.

"What do I do now? What do I say to him? What do I say to Sylvie?"

"I don't know. But I know you'll know when the time comes. Just be open."

"You sound like a preacher."

She found that hilarious. "Ain't no preacher, just happy to meet yer."

She put both of her arms around me and we sat in front of the Cremo hugging and laughing as people looked at us with smiles, happy to see happiness.

Chapter Eight

Sylvie spoke a mile a minute the instant her bottom hit the booster seat.

"Today Emmie Mae and me—"

"I."

"I...were on the playground and we wanted to go down the slide, but you had to pay a pebble to go down the slide, so we got pebbles and slid down the slide. THEN Daniel started chasing us around the playground, so we ran up the fort but we couldn't go down the slide because we didn't have any pebbles, so we started screaming and then Daniel put Emmie Mae in a dip and KISSED HER right there on the fort!"

I wasn't sure whether to panic or burst out laughing. I chose the latter.

"Mommy, this is serious! He kissed Emmie Mae and she didn't want him to and so she shoved the slide guards out of the way and climbed right up!"

"And what did you do?"

"I ran the other way, of course. No boy is going to kiss me!" She crossed her arms and pouted.

I wanted to freeze this moment, preserve it for when she turned thirteen.

"That sounds like a rather dramatic recess."

"Uh-huh. Sure was."

"What else?"

"We had show and tell and Heath told us AGAIN about how his

mom got a speeding ticket. I think his mom must get speeding tickets every week. But this time she was in a city in another place and she went up a tower that goes far, far into the sky—"

"The Empire State Building?"

She cocked her head, curls cascading. "Where's that?"

"New York City."

"That's it! And he had a picture and Mom, that building is REALLY BIG!"

"It is."

"Have you been there?"

"I have."

Her eyes grew large and I think she looked at me as if I were a superhero. It was a good feeling. Of course I'd been there on a school trip back in high school and had been so petrified of heights that I kept my back against the wall the whole time and refused to look over the edge. But she didn't need to know that. I considered telling her that I'd rappelled down the side of it but she might share that next week, causing an immediate teacher conference.

"Was it SO BIG, Mommy?"

"It was SO big."

She looked out the window. "I want to go there some day."

"Okay."

"You'll take me?"

"Sure."

"YES!" Complete with fist pump.

"So Sylvie, there's something I need to tell you."

"What, Mommy?"

She was looking at me so expectantly that it broke my heart. It broke my heart that she would be so excited about the news I had to tell her, and yet I had been so devastated to learn it.

"Your father is in town."

"DADDY!" She started bouncing up and down in her booster seat, chanting his name.

"I'll let you call him when we get to Momo's house and invite him over for dinner."

The chanting continued.

With every repetition, my heart sank further into my chest.

♥

I didn't need to tell my mother. The chanting told her all she needed to know. She gave me a look, I nodded, and she got out another place setting for dinner. Sylvie skipped off with my cell phone and I collapsed at the dinner table, my head on my arms.

"Mom, this sucks."

"Oh honey, it will be okay. This had to happen eventually and at least now you can just get it all over with."

"This sucks." Really, with my face on the table, it sounded more like, "Thshhh shahhx."

"Here's what we're going to do. We're going to have a civilized dinner, I'll put Sylvie to bed while you speak with him, and then we'll kill him and throw his body in the lake. Simple."

I looked up expecting to see a smile but she looked strangely serious.

"Thanks, Mom, but I don't think I'm capable of murder."

She considered that and gave me the smile I'd been expecting. "I am."

"Mom, be serious. What am I supposed to say? How am I supposed to act?"

"I can't answer that. I can only say that you should say what you need to say and do what you need to do. You're the only one with your heart. Speak it."

"You're such a hippie, Mom."

"Not likely. I did offer to kill him."

"That won't be necessary."

"I'll be on call."

I sighed. "Mom, Jesse slugged Richard in the bakery today."

She dropped the fork clean into the frying pan of okra. "Repeat that."

"Jesse slugged Richard."

She smiled. "I knew I liked him."

"MOM!"

"Okay, fine, fine, so Jesse's got a temper. Just something to keep in mind. I'm sure Richard deserved it."

I was about to inform her that she was totally downplaying what had been a truly humiliating experience in front of my boss when Sylvie skipped into the kitchen and handed me back my cell phone.

"Daddy says he's staying down the road at the Wayside Motel and he'll be here as soon as he can."

"Great."

"Mommy, are you excited to see Daddy?" Her voice betrayed her true curiosity.

What was I supposed to say to that?

"I'm definitely anxious to talk with your daddy."

She stared at me, trying to figure out what I meant. Then she gave up and smiled as beautifully as ever. "Okay!" And she skipped off to get her bookbag.

I turned to my mother and ran my hands over my face. "Mom, this is a disaster."

"No, honey, the way you look right now is a disaster. Go get a long, hot shower. I'll entertain the asshole until you get back."

"Just do me a favor, Mom, and don't curse in front of Sylvie. It might come up in the custody hearings later."

She nodded and crossed her heart. "Yes, ma'am."

I trudged upstairs and stripped down, tossing my clothes on the floor without a thought. Then I fell back on the bed and stared at the ceiling. How had this day gone downhill so quickly? One moment Jesse was asking me on a second date, and the next my soon-to-be-ex-husband was lying in pink icing nursing a busted lip.

I forced back the tears and dragged myself to the shower where I turned up the water so hot that it colored my skin red.

I closed my eyes and opened my mouth. I swished the water around and let it pour out between my teeth. I massaged shampoo into my hair and breathed in the fresh scent of apples. I scrubbed my skin, between my toes, and splashed my face.

I had steamed up the bathroom so well I couldn't see myself in the mirror when I climbed out, so I wrapped a towel around myself and tiptoed down the hallway to my bedroom.

I pulled on a light sundress and brushed out my wet hair. I wasn't going out of my way, but I could at least remind him of what he was losing. I blew my hair dry and as I switched off the noise I heard it—his voice, following quickly by Sylvie's laughter.

I sat on the bed, tears burning my eyes, my chest so tight I thought I might be having a heart attack.

"Breathe. Breathe." I whispered the word over and over, rocking on the edge of the bed, running my toes over the carpet. I willed myself not to cry.

At last I wiped my eyes and nose, walked to the bathroom to check the mirror and make sure I didn't looked like a drowned mouse with my pink nose and flushed cheeks, and took one final, deep breath.

"You are okay. You are okay, Amanda."

But I couldn't fool myself. I'd have to fake it.

I peeked into the living room and saw Richard in an old arm chair, Sylvie snuggled up in his lap, kissing his face. He kissed the top of her head and I could see that he was trying not to cry.

Curse him for being so human.

Sylvie saw me being so ridiculous around the corner.

"Mommy! Daddy's here!"

I emerged from the corner, smiling fakely, fighting the tears that were blurring the image of those two cuddled up together. I was somewhat thankful for that.

"Amanda, you look great."

"Thank you."

Awkward silence. But not for Sylvie.

"Mommy is beautiful. Isn't she so beautiful, Daddy? She's the prettiest Mommy in the whole world!"

"DINNER!"

Thank you, Mom.

Sylvie held Richard's hand and led him into the kitchen where our places were set. In her infinite wisdom, my mother had set Sylvie across from me, next to her father.

After the blessing, we passed the bowls and plates, Sylvie chattering constantly about how much she loved chicken and how she didn't like black-eyed peas and how she loved mashed potatoes, but not with gravy. And how she really, really loved sweet tea.

Richard looked at me skeptically but I didn't give him the benefit of a shared commiseration over Sylvie's soon-to-be-rotten teeth. I wondered if he had really agreed with me about that or if he'd just given in on that one over the years.

"So, Richard, what brings you to town?" Mom, seriously?

"Well, I missed my girls. Thought I'd stop by and see my little princess, and have a talk with Amanda."

"How nice."

"Daddy says he has to go back home tomorrow, but that I can come see him soon."

You know the expression 'shot daggers with her eyes'? That's what I did.

"Well—I just suggested it really. There's no formal time for it—I—"

"We'll discuss it," I said.

And thus the most awkward dinner of all time became the quietest dinner of all time. Sylvie told jokes, her favorite was, "What do you get when you cross a rooster and a crocodile? A crock-a-doodle-doo!"

My mother did pipe up at one point to mention my recent heroics.

"So, Richard, have you heard that Amanda Jane is something of a local hero ?"

I shot her a look. Seriously?

"Really?" He looked first at me, then at my mother, but it was Sylvie who answered.

"Oh yes, Daddy. Mommy got the police to go investigate why Momo's water was all gross, and they found some bad people down the road and locked them away!" She so sincerely smiled at me…it was true admiration. I felt kind of proud.

Richard screwed up his face. "I don't follow."

"Oh, Mom's river water was polluted, so I found out the source of the pollution and had the proper authorities alerted. No biggie."

Sylvie whispered to her father. "Mommy is saving the earth."

He looked overly impressed for her benefit, but when he turned to me, his look was sincere.

"That's great, Amanda. Wow. Just great."

And that was the extent of the dinner conversation.

After dinner, Sylvie insisted that Richard put her to bed, so I helped my mother clean up the kitchen. She didn't say much; I think she knew she shouldn't. All she said was, "You're doin' right, sweetheart."

Richard walked reluctantly back into the kitchen. "Well, she's all tucked in and nearly asleep already. I didn't want to leave—she's so beautiful when she's sleeping. Like an angel."

"Let's go on the porch and talk, Richard."

His eyes fell to his shoes like a child. "Okay."

I closed the glass doors behind us and gestured to a chair. We sat next to each other so we could look at the world and not each other. I looked at the stars, dim on this cloudy night. A rumble of thunder in the distance seemed to echo my feelings.

"Richard, what did you say to Jesse to make him punch you in the face? Good job covering it up, by the way, did you use make-up?"

He blushed. "Maybe. And anyway, it doesn't matter. I just don't like that guy."

"Obviously."

He exhaled loudly. "Amanda, I need to say some things to you."

"Yes, you do."

"I'm so sorry." He exhaled deeply and I heard him shift awkwardly in his seat. I hadn't turned on any lights except the living room lights that leaked through the glass doors. All I could see was the silhouette of his face.

"I'm so sorry, Amanda. I screwed up big time."

"That's an understatement," I mumbled.

"I know. I know!" I heard the exasperation in his voice. "I'm an idiot. And I'm sorry. I let you down, I let Sylvie down, I let myself down. And I'm sorry."

"Thank you."

"I'm not asking you to come back..."

"I wouldn't."

There was a pause while he took a deep breath. "I know. And I don't want you to."

I was about to stand up and walk away. How dare he?

"Wait! Wait—I mean, you look so great here. Sylvie's great here. I know now, what we had was broken, broken, and neither of us said anything. I'mnotblamingyou!" He must have noticed I was about to go Southern Crazy on his ass. "I'm just acknowledging what I think we both knew. And so I came here to try to end this in a congenial manner. I want to talk about what's going to happen next."

I sighed and leaned back in my chair. For the first time in months, I felt relaxed when I thought about the future.

He seemed calmer now that I was settled back in my seat, nails no longer in a claw position. "Here's my proposal—can I tell you my proposal?"

"Of course."

"Sylvie stays with you—of course. I get to come visit once a month, for a couple of days. I'll stay at a hotel. Or if you're coming to Charlotte you'll let her come stay with me—maybe overnight?"

"That's a big maybe."

He sighed. "And then at holidays, Christmas at least, Easter, we come together. In whatever form that means. If you're marri—" His voice cracked and we sat there in silence.

"That sounds fair. And how do we handle this legally?"

He cleared his throat. "I'll have my lawyer draw something up."

"I'll have David look it over."

"Okay."

"Okay."

What more was there to say? Here sat two adults, discussing the end of their marriage.

I thought back to when I'd married Richard. I'd been so happy, despite the wedding. His mother had taken me by the arm and spent the majority of my reception dragging me from 'cousin' to 'cousin.' But I didn't care; I was in love. The cake topper had been stolen at some point between the cake arriving at the reception and the reception actually beginning. But I didn't care; I was in love. My uncle Joel got disastrously drunk and made a ten minute toast to my virginity. But I didn't care; I was in love.

And when we drove off from the reception, we pulled over just around the corner and burst into laughter thinking of all of the ridiculous antics of our families. But we didn't care; we were in love.

And now here we sat, in silence, on a stormy night, on my mother's back porch, calmly discussing the fact that we were no longer in love. Folly ushered in our marriage; folly stretched across the finish line. And here we were.

"Richard, I will always respect your love for Sylvie. Whatever happens between us, as long as you love her, I can't help but respect you for that."

"Thank you."

"You don't deserve it, of course."

"No, I don't."

"But all the same...I'm glad we can come to this arrangement. It's what's best for her."

"I don't want her to have Christmas only halfway. That's no way to go through a childhood. I'm just so thankful you'll allow me to stay in her life."

"Of course. You might be an ass, but you're her father."

He chuckled to himself. "Seems like a paradox."

I shrugged and looked over at him for the first time. He was nervously picking at his cuticles, a habit that had made me feel irrationally angry on many occasions. Now I just saw a sad little boy, alone and lost.

"Richard, I'm so angry at you."

"I know."

"No, I don't think you do. You embarrassed me. You humiliated me. You made me feel like I wasn't good enough."

"I'm sorry."

My hand flew up. "Let me finish." Here it was—the great purge. "You betrayed me. You betrayed my love, my hopes and dreams, your daughter. And for what? A blonde with long legs and big boobs."

"Amanda, please know that it was no reflection on you—"

"Stop. Just leave it at that. I know you're sorry."

"I am."

"Me too."

I felt released, lightened, fulfilled.

"Amanda, can I ask you a question. Who was that guy today?"

Abashed.

"His name is Jesse and he's a friend of mine."

I heard him swallow. "A friend?"

"Yes. A friend."

"Okay. Does he know Sylvie?"

"Just a little. He works for my mother."

"Oh. Okay."

I felt a drop of rain hit the top of my head and when I looked up I was hit in the eye.

Richard leapt up. If I was citified, he was metropolized. "Geez, guess I'd better get going. I won't be able to find my way back to the motel."

I stood and the bottom fell out. Rain poured upon us and I pushed Richard under the overhang, against the wall.

"You'll have to make a run for it—do you want an umbrella?"

"No, no I'm fine. I'm fine, thanks."

I saw him in the light now. He looked so old despite the fact that we were really quite young. Bags hung loose under his eyes and gray hair peppered his sideburns.

I don't know what got into me. I don't make it a habit of kissing total jerks, but for whatever reason, call it nostalgia, I leaned over and gave him a peck on the cheek.

"Thank you for loving our daughter."

He looked me in the eyes and the corner of his mouth rose slightly. "I love you, too."

I took his hand and gave it a squeeze. "Let's not get carried away. It ain't Hollywood, Richard."

He laughed. "So feisty, Amanda. Don't ever change."

"It isn't likely."

"And let me mention one thing that I'm finding kind of curious." He grinned. "Since when do you say 'ain't'?"

My stomach flipped and I felt an overwhelming sense of gratification sweep over me.

"Since I became a country girl again."

Before I could stop him, he put his arms around me and pulled me close. His words in my ears stuck with me long after he'd driven away. "That's who I fell in love with, Amanda Jane. I'm so glad she's back."

And then he ran off into the wet darkness.

Curse his kindness. I'd rather think of him as a total bastard.

❤

My mother had retreated to her bedroom where she'd fallen asleep, fully clothed, watching Trebek, so I peeked into Sylvie's room on my way to bed. As soon as the light fell across her she popped straight up, causing me to gasp aloud.

"Sylvie! You're supposed to be asleep, sweetie. What's wrong?"

The look on her face hurt my heart. She'd clearly been crying, tear stains plastered hair across her face. Her bedspread was covered in snot from her runny nose.

I went to her, sat and took her in my arms. I could feel her tiny body trembling and her words shook so violently I couldn't understand her. I pulled her to my chest and breathed with her to slow her pace. When she was finally breathing regularly, she spoke again.

"I want Daddy to stay."

"I know baby, but Daddy has to go home."

"I want to go home, too."

I smoothed her hair and she turned her sincere face toward mine.

"I thought you loved being at Momo's house."

"I do, but I miss Daddy more. Can't we go home, Mommy?"

I started rocking her, or maybe I was rocking myself. "Honey, we can't go back there. This is our home now."

"Why?"

"Because Daddy and Mommy aren't going to be married anymore, remember?"

She climbed out of my arms and turned to face me, perched on her knees.

"Why not?"

I thought I'd side-stepped this conversation. I should have known better.

"Well, Daddy and Mommy have just decided that we are happier living in different houses."

That was so pathetic.

"Don't you love each other?"

"Of course."

"Then why aren't you married? I love Noah at school, and I'm going to marry him."

"Sometimes love is not enough."

Geez, wasn't she a bit too young for this?

"I don't get it, Mommy."

I took a deep breath and found myself praying to God for the first time in years.

God, please give me the words to say to her. Please help me. Help me. I can't do this.

"Sylvie, Mommy and Daddy are still a family, but we're a family that's going to live in different places. I want to live here, in the country, and your daddy loves the city. We still love each other, but we can't live together anymore."

I was just patting myself on the back for an argument well made when Sylvie did the unthinkable—she started screaming.

"THAT'S STUPID! THAT'S NOT A FAMILY! A FAMILY IS TO-GETHER! A FAMILY LOVES EACH OTHER NO MATTER WHAT! YOU TOLD ME THAT! YOU LIED TO ME! YOU'RE A BIG FAT LIAR!" And she jumped off of the bed, threw herself to the carpet, and started beating her tiny fists on the floor, calling through her tears, "A liar! A liar! A liar!"

I knelt beside her and tried to wrap my arms around her but she shoved me and crawled to the corner of the room where she faced the wall, knees to chin, arms wrapped around herself.

I felt completely helpless. This was my sweet girl, my Sylvie, my obedient, reasonable, calm child who had never thrown a tantrum in her life. At least not like this. So I did what any self-respecting parent would—I blamed her father. Was it coincidence that this happened just after he left? Was it coincidence that the one who tucked her in was the one person who would no doubt plan the seed of lies in her pretty little head? The one who was obviously quite good at lying? At turning people against each other? At ruining families?

"What in Sam Hill is goin' on in here?"

My mother had evidently been awakened by the eruption of Mt. St. Sylvie and now stood in the doorway, bleary-eyed and obviously as taken aback as I had been to hear Sylvie screeching and pounding the floor.

"Sylvie is upset that her father left."

Her little voice was barely a whisper. "I want my daddy."

"Oh, little beany bean." My mother crossed the room and put her hand on Sylvie's shoulder. "Your daddy had to go back to work. But you'll see him again soon."

"Tomorrow?"

"Probably not tomorrow, but I'll bet you can talk to him tomorrow, and you can tell him you want to see him soon."

"Why not tomorrow?"

My mother looked at me, giving me my cue that I needed to step in. I crawled across the room and sat behind Sylvie, not touching her yet, but close enough to see her shoulders trembling.

"Daddy has to work, angel. But you can call him tomorrow."

"Will I ever see Daddy again?" She started to cry again and I put my mouth close to her ears.

"Of course, baby. That's what we were talking about outside. You'll see him all the time."

"You promise?"

"I promise, baby."

She wiped her eyes and her nose and snuggled against my chest. My mother gave me an approving smile and quietly slipped out of the room.

"I understand, Mommy. It's like when someone dies. You still love them, but they just don't live with you anymore. It's just the way it is."

I'd say she was being rather profound but it echoed a conversation we'd had back in May when David the goldfish had died.

"That's about right."

"But we're lucky that Daddy isn't dead. So we get to see him sometimes."

"Yes."

"Okay. Thank you, Mommy. Thank you for not letting Daddy be dead."

You have no idea how close it came...

I gave her a kiss on her sweet little nose. "Honey, I love you so much. Can you be happy living here?"

"With Momo?"

"With Momo and Mommy. And Daddy sometimes."

She searched my eyes and then snuggled back down into me. "Yes."

When I was sure she was asleep, I crept downstairs and called Jesse.

"Glad to know you're still talkin' to me. Sorry about today, Mandy. That guy just got me in a sore spot."

"Yeah, well, I think the two of you got me into a sore spot. You know my boss was standing right there when you slugged him."

"I know. I'm sorry." There was a pause. "Although she looked rather gleeful about the whole thing, to be honest."

I rolled my eyes. "For Beulah, the image of two good-looking men brawling amongst her cupcakes is probably a fantasy come to life."

He chuckled. "I hope you don't get into trouble."

"Oh, no worries. I'll go in early on Monday and fix everything that was ruined."

He sighed. "I wish I could help."

"You could do me a favor and try to control that temper of yours."

"Fair enough."

I paused, considering what I should tell Jesse about my conversation with Richard, about my conversation with my mother regarding Patsy Cherry. But in the end I decided I'd had enough drama for one night. I didn't have any fight left in me, not to mention any tears.

"Okay, I gotta get back to bed before Sylvie misses me."

"Okay then. I am truly so sorry, Mandy."

"Yeah, yeah, tough guy. Guess it's good to know you're willing to defend my honor." I smiled in spite of myself.

"Any time."

"Night, Jesse."

"Bye."

I climbed back upstairs and into bed. Sylvie was lying on her side, her curls damp with perspiration. When I woke up the next morning she had her arm thrown across my face and her legs dangled off of the bed. It was the sweetest thing I'd ever seen.

Chapter Nine

Jesse showed up at six o'clock sharp. I was at the table, playing Go Fish with Sylvie, letting her win at least every third hand, to teach her how to be a good winner, of course.

"Hi, Mr. Jesse!" she sang as he walked into the kitchen dressed in jeans, a flannel shirt, and that hat. I know I say a lot of about the hat, but really, it was so incredibly Jesse.

"Hi, short stuff. Whatcha doin'?"

"Playin' Go Fish. Wanna play with me?"

He looked at me, eyebrows raised.

"Go ahead, Jesse, I need to go finish getting ready."

I handed him my hand of cards and hurried upstairs to run a brush through my hair and put on a little make-up. I looked at myself in the mirror and realized that Jeannette would be proud. I had put on dark jeans, a flimsy black top, and—wait for it—boots. Sparkly body powder, red lipstick, mascara—I was feeling kinda saucy. I sashayed down the stairs like a scarlet woman.

"Mommy—you look SEXY!"

Well that was unexpected.

I froze in the doorway, then went right into 'Mommy Mode,' hands on hips. "Sylvie, where did you hear that word?"

She looked at her hands, her little mouth turned downward in sincere shame.

I knelt at her feet and took her face in my hands. "You're not in trouble, baby, it's just that 'sexy' isn't a word you need to be using."

"Noah said it."

"I'm sure he did. But it isn't a nice word."

She looked into my eyes. "Why not?"

And how, I ask, is one supposed to explain 'sexy' to a five-year old?

Jesse and my mother were standing side by side, arms across chests, looking on in enjoyment.

I took a deep breath. "Well, sweetie, when you call someone 'sexy,' you are basically saying that what they look like is more important than what kind of person they are." I leaned back and shot a smug look at the audience.

Sylvie twisted up her face. "What kind of person they are?"

"Yes, it means you care more that someone is pretty than if someone is nice—kind to others."

"Okay, Mommy. I won't say that word anymore."

"Thanks, sweetie." I kissed her forehead, stood, and brushed my shoulder as I turned to my mother and Jesse.

"Mommy, is Mr. Jesse taking you to dinner?"

"Yes he is."

"Is he going to be your boyfriend?"

I froze mid-shoulder brush. Jesse looked like he was about to burst with laughter.

I twirled around to face my child. "Jesse is just a friend, Sylvie. We're just two friends going out to dinner."

She spoke with a knowing tone, "Are you gonna kiss him?"

I got right into her angelic little face. "I'm gonna kiss YOU!"

"No, Mommy!" She squealed as I tried to kiss her all over her face and neck.

"Okay, okay, Mommy's going out. Be good for your Momo."

"Always!"

She puckered her lips and I leaned down to meet her tiny kiss. "Sweet dreams."

"Night, Mommy. Night, Mr. Jesse. Have fu—u—u—n!"

"Be go—o—o—d!"

She smiled sweetly as we walked out the door and to Jesse's truck. When he had me settled in and had climbed behind the wheel he turned to me and grinned suspiciously.

"I hope you're ready to go back in time."

"Wow. Okay. Yeah, I'm ready."

He turned on the CD player and a teentybopper girl band that had been popular when we were in high school blasted through the truck. I cracked up laughing as he pulled away from the house, singing at full volume in a pseudo-female voice. I pulled a hairbrush from my purse and sang along as loudly as I possibly could. He rolled down the windows and our voices echoed into the waning evening light.

Twenty minutes later we pulled into the parking lot of my junior high school. I looked out the window and saw the marching band lined up and marching up the hill that led to the high school football stadium. No. Way.

"Jesse, are we doing what I think we're doing?"

"Friday Night Football rained out—rescheduled for Saturday night! Just our luck!"

"You have got to be kidding me."

"No, ma'am. And look, I even managed to play this so that our alma maters are battling it out tonight. How's THAT for planning?"

"I call it luck."

He shrugged. "Maybe. But it's awesome either way."

I let myself out of the truck and looked around me where families were tailgating in the junior high parking lot. Grills, ice chests, the occasional keg. I'd forgotten just how seriously these people took high school football.

Growing up, you were trained to root on the high school team from elementary school. Every Friday the varsity cheerleaders would wander through our school—shouldn't they have been in class?—collecting fifty cents in exchange for a red ribbon with gold letters proclaiming that the Big Red would win. The ribbons affixed to your shirt with a large, gold foil football sticker.

And then at precisely two-thirty every classroom would open its windows and every student would scream in unison, "GO BIG RED!"

A rite-of-passage in junior high was to walk underneath the bleachers from one end of the field to the other. Since this was where teenagers disappeared to do drugs, drink, and make babies, this was quite a task. I completed the rite in seventh grade, running all the way with Dana's hand clasped in mine.

And then high school. On Friday mornings the cheerleaders would toilet paper the football players' houses and hang signs in their trees. I never understood this because to me, TP-ing was vandalism, an act my mother claimed was punishable by death, but the popular kids loved it. You were really 'somebody' if your house was TPed. Ridiculous.

And if you weren't at the game, you'd committed social suicide, so every kid, from the most popular to the most dweebie, was there, cordoned off into little sections of status. I had stayed with the marching band flag line after my failed cheerleading attempt, so I got to sit in a reserved section. I sometimes wondered if we'd get a little more respect from fans if we boycotted a couple of games, refused to play the fight song when the team scored a touchdown. But sadly, the band director needed a job, so we played along. We didn't watch the game though. That would be crazy.

And now here I was, all grown up and back at Richland Field.

Jesse appeared next to me and took my hand. His accent was thick as he said, "Ready for this, little lady?"

I sighed and looked up into his eyes. They were laughing and I couldn't help but play the part.

"Ready, cowboy."

We walked up the hill, which was painted with red cat paws for the Northeast Cougars. When I was in marching band, I stomped up this hill so many times I'd lost count. And yet now the hill seemed insurmountable. It couldn't possibly be the fact that I wasn't eighteen anymore, could it? After all, I was supposed to be going back in time tonight.

By the time we reached the top, I was panting, couldn't speak, and had decided that I would start jogging around the farm in the evenings, beginning the very next night. Jesse put his arms around me and laughed. "Are you okay?"

"Yes," I panted. "Fine."

We bought our tickets from some sweet teacher spending her Saturday night making a little extra money at the gate and walked into the stadium. I felt my stomach leap into my chest as I took it all in. In a football town, the stadium is the heart, and it is decked out as such. A brick wall surrounded the field and pristine metal bleachers rose into the sky to the immaculate press box, nicer than the one that had been at my college. A voice called advertisements over the stadium intercom as the boys warmed up on the field. The lights were on and bugs were buzzing around them, occasionally ramming headfirst into the plastic cover.

"Want to sit or should we go ahead and get somethin' to eat?"

I looked at him as if he'd just offered me a gourmet meal. "Tell me they have suicide dogs here."

He squeezed my hand. "That's why I like you, Mandy. And yes, they've got the dogs."

Suicide dogs were local slang for a chili cheese slaw dogs, usually dressed with ketchup, mustard, and onion, as well. You can guess how they got the name.

We made our way through the crowds of teenagers decked out in their letterman's jackets despite the fact that it was nearly eighty degrees. I felt sorry for them. I remembered being a teenager, trying so hard to fit in with whatever was the 'right' thing to do, even if it meant a heat stroke in the stadium bleachers. I looked at these kids walking around in their little shorts and peasant shirts, the boys so incredibly awesome in their suede flip flops and button down shirts with shorts. They flipped the hair out of their faces like they were cool. It looked like a nervous tic to me. If I were one of these girls, I would be truly disturbed if a boy flipped his hair more than I did. But I guess I'm just old-fashioned.

I was just considering the trials of youth with I heard the words I'd come to dread.

"Amanda Ja—a—a—ne!" It was a deeply accented, high-pitched drawl.

I probably looked like a raccoon caught in the porch lights as I whipped around, searching for the owner of the voice.

Jesse cleared his throat and I looked in front of me, on the other side of the concession stand counter.

It was my high school Chemistry teacher, Mrs. Hollings. She was a thing of legend at Northeast, and not only because she had been an amateur alligator wrestler. Yes, that's right. There was a picture above her blackboard in which she was nose-to-nose with an alligator. The thing was, Mrs. Hollings was petite and adorable. She had blonde, curly hair—now probably artificially blonde—and a big, red-lipsticked mouth. And did I mention the sugar-sweet Southern drawl?

"Amanda Jane Rawberts! Look at yew! Oh, my gawsh, but ah woulda recuhnized yew anywhar!"

She reached across the counter and threw her arms around me. Yep, still smelled like baby powder. Trademark.

"Mrs. Hollings, it's so wonderful to see you, too!"

"Hun, are yew back in tow—on? Fer good?"

"I don't know. Just back for a little while, trying to figure things out."

She nodded and squiggled up her nose. "Ah know how that goes. Good fer yew, sweetie." Then she looked oh-so-nonchalantly at Jesse. "And who's yer yung ma—yun?"

I blushed like a teenager caught holding hands in the hallway.

"This is Jesse Gregory."

"Ma'am." He shook her hand. Kinda cute.

"Nice to meetcha, Jesse. I wuz Amanda Jane's Cheemistry teacher back in hah—school."

Jesse nodded.

"Okay yew two, whatcha havin'?" She took a pen hidden behind her ear within the blonde locks and held it poised over a note pad.

"Um…I'll have a suicide dog and a Coke, please."

"No fries?"

Jesse piped in. "A large fry, please, and two more suicide dogs."

"Boy, you wanna die tonight?" Mrs. Hollings winked at him.

"No, ma'am, but if I do, I want it to taste good."

She laughed…giggled, really, and then took our money and screamed our order behind her.

Within seconds the food had arrived and I was hugging Mrs. Hollings goodbye and following Jesse to the condiments barrel. A barrel, that's right, with a ketchup and mustard set poised on top, holding down the napkins. It was such a contrast to the press box.

We dressed the dogs and pushed our way to the bleachers and all the way to the top.

I felt so all-American sitting in my football stadium eating my hot dog when the band marched on the field for the National Anthem. I wished I'd worn a blue jean jacket.

We stood and Jesse took his hat off as the band completed the pre-show, and then the cheerleaders came cartwheeling out and…yes, Russian-ing. They formed their girl-towers and held a huge sign that read, 'Bruise the Bruins!' The fight song played, the teenage boys burst through the banner, and I laughed so hard I cried.

And yet, when it came to it, I was cheering so loudly that at one point I noticed Jesse was just staring at me with a look on his face that reminded me of a kid on Christmas morning.

"What?"

He just shook his head and smiled. "I don't know where you came from."

I played dumb. "Um...the country?"

He pulled me into him. "I'm so glad I met this country girl."

At halftime I really broke free as I cheered for the marching band although no one else was.

"Go band! Go ba—a—and!"

I was getting so involved I barely noticed that Jesse had joined me in my salute to the band. I truly believed he had no idea what he was doing, what they were playing, or what some of the instruments even were, but he cheered nonetheless.

During the final minutes of halftime, when the band had finished, the boys were back on the field, warming up, and the fans had emptied the stands to refill their popcorn tubs, I sat alone, my date being one for a quick refill before the second half. I was scanning the crowd, searching for my man when I heard my name in a sort of hesitant tone. This whole, 'Let's call Amanda Jane's name before we give her a chance to see we're here' thing was getting old, but I turned to the side and shaded my eyes against the stadium lights. There stood...someone I had never met.

"Um...yes? I'm Amanda Jane Roberts."

I realized too late. The narrow eyes, the puckered mouth, the close-cropped blond hair. It had to be—

"Robbie Prescott Foxfire. I believe you work for my mama."

Well, if this was a pick-up line, it sure as hell wasn't working.

"Ah, yes, of course. She's mentioned you." I stood and stuck out my hand, which he looked at confusedly before shaking. I guess he wasn't used to the kind of woman who shook hands. That's to say, the kind of woman who had confidence.

"You here by yourself?" He grinned and stuck his hands in his pockets. Seriously, was he attempting to sound like a total creep or was it just the way he operated?

"No, actually, I'm here with someone."

"Oh yeah, who's that?"

Now he was really getting on my nerves. How about a question about me? Maybe how my day was or if I needed a refill of my Coke. Or even if I had plans after the game.

"Jesse Gregory."

"Oh, yeah, Jesse Gregory. I remember Mama sayin' he came in the store the other day and made a scene. You sure you wanna be hangin' around a man like that, darlin'?" He gave me one of those smiles, one of those of-course-you-wouldn't smiles. I wondered if he expected me to have some kind of sudden recognition and ride off with him.

"I think I'm doing all right, thanks."

He actually looked surprised. "Well, if you change your mind, darlin', well, I'd love to take you out some time. You're mighty pretty, and Mama says you're a good girl."

"Well, I'm so glad she thinks that of me."

He nodded and sucked at his teeth. It gave me the shivers.

"If you're free after the game, I'll be over at the Tipsy. They got karaoke on Saturday nights. Love for you to join me."

"That's very sweet, Robbie. I think I'll turn in early tonight. I have a daughter at home and—"

"A daughter?" Now the shock was real. Ah, Beulah, you sly little lady. Left out a fairly substantial detail, did you?

"Yes, she's five. A handful, but just as sweet as she can be. I'll bet she'd love a good round of karaoke!"

He sucked through his teeth harder. "Yeah, well, Tipsy ain't no family place. But uh—say, I gotta run, Amanda Jane. It sure was nice to meet you." And with that, he was gone.

I had always judged men who ran as soon as they found out a single woman had a child. Tonight, though, I found myself pretty thankful that such a trait was in some men.

Jesse returned just at that moment with a tub of popcorn and a fresh Coke.

"Did I miss anything?"

"Nah, just some guy tryin' to pick up your date."

He looked incredulous. "Seriously? I was gone ten minutes!"

"Better be careful, Jesse. Evidently this lady's still got it." I winked at him and he tossed a piece of popcorn at me.

The second half was a dud for Jesse. We beat county 35-7. It was a pretty good show.

And as I was used to the pickup truck by now, the post-game wasn't so bad either.

We won that night. The football team, I mean.

❤

On Monday morning, I called David while I was mixing chocolate cake batter with caramel.

"Okay, AJ, so I spoke with my contact at local law enforcement. Did you know that when they contacted the owners of the land you saw down the river, and went to see what you saw, they found the trash chute as well as about fifty cats?"

"Fifty cats?"

"Yeah."

"I didn't see any cats, Dave."

"They were all inside."

I felt nauseated.

"Don't worry, animal control took them and everything's fine."

"Man, my heart hurts, Davie."

"I'm proud of you. You come home and jump right into philanthropy."

I rolled my eyes. "Let's not get carried away. I just wanted my mom's fields to get clean water."

"Yeah, okay, you do-gooder. Whatever."

"Hey, how's the boy toy?"

He chuckled. "Wonderful. As a matter of fact, I think I'm going to introduce him to my mother pretty soon here."

"Ooh, brave."

"Brave. Stupid. Both."

"Brave. Hey, I made out in a pickup truck with the boy again."

"Naughty."

I smiled as I remembered our laughter as I leaned on the horn and scared every living creature in that field, including myself.

"You should try it sometime. Anyway, gotta go. Love you, Davie."

"Love you, goody-two-shoes."

I hung up and added a bit more caramel. I poured the batter into a couple of cake tins and allowed myself a tiny lick of the spatula.

Beulah bee-bopped back into the kitchen carrying an empty tray.

"Who were you talking to, my dear?"

"I'm sorry?"

She smiled. "I heard you on the phone and I'm nosy, in case you haven't heard, so I'm wondering who it was. You never talk on the phone at work."

"Just my friend David."

"David?"

"David Harrison."

Her face fell and she showed that look that says, "Oh, David HAR-RISON."

We worked in silence for a minute while I digested her reaction. But I couldn't get past that smug look on her face. Suddenly I spun around, gesticulating with a whisk I'd just picked up from the crock of tools.

"Beulah, why did you respond that way when I told you who I was talking to?"

"I don't know what you mean, dear." So artificial. And she didn't even look at me.

I shot fiery daggers from my eyes into her back.

"I mean, why did you look at me as if I'd said the name of some horrible person."

She shrugged with a sigh. "He's not a horrible person." She turned toward me and looked me straight in the eyes. Her voice dripped with condescension. "He's just a degenerate, sweetheart."

I think I went blind for a moment. Really. I didn't see anything and then when the world came back into focus it was just Beulah, standing there in a freakin' gingham dress with a damn little cutesy apron that screamed Betty Crocker Wannabe. I hated that outfit.

"Beulah, I cannot believe you just said that."

She sighed and looked at me as if I were an ignorant child. "Honey, I'm sure he's a nice boy, but his life choices are not what God teaches of his children."

Really. I think I must be destined for early vision loss. Because I went blind again. I should have that checked.

I stuck the whisk in her face. "Beulah, God says to love everyone. He says not to judge others. He doesn't say to treat someone like dirt. No matter whether you ignorantly think his 'lifestyle'—" that's right... get her with the air quotation marks! "—is a choice or not."

She clucked her tongue like old women do and shook her head. "I feel sorry for your mama."

And now I was on fire. Crazy. Burning. Out of control. Fire.

"Excuse me?"

"To think she raised such a girl who would not only approve of those who balk in the face of God, but who would commit adultery in front of the entire town."

"What are you talking about?"

"I know you were at the football game the other night...on a date." She spat the word.

"So?"

"So, my dear, in case you have forgotten, you are still married." She pointed to her own ring finger.

"Are you kidding me? You sent your son to flirt with me! You stood right here several weeks ago and suggested I go out with him!"

Her eyes narrowed and I realized what this was all about. This was about my rejecting her most perfect offspring.

"Once your marriage is dissolved. Until then, you, my dear, are living a sinful life with that Jesse Gregory."

"I can't believe you."

"I can't believe your mama hasn't tried to rein you back in. Then again, I haven't see her at the church in a while, so—"

"You bitch."

She gasped and her hand flew to her heart. Somehow that just made me even angrier. Thank God that whisk wasn't a real weapon.

"I quit. But I want you to know that my mama has more religion than any judgmental, superficial witch like you!" Immature, I know, but sue me. David is like a brother.

Beulah just kept making shocked sounds as she looked around, gape mouthed, as if the pots and pans would back her up.

I tossed my whisk in the sink, poured the chocolate caramel batter on the floor, flipped off the timer on the oven so the cake would burn, and marched out of the bakery.

I had just broken one of the small town Ten Commandments— Thou shalt not challenge an old lady's religious beliefs.

❤

I rolled down the windows of the car and turned up the music as loudly as possible. I also stopped at the Cremo for one last milkshake in case I really was marked for damnation. But who the hell did she think she was? God? What gave her the right to label my best friend...a man she didn't even KNOW. And to judge me for not falling for her disgusting, inappropriate soon. *My* mama should be criticized? I was still cursing her when I noticed the flashing blue lights in the rearview mirror. Seriously?

Pulled over on the side of a country road, I was horrified as pickup trucks kept driving by slowly, the travelers gawking to see who'd been pulled over. I'm sure they were disappointed to see an unhappy young woman who surely did not have illegal drugs in the trunk. There's something about me that people just find innocent, people other than Beulah May Foxfire. I gave up when I was sixteen and decided to just embrace the innocent look.

Sunglasses and a hat. Of course.

"Ma'am, could I see your license and registration please?

I already had it ready. He looked impressed. That was a good sign.

"I went to school with an Amanda Jane."

I rolled my eyes. "It was probably me. Small town."

He took off the sunglasses and peered into the window. "Nope, I don't think so. This Amanda Jane was a redhead."

I nodded. "Oh well."

"Yes, sir, she was the prettiest thang in school. Cheerleader."

I rolled my eyes away from him. "Well, that is definitely not me."

"Never gave me the time of day. I was in the band, you know. Drums."

"Oh yeah? Me too—in the band. Not drums."

"Which school? I see we're about the same age." By this time he was crouching next to my car so our faces were eye-level.

"Northeast."

"Me too. Hmmm...Name's Scott Trilley."

Scott Trilley. Bingo!

"Oh, Scott Trilley! Yes, I remember you. You were a couple of years behind me. You might remember me as the flag twirler who fell flat on her ass that rainy night at Southeast. You know, the night everyone's feathers were flying off of their hats?"

"Oh yeah." He laughed. "That was a hell of a night."

"Yeah, remember how the other band poured Crisco all over the bleachers where we were supposed to sit, so we just went and sat on the home side?"

"Yeah, that was awesome. And at halftime all their fans were cheering for us. Liked us better than their own. Man, that was a good time."

"I know."

He suddenly remembered himself and stood up, clearing his throat.

"So anyway, do you know how fast you were going?"

"Yes, Scott, I do. I just quit my job and I guess I was a little bit mad at the world."

"Well, don't take it out on the road, okay? That ain't safe."

"I know it. I'm sorry."

He smiled. I'll give you a warning this time, for old times. But please be safe, Amanda Jane."

"Yes, sir."

As he started writing, he spoke hesitantly. "Say—weren't you friends with that girl...Dana? Was that her name?"

"Yes, I still am, as a matter of fact."

He grinned. "She married or anything?"

I felt bad breaking his heart after he'd been so nice to me. "I'm afraid she is, Scott. And with a slew of kids, too."

He shrugged, the smile still on his face. "Ah, well. She was a looker. Gotta take the opportunity when you can."

I nodded and started to fasten my seatbelt.

"You married, Amanda Jane?"

Well, this was unexpected. I'd never before dodged a ticket only to be hit on by the cop right after he'd basically hit on my friend. Worse, I didn't really know the answer to the question.

"Sorry, Scott. I'm spoken for."

"Oh well, I'll find my girl someday. Now be safe out there." He tipped his hat and walked away.

And that was the first time in my life that being pulled over for speeding had actually had a therapeutic effect on me. I felt much better as I drove the rest of the way home, except that Scott followed me the whole way, presumably to see where I lived. That was a little creepy, but not unexpected around here.

I found Mom in the fields working the fall maintenance on the berries. She was in her own little world and when I spoke her name she dropped her clippers and nearly jumped into the bushes.

"Amanda Jane! What in the world are you doin' here? You scared the tar outta me, baby!"

"I quit."

She dropped the clippers again and I scooped them up for her.

"You quit?"

"Yep. Quit. Can't work for that woman, Mama. She's too ignorant and nosy."

"Well I think we all knew that already, darlin'. What'd she do this time?"

I recounted the story for her and my mother just shook her head.

"I feel so bad for that boy livin' here with these people. Not all of 'em, of course, but so many are just downright ignorant. He's such a nice boy. Who cares? And who cares about Beulah's opinions anyway?" She clipped a bush rather violently.

"So now I have no job once again, Mama." I sat down in the grass and leaned back on my hands so the sun shone on my face.

"Well, sometimes you just have to stand up for what you believe in, even if it means walking away from somethin'."

I listened to her clip for a few minutes, the little 'chink chink' amidst the quiet of the outdoors quite welcome to me.

I crouched and started gathering her clippings and tossing them into the back of the cart she used to carry them to the burn pile.

"Amanda Jane, you ever consider opening your own bakery?"

I laughed out loud, "I think the memory of the last bakery that tried to open in this town is enough reason not to."

She stared at me. "Is it that you think you can't? 'Cause I assure you, honey, those special little pastries you make would bring people in."

"Mom, you can't run a bakery on pastries. You have to sell cakes. And Beulah has the monopoly on cakes in this town."

"That's the most ridiculous thing I've ever heard." The clipping was becoming feistier.

"Well, it's the truth. I don't know. Maybe I could go to a temp service or something."

She turned to me and put her hands on her hips. "You're starting a bakery. I'll front you the money."

"Whoa, Mom, that's not poss—"

"I don't want to hear another word. Now get that little unmotivated fanny of yours up to the house, get on that Gaggle, or whatever it is, on the computer, and find out how you do this."

"I figured I'd take a couple of days to relax and—"

"Ain't no time to relax!" Now she was pointing the clippers at me. I instinctively put my hands up in defense. "Now's the time to act! When you've got a fire in your belly! Now get to the house and get cookin'!" She turned back to the bush she'd been working and that was clearly the end of the conversation.

I trudged back to the house and sat on the back porch with the newspaper. I turned to the editorials and read about state's rights and the evil democratic candidate for state senate. But the highlight of the paper had to be 'On This Day in the Civil War,' a daily section surely dedicated to local history buffs. I flipped to the want ads and almost immediately slammed the paper onto the porch. Damn it, I was NOT working at the Nut House! I marched inside and sat myself down at my laptop, which had remained in a dormant state since I'd arrived.

"This is ridiculous," I whispered to myself as I started up the internet connection.

An hour later I shut down the computer and left to pick up Sylvie from school. On the drive, I mused over all that I had read about my mother's crazy idea. The good news was that my degree from culinary arts school had prepared me for the operation of the place, and also had gotten me a food handler's license, so I knew what that was about. The bad news was that this would cost an awful lot of money, money that I certainly didn't have and money that I refused to take from my mother.

But once the words had sunk into me, they'd turned into hope, and I'm a sucker for romantic ideas. So by the time I pulled up at Sylvie's school I'd formed a plan.

"Mommy!" the little voice squealed as she hopped into her booster seat and buckled up.

"Sweetie!" I sang back, turning to look at my beautiful little girl. She had a sticker on her hand. "What's with the sticker?"

She smiled shyly. "Austin gave it to me in the home living center. We're getting married next Tuesday."

Well, that was unexpected.

"Congratulations, but don't you think I should meet Austin before you get married?" I pulled away from the school but kept one eye on the rearview mirror where I could see her looking longingly out of the window.

"Okay, Mommy. I'll ask him over for supper. And Barbies."

"Sounds good. So how was school today?"

"Awesome! We had music class and we sang the Johnny Appleseed song! And then we ate apples! Yummy!" And she burst into song, "Oh the Lord is good to me! And so I thank the Lord! For giving me, the things I need, the sun and the rain and the apple seed. The Lord is good to me!"

I was pretty sure that you couldn't sing songs about the Lord in public schools, but then again, we were in Carroll, Georgia.

"How was work, Mommy?"

"Oh fine. I quit my job today. What do you think about Mommy opening her own bakery?"

She met my eyes in the rearview mirror. "That's an awful lot of baking, Mommy."

"Well I would have helpers, sweetie, just like I helped Miss Beulah."

"I can help you, Mommy. I'm a really good mixer!"

"Yes you are."

"And I can pour!" She was getting really wound up now, the seat belt straining against her excited little body. "I can put on sprinkles, and icing, and candles on the birthday cakes!"

And as a matter of fact, I was getting kind of excited, too.

❤

That night I called Jeannette.

"Jeannie, I'm opening a bakery."

"What the hell? What? I thought you were already working at a bakery."

"I quit."

"Hmmm...should I be proud?"

"The boss was a bitch."

She gave a cat call so loud I had to pull the phone away from my ear. "Woo-HOO! Good for you, Miss Independent! You slay that bakery bitch! You show her who's the Julia Child of the South!"

"Yeah, well, we'll see."

"Well, I plan to see myself."

I was taken aback. "What?"

"I'm coming to see you. It's clear you're never coming back to Charlotte and so if I want to see my best friend, I'll have to buy some camo and put the car in four wheel drive."

"Jeannie, does a BMW have four wheel drive?"

"No. It's a metaphor."

"Yeah, okay. But I'm really excited, Jeannie! When are you comin' over to these here parts?"

Her voice was firm. "First of all, don't EVER speak like that again. I'm coming to visit you, not the redneck version of you, and second, I was thinking about this weekend, if that's not too short notice."

"Mom will be thrilled. She loves guests, and she loves cooking Southern country delicacies for newbies."

"Promise me no squirrel gravy."

"Jean, we're country people, not mountain people."

"Okay. But seriously, do I need to buy...sneakers for this trip?"

"I think flip flops will do."

"Thank God. But seriously, do you see what I'm willing to do for you?"

"I do. And I'm so thankful, Jeannie. But there is something you might want to get."

"Oh Lord. What?"

"Blue Jeans."

Silence. In the ten years I had known Jeannette, I had never seen her wear blue jeans. She was totally anti-denim. Except a jean mini skirt to rock concerts. But that was it.

The first time I'd seen Jeannette, I'd been walking out of Bean Town, a small coffee shop in midtown, hurrying back to my first job out of college—Bath and Body Works. She was perched on a bench in front of the office I would soon be joining, decked out in black heels, black suit, black sunglasses, and black hair. She was on the cell phone, sipping from her Starbucks cup, and I thought 'I want to look just like that.'

"Jeffrey, NO! I said NO! I will NOT bring dinner home again tonight! I'm perfectly capable of cooking a delicious meal for us, and I am tired of you not giving me the chance. I'm cooking tonight, dammit, and that's THAT!" She'd hung up the phone and taken a long pull on her Frappuccino.

"Excuse me." I was much more forward then; I blame it on naiveté.

She looked up at me from behind the huge black sunglasses.

"I overheard your conversation. Can I make a suggestion?"

She nodded.

"Lasagna. It's easier than you think and it will really impress him." I smiled and started to walk away.

"Wait, please!" She was standing when I turned around, and she gestured to the bench.

I knew I'd be late for work, but as I wasn't really into being surrounded by battling floral scents and giving hand massages to total strangers, I took a seat.

"Can you tell me how? I mean, he wants take-out because I really can't cook. It's true. I totally suck. But I want to be good. I want to be a good housewife." She looked down at her perfectly manicured hands. "We're engaged."

"Congratulations."

"Thanks."

"I can't tell you what to do. But—"

"I'll screw it up."

"No. No, I did not say that." I took a pen out of my purse and scribbled a quick recipe on a napkin. I put my phone number underneath.

"God bless you, um..." She looked at me, I would say 'searchingly' but as I couldn't see her eyes behind the sunglasses, that would be presumptuous.

"Amanda." I'd dropped the 'Jane' in college.

"Thanks, Amanda." She held out her hand. "Jeannette."

"Nice to meet you. And good luck."

Of course seven hours later I was on the phone with her, walking her through every step. By the next weekend I was grocery shopping with her, and I spent Sunday teaching her how to make chocolate chip cookies from scratch.

The rest, as they say, is history. The guy didn't work out, but the friendship did. I taught her to cook, she taught me to dress. Symbiotic. And now she was coming into my world.

"I can't wait to see you, Jeannette."

"I'll pack bug spray."

♥

Things were looking up. That night I tucked Sylvie into bed, cleaned up the kitchen while my mother knitted on the couch with her game show lover, and then went out to the back porch for a little quiet time.

I pulled a blanket over my legs and folded myself into a chair, while gazing up at the stars.

I thought about the path my life had taken to this point. When I'd left Georgia, I'd tried so hard to leave Amanda Jane behind. I'd married a handsome, successful man who could be so sweet and loveable; sure, he had his moments, and Jeannette seemed to lock onto those, but he had done some sweet things as well.

Richard had proposed in Charleston, South Carolina. He'd rented a beach house for the weekend and booked dinner at a high-class restaurant overlooking the ocean. After dinner we'd gone to the beach, taken off our shoes, and danced on the sand to the music coming from an open-air bar high above the restaurant behind us.

I remember Richard had fallen in the sand, legs sprawled, sand everywhere, and he looked so helpless lying there in his nice pants and shirt. He'd laughed so hard he couldn't get up. It took all my strength to haul him to his feet.

And when he'd finally recovered himself—and gotten the sand out of most major orifices—he'd taken my hand and led me to the ocean's edge.

It was a beautiful night, calm, serene, although really damn windy— but that's just the Atlantic Ocean for you. Music was playing—okay, so it was "I Shot the Sheriff;" it was the beach, after all. He got down on one knee in the squishy wet sand, and asked me to be his wife.

I'd pounced on him, full-on country girl, slathered him with kisses as he fell back into the sand.

We were wet, dirty, and totally in love.

And now here I was. Alone on my mother's back porch.

I shook my head. Ridiculous. If he wanted a country girl, then he would have cheated with a girl from the sticks, not a girl from a bottle and a bad plastic surgeon.

The bell rang signaling that someone was coming up the driveway. I looked inside and saw that it was nine o'clock, far too late for a casual visitor.

My mother looked at me through the glass doors but I shrugged my shoulders and mouthed 'I'll handle it.'

The back porch wrapped around the side of the house and as I walked around I saw that headlights shone right on me as a pickup truck pulled up to my house.

Doors slammed, and I could just make out two men emerging from the darkness. Something in my chest tightened, call it 'woman senses,' and I pulled myself as tall as I could. I remembered my mother's words when I left for college, "Walk with a purpose. Men are less likely to bother a girl if she looks like she's paying attention and determined to get somewhere."

"Evenin', ma'am." A tall, thin, older man nodded to me behind a grimace.

I nodded back, and as I did, I saw he had a pistol tucked into the waistband of his dirty jeans. A quick look told me that the other man, who must have been his son, had a gun as well.

"What can I do for you gentlemen?" My voice was shaking, but I tried to sound 'purposeful.'

"We came to inquire what business it is of someone in these parts concernin' my family's land."

What? My face must have asked the question. The son continued for his father.

"Someone reported us to the po—lice, and we're here to let whoever that was know that we don't 'preciate it very much." He put his hand on the pistol.

Dear God. Please let me not die here on this porch. That wouldn't be fair, and I think you're a pretty fair guy. Please make them go away. Please. Please. Please.

"Gentlemen." My mother's voice cut through my stunned silence. I turned around and found her standing there with her shotgun in her arms, her chin raised so high you could see straight to her brain. "Is there a problem?"

The older man stepped back. "Yes, ma'am, I believe there is. Someone in this area reported us to the authorities, and that ain't gonna be tolerated."

My mother never blinked; she just stared at them. It was a look that took me right back to childhood and sent a shiver down my spine. For the life of me I don't know why these men weren't running back to that truck as fast as their scrawny little legs would carry them.

"What's not to be tolerated, gentlemen, are two things I see happenin' here. One is the pollution of the river that's preventing us farmers from watering our crops with clean water. The second is you threatening my daughter. So be gone and never return, or we'll have the police back to your place faster than you can say, 'Oh, shit.'"

The younger man looked nervously at his father, but the elder was trying to have a stare-down with my mother.

She narrowed her eyes. "Get off my property." She turned to the house. "Come along, Amanda Jane." And as we walked away I heard those two leave the porch and get back into their truck.

My mother locked the doors. "Do me a favor, darlin', and check the other doors. I don't expect any surprises tonight, but you never can tell with some people."

"Yes, ma'am."

"And Amanda Jane."

"Yes, Mama?"

She smiled, her eyes crinkling in the corners. "You gotta carry through with the purpose. You started off strong, but don't falter."

I nodded.

"And it helps if you're holding a gun."

The next day I called Jesse bright and early to report the threats.

"Trash." That was his verdict. "Mandy, there are many different kinds of people in this world, and those people are trash."

"Isn't 'trash' a bit harsh?"

Silence on the other end of the phone.

"If they set so much as one toe near you again, call me immediately."

Okay, this was a slightly scary Jesse.

"Jesse, I think my mama can handle this."

I heard him exhale. "Mandy, this lights me up. I've half a mind to go back down there right now and take care of this whole mess."

Okay, so a chink in the armor at last. The incident in the bakery had only been the opening act...Jesse had a temper!

"Um, I think they just needed to get it out of their systems. You know, 'big talk' and all. I'm sure it's fine now."

"Are you defending what those two jerks did?"

Was I? Geez, it sounded like it.

"No. No, of course not. It's just that I'm not that worried now."

"I am."

"Clearly."

Were we—fighting?

I tapped my fingernails on the bedside table as we sat in silence. At last he exhaled once again and spoke more softly.

"Sorry if I sounded a little crazy there. I just can't stand the thought of someone treatin' you and your momma that way."

"I know. Thanks." Faker. FAKER.

"I mean, it's just..." He sighed.

I started squirming a little. Where was this going?

"I just...aw, dang it." His frustration was evident by the tone of his voice.

"What's wrong, Jesse?"

"I think I love you, Mandy."

Okay. Yeah. Well, that was unexpected. Um...

"Wow, Jesse."

"Don't say anything. I'm gettin' off the phone now and I need you to just think about that, and I'm gonna not think about how I said that, and then later on we'll figure something out or else we'll never talk about it again, okay?"

"Okay."

And he hung up.

Well that was about the strangest declaration of love I'd come across yet.

♥

I wasn't sure what to think, so I decided on retail therapy...or retail distraction, to be more precise. So I took a tiny bit of my mother's 'investment' money and went to the store. There was nowhere in town to buy proper baking tins so I had to make do with whatever Wal-Mart had on its shelves, but I was pleasantly surprised by what Bluebell's, the local grocer, had to offer. They had a specialty section with paste food coloring, exotic extracts, and fondant! I could only assume this was Beulah's doing, but I was happy to capitalize on it. As I checked out, with my obvious bakery items and five tubs of shortening, I wondered if the cashier would pick up the phone and tell ol' Beulah that a young lady had been in here snatching up her emergency supplies. When the woman took my money, she looked at me a little suspiciously, so I said, "My daughter's birthday cake...we have a big family," and smiled. She totally bought it.

I brought my supplies home and spent the afternoon creating petit fours and gourmet cookies as well as a few tiny crème brûlées. I didn't have an official pastry torch, so I improvised.

Mom came into the house for lunch, and I served her a sampler platter.

"Honey, these are delicious!"

"Thanks. It's been a while since I've really made what I love. But I think I'm going with a European theme. It doesn't directly rival Beulah's and it's something people would be interested in. I've never met anyone who didn't sigh when you say 'France' or 'Italy.'"

She nodded, popping another petit four in her mouth.

"And I know what you should do first." I was deciphering the words around the cake that filled her mouth. "You should contact the independent stores and restaurants and see if they'd want to buy some of this to sell."

Genius! I threw my arms around her. "Mom, you are so business savvy! That's brilliant!"

She shrugged. "Common sense, I guess. Now how 'bout a cookie?

Gotta test that one, too." She took a bite, closed her eyes, and moaned. I can't blame her. There's really nothing like a chocolate chip oatmeal cookies warm from the oven.

Mom volunteered to pick up Sylvie from school while I researched local food providers on the internet and in the phone book and begged them to try my sweets.

"Hi! My name is Amanda Jane Roberts and I'm a local baker specializing in French pastries. I was wondering if you'd be interested in selling some of my sweets at your bakery or deli counter?" *Pretty please? I'm a single parent and I have no job and I really, really need you to buy these cookies! With sugar on top?*

But if I heard 'Well, bless your heart' one time, I heard it twenty, and after nearly twenty-five phone calls to locations within a thirty mile radius, I had five takers. Maybe that should have been disappointing, but considering the idea was still fresh, I was pretty psyched.

"Mommy! Can I help you pour?" Sylvie was calling out her request before she'd even opened the front door. She dropped her bookbag on the floor and ran to throw her arms around me.

"Whoa...I guess Momo spilled the beans?"

Her eyes were so earnest when they looked at my face. "I didn't see any beans."

I couldn't help but laugh at that. "It's a figure of speech! It means she told you everything." I buried my face in her neck and kissed her like crazy.

"She's very proud of her mama...I am, too." My mother set her purse on the kitchen counter and went over to the fridge. "Geez, Amanda Jane, where's MY food? All I see in here are eggs, milk, butter..."

"Well, Mom, I have five orders to get done over the next few days."

She looked at me, impressed. "Wow. And how are you going to get all that done, darlin'? You gonna call in Jesse, stick an apron on him?"

Sylvie started giggling and clapped her hand over her mouth. "Jesse isn't a girl!"

"Boys can wear aprons, too," I told her matter-of-factly.

She looked disbelieving at me and kept smashing her giggles.

"Anyway, no, I don't plan on calling in reinforcements just yet. I think I can handle it. Oh, by the way. I forgot to tell you in all the excitement...Jeannette is coming to town this weekend. Is it okay if she stays here?"

"Aunt JEANNIE!" Sylvie began to dance around the kitchen.

My mother was equally excited. "The famous Jeannette! Can't wait to meet her...what should I cook?"

"Anything fried. She plays at being healthy but that girl can put down crap like nobody's business."

"Ooh, Mommy! That's a bad word."

She and my mother both stood, hands on hips, giving me a disappointed look.

"Sorry, sorry. " I put up my hands. "I'll be good. Now, Sylvie, let's get you started on homework and Mom, I'll help you get cookin'. "

My mother put her hand over her heart. "Oh, honey, you just showed your twang."

I rolled my eyes. So I dropped the G. I'd done worse.

❤

After I tucked Sylvie into bed, I settled in with my mother on the back porch. Jesse had called earlier and I'd told him about my orders. He planned to bring some pastry boxes to me the next day, said he was driving to Tennessee to get some honey jars so he'd be able to stop by the restaurant supply store. He'd pick up some real baking tins for me as well.

The night was beautiful. It was just getting to have a bit of a bite in the autumn air, a crispness that suggested the coming of cold weather. A cool breeze danced through the trees, and I could hear a tractor drumming in the distance.

I wrapped an afghan around my shoulders and settled into a chair, a cup of tea in my hands, while my mother lit a cigarette that glowed in the darkness. In the moonlight I could just make her out.

I sighed. After the rush of the day, I was falling flat. "Mom, what am I doing? "

"You're setting a good example for your daughter."

I closed my eyes. "I'm not sure about that."

"I am. You're being strong, resilient, brave. You're taking those sour lemons you've picked and making them into a nice meringue pie."

"I hope so."

I felt a slap on my arm.

"Ow!"

"Honey, what is the matter with you? Have you been slapped upside the head with a fly swatter? Here, take a drag off my cig."

Well, this was new. "No thanks, Mom."

"Just as well. But you need to calm down. I don't know what'll do it. A drink, takin' the shotgun out and blastin' some branches off the tree, givin' it a good scream in the woods...but, honey, you need to get this out of you. You've gotten yourself all set up for amazing things, and you're holdin' yourself back."

"Mom, I'm fine. I'm not—"

"Honey, I've never laid much of a hand on you, but I'm about to slap you silly!"

I saw her face in the moonlight. She was serious.

"Amanda Jane, I've watched you fall deep into the shit of life, and I'm watchin' you claw your way out. When are you gonna realize that your life is right in front of you? You've got a beautiful daughter, a man who thinks you're kinda pretty, and an amazing way with those frou-frou things you bake. You've got it, baby! The Lord's provided for you...take it!"

She sat back and drew deep off of her cigarette. Then she stubbed it in out in an ashtray.

"I love you, honey, but you're missin' it. You're missin' it big time. Now go cry in your room and pull yourself together and get up in the mornin' ready to start again."

She walked over to me, kissed my forehead, and went through the glass doors into her room.

I stayed in my chair, my mother's words echoing in my mind. "You're missin' it." Maybe she was right. Maybe I was missing it. Here I was, just going through life, not actually believing I deserved all this and not believing that it would last for me. And she was right. She was always right.

I went upstairs, took off my clothes, and climbed into bed. I lay there fighting it, trying to avoid it, but I knew what I had to do.

Dear God...or, Father. Um...sir? I—uh—I don't know what I'm doing. Okay, you know that. Do you know that? I mean, I'm sort of on my own now. Well, I'm divorcing. Wait—you probably don't like that. Is that okay? So yeah, I have my daughter, who's awesome, and I think I'm getting my life together but I don't know what that means. I've changed so much. And I can't go back...not completely. But maybe that's good. Maybe I can take some pieces from all the versions of me and make them into... That sounds crazy. But I feel that way a lot these days. Yeah, you already know all this, don't you? And I'll bet you know how it's all going to turn out. I'm supposed to figure this out, aren't I? Well, anyway, thank you. Thank you for helping me. I'll try to do a good job. Amen. Oh—WAIT! If you're still listening, please take care of my mother, and my sweet girl. Thanks. Amen again.

I think I might have just been tired, but after my failure of a prayer, I actually felt a little lighter.

Chapter Ten

The next morning, I rose, took a shower, blew my hair out, and put on real clothes. I'd been working in sweats and t-shirts, but I figured a new attitude called for a pulled together look. And besides, Jesse would be dropping the boxes by that afternoon.

I dropped my sweet girl off at school with her little curls bouncing and she hurried into class, and then I went back to the Roberts Bakery, aka my mother's kitchen.

I turned off the television and, as soon as my mother was safely tucked among her berry bushes, I turned on some cooking music, a little Billy Currington, and set to work. Now it may not seem that country music is essential to baking tiramisu and truffles, but in fact, those delicacies could do with a little Southern sass.

I was up to my elbows in chocolate ganache when the doorbell rang. My eyes shot to the clock. Twelve-thirty…where had the morning gone? I looked around me and surveyed the battleground where the rolling pin and I had been in the throes of war for almost four hours. It was a disaster. Flour covered almost every surface. A large glob of what must at some point have been butter rested in the midst of a pool of chocolate sauce. I didn't dare look in the mirror.

I did run a wet washcloth over my face and clean off my hands before answering the door.

I could stare at that smile all day.

I gave him a quick kiss and took the boxes from his arms, leading him into the kitchen.

"Great Goodness, Mandy! What've you been bakin' in here?"

"A tray of tiramisu for Bluebells, a dozen chocolate truffles for

Bud's, one cake, sliced, for The Maple Grove, sixteen caramel cupcakes for Anita's, and five crème brûlées for The Deviled Egg."

He smiled broadly as he looked around, taking it all in. "Wow. You need help with delivery?"

"I would love some company. I'm planning to take them by this afternoon before I pick up Sylvie. I'm hoping that these will just be preliminary orders, that they'll call and ask for more, and in a larger quantity. I'm thinking of baking for each one on a different day of the week, delivering them in the afternoons."

"I'm so excited for you, Mandy. Doin' what you love. Doin' somethin' that makes other people happy, too."

"I don't know anyone who doesn't love a chocolate truffle."

He chuckled. "I have no idea what that is."

I noticeably responded to the shock I felt in that moment. He had no idea what a chocolate truffle was? Who was this guy? That was truly an earth-shaking revelation.

"Um...that's not normal, Jesse."

He shrugged. "Never had any truffles back home. Momma never made 'em."

How cute. "They're sort of special...I mean, not something you just make. Not like a chocolate chip cookie."

He subconsciously licked his lips. "My momma made the best chocolate chip cookies. Put oatmeal in them. Mmm, mmm. Best I ever had."

A challenge.

"Well, I don't have chocolate chip today, but try this." I popped a truffle into his mouth.

His eyes widened and he shifted his weight as he looked thoughtfully at the ceiling. He was very deliberate, really taking in the truffle.

But I'm an impatient woman. "Well? Well? What do you think?"

He took a napkin and wiped his mouth. "What do you call that thing?"

"A truffle."

He nodded. "I hate to curse in front of a lady, but the only word that comes to mind is 'damn.'"

I felt the smile creep onto my face. "I have two more extra."

"I'll take one."

I popped one into his mouth and, since I felt like a little indulgence was in order, I ate one myself.

He shook his head. "Damn."

"I can't exactly put that on the label, you know."

"I don't know. I think people would really respond to it."

"No doubt...but is it the response I want?"

He grabbed me and took me in a long, deep kiss. A kiss that tasted like chocolate truffle. Delicious.

Jesse finally unwrapped himself from me and went out to work in the field. I put Billy back on the stereo and started decorating and packaging my sweet stuff. The truffles were nestled in wax paper, the cake slices and cupcakes boxed in plastic containers, the crème brûlées and tiramisu slices in little cardboard boxes with plastic windows.

That's when I realized...what was I planning to label them with? A sharpie and cutsie block letters? I popped open my laptop and created a label, nothing fancy, just "A Taste of Europe by Amanda Roberts" and little French and Italian flags. Not ideal, but at least it existed. Thank God my mother had some labels from the pints of berries she sold at Bluebell's.

I slapped those puppies on and loaded them in some cardboard flats I pulled out of the storage room. I'd just wedged and buckled them all into the backseat of my car when Jesse pulled up.

"Need some help?"

"Got it...just a driving partner."

He grinned. "Yes, ma'am." And then he pulled himself into my car, folding his legs to fit.

"Oh please, Jesse. I've got that pushed all the way forward for Sylvie in the back. She has a bad habit of resting her dirty, muddy shoes on the back of the seat."

He slid back and stretched. "So much better."

"So what's new on the farm? I've been buried in dough and glaze."

"End of a good season. We've got one of the large pastures out to rent for some cows one of these city people own to get some country credit. Soybean field looks good. Garden's gettin' goin' good now. All in all, it's great. Your mama's doin' a nice job with those berries, cuttin' 'em back an' all."

"Good. I'm glad. She loves this place."

"I know she does. And she loves you, too."

"I know."

There was silence as I started bumping down the driveway, Jesse's hand in the backseat holding my livelihood steady.

He shifted awkwardly. "So Mandy, I was thinking. Wonderin', really. And maybe it's none of my business, so I beg your pardon if it isn't..."

I was getting nervous. What was coming? Was he proposing? Was he breaking up with me? Oh Lord, please let him not bring up the whole "love" thing right now.

"Are you plannin' to hang around here? I mean, to make a life here?"

I couldn't look at him. I was afraid I'd see something so soft, so full of longing that I'd have to pull over.

"That's absolutely your business, Jesse. And yes, I'm planning to stick around for a while. Sylvie loves school, despite the language barrier—"

"Maybe there's a class for that."

"Private tutor. And anyway, I'm starting to realize a few things about myself, and about my mom...I just think this is where I'm supposed to be right now. So yeah, I'm sticking around."

"Good." He relaxed back into his seat.

"Any other questions?"

He thought for a minute. "Sure. I've got a few, actually."

Awesome.

"Favorite color?"

Okay, I could play this game. "Blue."

"Favorite food?"

"Mom's meatloaf."

"Favorite drink?"

"Water."

His face snapped toward me, a look of complete shock plastered upon it.

"Water?"

"Water. I'm classy."

"You're unpredictable, that's for sure."

"What can I say? Is it alluring?"

"Absolutely."

"Good."

"And now I get to ask the questions."

He rubbed his hands together. "Let me have it."

"Favorite color?"

"Pink...okay, just kidding. Blue."

"Favorite food?"

"Corn bread...with or without pinto beans and onions."

"This is making me hungry."

"Let me cook dinner for you again sometime."

"I'd love it. But I'm not done with the interrogation!"

"Okay, okay," he laughed, settling back once again.

"First kiss?"

"WHOA! That's a whole different line of questioning." He looked shocked at the change in questioning, but I kept my game face.

"It's legitimate."

"Oh, sure. Okay, then...sixth grade. Emily Waters."

"Cute! Awww!" I fluttered my eyelashes at him.

"Eh...stop it." He rolled his eyes. "You're making light of this but that was love." He looked so sincere and yet there was laughter underneath.

"Sorry...I know that Joshua Richardson is very important to me."

"Who's this guy?"

"Kindergarten."

"Kindergarten!" He whistled. "Early start, Mandy?"

"What can I say? I'm a girl who goes after what she wants!"

"Clearly."

"Jesse, I have to ask you something."

"Okay."

"How old are you?"

He burst out laughing. He laughed so hard that tears streamed down his face. He pulled himself together long enough to choke out, "Guess."

"No. Absolutely not. Bad idea."

"Oh, come on. It'll be fun!"

"No it won't. It will be embarrassing and horrible."

"You're hilarious. Just guess."

I refused to speak. Very mature, I know. I learned it from my five-year old daughter.

"Mandy? Are you here, Mandy?"

"Yes."

"How old am I?"

I sighed. "Fine. Well, I'm thirty-two, so I'm going to go with... thirty-two."

His face was shocked and his voice suggested pure horror. "You're... you're thirty-two?"

Now this was freaking me out. I looked from the road to him and back. I considered pulling over so as not to drive us right into the ditch.

"What? What? I'm thirty-two…is that bad?"

"It's just I'm—I'm…"

Oh Lord. What? WHAT?

"I'm only twenty."

"Bull!"

He grinned. I wanted to slap it off his face. Or kiss him. Damn, that was a real problem.

"Naw, no worries, Mandy. I'm thirty. A younger man, but I think that's okay."

"I would hit you right now, but I'm driving."

"I think that's against the law."

"I think a man wrote that law."

"Whoa-ho! Feisty, Mandy!"

"I am my mama's daughter." I caught myself. The twang.

"You are certainly that. I just hope you aren't as good a shot."

"I hope I never have to shoot you."

He laughed. "Is it strange that I find that incredibly sexy?"

I felt my face flush…oh, who am I kidding, my whole body was on fire.

"Nah. I think that's pretty normal." My face hurt from smiling. "Okay, confession time."

"Oh geez."

"When you tip your hat…I think I'm going to pass out."

He tipped it and lowered his voice seductively. "Like this?"

I sighed loudly. "That's a hazard. I'm driving the car!"

He turned toward me and tipped it again. "It's a chance I'm willing to take."

"Seriously, Jesse?"

He leaned farther in my direction, tipped it, and said in a deep, John Wayne voice, "Howdy, little lady."

"You're going to make me drive off of the road!"

And that's when he tipped it about ten times in five seconds.

By this time I was beside myself laughing. "You're a mess."

"Well, as long as I'm a sexy mess."

"You are. You definitely are."

We pulled up to Bluebells and I led the way as Jesse carried my box of tiramisu cartons.

The glass doors slid open and I was greeted immediately by Georgina Blue, the granddaughter of Jebediah Blue, founder of Bluebells Grocery. Georgina was seventeen and perky as a damn Chihuahua on speed. She rang up groceries so quickly I wondered if the actual cash intake matched the outgoing product flow.

"Hey! Welcome to Bluebells!" I'd never felt so welcome.

"Hi, Georgina. I'm delivering the tiramisu you guys ordered."

"Oh, thanks, Ms. Roberts! Just let me get my daddy." She skipped to the back of the store and Jesse and I stood at the front counter.

"You know, when I was a kid," I whispered, "I used to come here with my mother and when we got to the deli counter Georgina's grandfather would give me a couple of slices of honey ham. I loved it. Such a simple thing..."

The doors slid open and my breath caught in my chest. I grabbed Jesse and yanked him and the box of tiramisu behind the counter, crouched among the paper grocery bags.

"What the—"

I slapped my hand over his mouth. "Beulah!" I whispered.

Beulah Mae Foxfire had just sashayed into Bluebells with her oversized faux Louis Vuitton and her red hair perfectly coiffed. She walked right past us humming happily.

"How old are we?" Jesse whispered.

"What?"

"We're hiding behind a grocery store counter. How old are we?"

"Twelve...now hush!"

We crouched in silence, listening to Beulah's heels click as she walked away.

"Ms. Roberts?"

I popped up immediately lest Georgina call my name more loudly.

She cocked her head to the side in confusion. "What are you doing back there?"

"Huh? Oh—I—"

Jesse cleared his throat. "We were looking for a pen. She wanted to put her phone number on the box just in case you wanted to order some more."

"But we have her phone number, of course. That's how we ordered these in the first place."

I slapped my head in exasperation. "Of COURSE! Of course. I guess I'm just tired from all the baking."

"Are you baking for other stores, too?"

"Not tiramisu...other things. A girl's gotta eat, you know." *Haha... heh.*

She smiled. "I know. I'm just really excited about this and I'm hoping we'll be able to get a few other things from you, too. We're going to put them in the bakery area back by the deli, where the breads and cakes are. And we'll put a couple of slices on the deli counter so people can't help but see them when they're planning meals. We've had your mama's business here all these years, it's excitin' to have yours now, too."

"Sounds great—thank you so much for your business."

She handed me an envelope and took the box from Jesse. "No, thank you. I've heard rave reviews of your baking. I'm buying one myself."

"Well, thank you. And please let me know if you'd like to order more—or anything else, for that matter."

"You got it, Ms. Roberts."

As we walked out of the store I held the envelope to my chest. The first money I had made on my very own. It was kind of a proud moment.

Fortunately Beulah didn't follow us on our route. I would have been embarrassed to be found crouched behind the counter of the Maple Grove Café where Miss Eudora Lee, who was about one hundred years old, sat in a chair punching numbers as you handed over your ticket. I felt fairly secure that she would slap me if I set so much as a pinky toe in her territory.

Each vendor was as gracious and complimentary as Georgina had been and they each assured me that they would call on me again. It was really affirming, I have to say. For a citified transplant crawling back home on her hands and knees, I was doing okay.

For Sylvie, it was like Christmas when Jesse arrived with me to pick her up from school. The teacher was holding her back from the car line by her backpack as we drove up, and when it was safe for her to cross, she practically ran to the car.

"Mr. Jesse! Mr. Jesse!" She looked through the open window at him and smiled with that perfectly angelic look that children do so well.

"Well hello, Miss Sylvie. How was school?"

"Awesome! We learned about the rainforest! And we made snakes out of ties and saw pictures of yellow and pink frogs!"

"Wow...that is awesome."

She climbed in the back and buckled herself, still talking a mile a minute about the rainforest.

"Did you know that 'rainforest' is a compound word? And did you know, Mr. Jesse, that if we throw trash on the ground instead of in the recycling bin, we could kill the rainforest? And if we don't have the rainforest, we won't have any CHOCOLATE!" She looked horrified.

I couldn't help myself. "And then Mommy wouldn't have a job, huh?"

"Mommy, we need to buy some recycling bins!"

"You can tell your grandmother that." I shared a look with Jesse that showed we both knew full well that my mother would look at us as if we'd lost our minds. The only place our trash went was the dump.

"I will." She looked so determined as she gazed out the window, sighing longingly at the trees.

When we pulled up to the house Momo was on the front porch, in a rocker, sipping tea. That was never a good sign. The only times I could recall her sitting on the FRONT porch were times I was late for curfew. She had smiled at the boy, opened the door for me, and then shut the door and shut me down.

"Amanda Jane, what in the world have you done?"

Sylvie gave me a sympathetic look and took her book bag into the kitchen.

"What now? What could I possibly have done?"

"Did you see my kitchen today? It looked like a chocolate dawg let it all out in there!"

Okay, so I was in a rush and didn't have time to clean before I headed out to make deliveries. I'd planned to clean it all up when I got home, long before my mother was set to start cooking dinner. I guess she'd decided to get going early.

"Amanda Jane, you can use the kitchen—lord knows I'm just thrilled you're doin' somethin' besides lyin' around on that couch readin' old Agatha Christie novels—but you've got to be a bit more responsible."

"Sorry, Mom. I was planning on cleaning before you came in-side..."

"You gotta manage your time."

I nodded. She was right. By now the chocolate and icing had prob-ably hardened, which would make it ten times harder to clean up. I turned and walked silently into the kitchen. It was spotless.

I spun around. "Mom, I didn't want you to clean it all up!"

She put her hands on her hips. "Do you think I could exist here for two seconds with that mess all around here? I came in to get a glass of water and spent the rest of the afternoon cleaning! And for that, you're cookin' dinner. Make it good."

"Yes, ma'am."

Sylvie whispered, "Mommy didn't clean her room."

I was about to lecture her on respecting one's elders but my mom called something over her shoulder and she walked from the room, waving her hand dismissively. "And there are at least six messages for you on the machine."

Six messages? For me? That was odd. I didn't think I knew six people in this town who would actually set out to talk to me.

I pressed the button and leaned against the counter, still thinking about how stupid I'd been to leave the kitchen in such a state.

Beep. "Amanda Jane, this is Georgina from Bluebells. We've sold out of that fancy stuff you brought in here, and it's only been a couple of hours. People keep askin' for it. Any way you could bring us twice as much tomorrow? And Daddy says he'd like a list of what all you can make as well. Thanks!"

Beep. "Hi there, my name is Rachel Landry and I had a cupcake at Anita's today that they said you made. I was wonderin' if you'd be interested in making a couple of dozen of those for my daughter's birthday this weekend? Call me if you're able. Rachel Landry. Thanks."

Beep. "My name is Rita Evans. I had one of your crème brûlées today and it was just delicious! I'm wondering if you have a store I could visit or a website so I can see what else you make. I'll be needin' a weddin' cake for my daughter in December and I'm really hopin' you bake cakes as well. Call me, please. Thanks so much."

There were six of them. Six people wanting to order something from me. I sat down at the table with Sylvie and rested my head on my arms. This was overwhelming. Wonderful, but overwhelming.

I took a couple of deep breaths and then I felt my mouth spread into a huge smile. I started laughing, my shoulders shaking uncontrollably.

I heard Sylvie leave her place and come stand next to me. She put her hand on my back.

"Mommy? Are you sad?"

I turned my head and found her sweet little face close to mine, her tiny brows furrowed in worry.

"No, baby. No, I'm really happy."

"Did all those people want you to bake for them?"

"They did."

Her face lit up. "That's awesome!"

"Yes, it is definitely awesome."

She gave me a big kiss and then ran off to find her grandmother, her shouts of "Mommy is a baker! Mommy is a baker!" echoing through the house.

I sat up and leaned back in the chair, looking around me. Who would have thought I'd find my future in this kitchen my mother had been cooking in for forty years? I went back to the phone, grabbed a notepad, and took down the orders. Things were looking good indeed.

♥

I realized pretty quickly that I was going to need a system of organization. Of course I'd spent most of my professional life organizing things, so a quick trip to Walmart with the money I'd made from the first order was all I needed. I chose a pink Rolodex that I could keep clients' information in, more labels for the containers, an official looking order pad, a financial ledger, and a cute new apron, just because. I dropped off the day's orders—all five locations again, plus a convenience store that decided it wanted some fresh brownies to sell after the owner had dinner at The Maple Grove the evening before.

I picked up Sylvie from school, dropping by the teachers' lounge a box of cupcakes and little business cards I'd printed the night before.

And thus my week flew by. I was baking all morning, delivering in the afternoon, picking up Sylvie, and coming home to address the books and supplies.

"You know," Jesse said on Thursday night as we sat on the back porch, "you really need to think about getting a space and hiring someone else to help you. This thing is really taking off and you won't be able to do it all yourself for very long."

I laughed. "I doubt anyone would order from me if they could actually be spotted doing so. Dana told me that she went into Bluebells yesterday to pick up dinner and Beulah was letting Mr. Bluebell have it for buying my sweets when she'd 'Been baking in this town for thirty years.'"

He shook his head. "I think this town would surprise you. Things have changed a lot. People are looking ahead more, looking for somethin' new, different. We're not just lookin' backwards anymore."

"Maybe. Know of any spaces up for rent?"

"Besides the storefront next door to Beulah's?"

I burst out laughing. "Oh, that would be rich. She'd find some way to burn me down but leave her place intact."

"Well, there's a little building on Thompson Avenue. It isn't Main Street, but all those little houses are turnin' into salons and clothin' stores. I think a bakery would fit right in there."

"Maybe. I can call and get some information—"

"Let me. You've got a lot to do."

I looked at him in the darkness, sitting in that chair, gazing up at the stars. I felt something like love well up inside of me. And I pounced.

It wasn't a hay loft, but it would do.

❤

By the next morning, everyone I knew in Carroll was working on 'Amanda Jane's Project' as my mother was calling it. Jesse had gone downtown to look into the building on Thompson Avenue, Dana was contacting the Nut House's suppliers to get some pricing for me, David was looking into business licenses and food handling permits, and my mother was calling up everyone she knew and raving about my sweets. I was busy in the kitchen, of course, having dropped Sylvie off at school with a cupcake in her lunchbox. Shameless advertisement, I know, but this was a family business after all.

At ten AM the phone rang. I let the machine pick up as my hands were covered in dough and I had the radio turned up so loudly it was easy to pretend no one was trying to reach me. Once the answering machine beeped off I managed to poke the play button with a clean icing bag tip and turn the music down with my elbow.

"Amanda, it's me. I'm on my way. Hope I brought enough bug spray and antacid. Anyway, I'll see you tonight! Oh—and if the GPS goes out, I'm a goner. Bye!"

Jeannette...I felt warmth fill my chest and I couldn't help but smile as I turned the music back up—a little too loud, but who was there to complain?—and got back to baking.

The troops reported in at about ten-thirty. Jesse knew the owner of the house on Thompson, so he'd gotten the information and wanted me to come by and see it. Dana had pricing for supplies and David had all the paperwork filled out.

"But you need a company name," David said casually. I could hear him flipping through the papers on the other end of the phone.

This had stumped me. Everything had been going on around me, and I'd never once thought about an actual name for the bakery.

I remembered being a kid, dreaming that one day I'd have a restaurant named AJ's Place. That didn't seem quite right now that we were here. In school I'd thought about The Iced Cookie or A Taste of France to be more specific. The latter seemed like a death knell in Carroll.

"I don't have a name."

"Then you don't have a bakery."

"That's ridiculous. I'm supposed to just come up with a name, just like that?"

"No, you're actually supposed to come up with a name during the process of planning to open your own business."

"David, I haven't planned jack squat. I baked some things, they sold, and suddenly I'm on the fast track."

"Indeed. And I need a name for the bakery."

His tone remained calm although I could hear a laugh starting from the other end of the phone. I had always been the indecisive one. I would agonize over what dress to buy for a dance, what title to put on an essay. When David, Dana, and I would go out in high school, I could never decide where we should eat or what we should do. And this was an important decision, much more important than whether we should eat at the old Depot or Pete's Pizza.

I tapped my foot on the wood floor, staring out the window into the woods looking for inspiration. I'm not sure what I thought would happen, maybe that a life-size cupcake in pink heels would come tiptoeing across the driveway holding a sign that said—

"I've got it!"

"Shoot."

"I saw a sign in a junk store once that said 'Calm Down and Eat the Cupcake.'"

"That's too long, AJ."

I rolled my eyes. "Obviously."

"Another question."

"Shoot."

"How are you going to pay for the start up? I mean, there's going to be rent, and remodeling, and—"

"You're freaking me out, Davie."

"Well, I think you probably should be freaked out."

I sighed.

The money I was bringing in was enough to expand, but certainly not enough to start a storefront. This was all moving so fast and I didn't know if I could keep up. Keep up with demand or keep up financially.

"I have no idea."

"Because I have a suggestion."

"Well praise God, what is it?"

"You just need to win first prize in the baking competition at the county fair."

I burst out laughing. "Oh, that's rich! What's the prize, fifty bucks?"

"Five hundred. Plus all you'll get from your booth and the orders you'll receive once people have tasted your delightful confections. "

"Excuse me? Since when is the prize five hundred bucks?"

"Since they moved to sponsorships and got some national names involved. You'd be amazed at the sponsorships that come in if you agree to use their products in the baking."

"Well, five hundred isn't enough anyway."

"It's enough for a security deposit. And the publicity, AJ."

"Beulah will be there, won't she?"

"And the chance to take down your adversary!"

"There's no way I can win. She'll already have the judges in her back pocket."

"You never know. People might be itchin' for something new. Come on."

"I don't know."

"Well you'd better know, because I already registered you and paid your entry fee and booth fee."

"David!"

"Not a word. I can't contribute much to this enterprise, so let me do what I can. Just do me a favor and give it your all."

"Thanks."

"And I need a name for the bakery."

"I'll get on it."

"I'll call back."

"Thanks, Davie. I'll come up with something."

"You always do, AJ."

The more I stared out the window, the more I saw that high-heeled cupcake trotting across the driveway. So I had a logo. But a name?

I made my deliveries in the afternoon, returned a few phones calls including Rita Evans who wanted to set up an appointment the next week to discuss wedding cakes, and picked Sylvie up right on time.

"I know, Mommy! 'Sylvie's!'" She smiled so sweetly I almost gave in. After all, Sylvie's Sweets had a nice sound to it. Poetic, in a way. But Sylvie wasn't a local name. And in this town, that mattered. No, I needed something clever. But what?

Sylvie called out suggestions all the way home: "Cupcake Surprise!" "Sweet Stuff!" "I Love Cake!" "Yummy!" I love my daughter, but she was driving me nuts.

Crawling up the driveway at last I noticed a red sports car peeking through the trees. As we pulled up in front of the house I recognized the personalized tag—GlmrGrl. Suddenly my anxiety lifted and I felt pure excitement. Jeannette Furman had arrived in Carroll, Georgia. Call the boys and tell 'em to get their boots on.

Chapter Eleven

Jeannette was dressed to impress. It was starting to cool off on this day in mid-October and she'd paired dark jeans with a button-up red gingham shirt. Hair in braids, cowboy boots with three inch heels, and a cowboy hat. Classic Jeannette.

She was sitting in her car, door open, swatting bugs when I jumped out of the car and ran to her.

"Jeannie!" I threw my arms around her and breathed in the familiar scent of Chanel No. 5 and cigarettes.

"Girl, this is like *Deliverance* land. I swear I haven't pulled the car over since I crossed the state line; I could hear the dueling banjos."

I slapped her playfully on the arm. "Yeah, Richard always called it 'The land that time forgot.'"

She grinned. "Where's my girl?"

"Aunt Jeannie!" Sylvie had freed herself and ran with her signature bounce to Jeannette who squatted down to enfold my daughter in her arms. "Aunt Jeannie, I've missed you! Have you come to stay?"

"For a couple of days, sweet thing. I've missed you too! How's kindergarten?"

Sylvie lifted up a stickered hand. "We get stickers for having a great week. I had a great week."

"Wow, that's pretty cool."

"We have recess on a big, big playground and lunch in a big, big cafeteria. And my teacher is really nice and my friend Austin and I are getting married!"

Jeannette cocked an eyebrow. "What does Austin's daddy do for a living?"

"He's a doctor."

She nodded. "Fair enough. I approve. Can I be your maid of honor?"

Sylvie nodded, her curls bouncing around her sweet face. "And Mommy is going to be there, too."

"I should think so."

"Come in, let me show you my Momo's house!" She took Jeannette's hand and dragged her to the house as I pulled her suitcase out of the car.

"Wow...first class service."

"This is the finest luxury cabin in these here parts."

Her face was a look of pure horror. "Seriously, I can't take that. Tell me your mother does not speak that way."

"Nah. She's all right. But the boy does a little bit."

"The boy!" She clasped her hands together in delight. "When do I get to meet him?"

Sylvie was fighting against a woman bent on interrogation, and she leaned forward as she reclaimed Jeannette's hand and dragged her up the steps.

"Sometime. Don't worry. I'm fully aware that he is the main reason you're here."

"Ha. The main reason I'm here is to check on you, my dear. I kind of miss having my best friend around."

Sylvie gave her the grand tour and we settled on the back porch with a couple of glasses of sweet tea.

Jeannette threw herself back in a chair, her braids dangling off the back, head tilted to the sky.

"Please tell me there's some moonshine around here somewhere."

"Not likely...my mother is many things, but a drinker isn't one of them."

She popped up and looked at me in dismay. "There's no alcohol on the premises?"

I shook my head. "Sweet tea is our hard liquor."

She let her head fall back. "The land that time forgot."

Sylvie set herself to drawing at the little table that my mother had set up for her on the porch. It had been mine as a child, and I remembered having many tea parties on the porch, leaves for napkins, cheese soaked in water, served in a measuring cup, for crumpets. I have no idea what I thought a crumpet was. And they let me into culinary arts school anyway.

"She's really beautiful, Amanda. She looks so much like you."

"Thanks."

Pleasantries now aside, Jeannette turned toward me in her direct manner, although it was a little difficult to take her seriously when she looked like she'd just come from a line-dancing party.

"How's she taking the separation?"

"Divorce, Jean. We're getting divorced." I felt my chest tighten and tears began to burn the corners of my eyes, which didn't make any sense because I had thought this thing to death and always came to the same conclusion.

"Wow. You're sure?"

I nodded, meeting her eyes. "Absolutely."

She narrowed her own, looking deep into me. "Good girl, I thought he was a complete asshole from the start!"

"What!?" I was shocked. I'd thought she'd really liked Richard.

"Mmm...girl, the day he told you—and I quote—'I really love what you have to say, but I was talking,' I thought I would punch him in the face."

"I don't even remember that."

She held up a perfectly manicured hand. "Or when he told you that if you let yourself go, he would still love you but he wouldn't be able to show you that he did."

Seriously—had he really said all this?

"OR! The ultimate! 'Honey, could you go out tomorrow so I can have the guys over? I feel like I just can't be myself when you're there.'"

I did remember that one. Superbowl Sunday. I'd spent the morning making homemade pizzas and brownies cut and decorated like footballs. I'd even iced a cake green and make edible goal posts. And then I'd spent the evening at the sports bar down the street, fending off drunk Carolina fans who were pissed that their team wasn't in the big game.

"Those weren't his best moments."

She snorted. "There weren't many of those. But he was cute, I'll give you that." She took a shot out of her sweet tea glass. I'd never seen anyone manage to make tea look like tequila quite like she could.

"Yeah, well, it isn't all about that. But he did have some sweet moments."

"Really?"

I cocked my head. "I think so. Can't really remember any at the moment."

She laughed, her head thrown back in complete surrender. I'd missed that laugh.

When she'd pulled herself together, she asked about Jesse. I wasn't sure where to begin. Where does one start when describing the ideal man?

"Well...he's extremely handsome."

"Define 'handsome.' Are we talking pretty boy or hot-daddy-kiss-my-face handsome?"

"Hot-daddy-kiss-my-face handsome."

"Hair and eyes...stats."

"Brown hair...short. Green eyes. Crystal clear. Amazing."

"Amanda, you look like you're about to float away to the moon."

"I am."

"What does he do?"

"He's a beekeeper."

She choked on the tea, beating her chest to try to cough it up.

"What? You've never dated a beekeeper?"

She looked at me with a twisted expression. "As a matter of fact, I haven't. And I've dated a mortician, a gynecologist, and a pimp."

"You've dated a pimp?"

She shrugged. "I think so. He wore leopard skin and carried a cane. Doesn't that just scream 'pimp' to you?"

"I guess so."

She nodded and took another shot. "No beekeepers, though. I'm not sure what I think of that. I mean, can the hotness extend to that horrible suit?"

"I haven't seen the suit."

"Of course not."

"He also drives the tractor for my mother," I added quickly.

She threw her hand out toward me. "That changes everything!"

I gave her a confused look.

"Amanda, there are few things in this world sexier than a man on a tractor...a man between the ages of eighteen and about forty-five, I mean."

"It's a Deere." I smiled at the hotness of this detail. Growing up, a John Deere was the Cadillac of tractordom.

Her face was blank. "I have no idea what that means."

Of course not.

"It's just a country thing."

She nodded. "Is it hot?"

"Yes."

"Then I like it!"

The porch door swung open and my mother emerged from the house with a glass in her hand. Sylvie threw herself on her Momo, attaching to her leg.

"Well now, sweet girl, how was school today?"

"Great, Momo! Aunt Jeannette is here!"

My mother dragged Sylvie along to shake hands with Jeannette. She gave her the up-and-down and looked to me for confirmation that the costume was for real, but she settled on a smile.

"I want to thank you, Jeannette, for being so sweet to my girls. Thank you for bein' there for Amanda Jane. You've been a great friend to her."

"I love your daughter." The braids were still just so distracting.

"Thanks, honey. And we're so glad to have you here. I'm fixin' a traditional country dinner for you this evenin'. We're gonna get some meat on those skinny little bones of yours." She winked and bent to unwrap Sylvie from her leg.

"Want to help me cook, sweet bean?"

Sylvie nodded and they went off, hand in hand.

Jeannette took out her cigarette case and fished out a stick. "Well, Amanda, tell me what you've been doing besides the cowboy."

I rolled my eyes. "I'm not 'doing' the cowboy."

"Sure. Whatever. If you're not, you should be. But what else? Tell me. What is there to do around here?"

I took a deep breath. Jeannette knew about my love of baking, she knew that it had always been a dream of mine to make sweets for my career. But she was also quite business-savvy.

"I'm getting ready to open a bakery."

She leapt off of the chair and 'Yeehaw'd' so loudly that Sylvie's face appeared at the window, checking to make sure we hadn't been suddenly killed by bear attack. Jeannette was skipping around the porch, ashes flying, tea sloshing out of her glass.

"Jeannie...Jeannie, I'm so happy you're so excited, but calm down! You're scaring my child."

She knelt in front of me. "This is wonderful! What's it called?"

Why did everyone keep asking? "I don't really know yet."

She looked thoughtful. "Well we need to think about this...I'm going to think on it."

"Please do."

"Tell me everything!"

I recounted the past few weeks for her, from my storming out of Beulah's to my first wedding cake order. I told her about the house on Thompson and how everyone was pitching in.

"I need to be a part of this."

"Oh Jean...you're already a part of this. Just by being so supportive—"

"Bullshit. I need to do something big. I'm naming the shop."

Oh Lord.

"Now, I'm sure there's something you can do..."

She stood up, her hand on her heart. The cowboy hat had fallen off when she'd danced around the porch so she looked a little bit more legitimate. "Amanda, I'm in advertising. This is what I do. I'm naming the store, I'm creating the logo...this is my part to play."

There was no fighting it. "Okay, but if you're going to do that, you'll need to see the clientele. I mean, these people don't know what tiramisu is."

She looked horrified. "Dear God, where are we?"

"Northwest Georgia. The mountains."

She leapt up. "I need to change clothes."

Once Jeannette was in her black leggings and oversized leopard-print shirt we sat down for a dinner of fried pork chops, creamy mashed potatoes, limp green beans, and carrot soufflé.

I had never seen someone so skinny devour so much food at a single sitting. In fact, she was eating so much so quickly that there was hardly any conversation at the table besides the usual retelling of Sylvie's day at school.

When she was finished, Jeannette leaned back in her chair and sighed. "I'm glad I changed into the elastic waist pants. That was gluttonous."

My mother smiled at her. "Does that mean there's no room for blueberry-peach cobbler?"

And in five minutes we were seated on the back porch, bowls of cobbler loaded down with ice cream balanced on our laps.

"Amanda, you must have weighed five hundred pounds in high school." Jeannette licked the last morsel off of her spoon and dropped it into the bowl. "Did your mother cook this way every night?"

"Almost. Once a week we had breakfast for dinner."

"I'm sure it was equally delicious."

"That is a fact." I rested back on the chair and Sylvie climbed onto my lap.

"Mommy, is Aunt Jeannie staying with us for a while?" She really had perfected the 'begging' face.

"Sweetpea, Aunt Jeannie is here for the weekend, but I'm sure she'll come back some time."

"Absolutely. If I ever move from this chair." She groaned in over-stuffed contentment.

"Can we go visit her?"

"Yes, when we go visit Daddy."

"When is that?"

Well that was a good question. With Thanksgiving around the corner some difficult decisions would have to be made.

"Soon."

Sylvie seemed content as she immediately changed the conversation.

"Aunt Jeannie, guess what I'm going to be for Halloween!"

Jeannette lifted her head enough to look curious. "A princess?"

Sylvie shook her head and I must say that Jeannette looked very disappointed. I imagined one day she would have a daughter who was a complete tomboy. Just seemed like divine providence to me.

"A ballerina?"

"Nope."

"A fairy?"

"Uh-uh."

"A witch."

Sylvie shook her head again and then looked over at me and burst into laughter.

"You might as well give up," I told Jeannette. "It's 'outside the box.'"

"Tell me then. What is Sylvia Jackson going to be for Halloween?"

"A race car driver!"

Jeannette's eyebrows shot up and she looked at me as if Sylvie had just announced that she was planning to dress as the yeti.

I shrugged. "She watched it with Mom all summer..."

"They go soooooooo fast! And wear super cool suits! And there's a girl now who does it, and she is so beautiful! When I grow up, I'm gonna be a race car driver!"

"No words, Amanda. No words." Then to Sylvie, "Sounds awesome! I can't wait to see the pictures!"

Sylvie nodded and leapt off of my lap to throw her arms around her "aunt".

"Sylvie...you need to go on upstairs and get ready for bed. I'll come tuck you in, in a few minutes."

"Mo-o-om! The sun isn't even all the way down yet!"

"I know dear, but it's time and we have a big day tomorrow."

"We do? What are we going to do?"

"Procrastinator. Go on up and brush your teeth, please."

Her little lip stuck out and she drooped her head as she moped inside.

We looked after her for a full minute before Jeannette spoke.

"She's an awesome little girl."

"Thanks. I think so, too, but I'm a little biased."

"I guess." She cleared her throat. "But I have some news of my own."

Well that perked me right up. "Yes?"

Her eyes brightened. "I'm moving to Colorado."

Time froze and my heart sank into my stomach. I could barely see her smiling face and I knew mine was one of devastation.

"Um—why? I mean, congratulations?"

She reached over and took my hand. "I got offered a job, much better than back in Charlotte, actually sort of in charge of some things this time. And I reconnected with this guy I knew from high school and he's there too...I just think this might be the time for me."

I knew I was staring at her. I knew I was being so, so awkward. But I also knew that I didn't know what to say.

"Amanda, say something. What are you thinking?"

"I—I'm just surprised. I mean, I'm going to miss you, Jeannie." Now my eyes couldn't hold in the tears that formed so quickly. I blinked but they slid down my cheeks and Jeannette came over and sat on my lap, wrapping her arms around me. "I'm happy for you. I swear I am. I'm just shocked, that's all. It's just—"

She tucked my hair behind my ear. "I know. There's a lot going on right now, but this is really exciting. And to be honest, once you left Charlotte, it just wasn't as fun anymore. Then this guy showed up, I sent my résumé just to see what would happen, and it's all falling into place. It's like it's meant to be, you know?"

I nodded because I really did know. I knew that what I was doing right now was completely right, and I knew she felt the same way.

"And I'll come visit. I'm not going until December anyway, but I wanted to tell you in person."

"Will you come for Thanksgiving?" My voice sounded so pathetic.

"Sure."

"Okay. Okay then."

She pulled back from me, cocking her head. "That's it? As long as I come for Thanksgiving everything's fine?"

"I guess so. I want you to be happy. I'm just selfish—I'll miss you."

"Well, just imagine me shacked up with some hot stud of a man who brings me breakfast in bed wearing nothing but an apron and I think you'll feel better about it."

"Does he do that?"

"No...but he hasn't been trained yet. Just starting out, you know."

"I'm sure you'll whip him into shape."

"Kinky cliché, Amanda. Now I know you're going to be okay."

I sniffled. "But that's not what's really got me upset, Jeannie."

She cocked her head. "What's that?"

"Are you gonna start wearing all neutral colors? Because when I think of Colorado, all I think of is green and brown."

Her hand flew to her chest. "Oh, honey, NO! Dear God! No, when I think of Colorado, I think of me in a bikini in a hot spring pool with snow all around."

I nodded.

She grinned devilishly. "A fuchsia, animal print bikini."

I sighed dramatically. "Okay, okay, you have my blessing."

I hugged her and went up to tuck in Sylvie while my mother kept Jeannette company on the porch. Smoking buddies.

But when I got upstairs, Sylvie wasn't in bed. She was in the closet with the light on and the door closed. It was very uncharacteristic for her.

I knocked and I heard her gasp and then lots of movement. When I opened the door, she was standing against the wall, head down, tears running down her face.

"Sweetie, what's wrong?" I went into full-fledged 'mommy mode' and knelt in front of her, taking her tiny hands in mine.

She simply sobbed and fell onto me, her head on my shoulder.

I patted her back and looked around as if the clothes could help me. That's when I saw what she'd done.

On the back wall of the closet, in colorful crayon, Sylvie had drawn a stick figure family, smiling and holding hands. There was a tall house and green grass and the sun all yellow in the sky. I was utterly confused. First, why had my obedient, sweet child drawn on the wall? She knew this was a huge no-no. And second, why had she drawn this and then hidden it behind some hanging clothes.

I turned my face into her hair. It smelled so fresh and clean.

"Sylvie," I whispered into her ear, "why did you draw on the wall?"

She sniffled. "I don't know."

Typical answer. Whenever she made a bad choice, this was the go-to reply to any interrogation.

I pulled her slightly away from me and tilted her quivering chin up so she could look me in the eye.

"Sylvie, what is this picture of?"

"I don't know." She was mumbling.

I took a deep breath, willing myself to remain calm.

"Honey, I know you know this was a bad choice. I just want to understand why you did it."

She sobbed again and I held her close and she let it all out, heaving into my arms. It was heartbreaking; this tiny, frail little person so clearly heartbroken.

When she'd gathered her breath, I pulled away again and held her hands.

"Sylvie, please tell me what the picture is."

"You'll be mad."

"I'm not mad. I'm disappointed you drew on Momo's wall, but I'm not mad. Why would I be mad about the picture?"

She looked down at our hands. She was subconsciously stroking my thumb with hers.

"It's us."

I looked over her head to the drawing. "Us?"

She nodded, the curls bouncing in happy contrast to her sadness. "It's me and you and Daddy."

In that moment, my heart broke into a million pieces. I couldn't breathe. I wanted to call for my mother, to have her come up here and fix this situation. But I couldn't. I squared my shoulders, praying that 'sitting with purpose' would work in this situation, and then I cocked my head so I was looking in her eyes.

"Honey, are you sad that Mommy and Daddy aren't living together anymore?"

She nodded and sniffled, wiping her nose on a sleeve.

"I am, too."

"You are?"

"Yes. I'm very sad. But I know that this is the right thing for me, for you, and for Daddy."

"I want Daddy to be here."

I took a deep breath, knowing I couldn't meet her on that one.

"He wants to be here, too. But you know what?"

She shook her head.

"He's here in your heart."

Yes, yes, I know it's cliché. But the beauty of childhood is that you don't know that these little sayings are cliché. To a child, they're just beautiful words.

"But I miss him."

I pulled her onto my lap and held her as if she were a baby.

"Honey, your mommy and daddy both love you very much. But we can't be happy living in the same house together. And that would make you unhappy, too."

She looked confused. How did one explain divorce to a five-year old?

"It's like at the end of that movie where the Indian princess has to stay behind while the boy she likes sails back to England..."

She panicked. "Is Daddy going to England!?"

Fail.

"No, no. Daddy is not moving."

Think, think. Oh, what the heck. We'll just go with the truth.

"As your mommy, I have to make decisions that are best for you. And I think that Momo's house, and your school, and your friends are what are best for you right now. I know they make you happy. And I know you miss Daddy but you can ask him to come visit whenever you want."

"Whenever I want?"

I nodded, and for the first time since I'd entered the room, my daughter smiled.

"I'm not sad anymore, Mommy."

"Good." I kissed her nose.

"But I have one question, Mommy."

"Yes, dear."

"Do you miss Daddy?"

I couldn't say no. And the truth was, I'm not even sure that would have been the honest answer. The truth of it was that I did miss Richard, at least, the Richard I had known and loved.

"Yes. I miss Daddy."

"But you have Mr. Jesse. Why not just have Daddy move here?"

Smart girl.

"I miss your Daddy like you miss Aunt Jeannette when she's away. But while they're away and we are here, we have to make new friends. And Mr. Jesse is my new friend."

"Do you kiss him?"

I wanted to sink into the floor. I figured that if I did so, I'd land in the middle of the living room on the sofa, so that wouldn't be too bad.

"Yes I have."

Her little mouth curled up into a grin. "Mommy and Jesse sittin' in a tree. K-I-S-S-I-N-G!"

I dug my fingers under her arms and tickled her as she shrieked and rolled away, running to the bed and throwing the covers over her head. I pounced and trapped her, then pulled back the cover and kissed her all over her precious face.

"Good night, little mess!"

"Good night, little Mommy!"

"I love you, little mess!"

"I love you, little Mommy!"

❤

As I lay in bed, I thought about how Sylvie'd come into her anxiety honestly. I've never been someone who could abide change. When I was seven and my mother rearranged the living room furniture, I'd come home from school, thrown myself across the couch, and cried as if she'd told me that we'd given Michael away. I was inconsolable, so much so that she moved the furniture back the next day. When my fifth grade teacher got married in the middle of the year and her name changed, I refused to make the change myself, and I even gave her a personalized pencil holder at the end of the year, with her REAL name on it.

Even in high school, when Dana lost her virginity to Billy Whitmire in that pickup truck, I knew it. She came over to my house the next day to study for chemistry and as soon as she sat down on the bed and I took one look at her face, I knew it.

"Oh my God! You had sex with Billy Whitmire! OH MY GOD!"

The look of horror on her face will always remain with me. She slapped her hands on her very red cheeks.

"Oh Jesus, do you think my mother knows?"

So you see, I don't handle change well.

And so that night I cried in my bed. Really it was an act of self-pity. Everyone needs a good pity party once in a while. Ramkie and I partied half the night.

❤

I awoke to Jeannette screaming in her bedroom directly under mine. I slapped myself a few times, wiped my swollen eyes, and nearly broke my leg tumbling down the stairs to her.

Her room appeared empty. "Jeannette?"

Her voice was a whisper. "Over here."

I found her crouched behind the bed in a cute little pink negligee. "There's something wrong with the creatures here!"

I looked around the room. There were no creatures in sight.

"I don't see anything."

She put her hands over her eyes. "I heard a scratching sound, so I went to the window and pulled up the blinds and I swear there was some kind of rabid, furry beast right there on the window screen."

I walked across the room, leaving her crouched in a tiny ball. "This window?"

She peered over the top of the bed and nodded.

I pulled up the blinds as quickly as I could and then dropped them as I fell backward. "Jesus Christ!"

The biggest, ugliest squirrel I'd ever seen was spread-eagled across the screen, his evil eyes huge and staring into my soul and his creepy little teeth bared and, I swear, drooling.

"It's horrible." I heard Jeannette's little voice from across the room.

"It's ugly as sin. Geez." I peeked through the blinds and looked eye to eye with the little creep. It really did look possessed. "My mother will handle this."

I paraded through the house and found my mother at the kitchen table with Sylvie, the former doing the crossword puzzle and the latter nose-deep in the comics.

"Mama, there's a squirrel on the window screen in Jeannette's room, and it's threatening her life."

She dropped the pages on the table, her eyes narrowing. "I'll take care of it."

Sylvie and I went back to find Jeannette still cowering behind the bed.

"You know, Jeannette, the squirrel is outside."

"Well clearly it's looking for something INSIDE, and so I'm staying put."

"Momo's gonna handle it," Sylvie proclaimed with complete certainty.

Jeannette's eyes were about as large as the squirrels. "And what exactly is she going to—"

BANG!

The pink negligee was a blur and Jeannette ran into the closet and shut the door. "WHAT THE HELL WAS THAT?"

Sylvie's giggles reassured her and she poked her head around the door frame. "Amanda, what in the world is going on?"

I looked at my daughter, rolling on the ground as she laughed, imagined my mother blowing smoke off the end of her shotgun, and then focused once again on my best friend hiding in the closet.

"That's how we handle pest problems in the country."

"Well remind me never to get on your bad side. Sylvie…shouldn't you be, like crying about the dead squirrel?" She looked to me. "Don't kids cry over dead animals?"

Sylvie pulled herself off the ground and put her hands on her hips. "A squirrel is just a rat with a furry tail."

Jeannette, for all her culture shock, looked impressed. "Indeed. That's true. Okay then…" she emerged from the closet and smoothed her nightie. "Well, now that that's handled, what's for breakfast?"

❤

Jeannette spent the morning on her laptop, designing a logo for my bakery. We still didn't have a name, but she'd created an image just the same, and it was even better than the cupcake in heels—a skinny, good-looking woman holding a larger-than-life cupcake topped with pink icing and a cherry on top. It was perfect, of course. I could see now why she wanted so desperately to move up in advertising; she was so much better than the credit she received in Charlotte.

At lunchtime, the bell on the driveway signaled and I saw the familiar truck rumbling down the driveway.

Jeannette ran to the window. "Is it him?"

"It is him."

She raced out of the kitchen and to the bedroom to freshen up. When she came back she'd pulled her hair into a perky ponytail and applied lipstick. I rolled my eyes. She'd once said, "If lipstick didn't exist then I might as well just go to a nudist colony," when the department store was closed and she couldn't get her signature shade.

"Hey now," I told her, putting a finger in her face. "Don't get any ideas. He's mine."

She held her hands up in defense. "No worries. I just want to make a good first impression in case I'm maid of honor one day."

"Do you still get to be a 'maid' of honor once you've—"

"Hush, hush. Your daughter is in the room. Shame, Amanda." She shook her head in faux consternation.

She practically crawled on top of me to see out the kitchen window, and when Jesse emerged from the truck, I heard her gasp.

He looked mighty fine today, which he pretty much did any day, but anyway, he looked mighty fine in his jeans and flannel shirt.

We got to the door before he could ring the bell and Jeannette threw it open, her face a bright, beautiful smile.

"Hi. You must be Jesse."

"Yes, ma'am. How do you do?" He tipped his hat, of course, and Jeannette, without any intention, breathed out, "Dear God almighty."

I elbowed her in the side as Jesse smiled, looking quite pleased with himself, and then I pulled her aside so he could actually enter the house.

"Amanda...that man is hot as hell!" She was staring, her mouth agape, and I expected a bit of drool to roll down her chin at any moment. I looked at Jesse who was leaning against the counter in the kitchen, talking with my mother. My heart fluttered and I felt my cheeks flush.

"Well, we don't really know how hot hell actually is...hope we never do, but he is a pretty damn good-looking man if I do say so myself."

"And you do."

"Yes I do."

We strolled into the kitchen, Jeannette still staring quite starry-eyed at my boyfriend—oops, did I say that? She stuck her hand out. "Sorry about before—I'm Jeannette."

"Nice to meet you, ma'am."

"Oh please, the pleasure is ALL mine." She smiled and I swear her eyelashes fluttered. My observant mother piped in immediately.

"Won't you all have a seat? I'm just gettin' some sandwiches together." She walked between them with a plate of chicken salad stuffed into croissants I'd whipped up earlier in the week.

"So, Jesse, Amanda tells me you're a beekeeper. What got a good-looking man like you into that line of work?" Jeannette was seated next to him of course, and had clearly gotten over her initial shyness.

"Well, my daddy kept bees so it seemed natural I should get into it. Makes a good deal of money—honey, raw honey, the combs. And of course I help out here. Mrs. Roberts was nice enough to give me a job workin' for her. I plow a bit here and there."

"Jesse really runs this place," my mother piped in. "He does all the real labor. And he's never refused a task I've asked of him. Not once."

Jesse grinned. "It's impossible to deny you much of anything, Mrs. Roberts."

She patted his hand. "You're a nice man. So glad you're seein' my sweet girl." She gave Jeannette a look that said, 'Back off, Missy' and Jeannette took the cue.

"I am too, ma'am."

Sylvie giggled. "Mommy and Jesse sittin' in a tree!" she sang...well, sort of sang as her mouth was full of sandwich. You couldn't understand the words, but let's face it, the tune is universal for humiliation.

Jeannette broke in. "So I do have to say that things in Charlotte are just not the same without Amanda. I have no one to get coffee with, no one to complain about work to, and worst of all...I have to cook all on my own."

"You were a great student, Jeannie. I've no doubt you're a culinary master by now."

"Well, I'm not starving to death yet, so that's something."

"So, Mandy." Jesse had that tone of voice one gets when about to ask a question he knows you're dreading. "Any ideas for the name of the bakery yet?"

You know, that chicken salad was so delicious, I had just stuffed a huge mouthful in when he asked about the name...funny how things work out. So I shrugged and chewed like a gluttonous squirrel.

"I know!" I could have predicted what Sylvie would say. "Sylvie's!"

"I love it!" My mother clapped her hands together.

I had to be the voice of reason. Unfortunately it took a minute to swallow the rest of the sandwich.

"It's a no-go. Around here 'Sylvie' is slang for 'high-falutin.' Can't do it. I want something that says what it is but in a clever way. You know, like 'Take a Seat' for a chair store."

Jeannette looked at me as if I were the biggest idiot on earth. "How many chair stores have you been to, Amanda?"

I waved her off. "The point is—I want witty."

We sat around, chewing on that one. Sylvie kept calling out various ideas, each of which included her name. My favorite had to be 'Sylvie's Cookies.' I mean, because that didn't sound completely wrong.

"Sweet Serenity"

"Sounds like a yoga studio."

"Sweet Nothings."

"A card store."

"Southern Sugar...No! Southern Sweetness!"

"Not my style."

Jeannette jumped up, waving her hands because she had a mouth full of potato chips. Can I add that she always condemned my craving for chips? I guess we all see the truth now.

"Let Them Eat Cake!"

I gave her a look of utter condescension. "So then I'll be beheaded, right?"

"It's clever."

"It's creepy."

Jesse raised his hand like we were in school and I called on him. "Craving?"

I thought about that one. Frankly, if it had been Jeannie or my mother I would have knocked it right down, but I gave Jesse a minute. Just one.

"Doesn't make it clear it's a bakery."

Silence. I think I'd frustrated them with my rapid-fire shootdown. My mother finally rose and started to clear plates. Jesse and Jeannie jumped up to help her while I cleaned Sylvie's face and hands.

"I've got some divinity for dessert if you're interested."

Jeannette looked confused. "What's divin—"

"THAT'S IT!" I dropped Sylvie's hand and stood up, my hands in the air. "THAT'S IT!"

They were looking at each other as if I'd lost my mind. Well, maybe I had, but I was thinking that this was a good one.

"Divinity is the number one best and most popular dessert around here."

"And damn hard to make," my mother mumbled.

"Exactly! So that's it! That's the name! 'Sweet Divinity!'"

Jeannette put her hands on her hips. "It sounds like a church."

"Even better."

Jesse started nodding. "I like it."

"It WILL look good with the cute logo I've made you—which is most definitely not religious."

"Mom?"

She looked stern. "You know you'll have to learn how to MAKE divinity if you're gonna use that name."

"You'll teach me."

She sighed. "This is gonna be interesting."

"'Sweet Divinity' it is! Make a sign!" I squeezed Sylvie who already had a piece of the white sticky sweet in her mouth.

"Ah wuv ich!"

My mother plopped a place of that sweet Southern confection in front of us and the pieces of candy began disappearing before Jeannette could decide if she really wanted to try it.

"What is this? No offense, Mrs. Roberts, but it looks like a white blob with some little brown things stuck in it."

My mother laughed through the gooey bite in her mouth. "Sweetie, it's nothing but sugar and egg whites, corn syrup, and vanilla. Well, and the pecans of course."

Jennette wrinkled her nose. "That sounds incredibly bad for you."

"Oh, it is." Jesse was leaning back in his chair, savoring the sweetness of what amounted to sweetened sugar in the form of sticky goodness.

"Then it must be delicious." I have to admit, it might have been the best part of my day watching Jeannette taste that divinity for the first time. Her look of curiosity transformed into surprise and then full-blown ecstasy. Needless to say she promptly scooped up two more pieces before they were all snatched from the plate.

I laughed, wondering if she'd be able to fit in her jeans after this visit.

"So you approve of 'Sweet Divinity,' Jeannie?"

She nodded and shoved another piece into her mouth.

On Sunday morning, Jeannette sat with my mother and me on the sofa, watching the church-of-the-week, a Southern Baptist out of Tennessee with a preacher who sweated more than an elephant in the Florida Keys.

"Mrs. Roberts, I like this. You get your church from the comfort of your own home." Jeannette was curled up in pajamas, a cup of coffee in her hands.

"Well, I'd prefer to actually go to church," my mother replied, eyes still on the knitting in her lap. "However, there's no church in a ten mile radius that doesn't have snakes, whether in crates or in pulpits."

"Snakes?" Jeannette smiled at me as if it were a joke.

"I'll tell you later," I whispered. "You don't want to know."

Her face blanched and she held her coffee a little closer.

"But couldn't these preachers be—uh—snakes, too?"

My mother didn't miss a stitch. "Honey, we've all got our own dirty laundry hangin' out to dry, you're just responsible for bringin' in your own. Any preacher could be a snake. But it's less clear on TV, and what I'm interested in are the words comin' out of his mouth."

Jeannette nodded. "But I have another question. How come you like the black preachers?"

I could hear the clicking of the needles. "They've got the spirit, sweetie. "

"Okay, so—"

The needles stopped working, and my mother looked at Jeanette lovingly. "Honey, we're gonna miss the Lord's word if you keep askin' questions."

And the little fashionista from the big city pulled her knees to her chest and whispered, "Amen."

❤

My mother filled Jeannette's car with food—meals in plastic containers, Ziploc bags filled with breads, a frozen strawberry pie she'd been keeping in the freezer, and a plastic baggie of divinity.

"That girl needs to eat more," she whispered to me as she carried a styrofoam cooler to the car. "She's never gonna get herself a good man lookin' like a string bean that's been strung."

"She's come a long way, Mom. Besides, expectations are different in the city."

She snorted. "They expect women to look like they're gonna collapse at any moment?"

"Sort of."

"Ridiculous. How's a woman supposed to birth a baby narrow as a Slim Jim?"

"Well, hopefully we're helping her out."

She nodded, sliding a plate of cookies into the backseat.

Jeanette came skipping out of the house holding Sylvie's hand. Sylvie was already crying, and I could tell my friend was trying to cheer her. I also noticed what a change had come over Jeannette in these two days. She'd left the country girl costume behind and now wore a pair of jeans with an old band t-shirt and sneakers...yes, sneakers. Her hair was in a messy ponytail. She looked naturally stunning.

"Sweet Sylvie, I'll be back soon!" She knelt in front of the little angel and wrapped her arms around her. "Besides, I'll have to come back for your mother's grand opening!"

"You promise?"

"I do." She kissed her little nose. "I'll be back before you even know it."

Sylvie nodded and wiped her eyes with a smile. "I love you, Aunt Jeannie!"

"And I love you, peanut."

Jeannette stood and hugged my mother, thanking her for helping fatten her up. Then she came to me. She pulled me to the side and my mother took the hint and led Sylvie back up to the front porch to wave.

"I'm proud of you, Amanda...or is it 'Amanda Jane' in these parts?"

I kicked some gravel and laughed at her false twang. "Yeah, turns out that's me."

She kissed my cheek. "I'm so happy for you. You've got a great guy, a sweet mama, a beautiful girl. And you're really doing something with your life...even here, in the armpit of the South." She said it so lovingly I couldn't help but laugh. "But really, I wouldn't have pictured it, but you fit here. This is you...the real you."

I felt tears burn my eyes. She was right.

"I'm really happy, Jeannie. But I miss you!"

She pulled me close. "I miss you. But I like you this way. And besides, I'll be back for the grand opening of Sweet Divinity!"

"Whenever that is."

She shrugged. "I might have to come back sooner then, to see my girls."

"Does this mean you kind of like the place? Maybe you'd want to start again here, too?" A girl had to hope.

She burst out laughing. "Hell, no!" Then she clapped her hand over her mouth and peered around the side of the car to make sure Sylvie hadn't heard her.

"I mean, the men are a-okay, but I can't take the wildlife, Amanda. I mean, look at my nails." She held up two chipped hands and sighed dramatically. "I can't live like this."

I pulled her close for a final hug and kissed her cheek with a smack. "Don't be away too long!"

"I'd say the same to you but I have a feeling you'll be away a lot longer than you think."

"I think you're right."

She hopped into her car, blew us kisses, and yelled, "I love you!" as loudly as she could, her words echoing behind her, and tore away in a cloud of dust.

My mother shook her head. "Now she'll have to wash that pretty little car."

Chapter Twelve

B right and early on the following Friday I was in the kitchen, working on my fifth batch of botched divinity. It was a rainy morning and my mother had been right the night before when she'd warned me: divinity cannot be made in a damp atmosphere. I'd closed all of the window and pumped up the AC but it didn't matter, the candy wouldn't set. I threw my candy thermometer angrily across the room, nearly striking my mother who ducked in the doorway.

"I don't have to say it, do I?"

"No. No, you don't. This damn divinity won't freakin' set, and I have NOTHING to present tonight at the baking competition!"

"Well you're certainly not going to be making any candy now that you've broken the thermometer, so that narrows down the options."

"I have nothing. It has to be special. It has to be uniquely southern for this crowd, and I'm fresh out of ideas. And ingredients."

My mother went to the cupboards and started poking around, pulling out a box of cocoa and some marshmallows left over from Sylvie's recent hot chocolate fixation.

"You can make a mud cake. I have Nana's recipe in my book."

I wanted to kiss her. In fact, I threw myself across the kitchen and covered her face with kisses.

"Whoa, Amanda Jane. Is that all it takes to get a little action in here?"

"Mama, you have saved the day!"

"I get that a lot."

I squeezed that woman so tightly I heard her gasp but I didn't care. I may not have been able to set divinity on a rainy day, but a mud cake...what could be more fitting?

I got started on the chocolate cake base right away. My mother offered to help but, being the stubborn woman I am, I told her I had to do this all on my own, so she helped how she could, by taking Sylvie to school and stopping by the store for another bag of sugar.

I was melting the butter in the saucepan, preparing for the creation of the world's best chocolate icing, when the telephone rang. I ignored it and listened to Sylvie's tiny voice on the machine, asking the caller to leave a message.

"Hello there, Amanda Jane. This is Beulah Mae Foxfire. I understand that you'll be entering the bake-off this evening, as will I, and I just wanted to let you know that if there is anything I can do to help, you being a first-time entrant, well, anything at all, you just let me know, honey. I would like to tell you that most bakers bring an assistant to help them at the booths, at least I do since so many people stop by to buy my baked goods. Anyway, I'm not sure if you'll need one or not, but I just wanted to give you that little tip. I look forward to seein' you this evenin'. Best of luck, dear."

I was frozen to the spot by that voice dripping with condescension. She was trying to psych me out like this was some kind of middle school basketball game where she and I were on the line. For a moment the mental image of that event made me laugh, but then I smelled the rancid scent of burning butter and I snapped back into the present.

Smoke was rising from the stove and my butter was a bubbling orange mess. How easily that woman had gotten into my head!

The answering machine's flashing red light was staring at me so I deleted that nasty message and cleaned up my mess before starting again on my icing. Not only would I win the damn competition, but I'd have the longest lines at my booth. I'd have lines so long the fire marshal would show up! Lines so long that cars would be lined down the street just to get into the fairgrounds! I'd show that Beaulah Mae Foxfire!

When my mother returned home I was sprinkling miniature marshmallows all over the chocolate cake, watching them begin to melt as they made contact with the warm, gooey cake. I poured the chocolate pecan icing on top, letting it all melt together before moving the whole thing onto the kitchen table to cool.

I must have been slamming things because my mother placed the sugar on the counter and then went out onto the back porch without a word. Smart woman.

Five hours later, I popped my last cake out of the oven and cut a couple of small pieces of the first one for my mother and me to try. I found her on the porch, smoking a cigarette.

"I can't do any work today, Amanda Jane. This damn weather's keeping me inside."

"Well, have a little cake, Mom. If you can't move, you might as well eat."

She cocked an eyebrow. "Is that what they say?"

"That's what I say."

We each took a bite in silence. It was perfect. Thick, gooey, sweet. Heaven on a plate.

"Amanda Jane, this cake would have made your Nana so proud."

"Thanks, Mom."

"And she'd be proud of you anyway. I am. Have I told you yet how grateful I am for you comin' home to me?"

"Oh, I'm the one who's grateful! Where would I be without you?"

She laughed. "I'm glad you say that now, 'cause there'll come a time when you'll be taking care of me and I'll be so ornery and cantankerous you'll probably regret comin' back."

"Nah."

She licked her fork. "I'm not gettin' any younger, Amanda Jane."

We sat in silence for a couple of minutes. I could hear a tractor way off, and I wondered if it were Jesse. A woodpecker was working on a tree right next to us.

"Mom, are you trying to have some conversation with me about... about you..."

"Amanda Jane, I'm trying to give you a warning. I'm already an old biddy. Are you sure you want to stick around here?"

I turned toward her and gestured with my fork. "Are you trying to get rid of me?"

"Have you lost your ever-lovin' mind? No, girl, I'm going to need you when I'm so old I can't get up and go to the bathroom by myself!"

"Ew, Mom."

"Maybe that wasn't the best example to convince you to stay."

"Maybe not." I couldn't help but smile as I considered just how ornery my mother would be when she got to the point where she couldn't be Miss Independent any longer.

"Anyway, what I'm sayin' is that I think I'll leave this house and the land to you..."

"Whoa, whoa whoa, whoa whoa! Mama, you're not that old!"

"Let's face it, pumpkin, when you're my age you'd better be ready to go kaput at any given moment. I could just keel over and die right here, right now."

"I don't like this conversation one bit."

My mother sighed and put her plate and fork on a wooden side table. "Honey, I'm just bein' responsible. I need somebody to know what I want. Listen, I've been livin' out here alone so long, I was afraid one day I'd just up and die and there wouldn't be nobody to find my body for days! I'd just hate that. Who'd want to ever come in this house again, and I've taken such good care of it for all these years."

"Mom, you sound morbid and just a little freaky."

"I sound a lot freaky, Amanda Jane. But the point here is that you're here now, so I don't have to worry anymore, and for that, I'm grateful."

"Um...thanks?"

Mom went inside and fell asleep on the couch watching soap operas so I headed off to pick up Sylvie and decided that it was about time my brother kept me company on the ride, so I gave him a call as I headed into town.

"Michael! It's your favorite sister, Amanda Jane, calling from Crazy Town!"

"Is that a twang I detect?"

"It is indeed, brother. I've been adopting the ways of the natives."

He chuckled. "How the heck are you, Amanda Jane?"

"I'm peachy. I'm actually on my way to pick up Sylvie from school."

"Mom told me she was having a hard time adjusting. Something about the accent down there. Is she doing better?"

"Much."

"I'm so glad. I miss that little munchkin. I'll bet she's grown a foot since Christmas!"

"Two feet, actually. She's going to be tall like her daddy."

"Speaking of which..."

"Not speaking of which."

"Fair enough. So then to what do I owe the pleasure of this call in the middle of the day? You know some of us are actually at work."

"Ha. Ha. Listen, Mike, Mom gave me a talk about dying in the house and no one finding her body for days."

"Oh yeah, that one."

"You've had this conversation?"

"Yeah, at least once a month until you arrived back home. Thanks for taking on the mantle, Amanda Jane. That one was getting a little old."

"I didn't know she was so lonely."

"I don't think she was. I mean, listen, she wanted us to grow up and build our own lives. That's what parents do. We both did the right thing. I guess you could just try to see that maybe a silver lining of your situation is that both of you get to spend this time together. And now neither of us have to worry about her dying and being found three years later surrounded by a bunch of cats."

"She hates cats."

"I know. I never really understood that. Maybe it's because they're like squirrels..."

"Michael, focus."

"Sorry, AJ."

"Okay, you've eased my mind a bit...I think. But are you coming home for Thanksgiving? I miss you. Sylvie misses you."

"Actually, yeah, yeah, I'm coming back. Besides, Mama tells me you're opening a bakery, so I gotta come support. You know, be an official taste-tester and all."

"Well, we'll see if that happens."

"The taste-testing or..."

I couldn't help but laugh. I may only talk to my brother a few times a year, but it always makes my day. Even if only to remind myself that I am clearly the superior child.

"The bakery, Mike."

"Well, I think we all know that the bakery is going to open. If there's one thing you got from our mother, it's balls. "

Obviously there were some complications in this statement, but I actually agreed with him.

Of course, I am partial to cats.

❤

When Sylvie got into the car, she was a stormcloud. She flung her lunchbox into the backseat and shoved her booster in place, yanking the seatbelt across her tiny chest.

"How was school today?" Yes, I know that the answer here is obvious, but I didn't know what else to say."

"Horrible."

"Oh no! What happened, sweetheart?"

"I don't want to talk about it."

"Did you have a fight with your friends?"

And there you have it. She burst into tears.

"Oh honey, what happened?"

The answer was indecipherable through the sobbing hysteria. I reached in the glove box and handed my little tempest a tissue. She took a quivering breath and tried again.

"There—is—a—c—club—and—I—am—not—in—it."

Thus it begins.

"What kind of club?"

"The Alphabet Soup Club."

"That sounds like a nice club. Maybe the people in it—"

"IT'S NOT A NICE CLUB!"

Okay, so cheerleading tryout rage has nothing on alphabet soup rage, as it turns out. My little angel had been replaced by some creature with a guttural, angry voice.

"Okay, so—"

"It's a club where they sit in a circle and they go around and each person has to say a bad word and that's not nice and when it got to me I refused to say a bad word and they threw me out of the club and now I don't have any friends and I'm so, so, so MAD!"

"Wait, did you say it's a club where you go in a circle and say bad words?"

"Yes."

"Um...what's one of the words someone said today?" I peeked in the rearview mirror and saw her eyes grow large. Then she burst into tears again.

"I can't sa—say it."

"It's okay, Sylvie. You won't be in trouble."

I was trying not to smile, truly I was, but the idea of a club of secret cursing was kind of funny. Besides, how bad could it be? Sylvie thought 'stupid' was a bad word.

She whispered something so quietly I couldn't hear, and in the mirror I saw her eyes lower to her hands.

"A little louder. Really, it's okay, sweetie."

"Okay." She bit her lower lip and met my eyes in the mirror. "Sheet."

My mouth fell open and for the first time I was thankful for the accents my daughter was exposed to every day. Clearly if she did try to use this word, it would come across as a reference to bed linens. But I was appalled that she would hear such a word in kindergarten.

"Oh, Sylvie, that's not a nice word."

"I wouldn't say it, Mommy!"

"I'm so glad. I'm really proud of you for that."

"It was a second grader who said it. She's the president of the club and she said if I wouldn't say it, then I couldn't be in the club."

"Well, why would you want to be in a club with people who say those words?"

"I just wanted to be with Noah."

Ah, fickle little thing.

"Did Noah say that word?"

She shook her head. "He said another one."

"Oh dear."

"The 'G' word."

Now, I have no idea what the 'G' word is, but I acted shocked.

"Wow. Wow, Sylvie. And what do you think of that?"

"I think he isn't very brave. We aren't friends anymore." She looked longingly out of the window. Cue the dramatic music.

"Well, I suspect this club won't last long, so I would be ready to be Noah's friend again once he realizes that this is a bad idea."

"Okay."

And now to feed her emotional need. Southern-style.

"Mommy made a new cake today. Wanna try it when we get home?"

She sniffled dramatically. "Mommy, you're the best!"

I wish I could bottle that up. I could use the reminder every now and then.

❤

As a child, I'd loved the country fair. Held on the grounds of an old mill, the event was a smorgasbord of everything Southern—clogging and fiddling, homemade ice cream and smoky barbecue, handmade quilts and homemade bird houses, an antique engine show and a Civil War encampment. And to every child's delight, a barn full of animals to pet and feed.

The fair officially opened on Saturday morning, but the vendors came to set up the night before, and the competitors—bakers, canners, barbecue masters, alongside artists and craftsmen—brought their competition pieces for the judging, which would happen later that evening.

We found Jesse waiting for us at our booth, shifting uncomfortably, his hands shoved in his pockets.

"Hey, Mr. Jesse!" Sylvie threw herself into his arms and he lifted her high in the air.

"Hey, little firecracker! You been helping your mama get ready?"

Sylvie nodded eagerly and proceeded to crawl under the front table and pick flowers...well, weeds, technically speaking.

"Thanks for getting the tent all set up. It looks great." I set down a box that contained the banner I'd had printed with Jeannette's fantastic logo, a cash box which was currently empty, and a carton of plates, napkins, and forks for tomorrow. "Though you don't look so great. What's going on?"

Jesse crossed his arms, a darkness coming over his brow. "Beulah's set up right next to you."

I felt the blood drain from my face and my stomach sank to the ground. "You're kidding me."

" 'Fraid not."

Well this was less than ideal. I knew we'd be competitors. Knew we'd run into each other in utter awkwardness. But I never for one minute considered that we'd be standing side by side all day, that the competition would literally be in my face.

"Can we move?"

"Now Amanda Jane, did I raise a coward?" My mother put her hand on my shoulder and when I looked I saw fire in her eyes. "This is just what you want. You want to show her what you've got. You want to make sure she sees it!"

"Actually, I don't. I want to sell my cakes with a smile and be content in knowing I've done a good job."

"Bullshit."

"Mama! Sylvie's right here!" I pointed under the table to where Sylvie sat, eyes wide, mouth agape.

"Momo, are you in the Alphabet Soup Club?" she asked in complete disbelief.

"The what?"

"Nevermind!" I placed myself between my mother and my daughter. "Okay, moving on. We need to get the banner hung and these tables wiped down and covered. Make sure we weigh them down with some big rocks. Sylvie, I have a job for you."

"Yes, yes?" She practically leapt out from under the table. Why are children so eager to do errands but not chores?

"I need you to find four big rocks to weigh down the tablecloth we're going to put on the cake table, okay?"

"Aye, aye, Mommy!" And with a salute she was off, running between tables toward the treeline.

"I got this, Amanda Jane," Jesse took the box from my hands. "You go ahead to the mill to submit your entry."

"Thanks, Jesse."

What followed I can only describe as akin to a religious ceremony. My mother opened the crate in which I had transported the cake sample. I had packed it in with newspaper so it wouldn't jostle in the car, and now I lifted it up and out with the delicacy one might use with a Fabergé egg. In my mind's eye, the sky cleared just at that moment, and sunlight came streaming in a direct line to my box, but maybe that's just my memory being overly dramatic. Yet in that moment, I felt I was holding the ark of the covenant. Or at least the secret weapon for smiting my enemies.

I walked so slowly toward the mill, the boxed cake cupped in my hands, my eyes never leaving the ground, seeking a root or rock that could mean me lying face down in the dirt, my precious cake a pile of mushed chocolate and marshmallow.

The old mill had been refurbished years ago and it still ran, the churning sound a welcome one next to the sound of the rushing waterfall that kept it going. On this night it was surrounded by people laughing and chatting as they came and went with their entries and exhibition pieces. I nodded hello a couple of times but didn't run into anyone I knew, amazingly enough, until...

"Well, Amanda Jane Roberts, it's so nice to see you again."

Patsy Cherry. Of course Patsy Cherry was sitting at the check-in table, bedazzled pen in hand, smacking on chewing gum and looking just as sickeningly pleased to see me as she would have been to see her first husband. Okay, that was rude. And she didn't have a first husband. That we know of anyway.

"Hi, Patsy, just checking in my entry for the baking competition."

She tilted her head and smiled even more broadly. "Well, bless your heart, Amanda Jane, you know that's just so sweet." She began flipping through index cards that I assumed listed all of the entries. "And what do you have in your box?"

"Mississippi Mud Cake."

"Oh, yum! I am just so glad I've agreed to help judge this year! I can't wait to have a bite of that."

And that was the moment I knew, for certain, that I would not win.

"You're lot nine. Second floor to the left."

"Thanks, Patsy." I smiled as syrupy as I could and took the flight of wooden stairs up past the central workings of the mill to the second floor which housed the canning and baking competitions. Beulah had already been there as evidenced by the cloche decorated with red swirls sitting smugly behind a monogrammed post-it with '5' written on it. I looked around to see if there was anyone to notice if I took a tiny peek under the cover, but the room was full of people bustling about with trays of cobbler and plates of brownies, so I swallowed my curiosity and located my spot.

I carefully opened the box and unwrapped my cake, perfectly preserved and moist, the marshmallows and icing mushed just enough to be thick and yet not take away from the chocolate cake. I could just see the specks of pecan poking through the icing. Perfect.

I had a small plate of my mother's china with me and I carefully transferred the cake, wiping the plate clean with a washcloth to make sure the presentation was perfect.

After I draped the plastic over the cake ever so gently to make sure nothing floated down onto it before judging, I took a look at the entries I could see. Gooey brownies, rich peach cobbler, a cupcake made to look like candy corn. All fantastic looking, but I knew that they wouldn't hold a candle to my cake. But whatever was under that cloche was haunting me, and we all know that the unknown makes the imagination wander to places you would rather not go.

I considered the irony should it be tiramisu or crème brûlée, and I laughed to myself. Probably a gourmet cupcake, a Beulah Mae Foxfire specialty.

Making my way back to the booth to help set up, I'd almost escaped the mill unnoticed when Patsy Cherry's sickeningly sweet voice cut through the chatter directly to my ears.

"Oh, Amanda Jane?"

Seriously? Why couldn't this woman just disappear? I halfway expected to turn and see her standing there with a clipboard, demanding that I do a Russian before she would qualify my entry.

MEGAN PREWITT KOON

"Yes, Patsy?"

"I assume Jesse Gregory is out there helping you all get set up?"

I nodded, my stomach suddenly heavy.

She smirked. "Would you tell him I sure do appreciate him taking me out the other night and that I look forward to doing it again real soon?"

I think I blacked out. Rage? Hurt? Confusion? I don't know what I was feeling, but I definitely felt my head swim and my eyes lose focus.

"Sure."

"You're too sweet. Almost as sweet as that sexy man. Quite a kisser, ain't he?"

She could see that she'd upset me, and that set me on fire. With absolutely no self-respect, I stormed out of the mill and strode across the fairground to my booth where Jesse was just climbing down from a stepstool he'd used to hang my banner. I didn't even notice how wonderful it looked.

"Jesse Gregory, I need to speak with you, please."

The tone of my voice must have betrayed my rage because Sylvie, who was working with my mother on straightening the tablecloth looked up at Jesse with genuine pity in her eyes and said, "Ooh, that's bad, Mr. Jesse. Mommy's really mad."

Jesse looked to her then back at me. "Yes, ma'am."

I didn't say a word as we walked to the amphitheater. We passed booths of crafts, people laughing, and kids running around—knocking over samples and dashing under table coverings. I didn't really see any of it. I didn't really hear any of it, either. I was too busy internalizing my rage.

I gestured to a wooden bench and Jesse sat, hands on knees. I guess he must have looked nervous, but like I said, I didn't really see anything.

I stood in front of him. "So I ran into Patsy Cherry in the mill. She's a damn judge."

His jaw dropped. "Amanda Jane, I—"

"Stop." I held my hand up. Signature move. "She said some things in there that took me really off guard. Things about you. And I know that there's a history there, and I've never asked questions because it isn't my business to."

"Actually, it is your business—"

"Stop." The hand again. "But I think you're right. It is my business now because you've done something, haven't you?" Oh damn it, the tears were coming now. "She said she saw you the other night, that you took her out, she said that you—you kissed her, and..." I couldn't go on. I was crying in earnest now. "And this is just the worst day ever. I'm going to lose the stupid competition, stupid Beulah is next to my stupid booth, and now I find out that my stupid boyfriend went out with his stupid ex-fiance and didn't even bother to tell me! This is embarrassing, Jesse! And now I'm crying and people are going to see me and I'm—I'm—I'm not okay!"

Jesse was on his feet trying to take my hand, but I kept pulling away. I was trying to be brave, I was trying to act like a grown-ass woman, but the truth is that I felt like a heartbroken little girl.

"Amanda Jane, I should have told you about this. And I was going to. In person. But I haven't seen you since—"

"Since you went on a date?"

"It wasn't a date."

His eyes looked so sad. He looked exasperated. But all I could hear were excuses.

"Then what was it?"

"I was at the Tavern just having a beer after work, watching the game, and she came up to me and I wanted to leave, but I felt bad. She looked bad and she started talking and then time just went by."

"She said you took her out."

"We walked down the street to the cafe. I bought her dinner. She was going through some stuff and I wanted to help."

"Well, you shouldn't have." God, I can be such a petulant brat.

"That's not fair."

"So?"

He looked at me as if he'd never seen me before. And I guess he'd never seen me upset, so that's accurate. He'd never seen me like this. And this was bad.

"Amanda Jane, I know you're a kind—"

"Did you kiss her?"

He looked at his hands. And that's all it took. My heart broke. I literally felt the pain in my chest, felt it break into two and the halves fall away.

"She kissed me. I didn't want it."

I stood up straight and pulled down my shoulders in an attempt to look confident.

"I need you to leave now."

"No. No, Amanda Jane, we need to talk this out. You need to know—"

"I know enough." And I spun around and stomped all the way across the grounds.

To his credit, Jesse did as I asked. When I turned around to look for him, he was gone. I felt disappointed. And then that made me feel confused. So I tried to shake it out of my head and kept walking.

At the booth, my mother and Sylvie were leaning on the table, clearly waiting to see what was left when the dust of my fury had settled.

"Everything ready? Let's go," I said, snatching my keys off of the table.

"Where's Mr. Jesse?" The little voice that would usually have melted my heart only made the pain worse.

"He went on home. Come on, we have a lot to do before tomorrow."

My mother raised an eyebrow at me but I ignored her, took Sylvie's hand, and marched toward the car.

"Mommy, I hope you win!" Sylvie was not to be discouraged.

"Thanks, Pumpkin. Me too."

I couldn't sleep that night. And it wasn't Beulah. And it wasn't wondering if a blue ribbon rested on my plate of Mississippi Mud Cake. It was Jesse Gregory. It was the broken look on his face when I accused him of cheating on me with Patsy Cherry.

In that moment, I had awakened all of the feelings I'd felt in the movie theatre last spring, the day I'd found out Richard was cheating on me. And I had responded without giving Jesse a chance to say his piece. And why? Because I didn't want to be caught off guard again. I didn't want to be hurt again. I wanted the upper hand for once.

So he *had* kissed her. He'd been drinking, ended up taking her out to dinner, and kissed her.

So much for the tipping of the hat.

The thought of it made me sick. Everything about him I thought I'd known, everything I thought I'd felt, everything I'd thought *he'd* felt...lies.

And as I lay in bed, staring at the ceiling, I felt the tears come again. Because I'd allowed myself to believe that I would find a good man. Because I allowed myself to believe in love again.

It was a rather impressive pity party, but around three in the morning I rolled out of bed and made my way downstairs to the kitchen. I turned on the light over the sink and stood still for a moment, looking out of the window. The moon was high, shining its glow upon the placid lake that lay just below the berry field. The human world was asleep but nature was still awake. And so was I.

I realized there was no going back to bed so I might as well get started. It was a crisp, cool morning, so I pulled out the new candy thermometer my mother had bought for me, still in the package.

"Okay, you little son of a bitch, let's make some divinity."

And then I got to work.

♥

I saw the sun rise through the kitchen window as I was spooning divinity onto waxed paper, twirling my spoon to make it look like a dollop of ice cream. I admit I hadn't quite gotten the hang of the twist yet, but my divinity had set, so I call that success.

Once my mother was awake, I got started on my Sylvie-approved chocolate-chip oatmeal cookies. She appeared in the doorway not long later, sniffing the sweet aroma.

"Mommy, can I have a cookie?"

"Good morning, sweetie. How about some breakfast first?"

"The cookies have oatmeal in them." She rested her head on folded arms as she perched on a stool at the counter.

"Nice try. I'll make you some toast."

"I've got it." My mother was a godsend. Before I'd washed my hands she'd popped two slices in the toaster and was peeling a hard-boiled egg.

"Someone was up early."

"Ha! Someone never slept!" I gave her a kiss on the cheek. "But it was a productive night of restlessness. Look!" I opened a tin and revealed my culinary masterpiece.

"Well, I'll be! Divinity!"

"Not enough to sell today, but enough to show I can do it!"

"I'm proud of you, Amanda Jane...how many batches did it take?"

"Don't ask."

My mother winked at me and went to take Sylvie her breakfast as I began boxing the cookies. I had baked several dozen and had them ready. After all, though Mud Cake was a tradition around here, there's nothing quite so classic as a good chocolate chip cookie. I was banking on kids being drawn to them and their parents buying it due to the Sylvie line of reasoning that they were somehow less of a guilty pleasure due to the oats.

"Amanda Jane, may I speak to you outside before you get ready?"

I sighed. I'd done such a great job of distracting myself from what had been a horrible evening, and now here was my mother, ready to dredge it all out of me.

"I don't know if I have time, Mama. I've got to get—"

"You have time."

When my mother speaks in that tone, you listen, so I found myself slouching out to the porch, a little petulance to drive me.

When we'd settled ourselves she started right in.

"What in the world happened with you last night? You go turn in your cake, come back and give Jesse the business, and then don't speak a word of it all the way home where you promptly lock yourself in your room until some time in the middle of the God blessed night when you get up and start making something that is named for the Almighty but that most people consider a recipe from hell itself. What am I to make of this?"

"You don't need to make anything of it, Mama."

She was exasperated. "Amanda Jane, I am going to ask you again. What's goin' on?"

I made the mistake of looking at her. Those big blue eyes, that earnest look that could bring the truth out of anyone. Here I was marching around like my own stormcloud was the darkest one, and there was someone trying to help me rid of it and I was just ignoring her. Making her feel awful too.

"I found out that Jesse had been out with Patsy Cherry."

"Honey, you already knew that."

"A couple of days ago."

"What?" She dropped herself into the chair next to mine and a startled slew of birds flew out of a nearby tree.

"I couldn't believe it either but he admitted it."

We sat there in silence, yet I could hear the happy notes of Sylvie's cartoons emanating dimly from the house. It was like an insult. I could tell my mother was thinking—she was tapping her fingers on the chair, her foot on the porch.

I looked out over the land, to the lake. I envied those birds floating serenely on the water. Not a care. No pressure, no expectations, no heartbreak...

"Have you lost your ever-lovin' mind?" My mother had risen from her chair and was standing tall over me.

"Um...what?" Had I dozed off?

"I didn't think I'd raised an idiot."

"Mama, what are you talking about?"

She pulled me up from my chair and took me firmly by the shoulders, yet the look in her eyes was all concern and love.

"Honey, there is just no way that boy has cheated on you. No way. I looked in his eyes and I saw his love for you. No way."

"Mama, I hardly think a look in his eye—"

"Baby girl, he talked with me about marryin' you."

I fell back into the chair. My body went numb, my face slack. I could feel my heart trying to force itself out of my chest.

"He...he did what?"

"He told me one day that he thought you were the one. That he wanted your divorce to be final because he planned to marry you one day and he didn't know how long he could wait. And he meant it, honey."

This was too much.

"Then why did he kiss Patsy Cherry?"

"Well, what did he give for the reasoning?"

I sat up, feeling my face flush. "He just said he didn't want it. I didn't exactly give him a chance to explain himself."

She put her hands on her hips and gave me that look I'd receive when I missed curfew. It was terrifying. And if you've ever had a mama from the country you know exactly of what I'm speaking. Sorry for the heebee jeebies.

"Amanda Jane Roberts, you give that boy a chance. Think for just one moment the chances he's given you, the chances you've given yourself. You can listen to him. I'd bank this farm on the fact that he has an explanation."

I felt myself shifting in the chair and I couldn't meet her eyes.

"I guess I may have jumped the gun just a tad."

"Just a wee bit, darlin'."

"Do you think he'll be there today?"

She laughed. "He wouldn't miss your big day, sweetie. He's dedicated."

Unlike someone else I know, her expression seemed to suggest.

"Okay, so I—I guess I should get ready."

"Get ready to eat crow."

I stood up to go inside but she threw her arms around me and squeezed. "I know it's been hard on you, and I know why you reacted the way you did. He'll understand, too. Give him a chance."

"Okay, Mama."

"And if I'm wrong, he'd better watch out, 'cause I'm also a pretty straight shot."

I couldn't help but laugh as she kissed my cheek and slapped my rear end, sending me in the direction of the door.

"Now get your pants on. We're gonna be late."

❤

We arrived at the fairgrounds half an hour before opening, but it was already buzzing with vendors setting up their wares and musicians tuning up in the amphitheater. Beulah was at her booth when I arrived, boxes with little red bows lined up along the table, a three tiered display of cupcakes, cups of peach cobbler, and—on top—divinity. She had on her little apron and heels even in the grassy terrain.

"Amanda Jane! I'm so happy to see you all set up here. I'd heard you'd had a few little trinkets in some stores, but look at you! Do tell what's in those sweet little boxes!"

I smiled as insincerely as possible. "Just some cookies and Mud Cake, Miss Beulah."

"Mud Cake!" She clapped her hands together. "How sweet! Children's favorites! I guess that makes perfect sense as I see a sweet little girl right here!"

She leaned down to put her face in Sylvie's. "Is your mama a good baker?"

Sylvie, to her credit, never missed a beat. "My mommy's the best baker in the world, and she's going to win the bake-off!"

God bless her.

"Isn't she sweet."

"She's an angel." I lifted Sylvie and gave her a kiss on the cheek.

"Well, best of luck to you, Amanda Jane. I hope your snacks sell." And then she marched back to her booth.

"That woman's nose is stuck up so in the air, she'd die in a rainstorm," my mother whispered, shaking her head. "What a miserable little woman."

"That's for sure. And she's got enough to spread it around."

I looked down to catch Sylvie peeking into a box of cookies.

"Love, close that box. That's your college money."

She looked confused.

"I'll let you have one at lunch time. For now, would you like to help Momo get the money box ready while I go check on the competition?"

As I walked toward the mill, I looked for Jesse amongst the crowd. There were people forming a line up at the ticket booths now, and cars were lined along the edges of the road to get into the field where the Boy Scouts were parking cars.

At the mill I had to force my way across the porch as people were coming out from checking on their entries. I walked slowly up the stairs, strangely feeling like a lot more hinged on this than the prize money. It was my chance to establish myself, to advertise my business, to begin to build a life. My chest was tightening as the gravity of this otherwise superficial situation settled upon me.

On the second floor landing I turned into the baked goods room and scanned the entry table.

And there was the blue ribbon.

On Beulah Mae Foxfire's plate of damn divinity.

And on my plate—nothing.

I felt furious. I wasn't hurt. I wasn't disappointed. I was irate. There was no way that the dry chocolate cupcake at number ten had beaten my cake. No way at all.

In my mind I could hear Patsy Cherry's shrill voice: "I am just so glad I've agreed to help judge this year!"

It was rigged.

That twit had taken my man and had taken my prize.

She'd better give her heart to Jesus, I thought, because her butt is mine! I was going to make that melee in Beulah's shop look like a Sunday School picnic.

I don't remember going back down the stairs, actually, or bursting onto the porch, glaring around through the mob of smiling, happy families here to enjoy a day at the fair.

I don't remember walking down the porch steps of the mill or crossing past the barbecue stand to the rows of arts and crafts booth. But I remember seeing her. And where was she, you might ask? Why, she was Beulah's helper, of course. Now I know what you're thinking: Amanda Jane, you should consider your child sitting in the next booth before you run across there and jerk that woman bald.

Bless your heart.

I strode down the row, fully determined to take out Patsy Cherry, and yet, just as I arrived at my own booth I saw him.

Jesse Gregory.

Tall, handsome, repentant Jesse Gregory.

He saw me, and he tipped his damn hat.

I don't know what came over me, but all of my anger drained away. One minute I was standing there plotting my takedown of Patsy Cherry via Beulah Mae Foxfire and the next all my anger was gone and replaced with something far stronger. Before I could will myself to stay firm I was all over that man like white on rice. I would have liked to have seen the look on Patsy Cherry's face, but it wasn't worth it to stop kissing this man right there in the middle of the country fair.

I vaguely heard Sylvie's voice *ooh-ing* as if she'd seen something truly scandalous. I did hear my mother clapping.

I kissed his cheeks and I kissed his forehead and I kissed that sweet, sweet mouth of his. And then he kissed me back.

When Jesse finally set me down, he couldn't catch a breath before he started. "Amanda Jane, I'm so sorry. I didn't do anything, I swear to you. She was on me before I could stop her and—"

I put my hand on his lips. "I don't need to know. I trust you. I trust you and I love you, and that's all. That's all, Jesse."

He grinned. "I love you, Amanda Jane Roberts."

"I'm sorry I didn't give you a chance to explain."

He chuckled. "Yeah, you were a little bit scary last night."

"Well, just try not to make me mad in the future, okay?"

"Oh, don't you worry. Now I know what I'm up against. But listen, did you win?"

I laughed at myself. "I did. But not the baking contest, if you care about that kind of thing." And I kissed him again. And again.

"Mommy! This is embarrassing!" Sylvie was talking out of the side of her mouth.

"Yes, Amanda Jane, as much as I love a good show, I think we're here to sell sweets today." My mother had her hands over Sylvie's eyes.

"You're right. You're both right. Let's do this." I took Jesse by the hand and led him into the booth, assigning him to the cookies and

Sylvie to the cake. My mother would handle the money while I handed out business cards and introduced myself to each and every customer.

❤

The morning began slowly. Clearly Beulah had some fair regulars who stopped by her booth first thing to load up on their sweets. They glanced my way but I'm certain there wasn't enough bravery in the strongest of them to actually step foot in my direction. But as the hours ticked by, more and more people came to my booth. To be fair, most of them had children, and were of the younger generation. Dana stopped by just after lunch with the kids, and made it a point to come by after they'd eaten their cake to proclaim loudly and obnoxiously that mine was the best mud cake she'd ever had. Then she whispered to me that she had bribed her kids to go to the picnic table areas and talk loudly about the cake. Their reward would be a box of cookies.

That woman is a genius.

David came by, too, just after lunchtime. He bought five boxes of cake, "For clients," he said. I knew he and Lawrence would enjoy them later.

Beulah had a steady flow of customers, to be sure, but I was doing all right for myself. I didn't sell out by noon as I'd hoped, but by the end of the day I had just a few boxes left. I didn't know that I felt entirely reassured about the bakery. After all, I hadn't won, fair or not, and I hadn't outdone Beulah. Indeed, as I watched her booth out of the corner of my eye, it became more apparent than ever that I would have a difficult time building a client base that included any of the town establishment. And yet, that would be necessary for the big orders I'd need to stay afloat. But I decided to worry about that tomorrow and just enjoy this evening. Jesse and I had survived our first fight, and I had managed to get my business card into over one hundred hands.

And what do you know? Turns out this town loves Mississippi Mud Cake.

Chapter Thirteen

Monday morning Jesse drove me to the rental house he'd found on Thompson Avenue. I had always loved this street with its full trees and old houses. I was happy to see that the area had been somewhat restored, with lawyers' offices and gift shops taking over the homes that lined the street.

"When I was a kid, I used to think I would live in one of the big houses at the end of this street."

Jesse grinned. "There's still time."

I shrugged. "I suppose. But I think I'll settle for renting one."

"Well, let's be honest, you're pretty much going to be living in this bakery for a while."

"Good point. So which one is it?"

We passed by a beautiful brick house with a bay window in front and a latticed porch on the second story.

"Patience." He parked on the side of the road and came around to help me out. Taking my hand, he led me across the street and we started down the sidewalk. "I want you to see it from the sidewalk first."

"Okay." Well, that was kind of thoughtful. Or else frightening. Was something wrong with this place? Suddenly my excitement turned to anxiety. Oh heavens, was this some kind of asbestos-filled fixer-upper nestled among the beautifully improved houses? I envisioned a program on hoarders and suddenly worried that I was stepping into disaster.

"Here it is."

We had stopped in front of the cutest house I had ever seen. And yet it wasn't one I had ever noticed on this street. Funny how the big, brassy houses are the ones that draw your attention when you're younger. I guess it's only when you realize that the more house you have, the more you have to clean that the more modest buildings suddenly become really attractive.

The house was small but cozy looking with a yellow, wooden exterior and a white front porch. It had been outfitted with a glass-paneled door with a little bell hanging from the ceiling above it, and the pale green shutters were clipped back with white, heart-shaped metal latches.

"Oh, Jesse. It's perfect."

His face was one of childish glee and he squeezed my hand. "I got it right?"

"You sure did. Can we go in?"

"Sure." He led me up the stone steps from the road to the walkway and to the white wooden steps.

He knocked on the door and it swung open, revealing a young woman about my age, smiling and holding a folder of papers in her hand. When the word 'landlady' came to mind, I certainly didn't picture someone young and hot. In fact, I was wondering if this was the person Jesse knew...I felt a little jealous but then I corrected myself, my mother's revelation of Jesse's intentions echoing through my mind.

"Hi!" She smiled and held out a hand. "Sissy Hendricks."

I shook her hand and looked questioningly at Jesse who smiled at me with a wink.

"Sissy and I went to high school together. She married my best friend, Bryan. They own this little place, inherited it from his parents."

Relief. She was married. Now I could like this woman.

"Yes, this was Bryan's parents' first home, and they later turned it into a café."

"I don't remember there being a café here."

Jesse smiled. "You were gone for a few years, you know."

I blushed.

"Shall we go inside?" Sissy smiled and motioned for us to enter.

If I had been impressed by the outside, the inside was enough to make my face hurt from smiling.

The place had clearly been a cozy, sweet little café, and very well-kept. There was space for probably four small tables next to the windows that lined the walls. The dining area was separated from a kitch-en workspace by a wall with a white shuttered window to pass plates through. The front counter was white and clean and a glass display case—refrigerated!—stood next to it.

"This is adorable!" I clapped my hands together excitedly and I saw Sissy smile at Jesse and nod in approval.

We went into the kitchen, which was basic, but would do for now. Industrial range, ovens, and fridge with a decent amount of workspace. It was smaller than what I'd had to work with at Beulah's, but it would certainly get me started.

"I know it's a little small," Sissy said, "but I think it's a good starter space. And of course we'd be willing to discuss any work or upgrades you'd like to do."

"No, it's...perfect. Really perfect."

I spun around, my chest about to burst with excitement. "Where do I sign?"

♥

That afternoon, Jesse and I met David and Dana for lunch. David's eyes grew large when we walked in the door, and he gave Jesse a hearty hand-shake and me, a wink. But this was a business lunch. David took a look at the rental agreement, and Dana had price lists for me and ordering forms which she'd already begun to fill out. We sat around a table at the Maple Grove Café, plates of crumbs stacked in the corner, filling out paperwork. David had procured the applications for the various licenses I'd need and was meticulously asking questions while Jesse had tucked into a piece of coconut cream pie and nodded his approval every once in awhile.

"Sweet Divinity," Dana sighed, leaning back in her chair. "Sounds delicious even though I can't imagine eating a single thing right now. So, will divinity then be your specialty?"

I shook my head. "I'll have it all right. Can't be a Southern sweet shop without it. But my specialty will be, as always, the tiramisu."

The bell rang and we all turned automatically to see who had walked in. A young couple with a baby.

"Aw, how sweet," Dana cooed, looking up from her papers. "Young love."

Jesse reached under the table and squeezed my hand. I felt my heart race. What is he doing? Oh my God...is he thinking that WE should have a baby? What? I felt my face turn red and I faked a dramatic and completely unconvincing sneeze so I could rip my hand out of his.

David turned backwards in his chair as the couple walked by. "What a beautiful baby." He waved and made a most ridiculous face which, thankfully, the baby found hilarious and not horrifying. "I want a baby."

I took my free hand and placed it upon his. "And you shall have it, Davie. That can be our next project."

He grinned. "Are you volunteering, AJ? I'm not sure Jesse would approve of that, and frankly, I'm not sure I'm up for it."

I slapped his hand. "Cheeky."

His smiled melted away and he started fiddling with his fork. "Anyway, it's not likely that I'll get to have a baby. Not around here."

Jesse looked confused as he put down his fork and furrowed his eyebrows. "Am I missing something?"

We all looked at each other and burst out laughing.

The bell tinkled again and I looked up and choked. Seriously, I think my heart leapt into my throat and if I'd kept my mouth open it would have just flopped on the table and I would have died right there. Which I sort of wanted to do anyway.

Beulah.

She scanned the restaurant and when her gaze fell on me darkness seemed to cloak her features. I felt as if I were in a horror movie and the zombie had just located me amongst the innocent.

She smiled a false, sugary sweet smile and followed the hostess to a table in the next room.

"Oh my God, oh my God, Beulah's here." I turned back to the table and put my hands over my face as if maybe if I couldn't see her, she couldn't see me.

My friends, however, were not so smooth and began looking all around, David practically standing up to scan the crowd.

I punched his arm and whispered. "Sit! All of you! Maybe if we just ignore her, she'll go away."

David laughed. "Is she a bee?"

I shoved him. Hard.

Dana leaned toward me. "You can't avoid her forever, AJ."

"What are you, Dana, my mother? She saw all that I sold at the fair, no doubt she's heard about the bakery...I'm getting the check."

And as I turned to stand she appeared before me, a figure in sickly pink, from her lipstick to her fingernails to her little patent leather shoes. I thought I was having a heart attack. And when I spoke, it was so not smooth.

"Good afternoon, Beulah." Oh, that smile was SO fake. "I haven't seen you in a while. You look positively pink—um, wonderful."

She smiled too sweetly. "I heard you're opening a bakery, Amanda Jane."

"That's true. I am. Over on Thompson Avenue."

She nodded, still smiling. "I suppose you know that bakeries in this town don't have a very good track record. I wouldn't put too much money into the start-up costs."

My friends, God bless them, looked as if they were watching a tennis match as they turned first to one of us, then to the other.

I felt heat rise to my face. "Beulah, I'm not trying to compete with you."

"Oh, but you are." She fluttered her eyelashes. It was really disturbing.

"I'm really not. I'm just doing what I know how to do."

She took a breath and looked around to see who was watching.

"You know, you really weren't that great of a baker. When I hired you, I was just helping out your poor momma with her little lost lamb who came home. I wouldn't want you to get your hopes too high."

Jesse stood. He towered over her. Oh Lord. Temper, temper! "Ma'am, you're on the verge of bein' disrespectful. I'd ask that you please step away. She's not tryin' to hurt your business, just tryin' to make her way. Now please move along."

She looked shocked but nodded and backed away, scurrying back to her little corner.

Jesse sat and we all stared at him in stunned silence.

David spoke first. "Well that was very impressive."

He shrugged and took a sip of tea.

"Jesse, that was amazing. You just told off Beulah Mae Foxfire in the most gentlemanlike fashion I've ever seen!" Dana looked over to me, very impressed. "Girl, you've got yourself a MAN."

I forced a small smile. "And an enemy."

❤

Halloween night arrived and I went all out. Sylvie's costume was a hit at the downtown shops which all opened for trick-or-treating since so many kids lived on farms and thus, had no real neighbors to walk to. I remembered being a kid and not knowing how people actually celebrated Halloween. I thought that every kid walked store to store in a pagan procession, holding out baskets to be filled with candies, home-baked goods, and knick-knacks. I remember being in college, that first Halloween away from home. As I pulled myself into a fairy costume that was two sizes too small, I lamented the lack of homemade goodies we'd receive. My roommates looked at me in horror.

"You mean your mom actually let you keep the homemade things?"

I laughed. "Well, of course...why wouldn't she?"

Cassandra, my roommate from Chicago who was dressed as a naughty Catholic schoolgirl, froze, mascara wand in midair, and spun around to face me, sparkly pigtails slapping her in the face.

"I mean...razor blades?"

"What in the world are you talking about?"

Cassandra and Rachel looked at each other, which was kind of funny considering Rachel was dressed as a sexy nun. For the record, I found that wildly inappropriate.

It was Rachel's turn to try to talk some sense into me. "Poisoned candy?"

"What is this, Snow White?"

"You seriously didn't have to dump your candy out and let your mom pick through it before you could eat a single piece?"

"Why in the world would you do that?"

Cassandra piped in. "What was the best Halloween treat you ever got?"

I had to think about that. "Chocolate cupcakes with sprinkles. Geez, I loved those as a kid."

The naughty nun faced the mirror and rolled her eyes. "Wow, life sure is simpler in the sticks."

I didn't take it personally. In fact, once I figured out that their childhoods had been tainted by fears of razor blades in apples and poisoned candy, I felt rather bad for them.

So after several years of bags filled with Jolly Ranchers and Reese Cups, Sylvie was thrilled to have a basket filled with cupcakes, muffins, homemade crispy treats, and little toys.

My mother and I decided to try a neighborhood tucked behind the main road in town, and Sylvie endeared many people to her. I guess there weren't many pig-tailed race car drivers coming door-to-door. But when we got to the end of Willow Lane, Sylvie cocked her head to her side.

"Mommy? What does that sign mean?"

I cut short my conversation with my mother regarding the frustration of distributing candy to teenagers sans costume, with pillow case in hand—it makes me so angry, I swear I give them one Hershey Kiss and an evil stare—and looked at the sign posted in front of a large colonial style house.

"We are Christian. Our 'treat' is the grace of God. We will pray for you."

Seriously?

I sighed and looked Sylvie in the eyes. "Those people don't celebrate Halloween."

"Why?"

"They don't believe it's right."

"Why?"

Okay, I know that it's good that she's a curious little girl, but she sometimes picks the darndest times for her interrogations.

"Because they think Halloween is bad."

"Why?"

I sighed, totally frustrated. And then I had one of those Parent of the Year moments. Yes, parents, you know exactly what I'm talking about here.

"Because, Sylvie, they never got to go trick-or-treating when they were kids, and they decided if they couldn't have candy, then NO ONE should."

Her little eyes grew so large and she inhaled rather sharply. I suddenly realized that I had no idea how she would respond.

She stuck out her lower lip. "That is so sad, Mommy." And without a further comment, she grabbed three pieces of candy out of her little pumpkin bucket, marched up to the front door, and put it on the welcome mat.

I truly think my little girl might just save the world.

❤

The next night I sat on the back porch with my mother, in the dark as usual. Yet after all these months, I found the farm so peaceful. There was something truly beautiful about the silence…well, I should say about the human silence. There's nothing silent about frogs at night.

I had wrapped myself in blankets against the chill that had crept into the air. My mother had done the same, covering her lap with an afghan she'd crocheted last Christmas. The telltale light of her cigarette signaled the night.

"November first, two more weeks until opening day." Her voice was prophetic coming out of the night like that. Of course the hacking cough that followed it sort of ruined the aura. Allergies, of course. At this time of year, my mother claimed that every ailment was caused by allergies.

"I know. I can't believe it. So much has changed since I got here, but it doesn't seem that long ago."

"Changes for the better."

"All of them."

My mother stubbed out the cigarette and I saw her face lit by the moon and stars. She was smiling, a look of contentment spread across her face.

"You know, darlin', I think it was the Lord that brought you here."

I laughed. "I don't think the Lord wanted me to end up divorced."

"No, that's not what I mean. I mean that when life happens, you have choices. You could have gone anywhere you wanted. Could have stayed in Charlotte, could have gone somewhere new, and yet you came back here."

"It's home, Mom."

"I'm glad you feel that way. Remember what you said to me when you left for college?"

My stomach lurched and the familiar sense of guilt washed over me. "Do we have to bring that up?"

"Oh, come on, it's funny now."

"Seriously?"

She put on her 'sassy Amanda Jane' voice. So humiliating. "Mama, I love you, but I hate this place. I ain't never comin' back, so you'll need to find yourself a way to see me. I'll pay for a flight for you if I have to, but I can never look at dirt again."

I hung my head. "I am so ashamed, Mama."

"Nah—don't be. You were eighteen, had no idea about life. I think it's kind of cute."

"I'll bet you didn't think it was cute at the time."

"Are you kiddin' me? I said I had to use the bathroom before we left, and I ran and locked myself in the closet and laughed so hard I cried!"

"I thought you were cryin' because you missed me."

"Well I was, but I was missin' your innocence, your sweetness, your idea that you were so far beyond this place. I think I always knew you'd come back."

"I didn't know that."

"Liar."

I sat back in the chair, eyes closed, listening to the frogs. Maybe there is something to the fact that you always call the place you grew up 'home.' I remembered talking to Jeannette one day. She was going on and on about 'home,' and she wasn't talking about her apartment in Charlotte. She was saying, "Back in Cleveland, we have this amazing art museum."

I laughed. "We?"

She got this faraway look in her eyes. "Yeah, that's kind of weird isn't it? I always say 'we' even when I haven't lived there in ten years."

"I guess that's cause it's always home."

She scrunched up her mouth in thoughtfulness. "Then where am I now?"

There was something to that conversation I hadn't understood that day. Something fundamental about human beings. There's an attachment to where we come from, some pull that brings us back, if not in body, certainly in spirit.

"Mama, once the bakery's open, I can probably get my own place with Sylvie."

"I thought we'd talked about this."

"I know, I just—I don't know." I shifted awkwardly, looking up at the moon.

"Do you want your own place, a place you and Sylvie can call your own? Because I don't want you to stay here just for me. You're young, you have your own life. You're entitled to that."

"I know, I know. It's just—" I sighed, so confused.

"Just what?"

"It's just that I think I need to stay here for me. For Sylvie. I want her to have the childhood I did."

My mother started laughing.

"Mom, seriously."

I couldn't see them, but I knew the tears had already started.

"Honey, you just have no idea how glad I am to hear you say that."

My heart filled with love for her and I leapt up from my chair and threw myself on her. I think I nearly smothered her.

"Thanks, Mom. Thank you."

Her voice was muffled by my embrace. "Oh, honey, I wouldn't miss this for the world."

"I don't want to miss it either."

She pulled away from me and looked in my eyes. "I'm so proud of you.

"Thank you."

"You've found yourself. And you've found a wonderful part of yourself to share with your daughter."

"I don't know how I found I found it, Mom. I really don't."

She picked up my palm and kissed it like she use to do when I was a little girl.

"It's love. It's simply love."

"Of course, I don't know what I'm going to do about Jesse. I mean, if he and I were to get married, then where would we live?

"I've got plenty of land. I could use a next door neighbor."

I couldn't see her face, but I'm sure she winked through the darkness.

♥

The next couple of weeks were filled with paperwork, moving pains, and sugar...lots and lots of sugar. Jesse helped me paint the inside of the building, once I'd cleared powder puff pink with the girlie landlord. He went with me to Wentworth Hardware to buy lighting fixtures, tables and chairs, and to the kitchen supply store in Tennessee to stock up behind the scenes. Dana sold me several pieces of Nut House artwork at face value, my favorite being a little sign that read 'Keep Calm and Eat Cupcakes.' I hung it on the wall behind the cash register. After all, it was pretty much my lifelong mantra.

David got my licenses filed and approved. And, perhaps most importantly, my mother wrote check after check. She signed each with a smile, claiming that she was glad my father's alimony checks were finally being put to use.

Sylvie came to the bakery after school and did her homework at the little stainless steel tables Jesse had set up in the front room. When she finished and I'd checked her work, she came into the back with me and helped me sort items as they arrived in the mail, or helped me mix batter for experimental concoctions.

And all this time I was still baking for my usual customers, the store, restaurants, and clients who had tasted my cake and cookies at the country fair. Of course, I found out that just after the *Showdown at the Maple Grove Café*, Beulah had started taking baked goods to the same stores that sold mine, trying to push me out. Georgina at Bluebells assured me that my items were the bigger seller, and I took pride in that. It was good to see that I had some loyal customers of my own.

We printed Jeannette's logo on menus, stickers—Sylvie's favorite...I even found one on the inside of the toilet lid one morning—and flyers. Dana and her mother posted my flyers inside and outside the Nut House, and I had a stack of menus on the front counter ahead of opening day.

It was a whirlwind, and everyone took on a role. The Monday before I opened, I was sitting on the counter next to the brand new, recently programmed—thank you, David—cash register, looking around the bakery, when I realized how this place didn't just belong to me, it didn't just reflect my own dream. No, this was a family bakery. And the term 'family' extended far beyond bloodlines and ancestry. I could see their fingerprints all over the place. Quite literally.

Jesse walked inside from where he'd been finishing touch-ups on the white gingerbread trim and found me crying, wiping my tears with a pink napkin.

He wrapped his arms around me and I pulled him closer with my legs, holding him tight.

"What wrong, Mandy? Everything's okay."

"Nothing's wrong," I whispered. "Everything's right. For the first time in a long time, everything is right."

"Does this mean you aren't afraid Beulah's minions are gonna come torch the place before daybreak?" He said the words softly, as if they were words of love.

I shoved him back. "Well no, I actually hadn't even considered that until this very moment!"

He shrugged, that mischievous grin on his face. Then he tipped his hat.

I rolled my eyes. "You know that one doesn't work its magic on me anymore. I'm onto your tricks, mister!"

He tipped it again.

"Great goodness, just get over here and kiss me!"

And thus, the bakery was christened.

But as we sat on the front steps a little later, watching the cars go by, I began to feel sad.

"Jesse, can I ask you something?"

He took his hat off and ran his hands through his hair. He looked nervous, and I'd never seen him this way.

"Anything."

I took a deep breath. "Could you see yourself making a family with me?"

He didn't answer right away, just sort of flipped his hat about his hands and studied the sidewalk. I began to regret the question.

Well done, Amanda, well done. You've devolved your man back into an insecure boy, and now he's FREAKING OUT. I seriously thought about slapping him on the back, spewing forth a few hearty chuckles, and telling him I was totally kidding, but that never works on television, so why would it work in real life?

When the hat stopped moving, my heart stopped as well. He looked at me, narrowed his eyes, and smiled.

"I could, maybe."

Well, that was unexpected. To be honest, I'd sort of picture him throwing himself onto the sidewalk on one knee and proposing right then. In fact, I had the entire rejection already planned out.

I'm sorry, Jesse, but I'm just not ready. I'm just getting my life together. The bakery is about to open, Sylvie's just started school, and I think I just need some time to myself. I'm sorry. But ask me again in six months, okay? Cue smile.

Pathetic.

But I was totally unprepared for this response. It wasn't a no, and it wasn't a yes. It was Jesse.

"Okay. Um, well, yeah. So…"

Awkward. I could have sworn I heard crickets chirping in the distance. They were mocking me.

"Mandy, I think I was a little crazy that night I said those words… that I loved you…I mean, not that you aren't loveable, just—"

I held up my hand. "Say no more. You just sort of sent me into a state when you squeezed my hand as soon at that little baby said 'goo.'"

He looked confused. "What in the Sam Hill are you talkin' about?"

I looked at him with pity, like a little boy who didn't understand that his actions were inappropriate. God, I was speaking in my Mommy voice.

"Jesse, when we were in the café and that baby came in you...you squeezed my hand."

His mouth dropped open. "I was thinking of Sylvie."

Oh no. "What?"

He was smiling now, like the fox that got the chicken. "I was thinking about how you were such a great mom, and how it must make you a little sad to see that because Sylvie's growing up now."

I am an idiot.

"Oh."

"And by the way..." He put his hat back on. "That sneeze wasn't very believable." He winked at me and stood, holding his hand out to me.

I took it and stood with him on the sidewalk in front of my bakery, looking like a prize fool.

"Sorry, Jesse."

"Nah...I think it's kind of cute. Wait a minute..." He pulled back and looked at me warily. "Are you in love with me, Mandy Roberts?"

I have him my most intriguing smile. "I could be. Maybe."

❤

That night I was tucking Sylvie into bed when she dropped a bombshell on my perfectly satisfying day.

"Mommy, is Daddy coming for Thanksgiving?"

My heart actually stopped for a moment. So it's kind of a miracle I'm still alive and kicking enough to recount this horrid tale.

"Um...I don't think so. Why, sweetie?"

She frowned. Not one of those fakey lip-out frowns. No, no. This was the real deal. My heart broke.

"I just miss him, Mommy. I want him here for Thanksgiving."

"Well, honey, I'm sure he has plans."

"Will you ask him?"

"Honey, I don't think that—"

"Mommy, Thanksgiving is about togetherness. It's about being a family and forgiving those who do you wrong because they're your family. Just like we're all God's family."

She wasn't sweating so much that she needed a handkerchief, but she might as well have been. I could have slugged that television preacher! I'd have to have a talk with my mother.

"That's true."

"So ask Daddy."

I had no response.

"Ple-e-e-e-ease?"

"Fine."

"I love you, Mommy."

"I love you, sweet bean." I tucked her in and leaned in to give her a kiss when she dropped the second bombshell of the night.

"Can we say a prayer? Momo taught me one."

And yet, when I heard the question, my immediate response was, "Sure." After all, I'd been having secret late-night conversations with God for some time now.

Then my daughter recited the sweetest little prayer about 'Now I lay me down to sleep,' but I was a little disturbed when she started going on about 'If I should die before I wake...' That didn't seem like something a five year old should be worried about.

I finished tucking her in and stomped downstairs where I found my mother finishing up the dishes.

"Mom, you've got to stop letting Sylvie watch the TV preachers."

She turned to face me with a smile.

"I think it's good the girl gets a little religion."

"I'm fine with religion...in fact, I've been praying a little myself." I said this very smugly, which probably negated the sincerity of my previous prayers, but I think God could indulge me just this once.

"I'm so glad to hear that."

"Great. Now the problem is that Sylvie just preached to me some sermon about Thanksgiving and now she wants me to invite Richard to dinner."

My mother bit her lip. I couldn't tell if she was about to burst out laughing, or if she was just thinking really hard.

"Okay."

I was flabbergasted. I must have looked absolutely ridiculous with my mouth hanging open and my eyes as big as half-dollars. "Okay?"

She shrugged. "Sure. Seems reasonable. He is her father after all."

MEGAN PREWITT KOON

231

"Mom. No."

"Amanda Jane. Yes."

"No."

She nodded. "For your daughter."

I sighed ridiculously loudly and stormed out of the room like a petulant teenager.

"And Amanda Jane," she called after me, "if you let your mouth hang open like that, you'll catch nothin' but flies."

On the way to my room, I decided to pray.

God, if you're still listening after my flagrant showiness concerning these prayers, then I've got one for you. Please, please let Richard already have Thanksgiving plans. Please, please let him say no to me. Please, please, please.

He said yes.

God, I think I know why you're doing this... and fine. You're on Sylvie's side. I would be too—I mean, I am, too. Oh damn! Then I should WANT him to come. Oh geez, I just cursed in a prayer. Dag-nabbit.

❤

Opening day. November fifteenth. I hardly slept the night before and when I woke the next morning, the first thing I did was throw up in the toilet. Which is a great thing to do in the food preparation business.

I left at four o'clock for the bakery and was joined by Jesse and Dana who had offered to come early and help bake some fresh items. David said that it was in the best interest of business that he stay away from the kitchen, but that he would be happy to drive around town with a bullhorn and command people to come. I handed him some flyers instead and told him to stand outside the Maple Grove Café.

At six-thirty, I turned to Jesse and Dana who were both at their stations, took a deep breath and opened the front door.

There was no one there.

Well, that was anticlimactic, but I propped the door open despite the cold, told Dana to check that the coffee was hot and ready, and went back to the display case to add some muffins that had just come out of the oven.

My mother brought Sylvie by on her way to school and I served her my breakfast specialty—a fresh, warm croissant with orange marmalade and softened cream cheese on top. Sprinkled with crushed nuts, of course. That was Dana's mother's idea.

"I love you, Mommy!" She gave me a sticky kiss and whispered to me, "I have the coolest mommy EVER!" before she winked and skipped out the door with my mother.

At seven-ten our first customer arrived.

"Welcome!" I cheered, a bit too enthusiastically I guess because the woman looked frightened as I rushed to the counter.

She looked nervously at the three of us grinning so giddily about a real, live customer. "Hi...um, do you serve breakfast?"

"If it's baked, we sure do."

"Could I have a muffin then?"

"What flavor?" I handed her a menu.

Her eyes grew large. "Wow...so many to choose from."

"I recommend the traditional blueberry...it's a family recipe. But if you're looking for something a little different, try the pina colada. It's really quite heavenly."

She smiled. "I'll take one of each."

Awesome!

"For here or to go?"

"To go."

"Coffee?"

She sniffed the air. I have to admit, it did smell kind of scrumptious. Well done, Dana.

"Yes, please."

While I rang her up, Dana packed the muffins in a little box with a sticker on it and dispensed the coffee into the cups Jesse had bought in bulk at the office supply store.

I dropped a menu into her bag. "Please come back, and tell all your friends!"

"I will—thank you!"

She left with a tinkle of the doorbell and I started jumping up and down. "Yes! A customer! Eat THAT, Beulah!" I reverted back to my teenage self and did some warped version of a cheerleading herkey. Let's just say that was a very bad idea.

I hardly had time to work out the kinks in my leg as people began filing in, a few at a time, but enough to keep us busy all morning. Around eleven o'clock Dana had to leave for the Nut House, promising she'd send more customers our way, and Jesse had to go out to the farm.

It was a slow time, anyway. I figured the mornings were ours since

Beulah didn't open until nine and didn't serve breakfast items. Midday could be hers with her prime position on Main Street for the lunch crowd. The afternoon would be the battleground.

Luckily my store was closest to the elementary school, so the kids had to pass it to get across town, and I guess they begged their mothers to stop by because the traffic flow of children was steady for about an hour from two-thirty on. Sylvie arrived with my mother and set up her homework station at a corner table while Mom helped me with customers.

It had just slowed at about three forty-five when the bell tinkled and I'll be dag-nabbed if Beulah Mae Foxfire herself didn't saunter in, her eyes judging every detail of the store.

She peered in the display case as I helped an older man who wanted something for his sweet tooth. He winked at me as he said this, and I couldn't tell if he was trying to be cute or sexy. It's difficult to tell with little old men.

My rival sniffed as she saw my tiramisu and then made her way to the counter.

"Well, dear, I just came to wish you all the best, and to bring you a little opening day gift. She handed a bag across the counter. I was afraid to open it; something told me...rattlesnake.

But I opened the bag and pulled out a spatula. Not just any spatula. My favorite spatula from Beulah's store. I know it sounds ridiculous if you aren't in the business of baking, but when you find that one tool that just becomes an extension of your body, you know it's *the one*. I had missed this spatula.

"Beulah, I—"

Her red-nailed hand shot in front of my face. Her voice was still completely snotty as she spoke, and I realized that no matter this seeming peace-offering, the true battle was just beginning. "Say nothing of it. It's simply that I realized today that I have nothing to fear from you. You clearly own the breakfast crowd and I own the lunches. I have my loyal customers and I'm sure you'll have yours. I'm still not convinced, of course, that you'll make it. And I'll be damned if I won't fight you tooth and nail. But take the spatula. I have a better one back at the store."

She gave a little bow, turned on her heel, and sashayed through the door.

Neither my mother nor I knew quite what to say. We just stared at each other until Sylvie's sweet little voice piped up. Her nose was all scrunched up and she was waving her hand in front of her nose.

"Mommy, that lady wore too much perfume!"

I love that child.

Chapter Fourteen

As it turns out, I completely underestimated the people of Carroll, Georgia. They loved their tiramisu. It became a best-seller. And to my delight, the bakery seemed to be one of the go-to breakfast spots in town. The Maple Grove Café started ordering muffins daily so they could respond to the demand.

And about a week in, I even got my first full-fledged wedding order. Not just a cake. No, no. This future mother-in-law ordered the cake, groom's cake, and individually boxed cupcake favors for each guest.

Of course there was one drawback. Evidently this was a bit of a shotgun wedding, because I took the order on Tuesday for a wedding that Saturday night.

"Mama, I think I've bitten off more than I can chew." We were sitting on the front porch of the bakery in the two white rocking chairs I'd purchased with some of the opening day's revenues. Sylvie was inside working on homework. It was late in the afternoon, closing time, and I felt certain that any potential customers were home cooking dinner.

"Nah. You can do it. Might take a few extra hands in here on Friday night and Saturday morning, but you can do it."

I sighed. This was going to be a heck of a week, and Thanksgiving was right around the corner. The orders for pies and cakes were already starting to come in. I'd decided I'd have to cut them off at some point. But that was a good thing. I was on my way towards breaking even. Don't get me wrong, there was a ways to go, but I was determined to pay my mama back every penny by the one-year anniversary.

"Okay, I'm gonna go close up." I stood, stretched and walked back into the bakery to round Sylvie up and shut down the cash register. I hadn't been inside five minutes when the bell tinkled.

I assumed it was my mama.

"Almost done. You want to go ahead and take Sylvie on to the house?"

"Excuse me." It was a small, scared voice.

I looked up and saw a girl just about my age, plump, with a very sweet face and a mess of chocolate brown hair hastily pulled in a ponytail. She looked a little terrified.

"I—oh, sorry, I just—I thought you were my mama."

Her sad look turned to one of horror. Well done, Amanda. Now you've killed the girl's self-confidence.

"No, no...my mama is outside and I was expecting her to come in. I didn't even see you, just heard the bell tinkle and..."

A small smile—just the suggestion of a smile, really—crept into the corner of her mouth. When she spoke, it was almost a whisper and inhumanly high-pitched.

"I saw in the newspaper that you just opened and I hadn't had the chance to come by. Are you closing?"

I nodded. "Yes, but go ahead and pick something out...on the house." It was the least I could do after I'd implied the girl looked seventy years old.

"Oh, I couldn't do that. I'll just pay in cash and you can put it in tomorrow." She slid a couple of dollars onto the counter and pointed into the case. "Do you make your cupcakes with real sugar or that artificial stuff?"

Well I'll be. No one had asked that of me. Why in the world would someone think I used artificial? A chill went up my spine. The horror.

"Only the real thing here."

She relaxed. "Praise God!" she squeaked. My momma's got me on this low-sugar diet, and I think I'm gonna go off the edge!" She was smiling so sincerely now that I couldn't help but be drawn in by her.

"I'll take a mascarpone cupcake please." And she pronounced it correctly. I guess there's a first time for everything.

"Please don't be offended by this question," I said carefully, placing the cupcake in a box. "But how did you know how to pronounce that word? No one's said it correctly around here yet."

She blushed and studied her fingers. "I—I used to bake myself."

Well this was a revelation!

"Really? Where?"

Her eyes went everywhere except for me as she stuttered. I caught Sylvie looking up from her homework and listening intently.

"I—I—I went to school for it, worked at Beulah's for a while..."

Curious. "When did you quit?"

She tilted her head. "At the beginning of the summer...why?"

"I was your replacement."

Her face lit up. "I'm sorry!"

"Me too!" I shook my head and laughed.

She leaned toward me and whispered. "I quit because she told me I needed to eat less and sell more."

Really, that woman had no filter.

I narrowed my eyes. "She insulted my best friend."

The girl shook her head in commiseration.

"But anyway," I leaned back on the wall. "You were saying?"

"Oh, yes, well, not long after I left Beulah's I got divorced...moved back home with my momma to take care of her...and now, well, now I'm just waitressin' down at the Depot Track Restaurant."

I do believe it was in that very moment that I realized that there is, in fact, a good and gracious God. Here was a woman who understood what I had been through...and who could bake.

"Did you do cupcakes?"

She took a deep breath and forced herself to look me in the eyes. "I made the BEST cupcakes."

The cogs were turning in my head. I'll be damned. I was just lamenting to my mother about this huge wedding order and here comes a baker, after hours, wandering into my store.

I had a sudden epiphany and narrowed my eyes.

"Are you real?"

She looked confused, turned her head to look in both directions—I have to point out that when she looked at Sylvie, my daughter shrugged and gave her a look that suggested she had no idea why her mother was acting like a crazy person—and then turned her eyes back to me.

"Yes. I suppose I'm as real as you."

Well, that was embarrassing. I was pretty sure I was having a vision. But this was better anyway.

"How would you like to help me with a big order this weekend? I have a wedding on Saturday, and I sure could use someone around here who can bake. I have helpers for packing and serving the customers who come in on Friday, but I need some magic hands. What do you think? I can't pay much."

Clearly she thought that this was Christmas Day, because she screeched in that high pitched voice of hers, "Hell, yes!" and threw her arms around me.

I looked over her shoulder and saw Sylvie covering her ears. I do think I was temporarily deaf.

The girl was jumping up and down, nearly taking my neck off, and I was trying to peel her off of me.

"Oh thank you! Thank you!" Was she crying?

I put up a hand. "Can you come in on Thursday morning, maybe eight o'clock, so we can go over the baking plan and I can show you how we do things around here?"

She was nodding so enthusiastically, I was pretty sure her head was going to detach and roll away across the floor. That ponytail was going nuts!

"Oh thank you, thank you, Miss..."

"None of that. I'm Amanda Jane."

"Amanda Jane! I'm Misti Mason. Thank you. Oh, thank you! And you don't have to pay me; let me prove myself first. Oh, I'm so excited! I'll see you Thursday mornin'!"

She was wringing my hand, and then she was out the door.

It was eerily silent in the bakery.

"Mommy, she left her cupcake."

I grabbed the box and ran to the door. Misti was hugging my mother, telling her how wonderful her daughter was.

"Misti, you forgot your box."

She threw her arms around me one more time and squeezed so tightly I actually make a gagging sound.

Then she was gone.

My mother stood next to me as we watched her skip down the driveway.

"What an interesting young woman."

I smiled and kissed her cheek. "The good Lord has provided, Mama. Praise God!"

❤

Misti turned out to be a master of icing. I had planned on using her for the cupcakes and tackling the cake myself, but it was apparent early on that she was used to wedding cake décor. Her icing flowers were the most beautiful I'd seen. God, I wanted to eat those suckers myself.

We were putting cupcake boxes together on Friday afternoon when I heard the bell tinkle.

"Amanda Roberts!"

And I'll be a granny goat's fanny if it wasn't Wendell Jones.

"Mr. Jones!" I put down the box I was making and leapt up to give him a hug. He looked as if I'd agreed to marry him. "I haven't seen you in so long...what's kept you away? I was beginning to get jealous, you know." I put my hands on my hips and smiled. He blushed in return.

"Took me awhile to get to this side of town. I'm a creature of habit, you know. And this isn't my daily route. Missed you at Beulah's. She ain't nearly as pretty."

"Well, thank you, Mr. Jones. Can I offer you a cookie?" I walked back to the display case to procure him something sweet, and through the glass I saw it happen.

Wendell Jones could not take his eyes off of Misti Mason.

He had taken off his hat and taken my seat, and the two of them were chatting as if they were old friends.

I leaned further into the display case. Was Misti—blushing? No way.

I brought the cookie, wrapped in wax paper and stickered closed. Wendell didn't even notice me at first, and when he did, I think he remembered what he was here for. But to my surprise, when he spoke, it wasn't to me.

"Miss Mason, would you go for a walk with me sometime?"

Misti blushed—BLUSHED. "Oh, Mr. Mason. I couldn't. But my momma, I think she might be willing."

"If she looks anything like you, it would be my honor."

"I'll ask her."

"I'm mighty thankful, ma'am."

He stood and winked at me as he took his cookie.

And as he walked out of the store, he turned to me and shook his head. "Sorry, Miss Roberts, you missed your chance. I couldn't wait around for you forever."

"It's my loss, Mr. Jones."

He winked and went out the door.

Misti was beaming as I took my seat once again.

"What an adorable little man!"

I nodded. "He's a keeper."

"So sweet."

We boxed in silence for a few minutes, then I asked the question I had been fighting back all day.

"Misti, what's your mama like? I hear you talk about her, but I feel like I can't get the real sense of her."

Misti's smile faded. "Well, it is complicated, Amanda."

"Okay."

I thought that was all she would say, then she set down a box and leaned back in her chair.

"My momma is a wonderful woman, wonderful. But she's too worried about me. Always worried about my weight, worried that I'm not married, worried that I won't give her grandchildren. It makes me insane."

"I can see why. So...does she know you're helping me out?"

Misti lowered her head like a chastised child and shook it slowly. "She wouldn't like it, me being around so much food." Then she looked up and her eyes were determined. "What she doesn't know is that it actually helps to work at a place like this! I mean, after havin' my hands in sugar all day long, the LAST thing I want to eat is somethin' sweet! I swear, I leave here, and I just want a great big salad."

I nodded in understanding. It was the curse of the baker.

"Why don't you tell her that?"

She laughed joyfully. "She wouldn't believe me! I mean, it doesn't sound legitimate. Sounds like I'm makin' it up."

I shrugged. "You might try it. You never know."

"We'll see. I don't need her stormin' in here throwin' cake around."

I started laughing so hard that I hit the table with a fist.

"Oh Misti, that wouldn't be anything new!"

❤

I'd like to say that it was a beautiful wedding. That I cried and ran home to Jesse, proclaiming my undying love and devotion. But that would just be a bald-faced lie.

Saturday morning saw the whole cavalry gathered at the bakery. Misti and I were icing cupcakes faster than Dana and Jesse could put them into boxes. My mother was already at the church, making sure they were ready for us. Sylvie and David were in charge of putting stickers on the boxes—a Sweet Divinity sticker and a sticker I'd had printed with the bride's and groom's names and the date.

We finished ahead of schedule, and then David and Dana took Sylvie to Dana's house to play while Misti, Jesse, and I piled the goods into Jesse's truck. Thank God it was a sunny day.

We arrived at the church and carried our boxes into the reception hall. I couldn't really look around me because I was concentrated so hard on not dropping the multi-tiered cake that Jesse and I carried... me going backwards, which was truly a terrible idea. I think it took us fifteen minutes just to go through the door and over to the cake table as I moved at the pace of a dying turtle.

But when we set it on the table and carefully removed the box, I exhaled and allowed myself a look around.

Sweet Jesus.

Everything was gray. No, not silver. Gray.

I can safely say that I had never been to a gray wedding before now.

Gray.

The tablecloths were gray, the little crepe paper bells hanging from the ceiling were gray—had they been dyed?—the streamers were gray.

I walked over to one of the tables to put the cupcake boxes in place, and the pink stickers actually complemented the gray quite nicely, although I was now second-guessing the fact that I'd interpreted the mother's order of 'gray stickers with the bride and groom's name' as silver. What was I thinking?

As I placed the cupcake boxes at each setting, I couldn't help but notice the centerpieces.

There was a whole lot of greenery arranged around a votive. And jammed into the green foam that held it all in place, was a confederate flag.

No. It all made sense, and I had a distinct feeling that I was in the twilight zone.

Gray. The South.

Misti exhaled through her teeth. "Great God Almighty."

The bride and her mother chose that moment to come in and get a sneak-peek at the reception space. My mouth literally fell open.

The bride was so young...was I that young when I got married?

But although it was a shotgun wedding, it was an early one; she looked beautiful in a tight-fitted white dress. It was a beautiful dress, truly, it was. The train's the thing.

From the back of this mermaid-cut dress fell a train that started at the base of her back and flowed outward into a large circular shape she dragged after her. And the design on the train? I kid you not—the Confederate flag. I was astounded.

"Oh, Mama! Look at these sweet little boxes!" She ran up to me and snatched a box out of my hands, popping it open. "Ooh! Cute little cupcakes!" Then she threw her arms around her mama and I had to reach out and take the box before she dumped our hard work on the carpet.

I sort of thought she should be hugging me, as I designed the cupcakes, but there's something about a girl and her mama on her wedding day.

Of course my wedding day was a bit different.

My mama and daddy pretended to be civilized, and indeed they did a fairly good job. Richard's parents were much wealthier and presumably happily married, although I always thought his dad had had an affair—don't know why I thought that. Must have been the way he slapped the fannies of the female servers as they passed by with hors d'oeuvres.

My mama came storming into the bridal room minutes before the ceremony, pulled Dana's mother aside and started going crazy about something...her hands were flying and I silently thanked myself that my mother had left the shotgun at home. Otherwise I think this wedding may have turned into a funeral.

I asked Dana to go find out what the problem was, and she pulled her mama to the side once mine had composed herself and floated out the door.

Dana's face went completely white and I saw her mouth "NO!" to her mother. Then they both looked at me, then at each other, then they shook their heads, then Dana came back to me.

"Well?" I looked her straight in the eyes. Dana was never a good liar.

"Nothing. Just a little music snafu!" She giggled nervously. That was the Dana Clemens sign of deceit.

"Dana Clemens, if you don't tell me right now what is goin' on, I'm gonna get redneck on your ass."

One of the flower girls overheard me and started crying in the corner.

This was going just swimmingly.

Dana rolled her eyes. "Fine. Your mama was just in tellin' Richard good luck and she overheard his mama tellin' him that it wasn't too late to back out."

Fire. Burning, raging fire.

"Now, AJ, calm down." She put her hands on my face. "You are a confident girl. Richard loves you. You love Richard. That's all that matters."

"Fine words coming from you! You're the one who always said when you married, you married his mama, too!"

She bit her lip. "Um—that was a joke."

I pushed away and stomped out of the bridal chamber. To hell with tradition! Come to think of it, maybe this was where it all went bad, when I set the curse in motion. I marched straight to the groom's room and threw open the door.

There was Richard, shaking my brother's hand and—what? Hugging him.

I felt like a prize fool.

"Amanda?" Richard looked concerned. He knew I was completely superstitious, hadn't even let the wedding dress come into the house so he wouldn't see it ahead of time. I had slept over at the hotel last night so we wouldn't see each other until the ceremony. And here I was... surrounded by a bunch of confused men in tuxedos.

"Um...yeah. So, I just wanted to say I love you!" I'm worse than Dana.

"I love you, sweetie."

"Yeah." I slammed the door and ran back to the bridal room. Dana met me inside the door with powder and tissues.

"Calm down, AJ!" She began wiping my face and fluffing it back to perfection.

"Okay, that was a really stupid thing to do. But that woman! How could she do that?"

Dana shook her head. "I don't know. But let it be a lesson to you. You have to show her who wears the apron in YOUR house."

That one made me laugh. And so I let her finish my face and we went upstairs, and I got married.

And now here I stood, in the presence of the Old South.

"Congratulations."

The bride smiled and threw her arms around me. "Everything is beautiful. Thank you for such beautiful cakes."

"Of course. I wish you all the best."

Misti had been hanging back by the cake, putting the topper on and touching up the frosting. I quickly collected her and Jesse, who had hidden in the corner with the bride's father, yukkin' it up like only Southern men can, and we evacuated.

"What in the Sam Hill was all that about?" Misti had clearly never seen anything like that wedding, which made me hopeful for future bookings.

Clearly I had not given Jesse enough credit for the ability to gather information.

"Well, ladies, according to the father, the poor girl got 'knocked up'—his words—by a 'goddamn Yankee,' and so they planned the wedding as a message to him and all his 'damned Yankee' relatives."

We sat in silence for a minute, digesting the gray. It was Misti who piped up first.

"Well, as they say, 'The South will Rise Again!' I just hope that poor girl survives the wedding. Didn't go so well for us the last time around."

Jesse started whistling "Taps," and we all joined in as we drove down Main Street. In that moment, I realized that I didn't just own a bakery, I also had a bona fide employee. I'd draw up the paperwork tomorrow.

❤

The wedding had distracted me from Thanksgiving, but it was indeed upon us. Sylvie and I watched from the couch as the president pardoned the Thanksgiving turkey.

"Mommy, why do we eat turkey on Thanksgiving? Did the pilgrims eat turkey?"

"Honey, I have no idea."

"If I were a turkey, I would fly down to Florida at Thanksgiving."

I turned to her. "Don't you think people in Florida eat turkey for Thanksgiving?"

Her answer was very matter-of-fact. "People don't live in Florida, Mommy. Momo says it's just full of old Yankees."

I snuggled close to her. That's my southern girl.

The day before Thanksgiving Jeannette arrived in town. Don't worry, she wasn't wearing a Native American princess costume—I know you're disappointed.

Sylvie attached herself to 'Aunt Jeannie' as soon as one high heel hit the gravel driveway and barely let go for the next three hours. I was actually really appreciative of this as I had several pies to finish and get boxed up for customers.

"Amanda, this place is perfect!" Jeannette was sitting at a table in the bakery, making toilet roll turkeys with Sylvie. I had to give her credit—I have no idea where she got the idea to use the rolls, but they certainly helped the turkeys stand up. Last year we'd had a tragedy when one of Sylvie's turkeys went face-down into the mashed potatoes about three bites in. When the second turkey hit the cranberries we released them to the wilds and finished dinner.

"Thanks, Jeannie. It's just how I hoped it would be."

"So is Mr. Handsome coming to Thanksgiving dinner?"

"He is. He's down in Rome having Thanksgiving with his parents at lunch tomorrow, but he'll be here in time for dinner." He had also said that this would be the first of many Thanksgivings to share. I felt my heart flutter whenever I thought of it.

"Have you met his parents?"

"No, he told me he wanted to take me down there around Christmas time, that they would love me and that Sylvie would light up their home. I'm super excited to meet them."

"That's a big move. Meeting his parents."

"Yeah. A big move." I was basking in the promise of it when Jeannette, true to form, killed the mood.

"And tomorrow Richard will be here." It wasn't a question, and I saw her look at me from the corner of her eye as she glued a construction paper feather on the back of an empty toilet paper roll.

"Yes he will."

"Yippee." Deadpan.

Sylvie perked up. "I'm excited, too, Aunt Jeannie! I can't wait to see my daddy!" And she started bouncing up and down in her chair.

Jeannie kissed her head and came to join me at the counter where I was packing the last two pumpkin pies into boxes.

"Are you okay with this, Amanda?"

You know, that was an interesting question. I had given it a lot of thought, and the honest answer was yes. I was okay with it. Richard might not be my husband for much longer, but Sylvie was his daughter forever. If one good thing had come from the marriage—and to be fair, there were many good things in my memory—Sylvie was it. And what better time than Thanksgiving to remember how thankful I am for her.

"I am, Jean. I truly am. Thanksgiving is about family. And like it or not, Richard will always be family."

"You're disgustingly nice."

I shrugged. "I'm southern."

"Indeed, you are that." She grabbed the sticker roll and started sealing boxes. "I'm really going to miss you, Amanda. You know, when I move."

My stomach jumped and I felt a tear run down my cheek. "Oh, Jeannie, you'll have no problem finding a new girl to help you cook. Believe me, there are several in the world."

She gave me a look. "I think you know that you mean a little more to me than that."

"I do." I turned to wash my hands and wipe my face, and then went around the counter to hug her. "I love you, Jeannette. Thank you for all you've done for me."

"HA! I should be saying that to you, girl!"

The bell tinkled and my mother walked in, grocery bags loading her down.

"There's a poor old lady here with too many groceries...can I get some help?"

We took the bags out of her arms and started unloading the cans and vegetables. Jeannette and Sylvie went back out to the car to get the rest while my mother sat at the craft table.

We'd decided to have Thanksgiving dinner at the bakery. It just seemed appropriate when thinking about all the things we were thankful for this year.

My final customers picked up their pies with a flurry of kind wishes and thankfulness of their own. The last customer, Janey Cummings, had me bake her pie in her own pie dish. She clapped her hands when she saw it and announced that I had "Saved Thanksgiving." She had a family where everyone brought a homemade dish...no freezer section allowed. Well, Janey couldn't bake any better than a squirrel could, or so she said, so I helped her out in what I saw as a minor lie of omission.

At the end of the night, Jeannette, my mother, and Sylvie headed back to the farm and Jesse and I closed up shop. I sent Misti home to her family via Beulah's to deliver a small box of freshly made divinity candy from my display case. A peace offering of sorts.

I called Jesse that night to make sure things were going well with his parents.

"Mandy, I just want you to know that I am going to act like a gentleman tomorrow. I give you my word I won't make a scene."

"Yeah, the last time you and Richard were in the same room it didn't go so well. And that was the day I realized you have a temper."

"I do indeed. And I'm working on that. I want to be a better man for Sylvie."

How sweet. "I'd say you're doing all right."

"I can do better. And I will. I won't dare ruin any of that delicious food you and your mama have been working on. And I won't cuss, throw punches, or otherwise disturb the peace."

"I'd appreciate that."

"Although I might spit in his food."

"Jesse!"

"Just kidding, just kidding! I've got no anger against that man any more. He's Sylvie's father. I won't interfere with that."

I felt awkward. My mind was already in the future, wondering what it would be like if Jesse were her father, too.

"Be careful driving tomorrow. Be sure you keep that temper of yours in check!"

He laughed. "Be sure you keep that ex-husband of yours in check until I get there."

I laughed. "If he acts up, I'll just smash a cupcake in his face."

"Hmmm...he'll be expectin' that. Go for a whole pie. That'll show him."

"Okay. Bye, Jesse."

"Bye, love."

My heart stopped. Really, I think I almost died right there. I love that man.

Chapter Fifteen

Thanksgiving morning began with Sylvie in her pajamas clapping on the couch as she watched the televised parade and my mother bustling about, getting everything 'prepped.' Seeing as almost everything was at the bakery, she had very little to do, and this drove her crazy.

I wandered downstairs in an old t-shirt and sweatpants, my hair all a mess, and fixed a cup of coffee.

"Happy Thanksgiving, Mommy!" Sylvie called from her nest of blankets and pillows.

"Happy Thanksgiving, sweetie."

My mother shoved a plate of scrambled eggs, bacon, and cheese grits into my hands.

"Eat up! You'll need your strength!"

"Mom, it's Thanksgiving, not enlistment day."

She put a hand on her hip. "Honey, if you recall, the bastard Richard is comin' today. Now eat up, you need some color."

I took my plate to the living room and nestled alongside Sylvie who stole my bacon without once looking away from the screen.

Jeannette stumbled into the living room a few minutes later, plate in hand. She didn't say anything, and she didn't look like anyone would survive saying anything to her, so I just let her sit and nibble, knowing that she would pretend to graze but in fact gobble down every greasy morsel of the breakfast.

The parade over, dishes washed, I got Sylvie dressed in her Thanksgiving t-shirt and brown sweatpants, pulled her jacket on, and sent her downstairs to sit with Momo until it was time to go.

Jeannette was hogging the upstairs bathroom—surprise, surprise—and I had to knock three times before she heard me over her hair dryer.

"Amanda! Dear God, come in here and let me get to work!" She pulled me by the arm, shoved me in the shower, and set up all of her beautification tools.

"This is ridiculous, Jean," I called from the scalding shower. "I'm just going to get all gross and floury in the kitchen!"

"If you start with perfection, the worst you could possibly look is above average. Start with crap, you turn into shit."

Did I mention Jeannette was a philosopher?

She drew all over my face, insisted I wear a 'cute shirt' with my blue jeans, and finally let me go downstairs only after applying an insane amount of hairspray to my head.

"Mommy, you look beautiful!" Sylvie had loaded up her backpack with various art supplies and was sitting on the couch, watching *It's a Wonderful Life*. I'd never understood why this movie was always shown on Thanksgiving until this very moment.

When we pulled up to the bakery, Richard's car was the first thing I saw. Shiny. Sporty. Parked so that we couldn't get up the steps that led from the road to the sidewalk.

As Sylvie was straining against her seatbelt I motioned for him to move the car, and he did, making our access a bit easier.

He looked good, I won't lie. He'd had his hair colored and had clearly been going to the gym. But what was amazing to me was that when I saw him, I didn't feel anything extreme. No love, but no anger either. I felt—confident. I felt okay.

Sylvie ran into his arms, covering his face with kisses.

"Baby girl!" It was a sweet picture, these two, loving each other so much.

I was about to sigh when Jeannette whispered in my ear, "Better be sure Sylvie uses some antiseptic mouthwash before you kiss her again! Gross!"

I could always count on Jeannette.

Sylvie dragged her father inside and got him going on a craft project in the corner while Mama and I got going in the kitchen.

Jeannette wasn't sure what to do, so after a brief lesson I got her setting the table.

Dana and her family—mama, husband, and kids—arrived a few minutes later, and her husband and Richard took all the kids outside while the women came to help us in the kitchen. David was having Thanksgiving with his own mother...and Lawrence and his family. I said a quick prayer for him. Yes, that's right. It was coming pretty easily these days.

The bakery kitchen wasn't really big enough for all the women gathered about it, so I took Dana and Jeannette out front for a real introduction.

We sat at the table, listening to our mothers talk shop in the kitchen.

"God, if my mother were here, this would be a mess." Jeannette leaned toward us. "She'd be tryin' to put marshmallows on the yams."

Dana held a hand up. "Girl, we gotta get a couple of things straight. First off, this is a marshmallow-free zone. Second, never, EVER, call them 'yams.' They're 'sweet potatoes.'" She turned to me. "Am I right?"

I shrugged. "She's right, Jeannie. But maybe they use marshmallows in Colorado."

Dana nodded encouragingly.

"Or granola," I added.

Jeannette slapped my arm. "Stop...you're scaring me. Next thing you know you're gonna tell me they're not going to have that sweet tea you've got me addicted to!"

Dana and I looked at one another.

"Girls!" Dana's mama was bellowing from the kitchen.

We all hopped to attention and gathered at the counter.

"Dana, I need you to help mash these taters. Jeannette, come on back here, honey, and get ahold of this casserole...you can sprinkle bread crumbs, right?"

Jeannette nodded warily.

"Amanda Jane, you go on out there and talk to your ex-husband for a minute."

Well, that was unexpected.

"I'd like to remind everyone that this is in fact my kitchen..."

"Not today," and she slammed closed the shutters.

"Okay then..." I walked outside and saw the kids throwing a football in front of the house. Sylvie was cheering on the sidelines while Richard and Rusty played against the other kids.

I sat on the steps and shaded my eyes against the sun. Richard caught the ball, yelled "Touchdown!" and caught my eye as he made a victory lap.

"Yay, Daddy! Go, Daddy!" Sylvie did a really nice spread eagle, her imaginary pom poms waving like crazy.

"I'm out...even it up!" Richard came jogging toward me in his dress pants and button-down shirt.

"Looks like you didn't quite dress the part today," I teased, trying a smile.

He was panting as he sat next to me. "Well, this isn't how the Jacksons do Thanksgiving."

I nodded. "Yeah, we're more of a t-shirt and jeans kind of family."

"Or sweatpants." He glanced down at me with a grin.

I shrugged. "Cooking's hard work. I started out looking nice this morning."

"You look nice now." And he said it in a genuine voice, not some kind of ulterior motive voice, but just as a nice thing to say. "Yeah. So this place is really great, Amanda. I mean, the bakery. I'm really proud of you."

I looked in his eyes and could tell that he meant it. "Thanks, Rich."

He ran his hands through his hair. "I can't help but think I was holding you back from all this."

"No, no, don't think that." Part of me did want him to feel guilty; I kind of liked the feeling of inducing a good guilt trip on him. But the truth was that I'd held myself back just as much. "I could have done whatever I wanted. I just decided to do something else."

"And what was that?"

I shrugged. "Try to be a housewife." I barely got the words out before I burst into laughter, the tears starting down my cheeks.

Richard looked confused. "What are you laughing about? You were a great housewife."

"That's the problem!" I wiped my eyes and sniffled as I smiled. "I was good at it...but I wasn't very good at being myself. I'm NOT a housewife." I gestured toward the bakery.

"Clearly."

"Mommy!" Sylvie was calling from the other side of the yard. "What are you laughing at?"

"Daddy's funny!"

"I know!" She put her hands over her mouth to stifle her giggles and turned her attention back to the game.

"She's amazing. And you know, Amanda, she reminds me so much of you."

Sylvie chose that moment to try a new jump, and fell flat on her derriere. But, true to form, she pulled herself right back up and kept on cheering.

I raised an eyebrow. "Hmm...I think you have a point."

Now it was Richard's turn to laugh. "Remember the time we were walking into that swanky restaurant in midtown—"

"Hold it right there!"

"And you wore those ridiculous shoes and fell right down the stairs!"

"Not funny."

"Funny? It was wonderful! We got a free bottle of wine!"

It had always occurred to me as incredibly stupid to give a stumbling woman a bottle of wine...

"I blame my mother. She never would let me take ballet."

"Hah." Richard gave me a look. "I'll bet you were the type to insist that you could teach YOURSELF ballet."

I smiled. "Guilty as charged. I bought myself a book about ballet and practiced all the positions. I wanted to be just like the girl in *Flashdance.*"

"Wasn't she a stripper?"

I put my hands on my hips. "She was an exotic dancer, Richard, and when I was seven I thought she was just a dancer with very fringy costumes."

Richard was cracking up. "Did you dump water over your head?"

"In the shower."

He was in pieces now and I bumped his shoulder with mine. "Oh, pull yourself together."

"I never knew you aspired to be an exotic dancer. If I'd known, I would have installed a pole in the house."

"And a water bucket?"

"Absolutely."

I winked. "There's a lot you never knew about me, Richard."

"No doubt."

We sat for a minute watching our daughter, so joyful on the sidelines. Richard wiped his eyes with a handkerchief and stretched out his legs.

"You know, I do miss you, Amanda."

I sighed. "I miss our life sometimes. Some parts of it anyway. There were definitely some good times."

"Yeah. But too many not-so-good. Sorry I was a crappy husband."

"Is crappy the word I would use?"

He grinned. "No. You'd say 'shitty.'"

I nodded. "Much more accurate."

"But I had my moments."

"You did. First anniversary?"

"Ah yes, paper. I put all those cards around the house."

"'50 Reasons I Love You.'"

He nodded. "Yeah, that was a pretty good one, if I do say so myself."

"You were all right. You'll be better the next time around."

He looked sharply at me. "You think you'll get married again?"

I felt a smile spread across my lips. "Absolutely."

He put his hand on mine. "You deserve it."

"Thanks. You too, Rich. Everyone deserves to be happy, even you."

"I deserve that."

"Yes, you do."

"And a second chance."

"Yes. With a different woman, of course."

"Of course."

"Hey—thanks, Richard."

He had a goofy look on his face. "What for?"

"For Sylvie."

He laughed. "No, no. She's all you, Amanda. All you."

And for that comment, I was so very thankful.

It was at this moment that my brother pulled up into the driveway in his rented station wagon and came barreling out of the car.

"Hello, Family! Your long-lost relations have arrived!" He spread his arms and I nearly ran him over. My stupid big brother home for the holidays. I gave a quick hug to Louisa, his dear wife, as my mother hurried outside and filled her son's arms. And then I greeted Rebecca and Robert, who both took out their earbuds to hug me and then promptly plugged back in. I could see why my mother thought they were brats, but the way I saw it, they were just teenagers. Remind me to stop time before Sylvie gets there.

Michael took up the football and started playing while his kids sat to the side on their phones and Louisa joined the hands in the kitchen. Before five minutes were up she was telling Jeannette all about life in Colorado.

Richard was back in the game and I was just turning to head back into the bakery when I caught sight of Jesse's pickup truck coming down Thompson Avenue. I got that excited feeling in the pit of my stomach like you get before a first date. Elation, giddiness, and raw nerves.

"Mr. Jesse!" Sylvie was is his arms before he could fully stand up out of the truck.

"How's it goin', little miss?"

"Mr. Jesse, my daddy's here! Come meet my daddy!" She wiggled free and took his hand, leading him over to the football game which stood in awkward time-out.

"Mr. Jesse, meet my daddy." She gestured to Richard who looked ashen at the sight of this cowboy who had slugged him the last time they'd met.

"We've actually met, sweetheart." Richard stuck out his hand. With a raised eyebrow Jesse took it.

"That's true. But I think this is more of an official meeting. Richard." There wasn't the trace of a smile on Jesse's face, and he never moved his eyes from Richard's.

Looking at the two of them attempting to fake cordiality for the sake of Sylvie, I marveled at how I could have loved both of them. Richard was, well, Richard, a businessman whose idea of 'time away' was lying on the couch watching CNBC. Jesse was rugged...rugged and so, so sexy. And kind, of course. And wonderful.

Michael seized the moment to introduce himself to Jesse who laughed and informed my brother he'd heard a lot about him. Michael rolled his eyes. "Let me guess, the plants."

"It's a great story, man." Jesse was smiling now, and I saw that mischievous twinkle in his eye.

"I want to hear the story, Uncle Mikey." Sylvie looked so eager.

"Okay. Um. Well, once your Momo found out I was growing plants in my room and she took them and threw them out the window!"

Sylvie's grin turned into a frown and her brows furrowed. "Why would she do something like that?"

I piped in. "She said Uncle Mikey needed to clean his room, if I remember correctly.

"Well I sure am going to keep my room clean at Momo's house!"

"Yes, well," Michael continued, "that is definitely the lesson there."

"Dinner's ready!" Jeannette was standing behind us, yelling at full strength and beating a pan with a wooden spoon. Richard and I both clapped our hands over our ears.

He leaned toward me and whispered in my ears. "Jeannette hasn't spoken to me yet. Is she going to kill me?"

"Not if you're lucky. Although she probably won't speak to you or look at you either."

I winked at him and took Jesse's hand, calling toward the house, "Lock up the cupcakes, I'm bringing in the men!"

We all gathered around the table decorated with Sylvie's toilet paper turkeys. For each person she had made a turkey, and on its feathers she had written reasons she was thankful for the person. On mine she had written, "You braid my hair," "You tell funny stories," "I have fun with you," "You are very pretty," and "You love me very much." I felt tears burn my eyes as I realized she knew. She knew how much I loved her.

"Ladies, this is a sight to behold!" Rusty smiled as he passed the carved turkey to Dana.

"It was all Mama and Mrs. Roberts," she offered.

Both women humbly disregarded the compliments, as good southern women always do.

"Mmmm...cranberry sauce!" Sylvie licked her lips and spooned two large helpings of sauce onto her plate. I should have just set her place with the bowl.

I looked around me. There was my mother, rightfully at the head of the table, and Dana's mother at the other end. These women had formed me, sent me into the world, and welcomed me home. There was Dana and her family, the model of a functional family unit, so happy to be together. There was Michael, his wife, and his two kids, ear buds out now, laughing at their father who was fighting over the wishbone with Sylvie. There was Richard, seated, accidentally, next to Jeannette, who purposefully passed the food around him as if he weren't there. And he shrugged and waited, asking for the plates once everyone else had been served. There was Jesse, imperfect but pretty dang perfect for me.

And there was Sylvie. There was my life in blue eyes and a mop of curls. There was my future. I didn't know what would come for me. All I knew was that I was so happy where I was at this moment. My dream to open a bakery was looking promising, I'd found a guy who thought I was pretty great, and my daughter was thriving. What more could I ask for?

When everyone was served, we bowed our heads, and my mama said the traditional family prayer. Afterward, she went freestyle, thanking the Lord for everyone gathered here, and for everyone who couldn't be present today. She thanked him for family, for food, and for faith.

There's nothing like a good meal and family to help people put aside their differences. By the end of the night, Jeannette had even put a dollop of fresh whipped cream on Richard's pecan pie for him. Don't get me wrong, there was plenty of hurt around that table. Plenty of hurt and plenty of hard feelings. But there was also a lot of love.

Chapter Sixteen

Thanksgiving usually stirs feelings of togetherness, of love for one's fellow man, of gratefulness that we have shelter from the storm and food for our hungry bellies.

Clearly Beulah Mae Foxfire missed the memo.

The days following Thanksgiving had been filled with pick up football, turkey sandwiches, and naps. Richard and I agreed to a visitation arrangement wherein I would agree to spend one weekend a month in Charlotte so Sylvie could stay with him and he would come one weekend a month to visit her here. In addition he got the week before Christmas, Spring Break, and three weeks in the summer. David had a colleague call Richard's attorney to work out the legalese. Michael and his brood dropped their car in Atlanta and headed back out west with a promise to come back in the summer. The kids looked thrilled at the prospect.

And so life was getting back to the usual routine.

On Monday morning I arrived at the bakery before the sun rose to get going on replenishing the base items that hadn't been made since before the holiday. When I got to the front door, I found an envelope tucked into the door jamb. It was pink and perfumed so I knew immediately who had sent it. The note inside read, "I received your message loud and clear. If it's a war you want, darling, then it's a war you shall have."

I got a chill and looked around me in the darkness, searching for signs of an army in hiding, ready to fling muffins with slingshots or icing with blowguns. But all I saw were dark buildings and the occasional car passing down Thompson Avenue. I let myself in, flipped on all the lights, turned on the radio, and locked the door behind me.

What had I done? What 'message' had she received? All I could remember was sending the divinity by way of Misti. Wait—was Misti a spy?

I dismissed that thought immediately. Misti was too genuine a girl and besides, her story of leaving Beulah's sounded all too legitimate. So what had been wrong with the divinity?

I heated the ovens and checked my white board where I'd recorded all of the orders for this afternoon. I noted that there was a cake tasting tomorrow, so I'd need to bake a few test items today in preparation.

All the while I was racking my mind, trying to figure out what was so significant about that divinity? How had she interpreted that as a war decree?

Misti arrived at six o'clock, ready to get going on the muffins while I was working through croissants and planning the tasting in my mind; the joys of multitasking!

"How was your holiday?" I asked casually as I began forming the flaky little horns.

"Perfectly lovely. My mama really loved the pie crusts you sent home with me. Thank you so much for that. Saved us a lot of time on the day."

"My pleasure. I'm glad they went to good use. Seems like we'll be making some more just around the corner! I'm hoping that the Christmas season is going to be busy around here so you'll have to help me think of some Christmas specialties we can have on hand. Maybe some chocolate dipped candy canes...ooh, and some Rugelach! I'll bet we'll be the only place in town that Jewish families can purchase Hanukkah treats! We'll have to advertise that. In fact, I think I'll whip up some Rugelach and Bimuelos this afternoon if I have time so I can go ahead and get them in stores."

"Okay...Amanda Jane, I have no idea what those are."

I laughed. There was a tiny population of Jewish families in our town and clearly their delicious traditions had not spread to the majority of the population. I'd rectify that.

"Don't worry, Misti, I can teach you. The Rugelach in particular is easy-peasy. It's like a tiny croissant with chocolate and nuts.

"That sounds delicious."

"Oh, I assure you, it is. Maybe I'll buy a menorah for the window, too."

I saw Misti freeze mid-mix.

"Too much, maybe?" Baby steps, Amanda. "Now I have a bit of a mystery I'd love your help in solving." And I handed over the mystery note left for me this morning.

She nodded. "That explains this." She spread the day's newspaper on the counter. "I wasn't sure what to make of it, but now it makes sense."

Lying on my counter was a full page ad for Beulah's, "Now Serving Breakfast!"

That woman didn't waste any time, did she? And here she was, taking away my money-maker, the one thing that set me apart from her. What would I do? I was counting on that breakfast crowd for the cash flow until I established a client base for special orders. This was a disaster. And why?

Misti was still trying to reason it out. "That's so odd. When have you ever had a disagreement with her about divinity candy?"

And then I knew. I knew sure as if it had slapped me in the face. She'd won the country fair bake-off with her divinity. And she saw my gift as an affront, as if I had wanted her to see I could make it just as well—which was true, of course, but that wasn't my motivation for sending it.

"Oh, Misti. I get it. This is a complete misunderstanding. Okay, I'll just stop by this afternoon and talk it out with her. I'll explain things and then she'll see. She's a reasonable woman, right?"

Misti's look of doubt was all the confirmation I needed. I was screwed. There was no going back from this...this was, indeed, war.

❤

That night Jesse came over after I put Sylvie to bed and we decided to take advantage of the beautiful, clear night. It was on the cooler side, so we snuggled up in a nest of blankets constructed in the bed of his truck. I'd brought an arm load out of the house, a sight that caused my mother to raise her eyebrows and shake her finger playfully at me. Yes, that's right, I was lying down in the bed of a pickup truck with a boy. Don't judge. Or do; I have no shame.

We snuggled and looked up at the stars so clear out here where there wasn't any artificial light to dim them.

"Amanda Jane, I had a wonderful Thanksgiving with you and your family."

"Me too."

The sounds of a country evening were in full volume, frogs and crickets, the occasional owl calling from deep within the woods around us. Once in a while I would hear my mother laughing from the back porch and the sound filled my heart. In that truck bed, lying against the man I loved, in a place I loved, with all of the best people just a stone's throw away, I felt content. Settled. For the first time in a long time, I felt totally, completely happy. And so I decided to ruin it by bring up another woman.

"Jesse, why is Beulah Mae Foxfire such as nasty old biddy?"

He burst out laughing. "Oh, honey, that's like asking why the sun comes up in the east."

"I suppose."

We lay there in silence with me just fixated on the image of Beulah in her apron and red lipstick stirring up a kettle of some noxious brew whilst chanting an incantation to curse me. Jesse had other things on his mind.

"I want to tell you something, Amanda Jane."

"Mmhm."

"I need to tell you what happened with me and Patsy Cherry."

Could this day get any worse?

"I don't need to know that, Jesse. And I don't think I even care to know."

"Well, I need you to know, because...well, because I need you to."

I took a deep breath. "All right then. Let's have it."

He started stroking my arm as he spoke, and his touch calmed my tense body. I felt myself sinking into him.

"So you know we were together a couple of years ago. And to tell you the truth, it wasn't for very long. Her mama knew my mama from way back when and we ran into each other one day and were talking about that and then we just started seeing more of each other."

I was starting to feel sick now.

"Jesse, I don't need to hear this."

"I know, I just...it's really important to me that you do." He was squirming with nerves so I took his hand and gave it a kiss.

"Okay. Go on."

"So one day she came and found me when I was collecting honey. I saw her across the field and she looked just awful and..."

He paused. It endured horribly. It was as if I were stuck in one of those awful romantic movies where everything's going along just fine and then some bombshell hits and screws up everything.

"She told me she was pregnant."

BOOM.

I sat straight up and turned to look at him. "Oh my God, Jesse. I—"

"Wait, wait, Amanda Jane. There's more. You see she told me this and so I did what I had to do, right? I proposed. I knew I'd done wrong and I'm not someone to shy away from responsibility. It wouldn't have been my choice, you know. I mean, I didn't love her. I never loved her." His eyes were pleading and I didn't know what to say.

"Um...okay?" Smooth. As usual.

"And so we set a date and I bought a ring and I met her parents. And then one day she showed up crying again and I couldn't even hear what she was saying she was crying so hard. She told me that she wasn't pregnant anymore. The baby dissolved, or disappeared, or something. I still don't understand. So I broke it off. I mean, I wasn't in love. I doubt she was either. We just...I just..."

"Jesse, I'm so sorry."

He sighed. "There's nothing to be sorry for. There was nothing to miss. The doctor said this happens. Maybe it was God stopping us from making a horrible mistake, I don't know. It's just that I need you to know why it caught me off guard that day when you asked if I could see us having a family."

"I don't know why I said that."

"Well, I'm glad you did." He was smiling a little now, and he brushed a stray hair from my face. "And there's another reason I wanted to tell you that story, Amanda Jane. Another reason you had to know that I never loved that woman. That I've never really loved a woman enough to make that kind of commitment."

"And why's that?" I squeezed his hand.

"Because I am so absolutely in love with you."

I looked at this man in the moonlight, this gentle, kind, incredible man.

"I am so absolutely in love with you, too, Jesse Gregory."

I could see that grin in the light of the moon. "I am so glad. And yes. The answer is yes."

I turned around to face him, pulling the blankets around both of us. "Yes?"

"Yes. I can see myself making a family with you."

My heart beat wildly and my head went light. I felt a weight lift from my body, watched it sail off into the clear night.

"That's good to hear. Really good. 'Cause I can, too."

I snuggled into his chest. I could hear his heart thumping, could feel his body relax with the affirmation that we were in this together.

"So what happens next, Amanda Jane?

What a question.

"Well, I have bad news for you. I'm still married."

He chuckled. "I tend not to think about that."

"Me neither."

"So with that little unfortunateness cast aside, let me ask again. What happens next, Amanda Jane?"

"What's next, Jesse Gregory?" I grinned suggestively, taking his face in my hands. "Well, I don't really know, but I'd suggest you kiss me."

I didn't wait for his reply.

❤

At precisely two o'clock on Tuesday, my cake tasters showed up. The bell over the door tinkled joyfully and two young men entered my bakery, holding hands.

"Welcome to Sweet Divinity. How may I help you?" I couldn't help but wonder how in the world this couple had managed to arrive at my shop without a contingency of bamboozled locals trailing behind, watching to see if this certain mirage would disappear before their eyes.

"We have an appointment for a cake tasting. The name is Carr."

"Of course! Please have a seat up at the counter. Misti!"

God bless her, her eyes grew five sizes as she came sashaying out of the back with flour all over her face. "Oh, um, yes. Yes, Amanda Jane."

"Could you please take over the counter while I help these gentlemen with the cake tasting?"

"Um...yes. Of course. Let me, um...let me just wash my hands."

"And your face."

She smiled bashfully. "And my face."

I turned to the couple before me. "Now I don't recognize you two. Are you locals?"

The taller, dark haired young man chuckled and patted his companion on the shoulder. "This guy is local. Born and raised here. This is Patrick."

We shook hands.

"And I'm Taylor. We live across the state lines but we're in a bit of a pickle, and we heard that the two best bakeries in the region are here, so we thought we'd come and see for ourselves."

Mixed emotions. First, Hurrah! I've been placed on the same level as Beulah! Hoohee!!! Second, Oh geez, the showdown at the country fair was small peas.

"I suppose that other bakery is Beulah's."

Their faces were crestfallen. "It is...er, was...but she made it clear that she doesn't bake for 'our kind'—" he made air quotations "—so we really hope you can live up to the hype."

I'm sure my face betrayed my absolute disgust. I knew that Beulah had these views. That's why I quit...well, that and self-respect. But to actually act upon them to the detriment of her business?

"Well, Beulah is no friend of mine, so I, too, hope that my cakes just knock your socks off! When's the big day?"

They avoided making eye contact. We sat in silence for a full minute, the only sound Misti's whistling of the new Brad Paisley song.

Finally Patrick spoke. "Saturday."

"SATURDAY?" I admit, it was a little much. I hollered. I really hollered. But geezamineeza...Saturday?

Taylor took his fiance's hand. "You see, we'd originally booked Beulah's for the wedding. We'd heard about her from Patrick's family and so we figured, no problem. And everything was fine. I went and did the tasting when Patrick was overseas on a business trip. She was great. Professional. Kind. But when we went in last Wednesday to confirm everything, she told us she couldn't help us anymore. Claimed that she'd 'double-booked' and apologized, but it was half-hearted. We knew she was lying."

"I'm so sorry to hear that."

"So if this is a problem for you, please just say so right now."

"Oh, this isn't a problem. This is fantastic. I admit, Saturday has me a little stressed out, but let's just get this show on the road. Now what do you have in mind?"

Their faces lit up and we discuss the details before I brought out the sample plate. They loved my carrot cake, traditional with pecans and cream cheese frosting, as well as my half and half cake with that moist layer of chocolate separated from the vanilla with a raspberry filling. We discussed options such as using different flavors for different tiers. And then we discussed the Groom's cake, which Taylor insisted be his.

Patrick shrugged, "He is the chocoholic here."

At the end of an hour, I asked if they'd made their decision. They looked at each other and then Patrick spoke, "Amanda Jane, we're really a unique couple. I mean, I know everyone thinks they're a unique couple, but we really want this day to be memorable in every way. So is there anything unique you could do? Maybe a specialty tier on top of some kind? I mean, we're not having a cake topper, *per se*. We don't really go in for that whole 'two men in tuxedos' thing. So do you have a specialty? Or just something everyone will remember?

I felt the broadest smile appear on my face. The poetry of this moment was not lost on me as I replied, "I have a specialty, all right. How about a tiramisu wedding cake?"

It were as if I'd just told them that the cake would be made of pure gold.

We shook on it. It was official. I had taken my first client from Beulah Mae Foxfire. In fact the happy couple was so excited, they asked me to stay at the wedding as a guest. Plus one. I accepted gratefully and then got immediately to work. This would be the best damn wedding cake the world had ever known.

❤

I let Misti keep tabs on the shop while I picked Sylvie up from school and got her set up for homework at her usual table in the corner. Of course this was Kindergarten we were talking about, so 'homework' consisted of writing a few words on humongously lined paper and tracing the number three about fifteen times.

"Mommy, don't these teachers know that I can read already?" she whined as she wrote the word 'cat.'

"Well if they don't, they'll figure it out soon enough."

"Why do I have to do this?"

"Practice makes perfect." Cringe.

Sylvie put her head on the table. "I'm hungry."

Ah, the perpetual hunger of youth. I found a banana in back and peeled it for her. Thankfully she was replenished enough to finish 'cat,' but it took an apple and a bran muffin to get her through the fifteen number threes.

We finally closed up shop at six and Sylvie and I drove home to a meal of okra and tomatoes over rice, lovingly prepared by my mother. I really was spoiled. I didn't know when the last time I cooked a proper dinner had been. Jesse joined us, dropping off some honey for me to use at the bakery. I used it in recipes but also had it available as a condiment. Shameless advertising for my boyfriend's side business, but then again, it seems I have no shame these days.

Over dinner, I informed my family that this Saturday was all hands on deck.

"I really need to get this right. This is my chance to break away from Beulah's shadow and set myself apart."

"Don't put too much pressure on yourself, baby," my mother warned, gesturing with her fork. "Just know that we'll all be there. This is a family effort."

"Yeah, Mommy! I can help, too!"

"Jesse, this means you'll have to wear a suit on Saturday. After all, I'll need help with delivery, and we are definitely sticking around for this one."

Jesse sighed. "Amanda Jane, I may live in the sticks, but I know how to clean up. But wait...shouldn't we be wearing aprons or butler clothes or something?"

"Oh no, no, no. We are establishing right now that I will never, ever wear anything other than classy, professional clothes when I make deliveries or serve at events. No cutesy aprons. No chef hats. We dress to impress."

"Mr. Jesse, I'll bet you'll look ha—a—a—a—andsome!" Leave it to Sylvie to say what everyone else was thinking. And praying.

"I don't know about that, but I'll do my best."

"Well now I want to go, too," my mother stuck out her lip and her tiny twin followed suit.

"Me too!"

"Well little lima bean, I guess you and I will just have to eat our own cake here."

"And do our own dancing here!"

"That's right. You two go along and have your wedding date. Sylvie and I will have an elegant evening at home."

"Momo, can we have hot dogs with it?"

That girl's wedding will be a humdinger indeed.

❤

I prepped all week for the wedding. Poor Misti was working her tail off getting all of our other orders together and manning the counter at peak times. I was hitting up the liquor store for rum, driving to Tennessee for the best coffee I could find, and baking the layer cakes that would serve as the base, in addition to creating the world's most delicious groom's cake and petit fours for the guest favors. This wedding was a full-time gig.

And in the meantime I was also giving Misti lessons in divinity making. In a short time, it had become one of our best selling items. And now in December the weather was cool and didn't yet have the damp that winter sometimes brings with it, so we could still get our candy to set. Well, I could anyway. Misti was going to take some practice.

She had just plopped her first successful spoonful of divinity on a wax-papered cookie sheet on Wednesday afternoon when the bell tinkled.

"I did it! I did it!" She hugged me and I imagined sticky divinity candy in my hair. Oh well, nothing a little peanut butter couldn't get out.

"Let me go up front, you keep practicing. Work on the swirl."

Misti gleefully scooped up another spoonful as I pushed through the swinging doors.

"Welcome to Sweet Divinity. How may I help—"

Beulah Mae Foxfire was standing in my bakery. And she was furious.

I crossed my arms and took my stand, though I could already feel my legs shaking.

"Beulah. Well, what in the world brings you here?"

"Amanda Jane, I thought you had more sense," she said.

"I don't know what you could be talking about. How about cut the circumlocution and just get to it."

She stuck her red lacquered fingernail in my face. "Don't you dare start with your high-falutin' words just to try to show how much smarter than me you think you are! I've come here to talk some sense into you as someone who's been in this town just a wee bit longer than you, little lady."

"Well go right ahead, Beulah. But do make it quick. I've got a batch of divinity in back ready to be spooned." Ha! That's right, Amanda Jane. Bring up the divinity—show her whose bakery she's standing in!

"I came to recommend to you that you cut it out right now with this wedding you're baking for on Saturday. It will destroy your business."

And all of my confidence melted down into a solid ball of fury in my chest.

"Are you absolutely kidding me?"

"I am absolutely not kidding you. You do this, and the people of this town will turn against you. This is a God-fearing town, Amanda Jane. Maybe where you come from people don't take the word of God so seriously anymore, but here we do."

Without giving it a thought I found myself channeling one of my mama's television preachers.

"*This* is where I come from, Beulah. And I do take it very seriously. I also take care for human beings seriously and I take business seriously. And I can tell you right now that not only is the Lord himself grateful that I am making this wedding cake, but he is wholly disappointed in you for showing hatred in his name rather than love!"

She gasped aloud and her hand flew over her heart. Truth be told, I thought she might be having a heart attack.

"You poor, wretched girl. The Lord knows I tried to warn you."

"Besides, Beulah, since when is making a wedding cake a sanctified act? It's a cake. And I'm making a damn good one, too. Now if that's all you came to say, I appreciate your looking out for my business and my soul, but I have a little more faith in this town than you do, and I believe they will admire what I'm doing."

She scoffed. "You poor, misguided little girl. I don't know what else I should have expected from a woman who's datin' one man while still married to another."

If I'd been less of a lady I would have hurled a fork at her self-righteous face.

"Beulah, you may leave my store and never come back. But rest assured, I will be praying for you, that you come to realize that the world is really a pretty great place with a lot of loving people in it. Now go."

She narrowed her eyes in one final effort at victory, but to no avail. I gestured towards the door and she turned and stormed out.

Misti peered around the corner of the swinging door. "Is she gone?"

"For good."

"Do you think there's anything to that? That this wedding will hurt your business?"

"I don't know and I don't care. What's right is right, and that's what we're doing. Now let's finish up that divinity. I've got a wedding to prepare for."

❤

Saturday morning I got up at four in the morning, kissed a sleeping Sylvie goodbye, and drove to the bakery to assemble the cake. Jesse was already there and had the lights on and a cup of coffee made just the way I like—lots of cream, lots of sugar, and a little bit of coffee.

But I couldn't get past how handsome he looked. He wore a gray suit with a gray vest, a dark gray tie and a silver tie clip. His hair was parted differently and slicked back just a bit, and he was clean shaven, his signature stubble traded for a smooth chin. I walked straight up to him and rubbed his cheeks.

"You're so handsome."

"You're wearing sweatpants."

I gave him a condescending look. "Well I'm not going to get all messy in my fancy dress. I'm a professional woman."

I gave him a kiss and headed to the back to get to work.

Misti came in at six o'clock, just as I was putting the final touches on top—a chocolate lace heart I'd made the night before, after many failed attempts.

I changed in the bathroom, donning a conservative black dress and not-so-conservative red heels. Hey, a girl's gotta have a little *oomph*, you know? Besides, somewhere Jeannette was clapping.

"Now Misti, you know that if you have any trouble today, you just call me or shoot me a text."

"I know, Amanda Jane."

"If anyone asks, we are booked solid through next Wednesday, but we can take orders for any other day."

"Okay."

"And if you run out of something and don't have time to make it, try to to get them to purchase the Rugelach. If we can get them to taste it, they'll be hooked. Got it?"

"Got it." She looked horrified. "Amanda Jane, I don't think I can even pronounce that."

"Then just call it a mini chocolate nut croissant. Listen, Misti, you can do this. Okay, Jesse and I are off to a wedding. Have a wonderful day!"

She nodded, tears in her eyes. But I had confidence in our young Misti. In fact, I think she needed a trial by fire to show herself she could do this kind of work on her own.

Jesse and I carefully carried the cake to the back of my car where I'd created a makeshift nest as well as a support system made out of empty berry picking crates and styrofoam coolers. The groom's cake was already loaded as well as the smaller petit fours in their individual boxes. For good measure, Jesse hopped in the back with the cake. I silently prayed that today would not be the day that I was randomly pulled over by the police. That seemed to be a common occurrence for me here.

In honor of the day, I decided a little Billy Idol was appropriate, so I cued up "White Wedding" as we set off down Thompson Avenue and made our way to the Simpson-Muller House, a venue just over the state line that specialized in weddings and cotillions.

"Amanda Jane, I'm starting to worry about you. Is this really an appropriate song for today? I don't know it too well, but I don't think he's singing about a peaceful, blessed wedding day."

"Oh Jesse, don't you see. It's ironic."

"Sure."

"Okay, fine, any requests?"

"Something happy?"

I put on Kenny Rogers, "The Gambler," and we sang. Horribly, but we sang at the tops of our lungs.

Best. Roadtrip. Ever.

❤

When we arrived at the Simpson-Muller House everything was set. My own wedding day had been such a cattywampus disaster that I guess I'd assumed that all weddings were the same. But as we pulled in I saw that the florist had already arrived and was putting the finishing touches on the beautiful bouquets that accented the front porch railing, and a caterer was wheeling a silver cart laden with food stowed away in a refrigerated cabinet through the white gate that led to the back of the house.

Jesse and I took the groom's cake and boxed petit fours first and set them inside the house on a table that was set up exactly as Taylor had told me it would be. Then we went back for the cake and carried it through the white gate and to the back porch of the house, a sweeping veranda that met a large tent set up with heating elements scattered throughout. It was warm and cozy inside, and we sat the cake on a table away from the heaters, lest the tiramisu turn into a soupy mess before the hundred of guests could admire it and demand my business card.

Once the cake was set, we tended to the business of making everything look special. I adjusted the chocolate decorations on the cake and spread flower petals I'd collected from our hometown florist the day before all around the table. We unloaded the boxed favors and arranged them neatly inside. Finally, we tended to the groom's cake and made sure that the framed pictures that also rested on the table were adjusted to surround the cake and still be visible from every angle.

There were pictures of the two of them stretching back several years. Through haircuts and attempts at facial hair, pictures taken in front of Big Ben and at the rim of the Grand Canyon, pictures with parents and nieces and nephews and dogs. And in all of them, Patrick and Taylor looked like the happiest men on Earth.

Taylor came by the table to see the finished product, and I'm proud to say I saw a tear in his eye. He kissed me on the cheek and thanked me before rushing off to check out the catering setup.

"Should I be jealous?" Jesse whispered with a smile.

"Maybe. I mean, I'm going to be the center of attention for a lot of people here tonight, and you know what they say about the way to a man's heart."

He took my hand, making sure no one could see. "You certainly will be the most beautiful woman in the room."

"And the best with a whisk."

"Then I guess I'll have to keep close to you all night."

I sighed dramatically. "I guess so."

The guests began to arrive just as we'd finished, and Jesse and I stood back with the other caterers and providers as we watched the ushers seat everyone in the tent. I saw a few faces I recognized from town. Turns out Patrick's mother was a teacher at the elementary school. I recognized her as a sympathetic face from the great 'beench' debacle. I saw the owner of the Maple Grove Cafe and wondered how she was related to this family. I also saw the mayor, which really threw me for a loop. I saw a lot of business possibilities there.

But what impressed me most was that all of these people had driven out of their way to celebrate Patrick and Taylor. It warmed my heart to know that my town was not defined by the likes of Beulah Mae Foxfire. No. She was clearly in a class by herself.

It was a beautiful ceremony. And when the reception began and the cake was cut, I delighted in handing out slices to the guests as Jesse doled out the groom's cake. I had no fewer than twenty-three people come back to the table to ask me for my business card. A success, indeed.

The cake was gone by the time the dancing began, so I started boxing up the top tier for our grooms and cleaning up our supplies. It had been a long day.

I had just used a crumb scraper to clean off what must have been a very expensive tablecloth when Jesse appeared by my side, his hand out.

"May I have this dance?"

I was taken aback. "Jesse, we're working. I don't think that's appropriate."

"Do you think they care?" He threw his thumb over his shoulder to where our clients were dancing cheek to cheek in a world of their own.

"One dance." I allowed him to lead me just to the edge of the dance floor.

There are few things in this world I love more than being in the arms of someone I love. Those things are kisses from my daughter, my mother's laugh, and a pair of woolen socks. But on this afternoon, with the bright cold outside and the dim light and warmth of this cozy tent surrounding us, there was nothing I wanted more than for this moment to last forever.

"Amanda Jane Roberts?" The words were whispered into my ear.

"Yes, Jesse Rush Gregory?"

"I'm going to marry you one day."

My heart. My heart ached with yearning, and I think I blacked out a little. But that's okay, I knew someone would be there to catch me.

When the words came, they were in the voice of a confident woman.

"I know. I'm going to marry you, too."

When the music ended, neither one of us let go.

♥

And just like that, Sweet Divinity became famous in the tri-state area for its tiramisu cakes. And the locals still couldn't pronounce it correctly. We didn't shut down Beulah's, and I didn't want to. I stayed away from the specialty cupcakes, she stayed away from tiramisu, and we both stayed away from each other. The breakfast crowd was loyal, but I didn't sweat it. The Monday after the wedding I had more special orders than I knew what to do with.

Sylvie was invited to many a birthday party that winter, so long as her mama could make the cake, and so she became president of the Wedding Cake Club, an organization of little girls and boys who came to the bakery one Saturday a month to learn the basics of baking. It usually left the place a complete disaster, but it was well worth it to see the look of joy on that little girl's face as she showed her friends how to pipe on icing. No curse words required.

As for Jesse and me, we're still waiting. He hasn't officially popped the question, and I haven't officially said yes. Seems right to wait for everything to be settled back in North Carolina. I may still be a bit 'citified,' but there are some things that just seem just plain right or wrong. But we'll get there. I'm in no hurry.

The night of the wedding, Jesse and I pulled in the driveway round about eight o'clock. It was already dark and the evenings were starting to get bitterly cold, but I knew my mother was still awake when I saw the glow of her cigarette, a little speck of orange in the darkness. I kissed Jesse goodnight and headed for the porch where my mother sat covered with a crocheted afghan, the electric heater on full blast next to her. I plopped down in a chair and pulled my knees up under my coat.

"How'd it go, honey?"

"It was an amazing night, Mama. A beautiful wedding and a huge step forward with the bakery."

"I'm glad to hear it."

We sat in silence for a while, there on the porch. The chill in the air made my cheeks tingle and I could see my breath. But I didn't want to go inside. I refused to give in to nature's signal that it was time to hibernate. I scooted my chair a little closer to the heater and rubbed my hands together.

As the clouds parted and the moon shone brightly from above, I could see that my mother was holding back laughter.

MEGAN PREWITT KOON

"Mama, what in the world are you laughing at?"

"Just you, my girl, just you. You and your country boy and your small town bakery. God almighty, I never thought I'd see the day!"

"Yeah, me neither."

"My baby girl makin' homemade cakes and divinity with the best of 'em."

"Yeah, well, that divinity was a battle and I'm downright ashamed of all of the eggs and sugar I wasted in the process. I didn't think it'd ever turn out right."

My mother turned to me, her eyes shining in the moonlight. "Now that I'm thinkin' about it, sugar, life's a lot like divinity."

I couldn't help but chuckle. "Well, this one I've got to hear."

"Don't you laugh at me, Miss Priss. You see, with divinity, just like this one life we got, you gotta create the right atmosphere, you gotta have just enough patience, and you gotta know how to add a little flair with the spoon." She stubbed out her cigarette. "Sure, it's gonna kick you in the ass once in awhile, but the rest of the time, it's gonna turn out pretty sweet."

In that moment, sitting in the darkness with the chill of winter whipping against my skin, the wisdom of my mother filled me with warmth, and on that cold winter night, I knew, unequivocally, this is where I belonged.

"True words, mama, those sure are true words, indeed."

Let the choir say 'Amen.'

MEGAN PREWITT KOON grew up in the foothills of the north Georgia mountains, playing in mud and helping with the family farm. She earned her BA in English from Furman University in Greenville, SC, and moved even farther south to earn her MA in English from a joint program at The Citadel/College of Charleston. Though she now lives with her husband, two children, and literary feline in the greater Greenville area, where she works as a counselor and advocate for adult students, Megan loves going "home" to the Georgia farm where she can holler louder, wander through the woods, and leave make-up and accessories in her suitcase. You can enjoy her musings at meganprewittkoon.blogpot.com and follow her on Instagram, Facebook, and Twitter @meganprewittkoon

CPSIA information can be obtained
at www.ICGtesting.com
Printed in the USA
LVHW010834081219
639808LV00001B/64/P

9 781943 419975